OFF *the*
RECORD

Also by K.A. Linde

OFF *the* RECORD

RECORD SERIES BOOK 1

K.A. LINDE

Montlake
Romance

Text copyright © 2014 K.A. Linde
All rights reserved.

Published by Montlake Romance, Seattle

www.apub.com

ISBN-13: 9781477817490
ISBN-10: 1477817492

Cover design by Laura Klynstra

Library of Congress Control Number: 2013916745

Printed in the United States of America

To The Campaign,
For hundred hour weeks, Lights,
and Mama Dips.

Chapter 1

DAY ONE ON THE JOB

Liz Dougherty could barely hear herself think over the deafening buzz in the conference room. So much was going on. Reporters from all over North Carolina were piling into the Raleigh conference center waiting to hear State Senator Maxwell deliver a speech. Cameras were being set up, photography equipment lined the room, and voice recorders were poised and ready to capture every word the Senator uttered. Reporters milled around the room chatting with one another and directing their crews for the optimal angle. Liz hadn't expected her first press conference to be quite this . . . loud.

Hayden Lane stood completely calm and collected next to her. She knew he had quite a bit of experience with press conferences, and was grateful he had included her, but damn, was it intimidating. How could he be so composed?

Liz felt small enough standing next to the editor-in-chief of her college newspaper, but she felt like the tiniest minnow in the ocean compared to the legends in journalism surrounding her. She had joined the newspaper two years ago, and had put in her time, but she had always wanted to be a reporter. She had pushed and fought for it. She had watched for two years as other reporters took the prime spots, but as an upcoming junior she had the privilege of finally working her coveted position.

She had interned at home for newspapers and had taken more journalism classes than she could count, so she knew she was prepared. She had done her homework, but it didn't make her first real political press conference any less terrifying.

"You ready with the recorder?" Hayden asked, digging into his messenger bag and pulling out a notepad, pen, and digital camera. The equipment was nothing compared to what some of the top-notch reporters surrounding them had, but it would do the job.

"Yeah, I think I'm all set," she said, chewing on her bottom lip as she adjusted her navy blazer and teetered in her nude high heels.

"I wish we were closer. I'd love to get a question in." He peered around a camera to get a better look at the empty platform.

"Do you think we'll get a chance?" Liz asked, wide-eyed. In case she was given the opportunity to ask anything of the sitting Senator, she had prepared questions, but she didn't think it was a real possibility. Hayden would probably laugh at her if he knew how much extra work she had put into the questions. But it was her job and she couldn't help it. She had been so anxious last night anticipating the event, and it tended to make her meticulous. She hadn't even been able to sleep.

"Nah, probably not. If this guy is anything like his father, he'll make his announcement and get out of there. Easier to keep winning if you don't say too much. Know what I mean?"

She stared into Hayden's gorgeous face, and the full force of his charm hit her. She gulped and turned back to the podium. "Yeah, makes sense."

"I wish we could get one question in, though. I'd love to peg him down about education policy," he said.

Liz nodded. After researching Senator Maxwell's policy platform, she'd had difficulty narrowing her questions to the ten on education policy she had listed in her purse. He was a hard-core budget guy, just like his father, who was a sitting United States Senator. State Senator Maxwell had won his last two elections based on his broad, sweeping plan to balance the budget, and then he had done it. For the first time in twenty-five years, North Carolina's fiscal books were in order.

Not that she disagreed with the end result, but she wasn't sure how much she agreed with his approach to the matter: cutting anything and everything that might be deemed superfluous—and one of those items happened to be education. Her father was a professor at the University of South Florida in Tampa, and Liz couldn't imagine what it would be like to see all of his hard work slashed by a politician just out to line his pockets. Maxwell put business first and everything else after: Encourage small business, lower taxes, help the working class, but Liz didn't understand how he expected to help the working class when they couldn't even get an education.

"Lane! Lane?" a perky redhead called. She pushed past another reporter and all but attacked Hayden.

"Calleigh," Hayden muttered, hugging her back. "So good to see you. How's Charlotte treating you?"

"Amazing, of course. You should come and visit me. I could get you an interview," she said. She swished her red hair across one shoulder and smiled at Hayden like he was dessert.

"I might take you up on that when I graduate," he said. "Have you met our new reporter, Liz Dougherty?"

Calleigh seemed to finally notice that someone was standing next to Hayden. "Oh, hi," she said. "Are you taking over Camille's old job?"

"Uh . . . yeah. I've been mostly in editorials before this," Liz explained.

Calleigh Hollingsworth was a legend at the university newspaper. She single-handedly put the paper on the map last year by interviewing the President of the United States and busting up a sex scandal in the higher tiers of the school administration. Her byline had graced the front page of the university paper daily, and everyone at school knew her name. She had been offered a job at a New York newspaper, but had turned it down for Charlotte. No one knew why, but she was either crazy or a genius. Liz had only seen her in passing, and she was awestruck to be standing in the presence of someone with such fame.

"Well, I hope you do her some justice. I know Lane wouldn't choose someone incompetent. Good luck on the job," she said, turning back to Hayden. "Lane, drinks before you leave, doll. This is *not* a request."

And with that she traipsed across the room. Male eyes from all around followed her as she whisked past them and out of sight.

"That was Calleigh Hollingsworth," Liz said plainly.

"Yeah," he grumbled. "And I have to entertain her highness."

Liz giggled. "Do you not like her?"

Hayden shrugged. "She's good at her job, but so annoying. After she got that interview with the President, fame went straight to her head. She acts like everyone should treat her like a queen now."

"She kind of is a queen."

"And that's exactly why she acts like it!"

Liz didn't know Calleigh well enough to comment.

A hush fell over the crowd as a tall, leggy blonde walked onto the stage. A series of flashes went off as the reporters adjusted their camera settings, anxious not to miss anything that was about to happen.

"Was it leaked as to what he's speaking about?" Liz whispered into Hayden's ear.

He shook his head slowly, never taking his eyes or ca? the stage. "I haven't heard anything. I just got the buzz about ?, yesterday morning. Impromptu."

"Strange," Liz said. She watched the blonde's heels as she walked across the carpeted floor.

She was beautiful, almost unnaturally so, definitely unfairly so. Liz was happy to be on the shorter side most days, but not when that woman was onstage. And Liz had always thought she was above average in the looks department, with naturally straight blond hair that the sun highlighted in the summer, and blue eyes. She loved her pouty lips and high cheekbones, but her athletic build was far from that of the skinny minny standing onstage.

"Thank y'all for coming out at such short notice," the woman said, smiling at the crowd of cameras. "I'm Heather Ferrington, Senator Maxwell's press secretary. He is only available for a short while, but he will be taking questions at the end. Please keep them to a minimum. The Senator will be out in a minute."

As Heather walked offstage, all the reporters began speaking at once. The idea of actually getting an answer out of the State Senator was a real treat. His father had always kept the family rather tight-lipped. Speculation circulated that it was because they had secrets to hide, but with thirty years of service in public office the Senator had a clean slate. They were a model family, and no one was surprised when Brady Maxwell III followed in his father's footsteps. It was a logical step for him.

"What are the chances we get a question in?" Liz asked. She edged forward in the crowd as it moved inward in anticipation.

"Zero," Hayden murmured, resting his hand on her hip so as not to lose her as the crowd heaved forward. Liz felt her side warm at his touch and tried to keep from purposely leaning into him. "Try to see if you can get a little closer anyway." He urged her forward.

Liz followed his lead and nudged her way deeper into the cloud of reporters. One woman gave her a withering glare as she pushed past her, but Liz paid her no mind. Once she reached the best position she could stand in, she stopped and waited for the Senator to come out.

Besides his work in cutting money for education, he had blocked NC Pledge, a piece of legislation that would make it easier for college students who maintained a certain GPA to afford a degree. She knew that he was pushing these measures to balance the budget, but it came at the expense of the most important thing anyone could ever offer. Senator Maxwell had received a great education at the University of North Carolina Chapel Hill, because his parents could afford it and he happened to be an exemplary basketball player, but not everyone else had those benefits. Tuition hikes after his budget cuts only exacerbated the problem.

And she hadn't heard a sufficient answer as to why he had allowed the cuts to education funding, even encouraged this to happen. The only reasonable explanation she could consider was that he had kept certain measures in the budget that his big-time donors benefited from and had cut education to make up for it. This led her to believe that the only thing he truly cared about, as a politician, was the money coming his way . . . just like most other politicians.

Senator Maxwell walked onstage, and Liz's mind went blank.

She had seen a picture of him. Dozens, in fact. Probably more than that. What kind of reporter would she be if she hadn't?

She knew he was young. It was hugely controversial in his previous state elections that he had beaten two incumbent representatives at such a young age. But attractive? No, not attractive—gorgeous . . . breathtaking . . . delicious. She tried to stop her brain from continuing, but damn, pictures did *not* do him justice.

She wasn't certain why, but the ease of his stride stood out to her. He carried himself confidently in a damn sexy black three-piece suit. He had the air of someone who didn't have to take what he wanted, but was instead handed it on a silver platter. His dark hair was cropped short and spiked in the front, and his intense brown eyes surveyed the crowded room as if he were here to accept an award. He smiled at the reporters waiting for the inevitable photo op and adjusted his red-white-and-blue tie knotted at the top of his crisp white button-down. He was freshly shaven, accentuating his chiseled cheekbones and strong jawline, and ever-looked the part of the young State Senator he was.

As bulbs flashed in all directions, Liz stared up at the Senator, rooted in place. No wonder he had won election over previous incumbents. He could just walk into a room and win a crowd. It helped that his name was recognizable, considering he shared the same one with his father, but he didn't need any help winning when he had that body and charm. She wondered if the demographics on the election were 95 percent women. She would believe it.

"Thank you all so much for coming out here for this last-minute press conference," Senator Maxwell spoke powerfully into the microphone. His voice was like an addiction—pulling you in, making you crave more, making you feel as if you could never get enough.

"Liz, are you getting this?" Hayden asked, brushing against her shoulder and jarring her out of her daydreams.

"Yeah, sorry," she murmured. She fiddled with the recorder until the red button blinked, and tried to reorient herself.

"I know you are all wondering why I decided to come before you, here in Wake County, on this lovely Saturday afternoon." He leaned forward against the podium. "Let me tell you a story first . . ."

Liz felt the crowd draw closer to him, as if each person were practically hanging on the edge of their seat to hear him speak for just a second longer.

"I grew up here in the Triangle. My mom worked as a professor at the University of North Carolina, Chapel Hill. My father, as you well know, sat as a United States Congressman for many years and now serves you all as a Senator. I know the people here, because I went to school here, I played ball here, I met my first girlfriend here. I saw my friends go off to college and leave town just like many of you did. And I saw friendships fade with distance. My own best friend, Chris, moved to New York City, and I miss him every day." The crowd sighed with him at the loss of a friend. "When I thought about leaving, going off to the big city, making a name for myself— all it sounded like was leaving all the people I loved behind. So I decided to cut that out of my plans and focus on what I had always loved—and that was the people of North Carolina."

Liz hadn't even realized that a huge smile was plastered on her face as she listened to his engaging voice. She dropped her smile immediately, not wanting to get taken in by someone she disagreed with, and held the recorder out farther.

"I knew after living here my entire life that there was too much to do to leave my community for someone else's. That was Chris's plan, not mine. And I'm glad I stayed, because if I had left, I wouldn't have been here when my mom found out that she had breast cancer, or to see my brother and sister choose a college, or my dog eat an entire steak while we weren't looking one night." The crowd burst into laughter and glanced around the room at one another before focusing back in on the Senator.

"I want to take that same enthusiasm for my community and fight for what you believe in. That is why, as of today, I am announcing my intention to run for the United States House of Representatives in my home district."

Liz's mouth dropped open, and the crowd of reporters clambered forward, each trying to be the first to ask the Senator a question. She had been expecting a conference on a bill that had recently passed, North Carolina taxes, or really anything but this. It was practically unheard-of for a one-term State Senator to run for the House. They usually bided their time and waited to gain status and recognition, climbing the ranks before throwing their hat into the race. Brady had his dad's name and reputation to go off of, but would it be enough?

For some reason, even though she disagreed with him on some issues that were key to her, she could see Brady pulling it off. There was something about him that fired up a crowd and lit up a room. He had been all but bred for this moment, but you couldn't fake that charm and ease before the cameras. She knew firsthand, because she turned into a blabbering idiot with a camera in her face. She was already beyond ready to see how this election would play out.

A barrage of questions was thrown at the Senator as he smiled radiantly at the sea of flashing bulbs. Liz moved with them, excitement coursing through her body for the upcoming Q&A.

"Thank you for your enthusiasm. I'm ready to get started here in North Carolina. I'd be happy to take a few questions, though I don't have much time," he said, eyeing the line of microphones.

"Senator Maxwell!" a few reporters called. They threw their hands in the air as more raised their recorders and volleyed for his attention.

"How about Mr. Tanner," Senator Maxwell said. He pointed out a short, balding man with a *Raleigh News* badge on his shirt.

"Senator Maxwell, you've had tremendous luck in your previous elections. What prompted this decision when you've barely won the last two elections?"

"Barely won is still winning, George," Senator Maxwell said with a smirk. "But on a more serious note—I chose this race not for me, but for the people of North Carolina. I'm not running with any selfish motivation. I know what is needed to help the people here succeed and what they need in their daily lives. This is a fight worth fighting, and I intend to give it my all."

"Senator, can you give us insight into how you plan on beating the incumbent representative?" a tall librarian type butted in.

"We haven't talked strategy just yet, Sheila, but I think North Carolina can do better than what he's offering, and I'm the man for the job," he spoke confidently.

A commanding man in a faded button-down with his shirt-sleeves rolled up to his elbows chimed in next. "Senator Maxwell, your past opponents have already brought up the fact that your youth contributes to the image of your inexperience. What do you have to say to that?"

The Senator chuckled softly into the microphone before looking back up at the crowd of reporters. "I'm twenty-seven, ladies and gentlemen. The Constitution of the United States says that a member of the House of Representatives must be at least twenty-five years old. If the Founders of our great country believed that a twenty-five-year-old could get the job done, why don't my opponents?"

"But don't you think it will be a hindrance to your campaign?" someone shouted over the crowd.

The Senator shook his head. He had clearly been prepped for this question. "Not at all. I know North Carolina. I've seen my own father work for the people and my mother work for the people, and now I want to. How about we take one more," he said, cutting off the reporter and staring out at the crowd.

Liz shot her hand up in the air, pushing past another reporter in her haste. She *wanted* this question. She wanted to prove herself to Hayden and to herself.

"You there." Brady pointed into the audience. "An unfamiliar face with a familiar logo. I'd be happy to take a question from my alma mater. It's good to see them in the house."

Oh my God. Liz stared up at Senator Maxwell and saw that he was pointing right at her.

"Uh," she hesitated on her beginning. Why was she blanking on the questions she had planned to ask him? She had practiced for hours, and now standing there with the opportunity she was losing it all.

She locked eyes with Brady across the room and felt the heat of his gaze run through her body. She cleared her throat uncomfortably. She needed to get it together. She was a reporter, after all, and this was her job. He was handsome, but just a job.

Liz straightened considerably and met Brady's gaze head-on. She wouldn't back down from a challenge. "Senator Maxwell, during your time in Raleigh you consistently voted to cut education funding in the name of balancing the budget. Yet you've also voted to allow some of your biggest donors to avoid paying corporate taxes on their various business ventures. Can you please comment on how this helps better the lives of all North Carolinians, which you've repeatedly stated is your primary reason for entering this race?"

Everyone in the room seemed to hold their breath waiting for his response. Questions from the college newspapers were typically light and fluffy. Politicians chose them because it looked good on paper to include them. College reporters weren't supposed to ask a question that hit that close to home.

Liz could feel eyes judging and assessing her from all sides.

Had she really thrown his entire speech back in his face? Staring into those eyes, she felt a jolt of electricity course through her body. It was as if they were the only two people in the room in that moment. She held that gaze like a pro and watched as he changed his appraisal of her.

"That's an excellent question. It was painful for me to have to do that knowing how closely linked I am to higher education, but other aspects of the bill were unacceptable to me. I couldn't fully support the bill with those parts still in it," he stated.

Liz narrowed her eyes as he stealthily evaded her question, not even touching on the tax cut component. He really was a natural.

"Thank y'all for coming out and I'm sure I will see y'all again on the campaign trail."

He waved at the reporters, ending the press conference. Several people shouted at him for one more, but he never stopped his purposeful stride offstage.

Liz couldn't believe that had just happened. She had asked a hard-hitting question at her first press conference and alienated a sitting politician. She thought she might throw up any second.

Hayden reached forward and turned the Record button off. "Fucking amazing, Liz," he cried. He threw his arm over her shoulder and pulled her in for a hug. She folded into his chest. Any other day she might have reveled in the embrace, but she couldn't get the image of Brady Maxwell III's eyes out of her head.

"Did you see his face?" Hayden asked. "You stumped him. He didn't see that question coming at all. This is going to be an incredible article."

Liz smiled weakly, and tried to push down the rising taste of bile in her throat.

"Liz, are you going to be okay?" Hayden asked, holding her arms and looking into her blue eyes. "You look kind of sick."

"I feel a little sick," she admitted.

"Well, you have no reason to. Calm down. That was great. I'm so glad you came with me!" He released her and slung his messenger bag on his shoulder.

They got halfway across the room when Calleigh Hollingsworth headed them off. "What a question!" she said. "I knew Lane would pick the right person. I never saw Camille stump a politician."

Calleigh Hollingsworth was complimenting her. She might die.

"Oh, I don't think I actually stumped him."

"He hesitated, honey. That's enough for me," Calleigh told her before shifting her attention back to Hayden. "Some other reporters are coming with me to get a drink. I've already told them you're coming with me, and they're excited to meet you."

"I'm really not up for it, Calleigh. We have to get this story out," he offered.

"No way. Unacceptable, Lane. I'll see you tonight. Liz, you are more than welcome, of course," she said politely.

Liz looked at Hayden expectantly. She wouldn't mind mingling with other reporters, but if they needed to work on the story, she would go back with him. "What do you want to do?"

He shrugged, clearly preferring to leave.

"You're not even running the story until Monday," Calleigh told him stubbornly. She placed her hand on her hip and sat into the movement. "Come out and play. You're too uptight."

"All right. If Liz wants to go, then I'm game. Otherwise I'll just drive home and work on the piece."

"Liz?" Calleigh asked, pleading with her big green eyes.

"Uh . . . yeah. Sounds like fun."

"Great! I'll text you the details, Lane, and see you later," she said, waggling her fingers at him as she departed.

Hayden sighed and readjusted his bag on his shoulder. "I guess we're going out."

"Sorry," Liz said. She followed him out the door.

"Don't be. It wasn't likely that I would have been able to get out of it anyway. At least I have company now." Liz smiled, butterflies jumping around in her stomach. "Do you want to go get dinner? It'll probably still be a few hours before they go out."

"Uh . . . yeah, sure," she said. Was he asking her out?

"Cool." They walked into the half-full parking lot and veered toward his black Audi. Liz took a seat as Hayden popped the trunk open and deposited his equipment before opening the door and sliding onto the leather seat.

"Do you have a preference for dinner? I'm really craving Italian."

"Fine with me," she agreed easily. She didn't know how to judge the situation.

It didn't help that her mind was still captured by the Senator. The way his eyes found her in the crowd, the tone of his deep, husky voice, the borderline arrogance in his every movement was so . . . appealing in a way she had never even known before. It wasn't as if she hadn't been attracted to a bad boy in the past, and that was exactly what Maxwell portrayed under that charm, but she didn't know whether he really was that bad boy underneath the image of the upright Senator.

It was a paradox she wanted reconciled. Who exactly was Brady Maxwell?

Chapter 2
OUR POLITICIAN

Liz pushed open the glass door to the quaint Italian bistro, and a bell chimed overhead. "How did you find out about this place?"

"My dad used to take me here a lot," Hayden told her, grabbing the door out of her hand and holding it open for her.

"Thanks. I forgot you're from Raleigh. Your parents live here?"

"No, they moved to D.C. when I graduated. They didn't want me to go to D.C. public schools, but my mom always wanted to work on the Hill. So as soon as I went to college, they packed up and left too."

The waitress seated them in a maroon booth at the back of the restaurant and then left. Liz opened the menu and skimmed the choices. "Do you get to see them much? It's like a five-hour drive to D.C., right?"

"Yeah, that's right. I'm too busy to go home much right now, but it's all right. I get to see them around the holidays, and I'm flying back for the summer. Where do your parents live?"

"Tampa. I'm in the same boat. I'm too busy and it's too far to drive."

"At least you have the beach." He looked up at her over the plastic menu.

"That's true. Guaranteed tan on vacations. If I went home more, I probably wouldn't be so pale."

"You're not pale. Do you see this?" he asked. He pulled down the open neck of his button-down. She didn't know why, but the way he exposed the bare skin under his shirt to her made her flush.

She cleared her throat and averted her eyes. "Well, I guess I have that going for me, at least."

"Liz, you have everything going for you. Aren't you a Morehead scholar?"

"Yeah, but that's just academics. Book smarts," she said. "You have the whole paper, and everyone *loves* you."

"You could have the paper."

"You think so?"

"I've seen your work. It's really good. Plus, you're driven."

"Thanks," she said. It was what she wanted and what she had worked for. She appreciated that he saw that in her.

"I wouldn't have put you in a reporter position if I didn't think you were fully capable of moving forward."

"Well, you sure know how to motivate someone," Liz said, her face heating under the spotlight. She would love to be editor, but she knew that she had some work to do over the next year to prove that to everyone else.

Hayden made everyone *want* to work for him. When he was overseeing a project people worked twice as hard than if anyone else had initiated it. He had such a presence that he could seamlessly take over a whole room. Once people got to know him and witnessed his unfailing dedication to projects, they only loved and admired him more.

Liz certainly had fallen for that amazing presence. Plus, he was attractive. His medium brown hair was always shaggy and over-grown, curling at the ends and around his ears. It constantly covered his hazel eyes, which changed colors depending on his mood or attire. He had a runner's build and could be seen crisscrossing campus in his track shoes. Best of all, he always had a smile on his face. It was such a relief to walk into the office after a grueling day and be greeted by such a happy demeanor.

They ordered when the waitress returned. Hayden claimed the restaurant had some of the best spaghetti he'd ever had in North Carolina. Liz wasn't sure that was saying much, but ordered it anyway. She trusted his judgment. He had chosen her for this position, after all.

"So, do you think Maxwell will win the primary?" Hayden asked, taking a sip of his water.

"Definitely," she said without a doubt or second thought.

"You're so sure," he said. "What makes you think that? He's a young, first-term State Senator with no experience."

"He has his dad's name and career to run off of, and that's clean. People know it. I wouldn't count him out." Plus, he was attractive, really attractive, and that always helped.

"No, you're right. I was just curious," he said, smiling into his menu.

"What?" Her eyes narrowed.

"You were kind of staring at him when he walked onstage," he said. "Did you not know he was that young?"

"Stop teasing me, Lane."

"Hey, I don't blame you! He's a good-looking guy," he said with a devilish smirk as she glared at him.

"Don't be ridiculous," she said. Hayden had pretty much hit it on the head.

"You don't have to hide it from me. It was a pretty sharp three-piece suit."

"Hayden Lane! I think you have a crush on our politician," she said.

Hayden rolled his hazel eyes to the ceiling and pretended to fan himself. "You caught me."

Liz laughed. This was the most fun she had ever had with Hayden. She wasn't sure if it was because this was the first time she had ever been completely alone with him. They had worked together for the past two years on the paper, but it was a different environment. Plus, others had easily overshadowed her, like the star reporters, Camille and Calleigh. She liked seeing a more relaxed side of him.

"In all seriousness, though, it's going to be an interesting race," he said.

"That it is."

The waitress walked over and plopped the spaghetti down in front of both of them. Liz dug her fork into it and served it into her mouth. She was surprised: She had to admit that it was the best spaghetti she'd had in a really long time.

"So, what are your summer plans?" he asked, watching her devour the spaghetti. "It feels a little cruel to me, giving you this big story right before summer break."

She wiped her mouth with a napkin. "I appreciate the opportunity. I'd love to work as much as I can this summer. I feel like I'll be better prepared for next semester."

"Good. That's what I was hoping for."

"I don't have much planned for the summer, though. I'm taking a class in the journalism department. I think it'll be easy. What about you?"

"My mom helped me get an internship with the press office where she works on Pennsylvania Avenue in D.C."

"That's really cool," Liz said. She would die for an in like that on the Hill. She was one of the few staying behind for the summer.

"Hold on." He pulled his phone out of his pocket. "Hey, what's up? Yeah, we're just finishing up dinner." He ran his hand back through his longish mop of medium brown hair and listened. "Okay. Okay. Yeah, I know where that is. We'll be over soon. Bye."

He hung up the phone. "That was Calleigh."

"Oh yeah?" Liz asked.

"She just got to the bar. We can head out whenever you're finished."

"All right." She had suddenly lost her appetite.

She hated how anxious she was already getting about hanging around with Calleigh. Liz had virtually idolized her for the past two years. Hanging out with her felt a little surreal.

"Hey, is everything all right?" Hayden asked, his head tilted slightly to the side as he looked at her.

"Yeah, sorry," she said with a nervous laugh. "Just zoned out, I guess. What are you going to be doing in the press office?" she asked, returning to her dinner even though she wasn't hungry.

Hayden shrugged, still looking concerned. "Probably nothing interesting. Fetching coffee and doing research is all I anticipate. I doubt they'll let me do much else even though I have the training. I bet your class will be more interesting."

"But you'll be in D.C.! There's so much going on there. No way could it be boring, even if the work is slow. I'll just be in North Carolina researching political communication and reporting. You'll actually be living it."

Hayden kept his hazel eyes downcast. She didn't know what that meant, but the quirk of his mouth had her thoughts swirling. What was he thinking underneath that smile?

"You're going to visit, right?" he asked, raising his eyes to meet hers.

Liz swallowed and took a sip of the water. "You really want me to?"

"Yes," he answered confidently. "I need to see you this summer."

Silence lingered after his bold statement. Hayden not just wanted, but *needed*, to see her. She was blindsided by this new information. She wasn't sure if this was a date, and she had no confirmation. Not that his wanting to see her over the summer meant they were currently on a date.

Okay, now she just felt stupid and overly analytical. They couldn't start anything now . . . a week before he was supposed to leave for the entire summer. But she could visit him . . .

Blowing out a slow breath, she placed her fork back on the plate. "Well, then I'll visit," she said softly.

Chapter 3

HITTING THE BIG TIME

Walking into La Luna Lounge, Liz and Hayden passed the bouncer and entered another world. La Luna was as far from a place Liz would have chosen as they could get. She didn't mind going out, drinking, and have a good time, but not like this. She preferred low-key bars where she could sit and enjoy the company of her friends. Her best friend, Victoria, would have liked La Luna much more than Liz did.

The entrance was a large arching tunnel lit by dim blue bulbs that opened into an expansive open room. It was slightly reminiscent of a 1950s movie theater, with a small stage at the front, all red plush seating around the perimeter, and tiered balconies up above. The center of the room was taken over by an ever-growing mass of people dancing, and the walls were lined with liquor.

Hayden scanned the room for the group of reporters. Liz wasn't short, but she wasn't exactly tall either. From her vantage point, she couldn't see much more than the group of girls gyrating in front of her. The room was too dark for her to be able to pick anyone out of the crowd anyway.

"I think they might be over there," he told her uncertainly.

"Maybe we should get a drink first?"

He nodded, and they angled for the bar. There were three small steps that led up to it, and it gave her the extra height she needed to see above the crowd. Hayden had been right; she could see Calleigh's lush red hair from here.

"What would you like?" Hayden asked, drawing her attention.

"I guess just a whiskey sour."

Hayden ordered for both of them. The guy behind the bar quickly mixed the drinks, and Hayden handed over his card.

"Keep it open," he told the guy, sliding Liz's drink toward her.

"Thanks," she said.

She took a sip and tried not to wince as the alcohol hit her.

Hayden laughed at her pained face. "Not a big drinker?" he asked.

She shrugged. "I like drinking just fine, but I can't seem to get past the burn."

"You need to drink more, I think."

"You sound like my friend Victoria."

He smiled that smile that turned her insides to jelly. "I'd like to meet her sometime."

Victoria would be happy to meet him too. She was the more outgoing of the two of them and found it way easier to get people to love her. "You should. She's a character."

"I'm sure I'll get the chance."

Liz turned back toward the dance floor, not able to meet his gaze. Was he saying he would meet Victoria because he would be spending more time with her? Was he flirting with her? She wanted him to, but she was so thrown that she didn't even know how to respond.

"You were right. I spotted Calleigh," Liz told him, pointing in the same direction he had mentioned earlier.

"Great," he said, more enthusiastic than he had been before.

She followed him through the crowd, inching around the dancers. Hayden reached back, and she slipped her hand into his. A bolt of electricity shot up her arm. Her attraction to Hayden was only growing the more time she spent with him, and the way he grabbed her hand, pulling her through the crowd, made her feel flushed. She didn't want him to let go.

But he did.

"Lane!" Calleigh called. She stood in her four-inch black stilettos. Drink in hand, she surged forward, brushing past Liz, and flung her other arm around Hayden's neck.

Liz took a step away from them, holding her drink at arm's length to keep it safe. Liz wondered how intoxicated Calleigh was already.

"Hey, Calleigh," Hayden said, wrapping one arm around her waist when she didn't let go.

Calleigh took a step backward, straightened out her low-cut cream blouse. Her black suit jacket was discarded in the booth. She didn't *look* that drunk. She kept one hand resting on Hayden's chest as if she needed to steady herself. Her signature dark red hair—nearly maroon—fell down in front of her shoulders, with thick, chunky bangs falling into her ever-vigilant green eyes. Was Calleigh interested in Hayden?

Liz didn't think she stood much of a chance against Calleigh Hollingsworth.

"I'm glad you made it," Calleigh said. "Let me introduce you to my coworkers."

Calleigh grabbed Hayden by the crook of the elbow and pulled him toward the booth. Liz shuffled after them.

"Hey, y'all, this is my friend Lane, the one I was telling you about," Calleigh said. "Lane, this is Trent, Jenny, Monique, and Rick. They work at the *Charlotte Times* with me." They all nodded their heads and responded with their own salutations.

"Nice to meet you all," Hayden said with his charming smile.

Each of the guys wore a plain, square-shouldered suit jacket. Trent had light red hair, distinct against his green shirt. Rick was dark headed and stocky, with a dark blue shirt and silver tie combination. Monique was exceptionally tall with short black hair shaved on the sides and styled into waves on top. She wasn't exactly big, but she had a larger bone structure hidden underneath long black suit pants and a billowy black blouse. Jenny was a girl-next-door blonde, small and mousy, with a pale yellow shirt tucked into her khaki knee-length skirt.

"We've heard great things about you, Lane," Monique said.

Hayden chuckled softly, his eyes darting to Calleigh and back. "Thanks. I'm sure Calleigh exaggerates."

"I would never," she said, placing her free hand on his arm.

"You're editor now?" Rick asked, assessing him. Liz saw his eyes flicker to where Calleigh's hand rested on Hayden's arm. So, he was interested in her. Not surprising. Everyone was always interested in Calleigh.

"Yeah. I took over this past semester when Calleigh decided to take the job with y'all, and I'm continuing through my senior year," he told them.

"We were lucky to get Calleigh," Rick said.

"I think the last editor y'all got from Chapel Hill was Mr. Stewart," Calleigh said with a giggle.

Jenny rolled her eyes. "Let's not even bring him up."

The group laughed, all sharing a private joke that neither Liz nor Hayden understood. She was getting tired of being anonymous and was about to speak up, when Trent noticed her.

"Hey," Trent said, "aren't you that girl who asked Senator Maxwell his last question?"

Liz flushed with pride. She knew it was a good thing, but it felt odd that a reporter for the *Charlotte Times* had noticed her.

"Uh . . . yeah," she said. She took a step forward and stood next to Hayden.

"Sorry," Hayden apologized. "This is my reporter, Liz Dougherty."

"Well, great job," Trent said.

"Yeah, she's great, right?" Calleigh said, finally including her in the group. "Lane really knows how to pick 'em."

Liz pushed the implication in her words out of her mind. She didn't care one bit that Calleigh was probably talking about herself. Liz tried to look unruffled.

"That was a stellar question," Jenny told her, leaning forward. "It's nice to see the college papers asking bold questions."

"Yeah," Trent agreed, looking her up and down. "Bold."

"I guess I didn't realize how bold it was at the time," Liz admitted with a shrug.

She took a sip of her drink. She couldn't believe where she was and what she was doing. It was pretty amazing.

"Well, it was bold, all right," Monique said, twirling her hand in the air dramatically.

"I thought it was a great question," Hayden interrupted. "The kind of questions we need to be asking. Not those questions about his age and his past runs. We all know he's young. That's obvious. What people don't know about is his record. I bet we'll be hearing a lot more about it in the coming months."

There was the Hayden she knew. He had all these lofty ideals about how journalism should run; whether it ran that way or not was still up in the air, but he tried to keep things as idealistic as possible. She thought his philosophy kept things at the paper honest, and she appreciated the sentiment.

"Of course it was a great question," Calleigh said. "You guys should take a seat."

Calleigh reclaimed her seat, leaving just enough room for one person.

Liz stood off to the side as Hayden took the empty spot. Trent sent her a come-hither look and moved over so she could sit next to him. Liz tried desperately to avoid eye contact.

Hayden noticed she was still standing and nudged Calleigh over. Her green eyes glanced up at Liz, and she thought she saw a flicker of frustration.

Calleigh reluctantly moved down the booth, and Liz sat down next to Hayden. She sipped on her drink thoughtfully. Hayden had stuck up for her, and she appreciated it.

"Before y'all showed up, we were talking about Senator Maxwell. What do you know about him?" Calleigh asked, her mouth quirking up at the side as she looked from Hayden to Liz.

"Probably not as much as you do," Hayden said. "What have you heard?"

"Oh, nothing really," she said, waving her hand.

"Come on, Calleigh. You said you knew his sister," Rick prompted.

"Well, I don't really know her," she said with a smile. "I just know about her through a reputable source—my sister."

"Isn't his sister still in high school?" Liz asked. She remembered the biography she had read the night before.

"Yes," Calleigh replied. "She is, but she's graduating this year."

"What is a high schooler going to tell you about her brother that isn't already in the papers?" Monique asked. "I've heard he has a pretty clean slate."

"I heard he was engaged," Calleigh got out quickly. "Called the wedding off because she didn't have enough money or something . . . wouldn't fit into the family mold."

Liz narrowed her eyes. She hadn't seen anything in her research about his being engaged. Sounded like a rumor to her.

Hayden stretched and bumped Liz's knee with his own. She peeked up at him when he didn't move it away, but he was looking at Calleigh. Strange mixed signals.

"Is that all?" Trent asked. "That's not news, Calleigh. That's gossip."

"I don't believe he's as clean as he comes off. He's a politician! How is this guy winning?" She humphed.

Jenny giggled then. "Did you not get a good look at him?"

"You don't get a picture of him at the polls," Calleigh grumbled.

"You don't forget that face when you're voting," Jenny said with a smirk.

"I would hope that some people would vote for a person based on their policies and the kind of person they are, rather than on their looks," Calleigh spat back.

"I just hope people vote," Liz muttered under her breath.

"Preferably just the educated," Calleigh said.

Liz glanced away, not wanting to have this conversation. She had very strong opinions about this, and bringing it all up wouldn't be in her best interest.

"Oh, come on, Calleigh. Cut that crap," Hayden jumped in. "You don't honestly think we shouldn't let people vote if they haven't gone to college."

"But that's such a low bar, Lane."

"You're such an elitist," he said, shifting his weight closer to Liz.

"All right . . . high school diploma, but I really think you're selling America short," she said.

Liz wanted to keep her mouth shut. She swore she would. It wouldn't help anything to speak up, but . . . but she just couldn't stay quiet.

"I think *you're* selling America short by assuming that because people didn't go to college or never finished high school, they aren't able to form their own opinions about how they want this country or their community to run. Those are antiquated ideals, and if you looked more closely into the research on political campaigns, you would see that even without the same base of information, the majority of people know what is going on in this country. To say they shouldn't vote because they're not like you is . . . reprehensible," Liz said.

Thankfully, Calleigh didn't have a comeback. She just stared at her.

Did she find her a worthy opponent? Or was she plotting Liz's demise for speaking to her this way in front of all of her colleagues?

"I think voting rights were decided forever ago, and we should let it rest," Monique said. "I know quite a few of my family members who fit into the not-as-educated category who are *way* more informed than my brother, who is a biomedical engineer."

"There are always exceptions," Calleigh said with a shrug.

Liz kept herself from saying anything further. Exceptions were the rule as far as she was concerned, but she already felt as if she had alienated the woman she idolized in journalism. No need to push the envelope.

"Oh my God!" Calleigh shrieked out of nowhere. She latched onto Hayden's arm and a huge smile crossed her face. Liz didn't miss the way her fingers dug into his suit jacket or her knee pressed into his thigh.

"What is it?" Hayden asked, checking over his shoulder.

"Look! It's Tracey Wilson!" she said, pointing into the mass of people across the room.

"Yeah!" Hayden said in surprise. "It is. I haven't seen her in so long. I thought she was in Chicago."

"Me too," Calleigh said, snaking her hand under his arm. "Let's go say hi. God, it's been forever!"

Calleigh hopped up and started to drag Hayden along with

her. He looked back at Liz with a big smile on his face. "We'll be right back," he told her before disappearing into the crowd with Calleigh.

Great. Just what she wanted: for Hayden to disappear with Calleigh Hollingsworth. Not that she thought this was a date. It wasn't. Was it? Maybe she had misread his interest in her entirely. She had thought that they had a moment when he had asked her to come to visit in D.C. Now that he was running after Calleigh in a dark, crowded nightclub, she was reconsidering.

Liz crossed her leg and leaned back against the booth. Calleigh's coworkers started talking about the paper, and Liz pushed forward with the conversation even though Hayden had left. These people might be amazing contacts for her in the future if she decided to stay in North Carolina after graduation. She had been a little intimidated earlier at the prospect of being here with other reporters, but now that they were talking she felt right at home. This was what she wanted to do.

Trent kept shooting her looks as if he was going to make a move any moment, but she stayed engaged with the other people at the table and ignored him. She had way more interest in journalism than in the wandering eyes of one of Calleigh's coworkers.

Liz set her empty glass down in front of her and nodded along with what Monique was saying about spin media. She had taken a special topics class last semester that focused on spinning stories to make them more interesting to the reader. She appreciated that her area of interest was coming in handy and that she was able to contribute to the conversation thanks to her rigorous class schedule.

"Excuse me, miss," a waiter said. Liz glanced up in surprise at the waiter dressed in all black. He was carrying a tray with a cocktail on it. "Drink for you."

"Uh," Liz said, looking around at the other reporters, who had paused their conversation. "I didn't order a drink."

"A gentleman in VIP offered it to you."

"Sorry, I can't accept this. I don't know anyone in VIP."

"Oh, I'm sorry," he said, taking the drink back. "I was directed to give this to you by my manager. Must have been by mistake."

"Must have been. Do you know who sent it?"

The waiter shook his head. "No, but I can make an inquiry if you like."

"Yes, please do. Thank you."

She had no idea who would send her a drink. She was here with everyone she knew in Raleigh.

The waiter traipsed off to see if he could get more details about the person in VIP. She wished she had said yes now, but she felt weird accepting a drink from a stranger. She hadn't been in that situation very often.

"That was weird," Liz said. She turned back to face the other reporters.

"I can't believe you turned down a free drink," Jenny said.

"I didn't know who it was from."

"Still," Monique cut in, "it was free."

"If the guy wants to give me a free drink, he can come up and offer it to me himself."

The girls shrugged and returned to their conversation about spin media and how they thought it was going to affect the Maxwell congressional race. As interesting as the conversation was, Liz wished Hayden would come back. She grabbed her empty glass and tossed an ice cube into her mouth to suck on.

"Hey," Trent said, extricating himself from the conversation and sliding into the open position Hayden had previously occupied.

Liz smiled at him halfheartedly. She had been expecting this.

He scooted over until his entire leg was pressed against hers. "That was some great work you did today," he said, resting his arm on the back of the booth and leaning into her.

"Uh . . . thanks," she said, moving over an inch or two to put distance between them.

He bridged the space immediately. "So . . . are you and Hayden . . . ?" He trailed off.

"Are Hayden and I what?" she snapped. She was growing more and more uncomfortable by the second.

"You know . . . dating?" he asked her breasts.

"Do you date your coworkers?" she asked, diverting the conversation.

"I would if they were as pretty as you," he said.

Liz frowned. "I don't like to mix business and pleasure."

"So, then you're not together?" Trent clearly wasn't seeing that she was including him in the business category.

"No," she told him reluctantly.

"You know," he said, trailing his hand down her pencil skirt, "I find your attitude toward the Senator very attractive."

Liz stared down at his fingers on her skirt, and then brushed his hand aside. Why did he think he could touch her?

She tried to keep the anger out of her voice. "Did I have an attitude? I thought I was just doing my job."

He smirked, not even affected by the fact that she had moved his hand. And really, that look wasn't attractive. He didn't have the face for it. He should seriously reconsider his facial expressions.

"Whatever it was, I like it."

Liz grabbed her glass and tossed the last remaining ice cube into her mouth; anything to use as a distraction. He was still staring at her, waiting for her response, but she had none . . . except to tell him to get lost.

She glared at the empty glass. Why had she refused a free drink anyway? Another drink would be good right about now.

"So . . . are you interested in maybe . . ." he began, but she cut him off and stood abruptly.

"I think I'm going to go find Hayden," she told him, placing the empty glass on the tiny table.

"I'll go with you," Trent offered quickly.

She placed her hand on his shoulder, keeping him from standing. "Really. I'm fine," she said, then made a hasty exit.

Her feet carried her toward the center of the room, but there were too many people, and she decided better of it and began to walk around.

Just as she started skirting the crowd, she felt a hand on her shoulder. Expecting to see Trent following her with an irritating persistence, she reluctantly turned around.

"Ma'am," the waiter said, dropping his hand apologetically.

It was the same waiter who had tried to give her the whiskey sour, and he was still carrying it. Yeah, she needed that. She reached out and took it off of his tray. "Sorry about hassling you earlier. Thanks for the drink."

The waiter smiled. "The gentleman didn't wish to send his name."

Liz waved it aside. "That's all right. I appreciate it, whoever he is." She took a sip.

"He did request that you join him in the VIP lounge instead."

Liz stopped with the glass at her lips and eyed the waiter suspiciously. "You're serious?"

"Yes, if you'll come with me," he said, and began walking away.

Liz stared after him. Was he expecting her to actually follow him? She scurried forward more out of curiosity than anything. Her reporter sense was tingling and now she had to know the story. Who exactly was her mystery benefactor?

Chapter 4

AIRPLANES

Liz caught up to the waiter as he opened a side door that led to a flight of stairs. He held the door for her and allowed her to enter before him. They walked up the stairs and into one of the second-floor balconies that overlooked the patrons below.

The VIP lounge really wasn't anything fancy. No different from the room below except more sparsely populated and with way more staff. Okay, so maybe the booths carpeted in a red velvet material were a bit newer and the black high-topped tables and chairs had more shine to them. It sure was nice to have a long horseshoe-shaped bar in the center of the room all to yourself, but none of it was all that extravagant.

This certainly wasn't what she had been expecting VIP to look like. Where was the swanky furniture and crème-de-la-crème clientele? Apparently she had been watching too much TV lately. It wasn't as if she had suddenly been transported to Los Angeles. This was still just Raleigh.

"Who am I supposed to be meeting?" Liz asked the waiter as she took a large drink of the whiskey sour he had brought for her. She couldn't believe she was here right now. It wasn't her style at all.

"The man is in the corner," the waiter said, gesturing to the only full table.

"Which person?" Liz asked, her eyes scrutinizing the table.

"You can't see him from here. He's packed into the corner, but he's expecting you," the waiter said before disappearing into the stairwell.

"Thanks," she mumbled, taking another sip to calm her nerves.

It was now or never. She took a deep breath and slowly walked across the room. She wanted to look calm and collected, as if guys in VIP lounges bought her drinks all the time. As she got closer, a blonde at the table glanced over her shoulder and snickered. Why did she look familiar?

Liz had always been good with details. Her high school boyfriend used to make fun of her for being able to remember every aspect of their relationship—every date they had been on, what shirt he was wearing, the exact date of their first kiss, first dance, and first time holding hands—the list went on. The skill had manifested at an early age, and it was damn good in journalism.

Crap. Liz knew where she had seen the woman before. That was Maxwell's press secretary. Liz's heart sped up . . . could this be related to her question for Brady? That didn't seem to make sense to her. She was missing a piece of the puzzle. It couldn't be from Brady himself . . . could it?

A number of heads turned to face her as she approached. She felt heat rise on the back of her neck.

"May we help you?" a short, stocky guy in a charcoal suit jacket asked her. He was more than pudgy, with caterpillar eyebrows and beady eyes that swept her body. He was like Trent, but with the authority and self-importance of a VIP.

"I was sent over here by a waiter," she said. She held her whiskey sour up for their inspection.

"Did someone order a drink?" the guy asked, looking around the table with a knowing glint in his brown eyes. "Anybody?"

Two women in the corner buried their heads in their hands. The blonde looked amused, but said nothing. Now Liz was getting pissed off. Was this all a bad joke? Pick on a girl on the main floor . . . choose a likely victim? Was she being used for their amusement? She pursed her lips, feeling the edges pull down into a frown.

"Someone up here bought me a drink," she said frostily. "I doubt it was *you*. So, if you could point me to the individual who has some semblance of class, I'll be happy to get out of your way."

The man glared daggers at her. He didn't seem the type to approve of a woman with a mouth, and she couldn't seem to close hers when she got angry. Controlling her temper had never been one of her strong suits. He managed to stutter out a laugh before responding, "We have a feisty one here."

Liz rolled her eyes. She really didn't have the patience for this. "Fine. I'll take my drink and go then."

"Hold on a second, hon," he said, reaching out and grabbing her arm.

Liz gave him a pointed look and he hastily withdrew his hand.

"It's all fun and games. No need to get so irritated," he grumbled.

Liz shrugged. If he wasn't being helpful, then she didn't feel the need to be polite.

"Well, you're no fun. He's over there. Had to take a phone call," he said, pointing at a man leaning against the railing, partially obscured by a crowd of women.

"Thanks," she said, walking away as fast as could. She heard him grumble something under his breath, but she ignored him.

Liz reached the wall and was able to get a look at the guy talking on his smartphone.

Her heart sank along with her stomach.

Brady Maxwell III.

A sitting State Senator had bought her a drink. This was not real life. This didn't happen to her. Hadn't she just insulted him in front of a roomful of people? No, she had done her job. He had a pretty face, body, smile . . . okay, he was flat-out gorgeous, but it didn't mean she would stop doing her job.

Was she even allowed to be here? She was going home to write an article about him, and it wasn't all rainbows and sunshine either. She couldn't be *seen* with him. She looked down at her drink and *eep*ed! She nearly dropped it onto the carpeted floor. She had accepted a drink from a man she was about to write a scathing article about. Was she insane?

"Sorry, Jerry, give me one second," Brady said into the phone.

He turned to look at her and she froze. Her insides felt like Jell-O, or that wobbly feeling after getting out of the ocean after being tossed around by the waves. Her head was hazy, like a morning fog had taken up residence where her wit normally resided.

"Don't go anywhere," Brady demanded, staring at her intensely.

Liz looked away and then back up at him. Standing here right now was a bad idea. Maybe she should just head out after all. She wanted to know why he had bought her a drink . . . and he was so handsome, but she knew this had bad news written all over it. Still, she felt rooted to the spot.

She watched him finish his phone call and memorized every inch of his face in those couple minutes. Where he had been freshly shaven and clean cut early this afternoon, a five-o'clock shadow was growing in along his jawline. She could see that he liked to lick his perfect lips while he was talking, and they were slightly chapped due to the habit. He talked with his hands more when he was making a point, and she really liked those hands. She bet he had a firm handshake . . . a firm grasp. When he smiled, he got little creases around his eyes, making them light up with emotion, and the most adorable dimples formed.

Liz swallowed hard, trying to push down the growing heat rising in her core and her quickening pulse. Why did she feel like this? It hadn't been *that* long since she had been with somebody, and she wasn't one to get caught up. But just the thought of those strong hands grasping her hips was sending her imagination into overdrive.

She needed to shut down. *Now.*

"Thanks, Jerry. Tell Francine I said hello. I'll try to get by to play some ball with Matt this week. Yes, see you."

Brady hung up his phone and placed it into the inside pocket of his suit jacket. He turned to face her, leaning against the railing, and smiled. "You showed."

"Are you surprised?" Liz asked despite herself. He didn't seem like a man who didn't get what he wanted.

"You never know."

"Well, you didn't tell me who you were."

"Ah," he said, nodding. "Then you definitely wouldn't have showed."

Liz arched an eyebrow. He thought he had her pegged already. Well, he was in for a real surprise. She would have come up here for sure if she had known that he was more than some random guy, even if she would have been nervous as hell. "And yet I haven't left."

"I told you not to," he reminded her. "Did you like your drink?"

Liz looked down at it in her hand. Empty. When had that happened? "Yeah. Thank you."

"You're welcome," he said with the same smile that made her weak before.

Liz didn't know what she was doing here. Why had he bought her a drink, and why was he making pleasantries? This wasn't going to change her article. She wasn't sure if he really cared all that much about the college paper, but this certainly wasn't going to help him. Either way, though, she waited to find out what he wanted. She was too intrigued.

"Can I get you another?"

"No, thank you. I know my limits. I still have to get back home tonight." Why was she telling him this? Wouldn't no have sufficed?

"Are you sure?" he asked, his face a mask.

Something about him made her think he was tiptoeing around her. He still had the natural self-confidence she had seen in the press conference, but still there was something else, and she didn't know what it was. Did he want to know about the paper? Did he want to know about her article? Something didn't add up.

"Did you need something?" she asked, straightening her blazer.

"Need something?" he asked quizzically. His brows knit together. "Why would I need something?"

"I just thought . . ." She trailed off, embarrassed. "Just the paper . . ."

"Oh, no," he said. His eyes seemed to bore into her, searching her. She wished she knew what he was thinking or where this was going.

"Do you enjoy flying?" he asked abruptly.

"What?"

She was taken off guard. Did he want to take her flying? That was ludicrous.

"Flying, like in airplanes," he added.

"I don't understand."

"I never did. My ears popped, my parents argued, I never got a window seat, the lines were too long, and it always happened when I wanted to stay home."

Why was he telling her this? He didn't even know her name.

"I'd have panic attacks before boarding," he informed her. "Sometimes my parents would give me medicine to knock me out so I wouldn't hyperventilate."

"I'm sorry," she said, not sure how to respond.

"I grew out of it, of course. I had to, especially if I wanted to be a politician like my father, but I never forgot that feeling. My fingers and toes would get warm and tingle. I'd find it hard to swallow. My stomach would be racked with nerves. I couldn't focus properly on what was at hand. I couldn't keep my breathing even, and I also couldn't seem to suck in enough air. It was one of the most frustrating experiences of my life."

"I've hyperventilated before," she admitted—she wasn't sure why. "My sister made me run a couple miles to the store with her in the middle of the summer in Tampa, but I'm not a runner. I've never felt so terrible."

His eyes glistened as they stared into hers. "Then you know what I mean?" He waited until she nodded. "Well, I've never associated that feeling with anything good in my entire life . . . until you asked me that question today."

Liz's mouth popped open without any intention on her part. "What?"

Her question had been tough. She hadn't cared, though. She had wanted answers and all he had done was sidestep. She hadn't thought he had given it much thought, and he certainly hadn't thought about *her*.

"I think I hid it as well as I could, but I had to get off of that stage. I was suffocating under your scrutiny."

"Me?" she squeaked, losing all semblance of composure.

"And I wanted to know how you did that."

Liz didn't know what to say. No one had ever said anything like this to her before. She felt like an idiot staring up at him, getting lost in the endless dark depths of his eyes. How was she supposed to respond to that? Only two minutes ago she had thought this was some kind of joke. Now he was saying that she completely disarmed him. Him. State Senator Brady Maxwell III.

"You seem surprised," he said.

"Of course I'm surprised, Senator Maxwell," she said formally. "I'm not entirely sure how to even begin to respond to that. I wasn't doing anything on purpose. I just . . . asked you a question."

"You asked one hell of a question," he said, leaning forward into her.

"I'm not going to apologize," she told him, standing up taller in her heels.

"I wasn't requesting an apology."

"Then what?" she asked skeptically.

"I was merely complimenting your reporting skills. How long have you had this position?"

Liz narrowed her eyes. "You're complimenting my reporting skills?"

"It was a fair question," he told her.

"I know."

"Then why do you look like you might pounce? I'm not meaning to be critical."

She glanced away from his overwhelmingly beautiful face, over the railing, and out across the main bar area. It was a crowded night. How had he even seen her in the growing madness below?

"I just . . ." Her eyes gradually shifted back to his, and she gripped the railing harder. "I'm not certain where this conversation is heading."

"Why does it have to head anywhere?" he asked, scrutinizing her face.

She blushed and made the mistake of looking into his eyes. "I didn't . . . that's not what I meant."

He laughed. "It's all right. It seems you are more adept at sidestepping my questions than I was at sidestepping yours."

Had he admitted to dodging her question? Was this off the record? Had they ever clarified?

"Seems you're stuck here with me now. You're going to have to answer me," he said, taking another step toward her. His smile was playful. He was flirting with her . . . teasing her. Brady Maxwell was *teasing* her.

"I'd be happy to," she said boldly. "It's not like anyone is going to be writing an article about me."

"That's good. You don't need to be in the papers. Then everyone would know about you, and I think I prefer you here all to myself."

Her mouth went dry. She had no words.

"So," he said, deliberately reaching forward on the railing and sliding his thumb against her hand. Sparks ignited everywhere he touched her, and she felt her body reacting instantly to him. It was the same feeling she had gotten in that conference room when he had walked onstage. He focused in on her, and she couldn't breathe. "Let's start with your name."

She was pretty sure he had knocked the breath right out of her, but she found her confidence within and answered, "Liz. Liz Dougherty."

"Pleasure to meet you, Liz," he said, offering her his hand.

She placed her hand in his. "Handshakes and kissin' babies," she muttered.

"Such is the life. Though it's typically not this enjoyable."

"You seemed to enjoy yourself just fine today," she responded. "What made you decide to run?"

"Now, now, none of that," he said. She hadn't meant for it to come off as a reporter question, but it was her life, after all. "I didn't buy a reporter a drink. I bought Liz Dougherty a drink. And I want to know when I can see you again."

Everything about the situation told her not to give in. What good could come from that? She was a reporter and he was a politician she was writing a story on. They couldn't ignore that.

But for the life of her, she couldn't do it.

"You want to see me again?"

He dug into his pocket, pulled out his wallet, and extracted a business card. He placed it in her palm, and she fingered the thick embossed paper. It was an expensive card; that much she knew.

"I've already said I want to see you again. If you want to see me, give me a call on that number. It's my personal line. If you can't reach me, call my secretary at the number below that. I'll get in contact with you," he said with a penetrating gaze that made her believe he would. "I wish I could stay now, but I have some business to attend to."

She couldn't call him. She couldn't see him. It wasn't right for her professionalism or for her future career in journalism.

Maybe when she was finally away from him, she wouldn't feel as heated and desperate to be closer to him.

"Hey," he murmured softly, brushing his fingers across her jaw-line, "you want to see me. I want to see you. Call me. If you don't, you'll regret it."

Could he read her mind?

"I'll think about it," she whispered, entranced.

"I look forward to your call," he said, releasing her chin.

Her body was already missing his touch. She hated that he left her with the option, but he had already stated what he wanted. Now it was up to her. He wanted her to come to him willingly, and she certainly was willing. He had this undeniable, uncontrollable pull on her that she had never experienced with another man. He made her *want* to use this card.

But she knew she never would.

Chapter 5
MIXED SIGNALS

Liz walked in a trance back down the flight of stairs leading out of VIP. Her hand was clutching the business card Brady had given her, between shaking fingers. All of her attitude dissolved when she left, and she was wondering what the hell had happened.

Her feet hit the bottom of the stairs, and she exited the doorway back onto the main floor. She didn't know how long she had been gone or if anyone had noticed her absence. All she knew was that Brady Maxwell, a sitting State Senator, had said he wanted to see her again. And what had she said? *I'll think about it.* Really? Was she out of her mind? The man was the most gorgeous person she had ever laid eyes on, and the physical attraction she felt in his presence was off the charts. She would have gone to the ends of the earth for him, and still somehow she had told him she would think about it.

Not that it was a good idea to see him, but now that she was away . . . it felt like a much worse idea *not* to see him.

Liz tucked the business card carefully away in the pocket of her navy blazer and walked back to the table. Her head was down as she approached, her mind lost on Brady. He was all charm, and she shouldn't have been surprised. He was a politician, after all. She just had never expected . . . *him* . . . that he would throw her so off-balance.

She had a strong head on her shoulders. Her dad had always told her that. It was why she had worked so hard in high school to get a full scholarship to Chapel Hill, and why she pushed herself at the paper to become a reporter. It was the same steadfastness that made her a *long-term* kind of girl, and that caused her to always be the one who ended things with her various boyfriends when she felt the relationship slipping. She might stay with them longer than she should, but in the end, it was always her choice . . . it was always her. Yet here she was, swept away by some politician.

"Where did you run off to?" Hayden asked, jumping up from his seat as she drew near.

"Uh . . . I went to look for you." She wished she had a drink or something in hand. She didn't want to tell Hayden about meeting Brady. That would bring about a whole slew of questions she didn't want to answer with his enticing stare still burned into her mind.

"I only left for a second," he said a bit defensively.

Before she had met Brady, she would have taken all of this personally. After all, Hayden was the one who had run off with Calleigh, leaving her alone with people she didn't know. But now she wasn't focused enough to care. The card was burning a hole in her jacket.

"So did I," she said with a shrug. "Where did Calleigh go?"

"She's still talking to Tracey. I came back for you, but Trent said you ran off."

"Just came to find you is all," she told him again. "I think I'm ready to get out of here."

Earlier she would have stayed here with him all night, but now the mixed signals from Hayden were irritating her. Was he interested in her or not? Brady had been so up-front with her. Liz knew very few people had the self-confidence to pull off that attitude, but it wasn't like Hayden was lacking in that department. At least Brady had told her what he wanted . . . even if that situation had its own complications.

"Yeah, I'm ready to get back," Hayden agreed. "We have an article to write. I feel a long night ahead of me." He cracked that smile that she was so fond of, and she tried not to compare it to Brady's. That comparison wasn't even fair. "Let me just say good-bye."

A few minutes later they were walking toward the door of the bar when Calleigh appeared out of nowhere. Her burgundy hair seemed to have gained even more volume with the pressing heat in the room, and it only made her look more beautiful. Her bangs were falling haphazardly into her eyes, and she did nothing to push them aside as she latched onto Hayden's arm. "You guys aren't leaving, are you?" she asked, pressing into Hayden's side.

Liz watched Hayden disentangle himself from Calleigh's wandering arms and take a step away from her. At least this time she could actually tell that Calleigh was drunk.

"Yeah, we're heading out. It's late," Hayden told her. Liz didn't actually know what time it was, but it felt early.

"Hayden, you should stay here with me," she said, the coy smile wiped off her face and replaced with blatant desire. Hayden actually looked uncomfortable. Liz could live with that.

"Appreciate it, Calleigh, but we have to get back to Chapel Hill," he said.

"Thanks for the invitation, Calleigh," Liz said. "Really had a great time."

Calleigh looked at her blankly before returning her gaze to Hayden. "You're leaving with *her*?"

Oh, this wasn't looking good.

"Calleigh, let's not do this," Hayden warned with a sigh.

"I mean, after everything, and I haven't seen you. I just thought . . ." She trailed off. Calleigh actually looked affronted. She clearly hadn't thought the night was going to end like this, and Liz could only guess why by her comments.

Liz didn't want to think about it, but the visual kept coming back to her. Calleigh and Hayden. Hayden and Calleigh. Of course, it made sense. They were perfect for each other. She felt like a fly on the wall as they stared at each other.

"We have to go," Hayden said finally, ending the staring match. "I don't know what you thought you were going to accomplish tonight, but it's not like that. You know that. You've known that for a long time. I don't know how much more obvious I can be. What more do you want me to say?"

Calleigh looked at the floor, clearly hurt by his words. When she met his eyes again, hers were steely. Liz didn't want to know what she was thinking in that moment. "Fine. It's not like she's even a challenge," Calleigh said, tossing her hand in Liz's direction and talking about her as if she weren't standing right there.

"Calleigh," he said in a threatening tone, "keep it together. You're embarrassing yourself. Now, we're going to go. Good night."

Hayden gripped Liz's elbow softly and tugged her away from the ticking time bomb. She got one last glance from Calleigh, and she saw only a promise in Calleigh's eyes . . . a promise that Calleigh wouldn't forget tonight.

Liz stumbled out onto the blacktop parking lot. She felt the oppressive summer heat press against her suit, and she stripped her jacket off. Her mind was buzzing with the confrontation she had witnessed. Her body was still reeling. She couldn't believe what Calleigh had said. Liz didn't even really know Calleigh. She certainly wasn't a threat to her. Whatever had happened between

Calleigh and Hayden was something Liz wanted to forget . . . and knew she never would.

She stalked across the parking lot to his car. She hadn't even realized how furious she was until she started walking. How dared she say those things! Calleigh had power and prestige, but that did not give her the right to treat Liz like this.

"Hey," Hayden called, jogging to catch up to her long strides, "are you all right?"

"Fine," she muttered, walking faster.

He latched on to her elbow and pulled her up short. "Are you *really* all right?"

"What do you think?" she asked, sneering at him.

"I'd say no." He didn't let go of her elbow. "I'm really sorry about . . . all that."

"What *was* all that?" Liz asked.

"Calleigh and I were together last year before she took the job in Charlotte. It wasn't anything serious."

"She seems to think it's still something," Liz pointed out.

He shrugged. "I can't control how she feels. It's not whatever she thinks it is."

"Well, maybe next time you shouldn't go running off alone with her and then she won't think it's something," Liz said calmly. She couldn't believe that had come out of her mouth. It was what she was thinking, but never something she would normally say. Maybe Brady's frankness had gotten into her system.

Hayden dipped his head in surrender. "You're right. I didn't mean for it to come off that way."

"Intentions only go so far."

"True," he said, looking up into her eyes. She could see he wanted to say more, do more. But he didn't. She wasn't sure what was holding him back.

He was standing only inches away from her, and she knew she

would give in to him if he made a move. Even with Brady's words still ingrained in her head and Calleigh's stinging words ringing in her ears. She was mad at him, but it didn't hold back the crush that had been brewing inside of her for the past two years.

Hayden took a step in, and Liz's breath caught, her heart fluttering at a rapid pace. He was so close. She took a small step forward until their clothes brushed against each other and tilted her head up to look at him. He smiled at her and she sighed softly, waiting for the kiss she knew was coming.

His mouth quirked up at the side and then he backed up. She was so confused. She had given him an open invitation, and he had backed down.

Liz quickly turned toward the car, her face burning.

Hayden cleared his throat awkwardly. "We should get back."

She didn't even have the strength to respond, just walked to the passenger-side door and waited for him to unlock it. She didn't want to know what he was thinking. He had turned down Calleigh, only to reject Liz as well.

She would have been better off staying up in VIP. At least Brady had made his intentions clear. The hot and cold with Hayden was confusing at best.

Liz tossed her jacket inside and slid into the passenger seat of the Audi. The forty-minute drive back to Chapel Hill was quieter than the ride there had been. The radio was playing some hipster music that she wasn't really into, but it was better than the silence.

He parked outside of the small run-down house she rented on the north side of campus. The neighborhood wasn't all that great, but it was a short walk to the journalism school and was better than trying to find parking on campus. Luckily Victoria didn't care about the decrepit nature of the building, because it was so close to the bars on Franklin Street.

"Thanks for the ride," she murmured, grabbing her jacket and popping the door open. "I'll start working on the article."

She was all the way around the car when Hayden stepped out. "Liz," he called, stopping her from walking up the grassy path to her house. "I'm sorry about earlier."

Which part? she wanted to ask him. Was he sorry that he had run off with Calleigh? Was he sorry that Calleigh had been a bitch to her? Was he sorry for not kissing her when she had been expecting it?

Instead she just said, "It's all right." She didn't even know what she was saying all right to.

"It's not. Calleigh shouldn't take out her anger about me on you," he said.

Oh.

"Yeah, probably not," Liz muttered. "Night, Hayden."

"Liz," he called again as she walked away. She turned around reluctantly. "I *am* sorry."

She sighed and nodded. *Please be over quicker.* "I know you are. Don't worry about what Calleigh said."

"I just . . . don't want this to affect our . . . erm . . . relationship." Her ears perked up at that statement. "You're a great reporter. I wouldn't want you to think I'm using my authority or anything to come on to you. I would hate to lose you at the paper."

Liz's mouth dropped open. He didn't want to lose her at the paper? Like that was even an option. The paper was all she wanted. Was that why he hadn't kissed her? Was he afraid that starting something with her would be bad for the paper?

"Would you say you're coming on to me?" She hadn't thought that he was . . . not compared to Brady back at the club.

Hayden looked flustered, and she was glad. She had liked him for a long time and then after one evening together he was crushing it all. "I worry about how you took Calleigh's comment. I don't . . ."

"Just leave it, Hayden," she said wearily. "It's too late for this conversation. I'm tired."

"Right. Sorry. I thought I was clarifying, but it seems like I'm only more jumbled. I'll see you at the paper tomorrow." He stepped forward and grasped her hand unexpectedly. Despite everything, she was still glad that he was touching her. She was angry about the way he was acting this evening, but she couldn't hold back her feelings for him.

She saw him swallow as he stepped toward her again. She wasn't expecting a kiss, not after the incident in the parking lot. In fact, she didn't know why he was touching her at all, but she wasn't stopping him. And she didn't stop him when he pulled her into his arms.

They were strong arms, not particularly big but definitely not small. They fit well around her waist, and she could feel their definition as they circled her. Liz automatically wrapped her arms around his neck as he drew her into his chest. The hug was brief, but still, it was Hayden.

He broke away and looked as calm as before. She wished she knew what he was thinking, but unlike Brady, who broadcast his feelings all too clearly, Hayden was too much of a mystery. Maybe she wasn't supposed to know.

But she damn well wanted to.

Chapter 6

REPRINT

The article hadn't been as easy to write as Liz had thought. Each time she put pen to paper, the words got all jumbled. She wasn't saying quite what she wanted to say, and at first she couldn't figure out why. She had never had this problem before. Her writing was natural, flowing out of her like a river running downstream. But this one article had left her stuck.

She had dug in her blazer pocket and retrieved the business card Brady had given her. She flipped it over between her fingers, examining the high-quality card for an answer as to why she couldn't write about its owner. But that was reason enough. She was having a hard time being objective, extracting the Brady she had researched and interviewed from the man who had seduced her in the club.

You want to see me. I want to see you. Call me. If you don't, you'll regret it.

The words rang in her ears on repeat, tantalizing her, enticing her, commanding her. Thinking about him in that scenario—his hand trailing her jawline, his body so near, his charming air—clouded everything she was trying to do.

Liz couldn't write an article about *that* Brady, and yet that Brady kept creeping into her thoughts. He was morphing in her mind somehow from the man whom she disagreed with politically to a welcome invitation. She had tossed the card aside, hoping it would land somewhere she could forget about it so she could write the damn article.

It took her longer than she wanted to disentangle the two faces of Brady in her mind and write a clear and coherent article about the press conference. State Senator Brady Maxwell III was running for Congress. He wanted to represent her district to the House of Representatives. Yet he had given tax incentives to his big donors, which could be the reason he was slashing through the education budget. While she might agree with him on some other broader issues, the idea that he had done this just to line his pockets without forethought as to how it would affect thousands of people across the state left a bad taste in her mouth. She couldn't support someone who wouldn't even vote to help fund his alma mater, the place where his mother had previously worked as a professor, when he consistently ran on improving the quality of education. There. That would do.

The article ran Monday morning on the front cover of the school newspaper. It was the week before classes let out for the summer, and students were looking for any excuse not to study for their finals. Everywhere she looked her classmates had the paper in hand—passing hands between classes, perusing it over lunch, sprawled out with it in the Pit at the center of campus. It was literally everywhere.

Liz knew the paper was popular, but it was usually the kvetching column that drew them, where students basically complained all day. But when she glanced around now, everyone was staring at the front cover . . . at *her* article. She couldn't believe it.

She wondered how much of it had to do with Brady's picture covering the front page—there certainly were more girls looking at the article—but she liked to think that it was because of her writing.

Seeing her name next to Hayden's in the byline made her giddy. It was what she had always dreamed about. She finally felt as if she was living up to her own expectations.

"Hey, I thought you might be studying," Victoria said, plopping down across from Liz on the hard white-topped bench on the out-skirts of the Pit.

Liz broke out of her daydream and stared up at her best friend and roommate. "I-I was . . ." she stammered, though she hadn't glanced at the homework piled in front of her for some time.

"Psh," Victoria said, rolling her big brown eyes. "You were star-ing off into never-never land, because everyone on campus is going on about that hot politician you interviewed."

"I know, right? It's crazy," Liz said.

"Not *that* crazy. The man is gorgeous. Everyone is interested to see if he's going to make appearances here so they can go drool over him," Victoria told her, flipping her kinky curly hair from one side to the other.

Victoria was a voluptuous beauty with breasts that were always revealed in her low-cut tops and curvy hips always revealed in her tight skinnies. She was from New Jersey, with the northern accent and all that went with that. She wore a bit too much makeup with high penciled-in eyebrows, full red lips, and thick eyeliner. No one would have guessed that she was a Morehead scholar along with Liz, or that she was a lab researcher in genetics. But she didn't take herself too seriously like most of the other honors students did, and didn't bother with anyone who couldn't keep up with her wicked smart mind.

"Is anyone actually reading the article?" Liz asked.

"Was there an article attached?" Victoria smirked at her, arching one well-groomed eyebrow.

"Just the one I spent all weekend on."

"You could seriously use your time more wisely."

"Weren't you in the lab all weekend?" Liz leaned forward, her Carolina-blue blazer resting against her notes. She had the sleeves rolled up to three-quarter length because of the heat. It was a soft, breathable linen, and she had paired it with a neutral tank and white skinnies. Her typical platform heels had been exchanged for a pair of brown Oxfords. She missed the heels when they weren't on her feet, but it just wasn't practical when she had to walk to school.

"Not *all* weekend."

Liz sighed and waited for what she knew was coming. "Another professor, Vic?"

"Nooooo. He's just a TA. A PhD student in something useless . . . journalism maybe."

"Ha. Very funny. We're all laughing."

"Gorgeous. Totally not my type. I'm way smarter than him."

"And yet it doesn't stop you," Liz said, shaking her head.

"Why would I let that stop me? He has an office, Liz," she said, as if that explained it.

"Oh, I don't know. Propriety? Decorum?" Liz suggested.

"Well-behaved women rarely make history," Victoria quoted Laurel Thatcher Ulrich.

Liz let it pass, turning back to her notes. Victoria pulled out her oversize Audrey Hepburn sunglasses and leaned back on the bench to observe the mayhem in the Pit. It was said that if you sat in the Pit all day, you would see everyone on campus. Liz didn't know when anyone would have time for that, but it was impossible not to see someone that she knew when she was here.

But she hadn't really been expecting to see Hayden. They both practically lived in the journalism building near the Quad and in the newsroom in the Union off of the Pit, but after their parting on Friday things had been awkward. They had talked about the article, but nothing more, and she had left in a hurry Sunday after they had pieced it all together.

"Liz!" he called now, jogging up to her table.

Victoria propped herself up on her elbows and eyed him over the top of her extra-large sunglasses. "Hey," Liz said with a smile.

He looked good . . . really good. He wore brown Rainbows, pressed khaki shorts, and a Carolina-blue polo. The two of them matched.

"The paper is going insane. They asked for a reprint," he said, his face ecstatic, his hand running back through his shaggy hair. He tossed his head to the side to push the hair out of his eyes when it fell back into place. "I don't remember the last time we needed a reprint."

"Wow! Do you need help?" she asked, stuffing her notes haphazardly back into her folder.

"No. I should be fine. I have a couple guys who will make the runs, but I'm so glad I saw you. Reprints! All because of your article."

Victoria cleared her throat loudly, sitting up and crossing her legs. "What did I miss?"

"Oh, sorry," Liz said quickly. "Victoria, this is Hayden Lane, my editor at the paper. Hayden, my roommate, Victoria."

His face lit up and he stuck his hand out. "I've heard a lot about you. Great to finally meet you."

Victoria's eyes darted to Liz and back as she slid her hand into his. "I've heard quite a bit about you, Lane. People call you Lane, right?"

"Yeah. My friends call me Lane. Do your friends call you Vickie?" he asked, dropping her hand after they shook.

"No," she said plainly.

"Oh, well, I like it. Seems to fit you," he said with that charming smile. Liz tried to hide her own behind her hand.

"It really doesn't," Victoria bit back, not finding it funny at all.

"Suit yourself," he said, turning back to Liz. "Liz, I can't believe how well this all went. After the reception of your work, would you be interested in covering the campaign division for the paper? You're suited for it. I'd let you take it whatever direction you see fit. Consult me, but it's yours. I'd want you to start this summer."

Liz couldn't hold back her shock this time. He was handing over the entire *campaign* division to her! If she had thought being on the front cover was a dream, it was nothing compared to running her own column, her own division.

"What are you doing Saturday night?" he asked.

Her mouth fell open but she recovered quickly. After all that awkwardness, he was actually going to ask her on a date?

"I'm pretty open," she managed. She could feel Victoria's eyes on her.

"Great. There's this gala in Charlotte that I want you to go to. I have tickets, but my parents want me back in D.C. this weekend."

"Oh." Her heart sank. He wanted her to work. What was wrong with her? "Yeah, that'll be great. Just shoot me an email with the information."

"I will. I have to run, though. Reprint!" he said with so much enthusiasm.

Liz watched him jog into the Union and disappear from sight. As soon as he was gone, she threw her head down on the table and grumbled, "Could it get any more embarrassing?"

"He could start calling you Lizzie," Victoria suggested.

Liz cracked up despite her frustration. "I just . . . I swear he was going to ask me out."

"You've had the hots for that guy forever, right?"

"Yeah," Liz admitted with a shrug.

"Why don't you make the move? I bet he'd like that," Victoria said, as if she knew.

"I shouldn't have to," Liz said stubbornly.

"At least you have gala tickets," Victoria said.

Liz rolled her eyes. "Oh, who wants to go to a political gala anyway?"

"I don't know. You're asking the wrong person," Victoria replied, leaning back on her elbows and staring out across the Pit. "Just find a hot guy there and forget about your Hayden Lane problems."

If it was only that easy . . .

Chapter 7

JEFFERSON-JACKSON GALA

The Charlotte Convention Center was a modern-looking glass building set in the heart of downtown Charlotte. Nothing especially fancy, but large enough to hold bigger parties and conferences, and it even boasted a few high-end car shows. It was a staple for luxury political banquets for the state.

Liz kicked her flip-flops into the car and pulled out her pumps. It was a two-hour drive from Chapel Hill, and she wasn't about to drive that far in four-and-a-half-inch heels, especially not black leather platforms. She slid the heels onto her feet and stepped out into the parking garage. Her black satin dress fell to her knees, clinging to her athletic shape with a lace V-cut that hung softly off her shoulders. A matching black belt cinched around her waist and tied in the back, accenting her waistline. Her blond hair was loosely French braided across the front of her head and pulled into a messy bun at the nape of her neck, and she had gone for neutral makeup.

Grabbing ahold of the small gold clutch where her voice recorder was stored, she shut her car door and walked out of the parking garage. It was a short walk to the convention center, and by the look of the people walking in with her, she was headed to the right place.

Liz walked into the convention center behind a middle-aged couple holding hands and speaking in whispers. The entranceway was all high arched ceilings, long white pillars, and a red-carpeted floor leading down an extended hallway. It was impressive enough, but could use a little work to keep up with the clientele it boasted. Liz wasn't complaining, though. She still thought it was beautiful.

She followed the couple when they took a right down a hallway that opened up into a decent-sized ballroom. It was filled with several dozen white-clothed tables fit to seat eight. Each white-draped chair was tied around the middle with alternating red and blue ribbons. A bouquet of white flowers with faint red and blue accents rested in the center of each of the tables. A dance floor was completely open in the very center of the room, and a small stage was constructed directly opposite the entrance with an American flag banner across the back, two projection screens with the Jefferson-Jackson gala logo on display, and a large wooden podium. Chairs were already filling up as guests took their seats.

Liz wasn't sure how Hayden had acquired the ticket, because she wasn't seated in the back, where the reporters typically sat for press events. Not that she was working tonight. Well, not exactly. She wasn't carrying around a camera, at least, and the voice recorder was only for extreme circumstances. She was there primarily to listen, make contacts, and gather information on where she should be the rest of the summer for her later articles, not to write anything specifically about the event.

Hayden had handed over the campaign to her. It was all a bit overwhelming, and she had spent all week plotting out her summer classes and the political appearances she would have to attend. Hayden had given her a list he had already compiled, but he had been planning to add to that after the JJ gala. Now that was her job.

Her phone vibrated in her purse, and she pulled it out.

Have a good time. Wish I could be there with you, Hayden said.

She smiled. Speak of the devil.

Thanks. Me too. I just got here, but I'm not seated in the back. Where did you get these tickets?

My mom pulled some strings. I hope you enjoy it. I'm already missing Chapel Hill.

She wanted to tell him Chapel Hill missed him too, but really it was all too complicated for her to even insinuate.

Bet you're loving D.C., though, she typed. *Plus, your new job starts Monday.*

Nothing compared to running the campus paper, though, I'm sure.

At least it's paid.

True.

Can't beat Pennsylvania Avenue as far as internships go, Liz told him, not looking up from her touch screen and nearly running into someone.

There are better ways to spend your summer.

Liz smiled again bigger. Was he flirting with her? She never could tell. *Well, I have to go find my seat.*

Let me know how it all goes, and have fun!

Liz stuffed her phone back into her purse, on a high from the conversation with Hayden. He was missing Chapel Hill and the paper. He was texting her while away. He must miss her too.

She straightened out her dress, pressing her palms flat as they slid down the silky material. It helped relax her as she searched out her name card. When she located the table, she found Hayden's name instead. She wasn't that surprised since it was so last-minute. She was seated in the second row of tables nearest the stage on the right side. All in all it was a much better seat than she was expecting.

Liz placed her clutch on the table next to her nameplate and pulled out her chair. Her table was empty, but she didn't recognize any of the names of the people around her. She wondered who they were.

Her eyes roamed the ballroom. She recognized quite a few political figures and members of their staffs that she should probably get to know. She wanted to know where the politicians were going to be, or at least get the in on their events. It made things easier to plan. She had decided to primarily follow the Senatorial race, the House race for her district, the governor's race, and the local elections in Orange County.

The lights flickered in the room, indicating that the gala was about to begin. Individuals congregating together and mingling with their friends separated to return to their seats. Old wealthy white women who seemed to know one another surrounded Liz on all sides. They talked incessantly about local politics from several generations ago, and Liz tried to keep up as best she could.

A man in a black suit and blue tie walked purposefully onto the stage, interrupting their conversation. The room fell quiet as they watched him. He adjusted the microphone on the podium and smiled at the crowd. He was an older gentleman in his mid-to-late sixties with a bulging middle and graying hair. His square, wrinkled face was drawn and haggard.

Liz recognized him as Senator Mark Abbot. He had already announced his retirement, and individuals were clamoring for his seat, posturing for contention in the primary, and aligning themselves to be viable nominees.

"Welcome to the fifty-third annual Jefferson-Jackson gala," he called gruffly into the microphone. The crowd erupted into applause. Liz clapped politely along with them.

"Now I know you're all thinking, I was probably at the first Jefferson-Jackson gala." Light laughter ensued. "But I'll have to disappoint you in that regard. I have been to quite a few of these events, and I'll be the first to admit it's a damn good party. So thanks for coming out." Another round of applause followed. "You're probably all starving out there, wondering when this old geezer is going to shut his trap, but I do have to allow one more person to take the stage before we let you off the hook. I'll apologize up front that it's not steak, so you can all hold your complaints."

Liz chuckled. She had heard Senator Abbot speak before on campus, but she didn't remember him joking at all. Retirement must have really been calling his name.

"It's my pleasure to introduce my partner in crime on the Hill. We don't always agree on everything. Actually, if you look at our roll call records, we don't agree on much, but he's a good guy. In the political climate we find ourselves in these days, it's hard to find someone who can see the other side of the aisle, reach over, shake your hand, and politely say, 'I disagree with you.' No name-calling. No jabs. No animosity. I mean, I go get lunch with this guy once a week. And I'll miss that lunch when I'm sitting happily in my beach house in Wilmington ignoring politics."

Man, he was really working the crowd.

"Ladies and gentlemen, Senator Brady Maxwell Jr."

Liz swallowed in anticipation. If Brady's father was here, then surely Brady would be in attendance. She didn't let her eyes wander away from her work to search to see if he was here. But she would be lying to herself if she hadn't been anticipating his presence. Maybe even hoping for it.

The crowd applauded as the two gentlemen met halfway across the stage and shook hands. Liz noticed that they said something to each other and laughed before parting. Senator Maxwell was astonishingly handsome for an older gentleman. It was clear how much his son strongly resembled him. He was tall and distinguished, with dark brown hair growing in salt and pepper around his temples. His smile was infectious, and it wasn't hard to guess that he had the charm of his son. His black tuxedo was pristine, with a crisp white shirt and black bow tie.

"Thank you. Thank you," Senator Maxwell called out, quieting the crowd. "I'd like to take a moment to thank Senator Abbot for his kind words of welcome. I have a feeling I'm going to miss those lunches more than you are."

After a short pause to let the clapping die down, he continued. "Thank you again for coming out to the fifty-third annual JJ gala. I'm pleased to be the opening speaker for the night, especially since this event has so much personal connection to my family.

"Many of you probably don't know that my middle name is Jefferson, or why my great-grandmother insisted that it continue throughout the years. The firstborn son's middle name was Jefferson in every generation since the seventeen hundreds on her side of the family, and she can trace back her own lineage to President Thomas Jefferson himself. I am very proud to be Brady Jefferson Maxwell Jr. and that my son, Brady Jefferson Maxwell III, has similarly taken up his namesake and entered politics.

"As a descendant of the Jefferson household, I would like to formally welcome you. The gala has always held a special place in my heart for the rekindling of the past and the mingling of political company from both sides of the political spectrum. Our differences and how we handle the compromises make this country what it is today. I'm proud to be here tonight celebrating the achievements of the United States and this great state of North Carolina. A toast to you," he said, pointing at the crowd. "Enjoy the evening."

Now that his speech was over, Liz allowed her eyes to drift away from the elder Maxwell and out across the crowd of tables. She was excited and afraid to find him. Mostly because she hadn't called him.

The card had been sitting in her wallet all week, screaming her name. She couldn't allow herself to call, and certainly not after the article she wrote. What had she said about him? *Hypocritical. Power hungry. No vision. Interests lying in how deep his pockets could stretch, not with the people.* The comments were true. His record showed as much, and his ambitious desire to move up the political chain so quickly screamed that he was a man after power. Just like every other politician out there. *Don't be fooled by his pretty face and charming speech.*

Speaking of a pretty face, there he was.

Brady was seated at a table a row in front of hers on the other end of the room, and they were facing each other. He was matching his father in a tuxedo, and he looked perfectly put together. Her heart accelerated all on its own. Liz wondered if he knew she was here. It was unlikely, and she felt as if that gave her the upper hand somehow.

Dinner was served a moment later, and the room fell into hushed conversation mingled with the sounds of forks scraping against plates, glasses being refilled, and waiters' hurried feet. Liz tried to get into the conversations at her table, but none of the women was working on campaigns she was going to be following, and so she spent a lot of her time staring off at the handsome man across the ballroom and enjoying her roasted chicken.

The plates were cleared away, and the keynote speaker, Jeffrey Bakker, founder of the bipartisan organization People for a Better North Carolina, took the stage and delivered the final speech of the evening. Liz was surprised that he was such a good speaker and was able to engage the audience so easily. She wouldn't have expected these events to be entertaining. As he spoke his final words and walked offstage, the lights dimmed slightly and the party began. This was what she had been waiting for, the part where everyone finally socialized.

Most of the room gravitated toward the dance floor as music filtered in through the speakers. She had read about the event from what little information she could glean and knew that the night began with a traditional waltz. Fifty-three years of this event and they were *still* doing ballroom numbers around the room.

Liz, on the other hand, veered in the direct opposite direction. No way was she dancing. She didn't exactly have two left feet, but the last time she had willingly danced was when her mother had stuffed her into ballet lessons at the age of five. Two years of that nonsense and she had stripped quickly out of tights and grabbed a tennis racket. At least she could hit things that way.

Instead, she found the dessert table. Her favorite. She stared at the long table of desserts and zeroed in on the cheesecake. There was something about cheesecake. She couldn't say no to it—and it was Oreo. Double trouble and totally worth it. She didn't care if she had to spend all weekend in the Rams Head gym and on the tennis courts.

Liz took a piece and began to walk toward a group of people standing off to the side. She recognized one of the women as a press director for the governor's campaign. Handy person to know.

As she was about to interject herself into the conversation, she felt someone tap her shoulder. She stopped with her mouth open and turned around in surprise.

"Liz Dougherty," Brady said with a smirk, his big brown eyes staring straight through her.

Liz tried not to miss a beat, but something about him made her insides turn to mush. She hadn't expected him to address her in public.

"You seem to be everywhere, don't you?" he asked when she didn't say anything.

"I try," she said, trying for nonchalance. "And you're following in Daddy's footsteps, Mr. Jefferson."

"That's Senator Jefferson to you," he responded.

Liz laughed. "I didn't know you were related to the Jefferson family, Senator."

"Someone didn't do her homework," he said, tsking her as if she were a schoolgirl. "Whatever will we do with you?"

"I'm sure we'll think of something," Liz said, playing along. Her body was humming with the playful banter.

"I'm sure we will." The sentence hung in the air between them. Liz was holding her breath. His gaze was too intense. It was like the night back at the club when he had fixed her with that same stare.

"I read your article," he said, ending the silence.

Liz swallowed. Great. Why was he even talking to her after reading it? She hadn't been mean, but she hadn't been gentle either. "I bet you loved it," she said with a hint of sarcasm.

"Love might not be the right word. Is there something stronger than love?"

"Hate?" she offered.

Brady chuckled and shook his head. "I particularly like the part about me being—what did you say?—power hungry with my only interests in money? How did you write that, knowing I have other interests?"

He looked at her pointedly, and she swallowed hard. He certainly had other interests . . . like throwing her off balance.

"I was speaking politically. Talking about work."

"Well, are you working tonight? I don't see your voice recorder. No notepad . . ."

Liz shook her head. "No, not tonight." *Well, not exactly.*

"Good. Then our conversation is off the record?" he asked, raising an eyebrow.

She wished he hadn't clarified, but she wasn't going to write another article about him yet.

"Of course," she said, holding her hands up to show him she wasn't hiding a microphone or anything.

"Then would you like to dance?" he asked.

Liz shook her head, glad she had her cheesecake in hand. "No. Uh, no, thank you. I prefer my cheesecake to the waltz."

"Oh, come on. Everyone likes to dance when they have a good partner, and I happen to know where you can find one."

"Are you referring to yourself?" she asked, arching an eyebrow.

"Only the best."

"Sorry, I don't dance," Liz told him. She stuck her fork into the cheesecake to emphasize her disagreement.

He gave her a look that said he was calling bullshit on the remark and took the cheesecake from her hand. "You can have this later. Right now, we're going to dance." Liz glared. "Don't look so sad about it. I promise I'll show you a good time." The comment was laced with seduction.

He grasped her elbow softly in his hand and veered toward the dance floor. He placed her delicious-looking Oreo cheesecake on a table as they passed by.

"Why can't you find someone else?" she asked. She didn't really want him to do that.

"Are there other people in the room?" He placed his hand on her waist and pulled her close. Her breath left her in a whoosh with their bodies so close together, her left hand moving up to his shoulder, and their hands clasping together gently.

"How are the airplanes treating you today?" she managed to ask.

"Much better now that I have you in my arms."

Liz didn't get the chance to comment as the next song began and Brady swept her away into the crowd. She knew she was a bad dancer, but he was amazing. Was there anything he wasn't good at?

His hand held her easily in place and she dared a glance up into his eyes. They were smiling down on her, and she felt like the only person in the room under that gaze. Here she was, dancing with a sitting State Senator.

"I thought you said you didn't dance," he observed.

"I don't," she told him.

"Well, what are we doing right now then?"

"You're currently dragging me around a dance floor. I'm not sure I'm actually participating at all," Liz teased.

"At least you're humoring me," he said, pulling her against his chest.

She leaned her head into him and reminded herself to breathe. They were just dancing.

His hand pressed into her back, his thumb pressing into the soft flesh beneath her dress. The electricity rolling off of his fingertips and into her body was like a constant current wherever he was touching her. How was he able to keep their movements even? She was melting in his arms.

"I do have one question," he breathed into her ear.

"Um . . ." she hesitated, clearing her throat. "What's that?" Where were her reporter instincts? Why wasn't she pushing him away? Why couldn't she keep her heart under control?

"I was curious how you were able to speak so strongly about my character when you haven't had the chance to get to know me."

"My article was based on your voting record. It was an accurate portrayal," she responded unapologetically. His thumb trailed a circle into her lower back, soothing away her defenses.

"You should know that voting records don't always tell the whole story," he said with a smile. "Sometimes you really have to get to know a person before judging them so thoroughly."

"You're not going to change my mind about what I wrote, no matter how charming you are."

"So, you think I'm charming?" he asked with a smirk that said he already knew he was.

She humphed and looked away. The heat was still rising between them, and she didn't want to give him the satisfaction of giving in.

Brady's head tilted down toward her ear, and he whispered, "I'm asking you to get to know me. Is that so bad?"

It wasn't. Actually, with his mouth so close to her ear, it was sounding more and more like a better option than standing on this dance floor.

They left the sentence hanging between them as the song ended.

Liz dropped her arms to her sides reluctantly, and was surprised to find she actually wanted another dance. She had to agree with Brady; it was better when she was in his arms. And it felt like a weight had been placed on her shoulders when he let her go. But that wasn't what she was here for. She wasn't here to get to know Brady Maxwell. She was here to make connections and to make her time this summer at the paper tremendously easier. If she didn't take the networking opportunities seriously tonight, then she would be in for an upward battle the rest of the campaign.

"I think I'll go back to my cheesecake," she murmured, wanting nothing more than to stay.

"I think you'll stay with me."

"Is that a good idea?" Liz couldn't help but wonder how it might look if they were seen together. Not that she believed many people here either knew who she was or knew that she had written an article. They were probably safe, but she never felt like it surrounded by politicians and reporters.

"I think it's the only idea I care about," he told her as a matter of fact.

She swallowed hard. She knew what his intentions had been that night in VIP. Of course she had known, but without him in her presence she thought that maybe she had imagined how alluring and powerful his appeal was.

"I know I'm keeping you from your cheesecake," Brady said with a smile, "but you'll have to forgive me. I'm not letting you out of my sight."

"I think I can manage to forgive you," Liz whispered. If she could be more shocked than she already was, she didn't think it was possible. He was so forward . . . so different from all the other guys she was used to. She was sure that was part of his charm, but how could she resist it?

It worried her a bit—a very little bit at the moment—that she didn't even want to resist him. She had never had the impulsive demeanor of Victoria or the party-girl side of her college friends. Liz's world was rooted in reality, and she had always liked it that way. But she was starting to think that was only because she had never met anyone quite like Brady Maxwell.

And he was staring at her with an unrivaled intensity. She had the odd feeling that Brady Maxwell was seducing her. He had said that he wanted her at the club, but this . . . this was entirely different. This was him at his finest, and she wasn't just happily falling victim to his charming words, gentle touches, piercing eyes, and knowing smiles; she wanted this.

"Liz?" he asked discreetly, brushing his hand up her arm, sending shivers up her spine.

"Yes?" Her eyes fluttered closed at the electricity flowing through her body at his touch. They opened back up to stare into his eyes, and she felt her walls crumbling.

"We should go," he said, lust evident in his voice.

Even knowing it could be a bad idea, she nodded. "Couldn't agree more."

"I have a limo out front. Give the valet this," Brady told her, pulling a small slip of paper out of his pocket. "I'll meet you there."

Liz took the paper out of his hand and without another thought veered toward the door. This was not like her. It was not like her at all. One-night stands weren't in her repertoire. Yet here she was leaving the Jefferson-Jackson gala that she was supposed to be working for networking contacts to get in Senator Brady Maxwell III's limo.

How had her world flipped upside down so easily?

Chapter 8
NO ONE ELSE KNOWS

Liz was leaving the gala. She was actually leaving.

She took a deep breath and kept her feet moving toward the valet station. She had to force herself not to look over her shoulder at the party she was leaving behind. The evening was just beginning and she was walking out on the festivities.

It was deserted outside, and Liz briefly wondered if anyone would notice her absence. No one had known she would be in attendance, and she wasn't a name in journalism. Hayden was the only one who knew she was going to be here, and she didn't want to think about him right now. Liz tucked her gold clutch under her arm higher and strode to the valet.

"Can I help you, miss?" he asked with a smile.

Liz handed him the slip of paper Brady had given her and waited as he called for the limo. She tried not to think about her decision. If she thought about it too much, she wouldn't go through with it;

she wouldn't get into that limo. And she knew that if she didn't, she would regret it forever.

She wasn't prone to rash actions, but something about Brady made her insides flop. Her body heated despite the weather being balmy, comfortable, and beautifully breezy. She felt more as if she were sitting in the heat of her Tampa home than the cool North Carolina weather.

A long black stretch limo pulled up to the valet and he motioned her over.

"Here you are, miss," the valet said, pulling the door open for her.

"Thank you," Liz said, sliding onto the black leather seat. The door closed behind her and cast her into dim lighting.

She looked around, taken with the beautiful sleek interior. An uncorked bottle of champagne chilled in a bucket filled with ice. A flat-screen TV hung against the back wall, and a fully stocked minibar with an assortment of glasses took up a seat on the left.

Liz had never been in a limo before. Her high school boyfriend had wanted to get one for prom, but she had thought it was a waste of money. They had taken his dad's BMW instead. And Brady had a limo just for a gala event. What a different world. Liz found it ironic that this would be her first experience. Victoria would die to know the details, but there was no way she could tell her.

She knew that this was a bad idea . . . a really bad idea. If anyone found out that she had slept with Brady, then she could lose all credibility as a journalist. It would be career suicide for her. The paper had been the only thing she had wanted and worked this hard for. Maybe she shouldn't even be here. Maybe she should get out the other side and walk back to her car.

But she couldn't. She wanted to be with Brady. He had this pull on her, and their connection was like nothing she had ever experienced before. It might be wrong, but she wanted this to happen.

After a few minutes, the limo door opened and her heart rate accelerated.

For a brief second, a part of her thought that it was all going to be some ill-conceived practical joke. Hayden was going to be on the other side of the door with Calleigh Hollingsworth and the other reporters. They would be laughing at her for committing so thoroughly to their prank on the new girl. Because why else would Brady Maxwell ask her to get into his limo?

But then Brady's handsome face came into view. He looked at her, smiled that gorgeous, charming, incomparable smile, and she was lost once more.

"You stayed," he said, sitting down next to her.

"Are you surprised?" Liz asked, déjà vu washing over her. How often did this man get turned down that he would seem so surprised that she was near him? Didn't seem likely that it would be very often.

"This time, no," Brady told her confidently. The door slammed shut, casting them back into darkness.

"Do you often take limos out?" She broke his intense gaze and focused on her surroundings.

"Sometimes. I was an honored guest tonight, so the gala provided one."

"My lucky night, I guess," she said with a smile in his direction.

He chuckled. "I actually think it's mine. How else could I have impressed you?"

Liz tried not to gawk as she considered the question. She was pretty sure everything about him was impressive.

Watching his mouth quirk up at the side, she realized he was teasing her. That look of pure confidence did inappropriate things to her. She had the sudden urge to jump him right there in the limo. Normally that much cocky self-importance would have been a turnoff, but Brady was breaking every rule in her book.

The limo started moving then, taking them to their unknown destination. Liz didn't even want to know or else she might chicken out. She would rather step out of the limo with him at some unfamiliar place and simply follow his lead.

"You didn't have any champagne," Brady said, pulling the bottle from the ice and pouring them each a flute. The dim light fell across the label. Dom Pérignon. She shouldn't have been surprised, but she was.

"I wasn't sure I could," she admitted. Also, she was nervous as hell.

"Well, here you go." He handed her a drink. They clinked their glasses together, and she drank the champagne faster than she anticipated. It tasted like pure, bubbly bliss, way smoother than anything she had ever tasted before. He took a sip from his own glass and placed it by the ice bucket while she finished hers off.

"Want another?" he asked with a soft chuckle.

"Yes, please," Liz said, handing the glass back. Brady refilled it, and she took her time sipping the champagne. His eyes were watching her, and she wondered what he was thinking. Was he going to make a move? Was he waiting for her to make a move? What did he *want* from her? She had too many thoughts coursing through her head, and she was wishing she'd had more to drink at the party to calm herself down.

Liz finished her second glass and handed it back to Brady. Instead of refilling it, he placed the empty glass next to his own and pulled her close to him. He draped an arm around the back of the seat and he laced their fingers together.

Her heart was pitter-pattering in her chest at his nearness. He was so warm and comfortable, and God, did she love the way his hands felt connected with hers. He sent chills up her spine as the pads of his fingertips traced soft lines into her skin. Their hips touched on the leather seat, and she could feel his muscular leg

K.A. Linde

pressing against her own thigh. She crossed her legs at the knee as warm tingling sensations swept through her body.

He wasn't doing anything more than holding her hand, and her body was already molten lava. His breath was hot on her neck as he stared down at her. He seemed to be waiting for her to look at him, but she wasn't sure she could control her body at the moment.

"Liz?" he whispered into her ear. His forehead rested on her head as he breathed softly, waiting for her reply. She didn't think she trusted her voice to answer.

When she didn't respond, his mouth moved to her ear, nipping at it softly. He trailed his tongue down the side, causing her entire body to shiver in response. Nothing in her entire life had ever been so seductive, and she pressed her legs together in response. He must have known exactly what he was doing to her, because his grip on her hand tightened, and his other arm slid down to grasp her shoulder and pull her in closer.

"Liz?" he repeated, his voice a soft growl of desperation. Liz was sure that she would never want to hear her name uttered another way.

His tongue swirled around her earlobe, and her eyes fluttered closed, her head dropping back onto his arm in response. He tugged softly on the delicate skin, and she released a soft moan.

"Don't make me ask again," he groaned, his hand moving down her arm to circle her waist, grasping her tightly,

"Ye-yes," Liz finally muttered breathily. She was surprised she was coherent at all.

"Look at me."

She did what she was told without a second thought. Her head moved to the side and she stared up into his brown eyes. All she saw there was desire. He wanted her. Brady Maxwell, a sitting State Senator, wanted *her*.

Her world felt completely and totally upside down. Here was this incredibly handsome, unbelievably sexy man all but throwing himself at her. Yet, she had called him out in front of a roomful of people and written a negative article about him. Her mind was conflicted, but her body certainly wasn't. Her body was telling her mind to shut the fuck up and just enjoy herself, because she knew that she definitely would.

But what about her career? Could this damage her career? Liz tried not to think about it. She didn't want to think about it. She just wanted Brady.

As if he could tell that she was finished arguing with herself, his head lowered and his lips captured hers. His lips were soft and tender, but eager and demanding . . . just like him. As soon as he touched her, she wanted more.

Her hands ran up his suit and into his thick, dark hair, pulling on the strands. Brady groaned into her mouth, and Liz smiled, knowing she had found a weak spot. His arms reached all the way around her, yanking her against him and into his lap. Her dress fell askew as she pressed her warm body against him. Their tongues volleyed while Liz kissed him back with a ferocity that rivaled his own heightened desire.

How she had ever lived without his kisses in her life prior to this moment was an utter mystery. The raw intensity of their longing for each other surprised her. She had never felt so wanton before.

Yet, at the same time, she couldn't seem to control or stop it. Not that she wanted to.

They kissed feverishly for the remainder of the ride, coming up for air sparingly. Her lips were swollen and her breath was coming in spurts. She could feel every single place where her body was touching his like flames scorching through her skin.

The limo came to a stop all too soon. They slowly disentangled their limbs and separated. Brady refused to let go of her hand even as she attempted to straighten out her dress.

"I could stay like this with you . . ." he murmured softly, trailing off as he brought her hand up to his lips and kissed her there.

Liz wondered if he had meant to say *forever* at the end of that sentence.

The door clicked open behind her, and Brady broke away, cutting off whatever he had meant to say afterward. Liz reached for her purse and exited the limo with Brady close behind.

She realized that, unsurprisingly, they were at an upscale hotel in downtown Charlotte. It had an all-glass front and an imposing exterior, and Brady walked right into the hotel as if he owned the place. Liz tried to give off half the amount of confidence he had. She was sure that she failed, but it didn't matter. No one would spare two seconds to glance at her compared to him.

They walked right through the black-and-gray marble-tiled lobby with its dark mahogany walls, glass tables topped with strange, expensive-looking, ornamental glass decorations, and dark slate countertops. Brady didn't check in, and Liz wondered how long he had been in Charlotte or if he had checked in to the hotel earlier today. He punched the elevator for the top floor and it lifted them up immediately.

Brady smiled at her reassuringly as the elevator took its time taking them up. All she could think about was having his lips on her once more. Those beautiful lips smiling down at her and only her.

Liz had liked plenty of guys before, but it had never felt like this. Maybe it was because he was completely unattainable. Maybe it was because there was no way this could go anywhere at all. Maybe it was just because she wanted him. Simple lust that she was giving in to. She didn't even like him . . . not really. How could she like him if she didn't even know him and the only things that she did know about him, she disagreed with?

For some reason that didn't bother her as she thought it might.

Brady took her hand again when they stepped out of the elevator and showed her the way down the hallway. He chuckled softly to himself as he slid the keycard into the door.

"What's so funny?" Liz asked. He had such a great laugh.

"This is the presidential suite," he told her with a shrug.

"You're not the president," she said, arching an eyebrow.

"Not yet," he stated confidently, pulling her through the open doorway.

She rolled her eyes dramatically. "A little ahead of yourself, aren't you? Not even sitting in Congress and you're putting yourself in the White House."

"I didn't come here to talk politics with you, baby," Brady said, pushing the door closed behind them. "Lecture me after I'm done with you."

Before she had a chance to retort, Brady slammed her backward into the doorframe, her body colliding with the hard wooden door. She heard a dull thud echo around the room and wondered if the sound was as loud on the outside. Would people know what they were doing in the dark hotel room? Did she care?

She stared from under thick, black lashes at the man before her, seized with her growing desire. His hands came down hard and fast on either side of her head, rapping against the wood. She felt the vibrations ring in her ears, and her heart sped up double time. She stared up at him, trapped in his deep chocolaty eyes, lost to the world she lived in. His eyes consumed her, devoured her, absorbed her—and she was fully clothed.

Fuck! She wanted him. She wanted him badly enough that she all but begged him to continue. She could feel the heat radiating off of their bodies, the electrifying atmosphere, and the ever-present tension from the minimal space between them. He was so close, so damn close. His lips were hovering only inches above her, tempting her, teasing her. She swallowed hard, her chest heaving with the exertion it took to not throw herself at him.

"Brady," she groaned as his hand moved from the doorframe to trail gingerly across her cheek, flutter down the curve of her neck, brush against her exposed collarbone, and continue to her breast and waist. She thought she might combust.

"No talking," he growled, circling his arm around her waist and pulling her hips away from the wall. Her feet slid forward against the carpeted floor as he pushed himself against her, his lower half covering her body. Her breath caught at the feel of him through his suit pants. Damn!

Liz tried to hold her focus, but she was having trouble thinking about anything but what he was pressing up against her. She was burning with desire, and any thought of stopping had flown out the window when she had been thrown up against the door. Not that she had ever given any real thought to it to begin with.

Brady leaned forward, pressing against her harder, and kissed the same trail he had made with his hand. She whimpered, trying to keep from squirming at his slow progression. His grip on her waist tightened as he kissed across her breast and down her stomach. She could hardly keep her eyes open, but she had to watch him as he knelt before her.

She would never forget the day she brought a Senator to his knees. She couldn't keep the smirk off her face at the thought.

"What's that look for?" he asked, his eyes meeting hers. She tried not to look too devious. He immediately stood, and she bit down on her lip, looking up at him, refusing to break his rule. "You can answer," he told her.

"I was thinking about bringing a Senator to his knees," she said, her voice throaty and hoarse, trying to keep her desire in check long enough to speak.

"You think I'm the only one who will be on their knees?" he asked pointedly. She knew she would do just about anything for him if he continued. Brady moved forward and kissed her lips. She sighed into him, and he pushed her hands over her head. Breaking away from her, leaving her wanting more, he asked, "If I asked you to get on your knees right now, would you?"

Liz nodded without hesitation. She would do anything he asked in that moment.

"Good," he said, pleased. His hands found her waist again, gripping her securely and possessively. She never wanted him to let go.

Sliding his grip down across her butt and grabbing her thighs, Brady hoisted her legs up and around his waist. She immediately circled her arms around his neck and brought herself closer to him. He nipped at her bottom lip, causing her to writhe against him. What a tease!

He chuckled at her enthusiasm and managed to still her hips from their enticing motion as he carried her across the room. She could feel him digging his hands into the soft flesh on the backs of her thighs, holding her in place. She didn't know why, but that was making her even hotter than his teasing antics.

She hadn't gotten a glimpse of the room, as Brady had never flicked on the lights, but she could grasp that it was massive. He kicked open a partially closed double door that led to a master suite, and tossed her backward onto the king-sized bed. She lay sprawled across the comforter, her dress hiked up and one sleeve falling off her shoulder, but she didn't readjust. She could tell he was enjoying the view.

Her eyes followed him as he slid out of his jacket, then slowly unbuttoned each button on his stark white dress shirt. He shrugged the thing off of his shoulders and tossed it on the empty desk. His white undershirt came off next, and she marveled at him as he revealed the incredibly toned six-pack lying beneath. Why he would ever cover that up was beyond Liz's comprehension. She wanted to run her hands across it and lick her way down. He even had those gorgeous sexy lines that led right to where he was popping the button on his pants.

The zipper fell to the bottom, and her intake of breath was more than evident as his pants fell off his hips to pool at his feet. The erection beneath his boxer briefs was bulging, and she wanted nothing more than to take him right then and there.

He crawled across the bed toward her, and she suddenly realized how clothed she was in comparison. "Don't," he said immediately as she tried to shimmy out of her dress. She stilled her hands and waited impatiently. "I want to do it."

He reached out and grabbed her foot, yanking her flat against the bed and bunching her dress up around her waist in the process. She felt exposed in her cream thong, but the way he was looking at her made her forget all her worries. He was clearly enjoying her athletic build.

Brady's hands deftly found the side zipper and pulled it down to her hip. Sliding his hands up her sides, he pulled the dress over her head. As he tossed the dress to the ground, his eyes roamed her body. Liz met his eyes when they found hers, not breaking away despite the intensity of his stare. Her mind was lost in the depths of those dark eyes.

He didn't make a move for a while and she was growing antsy for his touch once more. How had she already gotten so desperate for him? Only a week ago, she had been standing in a sea of reporters while he announced his bid to run. Now she was lying under his heated gaze, nearly naked. She wasn't embarrassed or mortified by her actions. She would leave that for another day. Right now, all she wanted was Brady, however she could have him.

Liz licked her lips teasingly when his eyes shifted down to her mouth. "Are you going to kiss me?" she murmured.

"Senseless."

She smiled as he leaned down and brushed his lips against each cheek, her nose, her chin. She tried to angle her face so she could touch his lips, but he was totally in control. Moving farther down, his mouth traveled along her throat, leaving light kisses on her collarbone. His hands moved underneath her body, flicking the clasp of her bra and easing her out of it.

"Mmm," he groaned when her breasts were in full view. She knew she had a nice rack, and she couldn't deny it gave her satisfaction to see how much he appreciated them.

Brady's hands were on her breasts in a moment, massaging them until her nipples were hard. He pulled one into his mouth, circling his tongue around it until she writhed, then moved to the next one, showing it the same attention. She wound her fingers into his dark hair and tugged, never wanting him to stop.

His thumb replaced his mouth, stroking the peak to keep her heated as he traveled farther south down her flat stomach to the edge of her thong. He released her aching breast so he could hook his thumbs under the material and yank it off in one swift motion, leaving her completely nude beneath him.

Normally she would have felt self-conscious. No one usually assessed her body quite so thoroughly, but he seemed to be drinking in every single inch of her, admiring every curve, letting his tongue touch every ounce of flesh he could. And something about the way he looked at her dissolved all nervousness she might have had.

Brady was admiring her as if she were an angel fit for the heavens, and the way he was touching her made her feel like she had tasted ambrosia itself.

His hand came up and ran along her inner thigh and down between her legs. Liz groaned as he slipped one finger in and out of her.

"God, you're wet," he growled. He was clearly restraining himself.

"Brady," she moaned, her grip tightening in his hair. He looked up at her and landed another kiss on her stomach. "*All* I can think about is you fucking my brains out."

"Fuck," he said, gripping her inner thigh. His breath came out ragged for a second before he moved off the bed, dropped his boxers to the floor, slid on a condom, and moved over her.

Liz had less than a second of forethought before he entered her. She cried out at the hardness of his dick pushing farther into her, filling her completely.

"You feel so fucking amazing," he said into her ear when he was all the way in. Liz couldn't even manage a coherent sentence. Nothing had ever felt this good, and she was sure nothing else ever would. Her body throbbed all over, and she was aching for a climax.

She didn't even want to think about how long it had been since she'd last had sex. It wouldn't have changed how right it felt to be with him. She had always thought that the first time with someone new was awkward, but apparently Brady wasn't awkward with anything.

He began moving inside of her at an uneven pace—pulling out slowly and then slamming fast into her, causing her to whimper in pleasure each time. He kept up the pace until she felt her body tightening so hard she was close to convulsions. His breathing was rough as he pushed into her faster, reaching for an even deeper position.

Heat took over her body, starting at her toes curling against the mattress and rushing up all the way to her head. She felt the waves of energy pass through her, building up inside, and then rocketing from her core out. Her orgasm hit her like a punch to the gut. All the wind rushed out of her, her back arched off the bed, and she tightened around him until she was spent. Brady stilled within her, letting her ride out the pleasure.

When she was finished, lying with her eyes closed and a giant smile on her face, he pulled out. She groaned at the loss of him, already wanting more.

"Flip over," he commanded, grabbing her hips and turning her over. "I want you to come for me again."

Liz did what she was told as her body continued to hum. She felt a bit strange automatically moving onto her hands and knees at his request. She couldn't count the number of times she had refused the same position before, because she felt degraded. But after that orgasm and the promise of another, she wouldn't be turning him down. Absolutely not.

Brady entered her from behind, reaching even deeper than before, and she felt her body tense all around him. He was so big!

He didn't hold anything back this time. He reared back and then slammed into her over and over again, sometimes sending her entire body forward with the force of his movements. She could feel her body rejecting the pain as he forced into her harder and harder each time.

But at the same time, she found that she liked it. She liked how rough he was being, and each time he collided forward into her body, she wanted him to do it harder. His hands dug into her hips, and at times he would pull back on them, roughly smacking their bodies together. The pain mingled so perfectly with the pleasure that the lines blurred and she didn't know which she was enjoying more.

All she knew was that she was getting really close again, and he was getting even closer.

"Liz," he groaned her name, pushing into her again.

"Yeah," she moaned, her elbows dropping onto the mattress.

"I want you to come for me."

No arguments here.

"Fuck!" he cried out. "I'll keep talkin' dirty if you clench around me like that again."

Liz was too flushed to color at the comment. She liked everything he did at this point.

Her body didn't give her any warning this time. She saw spots with the intensity of it all, and buried her head into the pillow. She heard Brady grunt and then come, doubling over on top of her.

They both lay there, breathing heavily, unable to think, let alone move.

After a while, Brady moved out of her and padded to the bathroom to clean up. Liz collapsed forward onto the bed, curling up around herself. Exhaustion hit her with the strength of a bulldozer, and she felt herself drifting off.

Brady returned a minute later, replacing his boxer briefs and curling up into bed next to her. "Hey, your turn," he whispered, kissing her shoulder.

Liz grumbled but stood shakily and cleaned up. The overpowering smell of sex hit her when she walked back into the room, and she smiled lazily as she crawled under the covers. Brady pulled her close to him, cradling her in his arms.

"You're amazing," he told her, running his hand up and down her arm.

"You're pretty amazing yourself," she murmured drowsily.

They lay there together in the silence, absorbed in the ecstasy of their actions. Liz was nearly asleep when Brady spoke again. "Are you asleep?"

She yawned and rolled over to face him. "Not anymore."

He smiled sweetly at her and threaded his hand through her blond hair. She closed her eyes and let her mind drift again. He bent down and placed a soft kiss on her lips. "There's your kiss."

"You were right," she whispered.

"About what?"

"I'm pretty senseless," she told him.

He chuckled softly, giving her another kiss. "I like you like this. Not quite so snippy, are you?"

"You don't like me snippy?" she asked between yawns.

"Wouldn't change it for the world."

She smiled brightly at that comment and leaned into his shoulder. She was really enjoying the way he was playing with her hair. If he kept it up, she would be asleep soon enough.

"Tell me something no one else knows about you," he said, kissing down her jawline.

"Something no one else knows about me?" Liz opened her eyes and gazed up at him.

"Yes. I want something that no one else has."

"I slept with a Senator," she murmured, leaning her forehead into him to hide her face.

He chuckled softly and raised her chin with his fingers. "Are you embarrassed?"

"No," she said, blushing furiously.

"Oh really?"

"I'm not!" she told him.

"Fine." He planted a kiss on her red cheeks. "But you didn't answer my question. I already knew that. I want to know something no one else knows."

"That's all. That's the only thing no one else knows about me," she told him, biting her lip.

"You don't have any secrets?"

"You're my only secret."

"I'll keep that one," he told her.

Chapter 9

THE AFTERMATH

Life after Brady was like watching a film in black and white. It was really quite beautiful, but it felt like something was missing.

Liz went about her daily life—class, newspaper, sleep. It was all important, but it suddenly felt entirely too dull without him. She wasn't the type to get easily attached, and she found that she didn't understand her feelings toward him. They had spoken only twice, and for rather brief periods of time. She hardly knew him at all. Yet she had gone back to his hotel room with him. It made no sense. She wasn't *that* girl. When it came down to it, she couldn't decide whether she actually liked Brady or it was simply infatuation.

Either way, she didn't care. She just wanted more of him.

Instead she was stuck in her journalism class for the summer. The class was interesting, and she absolutely loved the professor. She'd had her the previous semester, and it was one of the main reasons she was taking the class. Professor Mires was particularly flexible around the summer session. She was allowing Liz to use her experience on the paper as her project for the semester, taking a huge weight off of her shoulders. It gave Liz a lot more time to focus on the local elections than she had been expecting, and she had taken to obsessing over campaign schedules.

Normally it would have been a light election season, picking up ferocity right around the time school started again in the fall. But since Senator Abbot and Representative Huntington had announced their retirement in the spring, contenders had started popping up like wildflowers. She was concentrating her efforts on the House campaign, and then would move on to the Senate. Three main candidates appeared on each side of the aisle for the House race, and Liz had opened her column with a daily focus on each of them.

Liz was on day six now, saving the best for last.

She stared down at the picture she had chosen of Brady out of the shots Hayden had taken at the Raleigh press conference. Brady's charismatic smile was missing from his face, and he actually managed to look serious. Liz wondered when this picture had been taken. He looked as if he were staring straight through her. She squirmed under his scrutiny and stood, stretching her aching muscles.

The paper was dead quiet, and all the lights had been shut off except for Hayden's office, which she had confiscated for the summer. She yawned, rolling a kink out of her neck. It was midnight, an hour past building close. She was glad she had the all-access key.

Liz shut down her laptop and stuffed it into her backpack. She had been working too hard, trying to drown out the inexplicable feeling of longing that had taken residence in her body. With Victoria gone for the summer, Liz was practically living at the office to escape the quiet.

She took one last glance around the office to make sure she had everything before shouldering her bag and leaving. She fumbled around for the light switch on the wall to illuminate the open office space. Just when she found it, she heard the phone ring in Hayden's office.

No one ever rang the paper this late. Turning back into the office, she grabbed the phone and answered, "Hello?"

"Hello, I'm trying to reach Liz Dougherty, please," a woman's voice said through the line.

Liz's eyebrows scrunched together in confusion. That was even stranger. People asked for a specific reporter only under rare circumstances. Hayden was asked for frequently, because everyone on campus knew who he was. Usually it was in relation to an article the reporter had written or requesting a follow up or, as with most of them, a friend who couldn't reach the person on their cell phone. But Liz had never been asked for by name.

"Um . . . yes, this is Liz. Who is calling? It is after hours," she reminded the woman. Though how she couldn't know that it was midnight was beyond her.

"This is Heather Ferrington, chief press secretary with State Senator Brady Maxwell."

Liz's mouth dropped open. Was she serious? When she had left Brady's hotel room last weekend, she had been certain it was the last she would hear from him. He got what he wanted from her, and though he said he would reach out to her again, she hadn't really believed him.

"Miss Dougherty, are you still there?" Heather asked.

Liz snapped out of her daydream. "Yes, I'm still here. How can I help you, Ms. Ferrington?"

"I've been informed that you are the contact for the campaign division of the paper; is that correct?" she asked in the most condescending fashion she could muster.

"I am."

"We've spoken with the university and set up a time for the Senator to speak publicly about his leap into federal politics. We have very few trips planned for the summer, but Senator Maxwell is making it a priority to speak at his alma mater," Heather told her.

Liz's mind was working overtime. Brady was coming here. To her school. Well, their school. Whatever! He was going to be in Chapel Hill to give a speech. This certainly wasn't a planned venue. The student body wasn't a target audience for the local elections, even though Liz was desperately trying to get them more invested.

During the presidential election her freshman year, the campus had been a madhouse, but students simply hadn't put in as much effort for the local politicians. Whether it was because they had a local representative at home (even though they lived at the school for at least nine months out of the year) or they were too busy with their social lives, it just wasn't a priority. She could count on the two party organizations, the Campus Y, and a few other politically active groups on campus to spread the word on their own, but sometimes it felt as if she were hitting her head against a brick wall.

But if Brady was coming to campus and it wasn't a planned venue for him, then he had to be doing it for a reason. And she couldn't think that that reason was . . . *her*.

"The university has approved space and even encouraged us to consider doing a series about the upcoming election. We're still considering that option, but as you are our contact at the campus paper, we wanted to let you know that this is an open press event. We won't be taking questions until after the event closes, at Senator Maxwell's request. We hope that you will be in attendance for this special occasion," Heather said in the same condescending tone.

It hardly felt like a press request, more like a demand. Liz's insides were squirming at the thought of seeing Brady again, but she wasn't comfortable with this conversation. Who called after hours like this? If this was about Brady, then he could damn well call her himself.

"Thank you, Ms. Ferrington. We'll take it under consideration. If you need to reach us again, please do call during office hours. We typically aren't working this late," Liz answered diplomatically.

"Look, Miss Dougherty . . ." Heather said impatiently. Liz was waiting for her to humph on the other end of the line. "Senator Maxwell's time is limited, and he's coming to the university. If your paper isn't interested in covering a prominent local official, I'd be happy to reach out to *Chapel Hill News*."

Liz held back the immediate bitchy retort that was hanging on the tip of her tongue. Did this woman think it was appropriate to *bully* a newspaper?

She took a deep breath before replying. "We would be happy to have *Chapel Hill News* on campus, of course. Please send over the details for the event, and a reporter will be in attendance. Thank you for informing us of this great opportunity," she said as cheerfully as possible.

"Wonderful, Miss Dougherty. Glad we're on the same terms. I'll shoot an email over to you with the details. Look forward to meeting you then."

"You too, Ms. Ferrington," Liz said as she hung up the phone. She had already met Heather once before, two weeks earlier. She wondered whether Heather would remember her, whether she knew that Liz had slept with Brady—if Heather herself had slept with Brady. No. She didn't want to think about that. She had spent too much time thinking about Brady Maxwell already. Most of it wondering whether she was ever going to see him in person again, or if she would be left with his shots on her computer screen.

Now that she knew she would be seeing him again, she was even more concerned with how the event would play out. Did no questions until after mean he wanted to see her afterward? What was his motivation for coming here anyway?

She had so many questions, and she realized that she was now very much awake. Sighing in frustration, Liz pulled her computer back out and booted it up. She wasn't going to bed anytime soon.

Liz woke the next morning with her head buried in the keys of her laptop. Grumbling to herself, she yawned widely and closed the monitor. She hadn't even known it was possible to actually fall asleep on her computer.

Running a hand back through her hair, she grabbed her bag and walked out into the main office. She hoped she didn't look as shitty as she felt.

"Morning, Liz," Meagan called cheerfully as Liz walked by. Liz waved at her halfheartedly, ready to get out of the office and back to her house. "Long night?"

"Yeah," she grumbled, trying her best to get away as quickly as possible. Meagan was a known big mouth. Once you got her talking, it was impossible to get away. She ran an opinions column that was relatively popular among the student body, but the column had no background in even basic journalism.

"I got some bagels from Alpine. Do you want one?" Meagan asked.

"Nah, that's all right. I'm about to go get some food."

"I'll come with you," she said, packing up her things.

"Really, Meagan, I've had a long night, and I'm sure you have a lot of work to do. I'll catch up with you later," Liz said, darting out of the office.

She made it down to her car, happy that it didn't have a ticket on the windshield. They started at forty dollars regardless of the offense. While she probably deserved it for staying in the service vehicle lot overnight, she was glad that fate had looked on her with good fortune. Returning to her house off campus, she took a quick shower to wash away the grime of the office. She scarfed down a bowl of Frosted Flakes and then hightailed it back to campus. At this rate she was going to be late for her class.

Liz was running too far behind to walk to campus or take the bus, so she would have to pay for parking in one of the few decks on campus. There were a ton of spots thanks to the summer session, but it was still an uphill hike to her class. Sweat beaded on her temples as she climbed the hill, reached the journalism building, and rushed into the over-air-conditioned room.

Professor Mires was Liz's favorite instructor, and she hated being late to her class. She slipped into the room right before the professor closed the door.

"Good to see you, Miss Dougherty," Professor Mires said.

"Morning, Professor," Liz said with a sheepish smile.

Professor Mires was a younger professor as far as they went, probably in her early thirties. She dressed like a fashionable hippie, with librarian glasses and her hair always pulled back into a messy bun. She was married to a guy a couple years younger than her who hung around her office all the time. All the girls swooned over him, because he was always bringing her flowers and leaving her love notes on her whiteboard.

Liz took a seat at the back of the room and pulled her computer out. She still needed to check to see whether she had received an email from Heather with the details of Brady's campus visit.

Her in-box lit up before her eyes as Professor Mires began the lecture. The majority of the emails were clothing stores asking for her business, and articles from the newspapers that she followed. And there at the bottom sat one email from a Ms. Heather Ferrington. Liz clicked on the email and read through it. Her stomach dropped when she saw the date. Wednesday. Next Wednesday. As in a week from now. Two whole weeks without Brady.

Liz knew she shouldn't have been disappointed, but she wanted him here sooner. Of course, he was busy running for office and all. There was no way he would be here today or tomorrow or any sooner. Not to mention the university probably didn't have immediate open space either.

But that left her another whole week to obsess about Brady.

A new message came in and Liz clicked back to her in-box. Her heart skipped when she saw who it was from. Hayden Lane.

She hadn't thought about him in a week. Before Brady had catapulted into her life, she had been so set on Hayden. They'd had their pseudo date before he left and then that awkward moment when he had basically said they couldn't date. She still wasn't sure what Hayden was feeling or if he was into her. Didn't really matter right now anyway. Hayden was in D.C., and she was aching in all the right places for a Senator she could never really be with.

> *Liz,*
>
> *How are things at the paper? I've been following your column and love what you're doing with it. Wish I could be there. I'm seriously missing it. Can't think of anything I'd like to be doing less than getting people coffee. Hope your summer has been more eventful than mine so far.*
>
> *I received an email from the Maxwell campaign's press secretary last night. They're doing a special presentation next Wednesday. Wasn't sure if she contacted you or not, but I thought I'd attach the email here. We should definitely be there. I think Maxwell's primary race will be the one to watch. Your last article about him really got the student body to pay attention for once. I'd recommend introducing yourself to him. I know you disagree with the guy, but it would be great for the paper if we could get an interview.*

Let me know how it all goes. Hope you're still considering
a trip up here. I'd love to show you around.

Hayden Lane
Editor-in-Chief

Liz read through the email twice, getting more irritated the second read through. She seriously wanted to have words with Heather Ferrington. Why did she call her at midnight last night if she had already emailed Hayden the details the day before?

Then there was the part about Brady. She had already introduced herself to him . . . *all* of herself. If she managed to find herself alone with him for an interview, she wasn't sure she could guarantee that it wouldn't happen again. If only Hayden knew what he was saying by pushing her toward an interview with Brady.

Her anger slowly deflated. Hayden kind of seemed to . . . miss her. He had asked about her summer and even asked her to come to D.C. to see him again. She hadn't thought he was serious about her visiting. Now she was thinking about when she could fit it into her summer schedule. Probably the end of July. Right after the journalism class let out would probably be best.

Taking a deep breath, she jotted out a reply.

Hayden,
The paper is great. Everyone misses having you around
to keep us in line, but we're making do without you. My
summer has been generally boring besides the column, which
Professor Mires said I could use for my class project. Sorry to
hear your summer isn't everything you wanted it to be. Do
they have you doing anything besides acquiring coffee?
I received this information from Ms. Ferrington just
before your email. I've already agreed that we'd cover it. I'll

*see what I can do about an interview. If he's read my article,
I doubt he'll give me one, but I'll do what I can.*

Liz cringed at the obvious deception, but it wasn't as if she could tell Hayden she had slept with Brady. She continued with her email.

*A trip to D.C. sounds great. What about after the end of
the term? I think I'm free late July, if that works for you.
Love,*

Liz paused. That was probably all wrong. She backspaced the valediction and tried again.

*Best,
Liz*

She hit Send and waited for a reply. She had taken too much time writing it to begin with. She had no idea what the professor was lecturing on now. It had been rough trying to say everything she wanted to say without going overboard. She had decided in the end to keep it as short as possible.

Liz didn't know how long it would be before she got a reply, but she couldn't text him while she was in class. So she waited. When the email didn't come, she finally gave up and paid more attention to Professor Mires's lecture.

Right before class ended, the return email popped up.

*Liz,
Yes, I exaggerated. I am doing some research, but it's
mindless. Save me from myself.
Late July it is. I asked off for the last weekend in July, so
don't change your mind.*

Go get back to work!

Hayden Lane
Editor-in-Chief

Liz smiled brightly and even laughed at his last line. Hayden wanted her in D.C. and he had taken the weekend off. She had plans to be with him for the weekend. Butterflies fluttered in her stomach as her remembered crush blossomed inside of her.

This was probably more realistic than Brady anyway.

Professor Mires completed her lesson and began packing up her bag. Liz and the rest of the students in the class followed suit. Liz shut her computer down and stuffed it back into her backpack. She had a lot of work to do before Brady came into town, and she knew she needed to get started tonight.

"Miss Dougherty, may I have a word with you?" Professor Mires asked as Liz walked past her.

"Of course," Liz said. She hoped she didn't get in trouble for being on her computer all class. She was normally more focused than she had been today, but with both Hayden and Brady swirling around in her thoughts, it was hard to concentrate on the lecture.

Liz stood off to the side while her classmates filed out of the lecture hall, leaving them all alone.

"I wanted to discuss the recent assignment that you turned in," Professor Mires said, taking a seat on the wood stool in from of the podium. "Was this from your newspaper column?"

"Yes, I thought you said it was okay for me to use that," Liz said. Her heart was racing. Professor Mires had never pulled her aside to discuss her academic work like this . . . no one ever had. She usually received high marks across the board.

"It is. I don't mind you using the articles for the assignment at all. I think real-life practicum in journalism is essential to improvement and potential job opportunities postgraduation. I am always pleased when my students go above and beyond the classroom," she said with a calming tone.

Liz could feel a "but" coming on at the end of that statement. The professor seemed to have more to say.

"I do have some concerns about the quality of the work, though," Professor Mires said, handing over Liz's paper.

She took it in her hands and saw the red ink scrawled all over the first article she had written about Brady. It was the one that had met with such fanfare from the students on campus. They'd had to reprint because of it. She flipped it to the last page and saw a big C+ circled on the page. Her heart sank. She had never received a C in her entire life. Not once. She could count the number of B minuses on one hand. What the hell had happened?

If she didn't improve this grade, she could lose her scholarship!

"A C plus?" Liz asked, her voice cracking.

"It's not that the article is poorly written. It reads really well, and it's polished."

"Then what's wrong?" she asked, skimming the comments on the front page.

"In journalism we strive for objectivity if at all possible. Had this article just been something you were writing for the student body and not for me, then it would have been sufficient, but you must think of your audience. How broad could it be? Who could be reading it? When I read the article, I heard your voice, which is very clear and solid, and then I heard your opinion on the Senator."

Her opinion on the Senator. How ironic, considering they had been in a hotel room together only a week ago.

"I think you have room for growth and your grade reflects that. Strive for objectivity in your writing. I don't want your opinions to bleed onto the page. You're not writing an editorial. I wouldn't have accepted editorials. Take a chance to look at the other side, do some more research, and then write an article that clearly states the facts," Professor Mires instructed her. "I'm not saying lose your voice or drain the page of emotion. I'm saying find a happy medium between the two. I believe you can do it, and I'll expect it to improve as we go forward if you hope to improve that grade."

"Thank you," Liz said, rolling the paper up in her hand for her to look over later. "I'll do my best."

"You always do, Liz," she said with a smile.

Liz walked out of the classroom in a daze. She had thought that she had been objective and looked at both sides this whole time. Now her professor was telling her the opposite, and Liz wasn't even sure where to begin. If she wanted that A, then she had her work cut out for her this summer.

Chapter 10

STAYING PROFESSIONAL

Liz sat with her friend Justin in the sound booth at the Great Hall auditorium, which the Maxwell campaign had been granted for their event. It was a large room built for five hundred, with a raised stage and podium. The Great Hall was a hot spot on campus, with a constant influx of student groups for theater productions, dance performances, a cappella shows, and the like.

Today it was covered in the red-white-and-blue signs the campaign had decorated it with, and each chair had a sign that had the Maxwell logo in the center—VOTE FOR MAXWELL in a circle with the words bolded. VOTE FOR was written like an American flag in red stars and stripes on the blue background, with MAXWELL in a stark, blocky white font. A globe focused on North America was at the center, reaffirming Liz's belief that Brady wanted to take over. The logo was a power symbol, and now it would be all over campus.

Students and faculty alike were filing into the room, taking the signs from the seats and sitting down. It was the summer session, but after Liz's articles and the work she had done building up to this, the room was pretty full. She wasn't sure why she had put so much effort into it, but she wanted the event to be successful.

Part of her wanted to say that it was only for the paper and her career. If more people came to these events and showed an interest, then her column would improve and she might be able to hit the front cover more often. At least overshadow another drunken debauchery scene on Franklin Street for once.

But the rest of her knew it was because of Brady. He was clouding her judgment. That was bad journalism. She wasn't supposed to get attached to the people she was writing about.

Objective. Neutral. Unbiased. Those were the words that came to mind when she thought of journalism. That was what her professor wanted her to strive for. Now all she was thinking in the midst of writing was *Brady*.

Brady. Brady. Brady.

He was about to get on that stage and talk about education policy, no doubt. This was the audience for that kind of discussion. If she were up there, that was what she would talk about. The very thought made her blood boil for so many reasons. She wasn't sure which one was the primary reason now.

Was she infuriated because he was actually going to try to discuss education with a sea of students whom she had informed his policies were garbage? Or was she heated because it would be the first time she'd seen his handsome face since leaving his hotel room nearly two weeks ago?

"So, you want me to record the whole thing?" Justin asked, squaring away his camera focused on the podium.

"Yeah. That would be great. We don't have the normal crew for the paper, and I wanted to make sure I didn't have to deal with video as well," she told him.

"No problem here. I'll be running sound and this thing will be running itself, thanks to my new tripod," he said, tapping his finger on the camera.

"Thanks, Justin," Liz said with a big smile. "Really appreciate it."

"Are you going to be in the booth?" Justin asked.

"Nah," Liz said, shaking her head. "I'm going to try to get a closer look. I reserved a front-row seat, but I don't know if I'll be able to sit still."

"First shindig all on your own, huh?" He fiddled with the sound equipment.

"Yeah. First campaign-related appearance on campus this season too," she told him. She wiped her palms on her high-waisted black skirt. She had paired it with a tucked-in V-cut Carolina-blue blouse that was loose and flowy, with little gold buttons up the front. Her nude suede heels finished off the outfit. She had chosen it all carefully and felt a little silly. She normally dressed nicely to begin with, but this had something . . . everything to do with Brady.

"It'll be fine. I've done shit like this before. Their crew tries to take over anyway. You probably won't have to do much," Justin told her.

"True." She tried not to think about it all. She stood as her nerves took over. "Hey, will you be able to splice this for me later? I want to get some of it up on the website as soon as possible."

"No way. Not tonight."

"Oh come on, what are you doing?" she asked, leaning her hip into the counter.

Justin shrugged noncommittally. "Stuff."

"Do you want me to pay you, is that it?" she grumbled. They had paper resources, but she wasn't in control of much. Normally she would have to get expenses approved through Hayden, but since he wasn't here . . .

"I might find some free time," he admitted.

"Fine, whatever," Liz said, turning to leave. "So difficult."

"See ya around, Liz," he said, chuckling.

"Bye, Justin."

Stupid AV abilities.

Liz walked out of the sound booth, frustrated with Justin. She had met him in her intro journalism class freshman year. He didn't really have any interest in writing and had made that blatantly obvious. The professor hadn't taken his shit, though, and forced him to complete all the assignments as written. Though she had allowed him some extra credit with his excellent videos.

Liz had forged a friendship with Justin from the beginning. He was also on scholarship, living in her dorm, and seemed to always be around. He refused to work for the paper or the UNC news channel, even though it was obvious that they could use his skills. He preferred to be freelance. They hung out sometimes with mutual friends, and he could be funny when he wanted.

Her heels clicked against the hard wood floor as she circled the room. She recognized some familiar faces in the crowd, but not that many. A group of girls waved at her as she walked by. She smiled tentatively and waved back, not used to people recognizing her. She walked purposefully to the front of the room and took her seat in the front row.

She felt a bit naked without her voice recorder, but she didn't really need it, since Justin was videoing for her. She pulled a small legal notepad out of her bag and flipped to the event page she had mocked up. She had a few questions that made the list. Some of them were from the Raleigh event and some of them were new. Heather Ferrington had said that she wasn't going to get to ask any questions until the close of the event, and Liz wanted to be prepared.

Her stomach flipped just as it did every time she thought about getting an interview with Brady after the event. Could she get that close to him again?

Liz pushed down the thoughts she had been harboring for the past two weeks. She was a professional . . . despite her actions. If her editor wanted her to get an interview, then she could do it. It didn't matter if it was Brady Maxwell or the President of the United States. This was her job, and she was going to take it seriously. She couldn't let her sexual attraction to the man mess up her career.

The buzz in the room died down as Heather Ferrington walked onto the stage. She was everything Liz remembered her to be—unbelievably gorgeous, with long blond hair, a tall, slim build, and a fresh gray skirt suit. She could have been a model, and Liz wondered what had made her become a press secretary instead. Did she see that Brady was going somewhere and jump onboard as soon as she could? Had she done *more* to get to this position?

Thinking about whether or not Brady had slept with his attractive press secretary wasn't going to get her anywhere. It was only going to make her jealous.

"Hello, Chapel Hill! Thank you so much for coming out today!" Heather said brightly. It was a completely different façade than Liz had seen from her before. With press she had been biting and strong; on the phone she had been condescending and demanding; now she was über-cheerful.

Don't underestimate her.

"My name is Heather Ferrington and I am Senator Maxwell's press secretary. Senator Maxwell is thrilled to be back at his alma mater today. Only a few years ago he was sitting in the same classrooms and attending the same events as you. He was playing basketball for your beloved team, and loving every minute of it. He cherishes every memory from his hometown, and appreciates you inviting him to come speak today."

Ha! Invited! Liz laughed to herself. Hadn't Heather called only a week ago and explained that they were planning Chapel Hill as an extra stop for the Senator? Would the lies always be boundless?

"Before the Senator comes out to speak, I am pleased to introduce your fellow student Leslie Chester, president of Political Action NOW and cofounder of North Carolina Students for Progressive Action," Heather said with a smile as she began the applause.

Liz sat up in her seat. She didn't know they were going to have an introductory speaker.

It made sense that they would pick Leslie. Leslie was scary, with her intensity behind the things she believed in, and she badgered the paper relentlessly for more space for her pictures, articles, and ads. It was a constant battle. Liz wasn't sure she knew anyone who actually liked her, but the girl sure as hell knew what she was doing.

Leslie Chester walked onstage in her modest two-inch heels. She was on the shorter side, with ashy brown hair and chipmunk cheeks. Liz suspected, like everyone else, that she would make a bid into politics one day, and she was dressed the part in a black pantsuit.

She stepped up to the microphone and cleared her throat. "Ladies and gentlemen, my fellow students, thank you for attending this momentous event on campus. As this is one of the very first campaign stops on Senator Maxwell's tour, I personally feel honored to be able to introduce him this afternoon."

Leslie went on to list off Brady's achievements and his career thus far in politics. It was without a doubt a rehearsed speech that the campaign had given her prepackaged. Liz knew all the highlights from her research, but paid close attention regardless. She never knew when they might throw a curveball her way that someone else might have missed.

"Chapel Hill, help me welcome our own alumnus, Senator Brady Maxwell III."

The crowd clapped, rising to its feet. Liz stood with them, her hands moving mechanically as she kept her eyes glued to the entrance.

There he was. He stepped one foot out onto the stage and then another. Liz swallowed. She had been staring at pictures of him for two weeks and could have sworn that she had every inch of him memorized. But now, with him on the stage, walking toward the podium, waving at the crowd, she realized that no memory could ever do him justice.

He had on another black suit with a solid blue button-down and red striped tie. The politician's red-white-and-blue seemed to be his MO, and she found herself thinking about the time she had seen him out of those colors . . . out of those clothes. She was having a hard time bringing herself back to the present.

His hair was perfectly styled, and his smile was overwhelming. She could almost feel his deep brown eyes scanning the crowd for her. Or maybe that was what she wanted to think. They'd had no contact since that night, aside from the tip she had received from his press secretary about the event. Yet the feeling remained.

Then his eyes found her sitting off to the side in the front row. They locked gazes for a brief second, but it was long enough for her entire body to tingle with warmth. His smile grew wider as he turned back to the audience. She would pay more than a penny for his thoughts in that moment.

"Thank you, Leslie," he said, shaking her hand.

"Thank you, sir," she said. She was staring up at him with a shock-and-awe expression that Liz was pretty sure she had never seen cross Leslie's face.

God, this guy can charm anyone! she thought.

Leslie quickly exited the stage as Brady made himself comfortable in front of the podium. Then suddenly, like turning a switch, he was in campaign mode. She didn't think she had ever noticed it before in the other speeches she had watched of his online. But with him so close she could see the difference. Likely no one else could, but he clearly had a campaign face of sorts, like an actor getting into character.

"Hello, Chapel Hill!" he said into the microphone. "It is so nice to be back in my hometown. How are y'all doing this afternoon?"

There was general applause among the audience. They were happy to be out of classes for the day and indulging in summer break. Most of them were interested in what he was going to say, but Liz was pretty sure that they would rather be at the pool working on their tans. She hated being so jaded about her classmates, but that had been her experience. And she wanted to change it, to educate and encourage her classmates to get involved. This was a good start.

"That's great to hear. I was just over at Top O eating before this," he said, talking about Top of the Hill, a local restaurant and bar. Brady paused as cheers rang through the crowd. "I swear the food gets better and better every time I go there. I can't even tell you how many things I miss about Chapel Hill—Pit sitting, lazy days on the Quad, dribbling circles around my friends in Rams Head."

Liz looked around to see the students nodding along. They all loved these things as well. He was appealing to their shared experiences. Clever.

"My four years at UNC were the best of my life, and I'm sure most of you feel the same way. You live and breathe the university as well as the community while you're here and want to see as much done for it as possible, but you won't always be here. Chris, my best friend growing up, followed me here to Chapel Hill. We were, of course, upstanding gentlemen as a part of the university."

The crowd chuckled. Liz knew as well as anyone that any basketball player at UNC was not only treated like a god, but was as far from an upstanding gentleman as they came. Had Brady been one of those guys? With his looks and charm, Liz wasn't sure he would have needed to rely on the fame. Then again, he didn't need it now, but he was smart enough to use it to his advantage.

"Chris graduated from UNC with me, and instead of staying here, he took a job in New York City. Likely many of you will do the same. You'll get the best education you possibly can from one of the best universities in the country, and then you'll leave," he told them frankly. Liz was curious where he was going, but she had her guesses. "You carry the weight of your university on your shoulders the rest of your life. Now, I know most of you are thinking about how great it is to have the UNC flagship stacked at the top of your résumé. Go ahead, admit it. I know you do."

His captive audience laughed, some jabbing their friends in the rib cage and whispering to each other.

"Now, stack on student loan debt, a struggling economy, poor job growth, and a depleted basis for internships, externships, and real-world experience that is crucial to success outside of these four walls. How heavy does that weight feel now?" The room quieted entirely. "That's what I'm here to address today: what I'm planning to do when I'm elected into office to offset these complications all students are facing pre- and post-education."

Bam! Liz felt like jumping up and down. She had been entirely on point from the very start. She *knew* he was going to address education at this event. It was a topic that resonated, and it was a fluff topic, because he likely would never be a part of any substantive education policy. His father was a budget guy, and a prominent member of the Senate Budget Committee at that. No way was his son getting stuck in education policy.

Now all she had to do was wait for him to slip up. She knew his education policy inside and out. Plus, she had the benefit of knowing ahead of time where his reasoning was wrong.

Liz listened to his speech with one ear to the ground for any slip-ups. She assumed he wouldn't talk about how his help in balancing the budget had cut funding for the university, but she paid close attention to make sure. Most of what he was saying was entirely symbolic, posturing and position taking on policy he would never be grilled on. It just happened to be policy she found the most important.

Near the end of his speech, Brady touched on exactly what she had been waiting for. "Some people are advocates for what they're calling NC Pledge, which provides a free college education for students who graduate from a North Carolina high school as long as they maintain a certain GPA. Sounds great, right? But where is the money coming from to support new students? How will that affect the growth in UNC system schools? Will that negatively impact the number of out-of-state students who attend North Carolina universities? In an already floundering economy, where will the support come from to stabilize a new influx of students, and where will those jobs come from? These are merely a few of the questions regarding NC Pledge that I am fighting for answers to. I need those answers to better assist you in the future and ensure that our educated youth just like you and me are getting enough help to find jobs once you graduate."

Liz couldn't wait to wheedle her way backstage for an interview. She had answers to some of these questions, and quite a few more that she would like to ask him.

Brady moved on to another topic and then wrapped up the speech. The whole thing had been less than an hour, but a significant hour. Liz had more questions scrawled onto her notepad than when she had entered, which she thought was a success.

And as distracting as his pretty face had been, she was proud that she had kept to her work as much as she could. Perhaps it was because they couldn't immediately disappear behind closed doors. Though that sounded like an appealing option.

Brady offered to stick around after the speech and talk to any students or faculty who were interested in speaking with him. Liz wanted nothing more than to rush over there and talk to him, but she knew she couldn't do that. Flipping her notepad back to the front, she tucked it into her purse and walked back toward the sound booth. Brady had a line of adoring admirers that could take up another hour of his time at least. Liz certainly wasn't going to wait in line. She would wait until he was done, then approach him for an interview . . . *just* an interview.

"How did it go?" Liz asked Justin when she entered the sound booth. She leaned against the counter, anxious to see how the material came out.

"Perfect shot," he said with a shrug, as if his work wouldn't be anything less.

"Great. I know your work is fantastic. I really appreciate you doing this."

"It's no problem."

Liz tore out a piece of paper from her notebook and handed it to him. "Do you mind getting all of this to me from the video?"

Justin scanned the paper. "You did all this while the speech was going on?"

"Yes. There are people who can multitask." She chuckled softly. "I know it's a lot, but I know the material will look great on the website."

"Yeah, I should be able to do all this. I can multitask." He winked at her in that typical Justin way and then started adding his own notes. "When do you want it?"

"Tonight would be amazing." She crossed her fingers, hoping he wouldn't charge more and just see it as a personal favor.

He nodded. "All right, Liz. For you."

Liz smiled. "Thank you. Can't wait to see how it turned out." She turned to leave, ready to wait out the flock of admirers.

"Hey, Liz?" Justin called as she reached the door. "What are you doing this weekend?"

"Working."

"Me and some of the guys are having a party over on Frat Court if you're interested," he said with a lazy shrug.

Liz never expected him to be in a fraternity. It still amazed her. He just didn't strike her as the type. "I'll let you know," she said.

The chances of her going to Justin's fraternity party were as close to zero as possible. He had invited her to more than she could count, and she had only been once. Victoria had come with her, and they had bailed around midnight. She didn't have Victoria this time to make it tolerable.

Veering back out into the auditorium, Liz made a survey of the room. The Advance Team was already hard at work breaking down the event. Fliers that had been left behind were being collected and stacked to one side. The sound crew was fixing the special accommodations that had been made for the Senator.

Heather Ferrington was off to the side talking to a shorter bulky man that Liz was surprised she recognized. He was the jackass who had made fun of her at the club that night after the press conference. It all felt so long ago. What the hell was he doing here anyway? Was he involved in the campaign somehow?

Pushing those thoughts aside, she found Brady amid the crowd. More than half of his line had dissipated. They had either given up on meeting him or he had barreled through people faster than she expected. He was the perfect politician—shaking hands, taking pictures, answering questions.

Liz spoke to a girl she recognized from class. She had liked the speech and had decided she was voting for him. Liz asked her if she could quote her on that. The girl giggled, but agreed. Another student gave her a testimonial about how much he liked Brady. A third student said that while Brady was handsome, she hadn't been sold entirely and she planned to research the other candidates more. Feeling that she had gotten the most out of the remaining students, she accepted those three as her sources and called it a day.

She walked over to where Brady was mingling with the remaining students. Leslie was among them, staring up at him with a gaga expression as he told a story. Liz wondered if she was infatuated with him like everyone else or if she was pushing for an internship with the campaign. If . . . when he won, it would look good on her already packed résumé.

"Ah, Ms. Dougherty," Brady said, looking up and directly at her, "just the person I was looking for."

Liz had enough good form not to look surprised when he interrupted himself to address her. "Senator Maxwell, always a pleasure," she said, thinking of other pleasures they had indulged in.

"You're here for an interview, I presume?" he asked with a smile.

"Of course. Are you ready?" she managed, keeping from darting her eyes toward Leslie with a *ha-ha!* expression.

"If you'll excuse me, ladies," Brady said sweetly to his crowd of worshipers.

"Senator Maxwell," Leslie cut in before he could leave, "do you think you will have time to speak after your . . . interview?" she asked, cutting her eyes to Liz.

"Another time perhaps. Ms. Dougherty has already requested the remainder of my time in Chapel Hill," he said, ending the discussion. "Right this way, Ms. Dougherty."

Liz followed him back up the stairs, to the stage, and through the side door that led them to the back of the auditorium. She was surprised at how empty it was; it had cleared out entirely. She guessed all of the students wanted to get back to the pool as quick as possible. She heard the door click behind her, and she slowly turned to find herself completely alone with Brady.

The air between them crackled with tension.

Two weeks.

Two weeks since her hands had threaded through his hair. Two weeks since she had circled her legs around his waist. Two weeks since her moans had taken over the hotel room.

She had missed him, and it was downright painful. How had she not noticed it when he had been onstage? She had stared up into his handsome face for a whole hour, her mind hardly drifting from what he was saying. Now here, with so little space between them, all she wanted to do was reach out and touch him, make sure he was real, make sure it had all really happened.

"How come you didn't find me sooner?" he asked, taking a step toward her.

"Didn't know you needed me to save you," she said.

"Well, you played along perfectly."

"I was actually coming to find you for an interview," Liz told him. The air seemed to be thinning the nearer he drew toward her. How was it suddenly so warm?

"Then you read my mind," he said with a smile. It was contagious and she returned it. "What questions did you have for me?"

He was mere inches from her, and she was having a hard time remembering anything she was going to ask him. All of her carefully prepared questions flew out the window, and all she could think about was his lips on her.

"Tongue-tied?" he said, his hand moving forward and running up her skirt to her waist.

Her breathing hitched and she strained to keep her eyes open. She couldn't let him completely distract her. She had questions. They were somewhere in her mind, and she needed to ask them. "You oppose NC Pledge for numerous reasons."

"I have problems with some of the specifics of the legislation," he said, circumventing her statement with the ease of a politician.

"You're blocking the legislation from moving forward in the state legislature."

"Was there a question in that?" he asked.

She swallowed, and tried to keep her thoughts on track. His thumb circling her hip bone wasn't helping. *Stay professional!* she yelled at herself.

"Why do you feel the questions you have posed regarding NC Pledge are enough to block landmark education policy in North Carolina? And how can the people of North Carolina, specifically this district, expect you to further our interests on Capitol Hill when you aren't even doing that here?" she asked, staring up at him with as much professional decorum as she could muster. She could see his campaign mask begin to slip on, and his eyes hardened. She had surprised him again.

"Until the legislature has agreed upon terms that I believe will actually benefit North Carolina," he said, pausing for dramatic effect, clearly wanting her to hear his words, "rather than hinder the slow growth within our state, I will continue to fight for better terms. I'll do the same on the Hill." He arched an eyebrow, waiting for a response, the rest of his face blank. She wondered how irritated he was under that cool, collected front.

Damn. He was good.

He hadn't actually said anything.

"But why wouldn't you want more students to attend college?"

"Of course I support students attending college."

"Did you have a basketball scholarship?" She already knew the answer.

"I did."

"Could your parents have paid for you to go to college if you hadn't had the scholarship?"

His hand tightened on her hip. "I see where you're going with this, Ms. Dougherty."

"Just a simple question, Senator," she said.

"Yes, my parents could have paid for me to attend the university."

"Do you know how many other students don't have that privilege? Please, Senator, explain to me why those students don't deserve a college education when you do?" she asked point-blank.

"I believe every student has the right to an education," he said sternly. His brown eyes seemed to bore into her. "I do, however, feel that NC Pledge does not satisfy a number of other demands, such as cost to the university system and future benefits in the workforce. These problems need to be addressed first."

"Can I quote you on that?" she asked, licking her lips as his hand moved to the small of her back.

"By all means, Ms. Dougherty," he said, pulling her against him.

She could see the mask slipping as he stared down at her. What was it that put him so on edge, and how did she manage to smooth that away so easily? She could do both within seconds, and both sides of him were incredibly appealing.

"Liz," he whispered, leaning down closer. "Are we done discussing politics? You know how much I like being lectured."

"I would say so," she responded, pushing her hands up his chest and around his neck.

Kissing his lips set off a fireworks display in her stomach. She pressed farther into him, gripping his back with the extreme intensity she was feeling. He responded with fervor, walking her back against the wall and kissing her as if it had been years rather than two weeks. His hands ran up and down her body, making her remember every place he had touched.

She couldn't get enough, couldn't breathe, couldn't think. There was just Brady. She felt as if she was lost in a world of him, drowning in him, suffocating in him. Nothing could feel more real or more enticing than this moment.

If she had ever been kissed like this before, then her memory was entirely faulty. His need was showing through with every grasp of her body, with every heavy breath from his lips, and with every swish of his tongue against her own. It wasn't even the first time they had kissed, but it was laced so heavily with the absence.

She had thought it was hot before, but she was practically perspiring with the heat rushing to the surface of her skin. He ran his hands down her body and between her thighs, sending chill bumps up and down her arms. He pressed his fingers against her most sensitive spot through her pencil skirt, and she groaned into his lips.

"Brady," she whimpered, her thoughts flying back to the hotel room.

"God I want you," he admitted, locking lips with her again.

She was aware as he swirled his fingers that she wanted him pretty damn badly as well. How had he cast such a spell? She just wanted to go home and let him have his way with her. She didn't care that she had promised herself it would only happen once. She couldn't be satisfied, couldn't be satiated.

She wanted Brady Maxwell.

"Come back to my place?" she asked boldly.

"I have a dinner I have to attend," he said as if it was the hardest thing he had ever done.

"Come after. Whenever," she nearly pleaded.

"I want to, but I can't," he said, shaking his head. He pulled her against him, hugging her tight. She held him, somehow knowing their time together was over for now. She felt a sudden loss. "Meet me tomorrow?"

Liz nodded. She would meet him anywhere.

He bent down and kissed her lips one more time, a lingering good-bye with promise for more.

Chapter 11

EQUALIZER

Liz yawned as she walked into the diner where she had agreed to meet Brady. It was a small, dingy-looking place that she had overlooked a hundred times before. She had heard that it had superb breakfast, but she was never awake in time to go unless she had class. And she wasn't going to wake up early. Her sleeping schedule was precious.

She hoped she looked okay. She wasn't a morning person, and her earliest class last semester had been noon. She had left her heels at home and opted for her brown-and-gold sandals. She had on short, cuffed white shorts and a long, see-through teal blouse. At least she had taken the time to do her hair, and it fell down to her shoulders in soft waves.

Tossing her Ray-Bans into her purse, she made her way to the back of the restaurant. If Brady wasn't here yet, she would rather take the farthest booth in the back and wait for him to arrive. That way she wouldn't miss him, and she could observe everyone else who was walking in.

She broke past the small bar area in the front where a few older gentlemen sat with coffee in hand as they mulled over their newspapers. The back room was pretty empty, only one elderly couple sitting in the front holding hands. Brady was already there, sitting with a cup of coffee in front of him.

"Good morning," he said with a cheery smile.

Her breath caught as she stared down at him. He was insanely good-looking. It actually hurt to look at him and not jump over that table to get at him. He was wearing a blue polo with dark jeans and a black Arc'teryx shell jacket. She was surprised to see that he wasn't in his typical attire. She wasn't sure if it was because their meeting was informal or because he didn't want to draw attention to himself. Either way it was nice to see him out of a suit. She blushed when she remembered the last time she had seen him out of one.

"Hey," Liz whispered. She took the seat across from him.

"You look well this morning," he told her, drinking her in.

"Thanks," she said, thinking the complete opposite.

As hot and heavy as they had gotten backstage yesterday, she didn't really know what he wanted from her. Why meet her here in a public place? Was he going to be letting her down easy? It hadn't seemed like that yesterday. He had initiated and pushed it further. She had just suggested moving it to a more private location.

And what was this dinner he had mentioned? Who had that been with? She didn't know, and she knew that it could have been any number of people from a girlfriend (though she hadn't dug one up yet) to his campaign staff to donors and anyone in between.

"You hungry?" he asked with a smile.

In fact, she wasn't all that hungry. She had too many questions to ask. The reporter in her was about ready to burst.

"They have great waffles. Do you like waffles?" he said.

"Yes," she responded. So, he was going for normal then.

"Coffee?"

"Definitely. It's early," she said, stifling a yawn.

A waiter came and took their orders. She seemed familiar with Brady. Apparently she had been working at the place all four years he was in college, and went to church with his parents. Liz shouldn't have been surprised, but she was. She sometimes forgot that everyone knew him here.

"I suppose I should go ahead and say that if anyone asks, we were finishing our interview," he offered.

Liz nodded, pulling out her recorder and setting it on the counter. "All right."

"You came prepared."

"Always. Should I turn it on?" she asked, raising an eyebrow.

Brady shrugged. "Not if you want to keep it."

Liz chuckled at the comment. She liked his humor . . . even if he wasn't actually kidding. She had no doubt he would take the recorder from her if need be, but he was lightening the mood. The veil of secrecy clouded the booth like a drape, and he was trying to sweep the curtains open.

"I think I'll just leave it there then. You can check my hands," she said, holding them up so he could see she hadn't touched the recorder.

Brady smirked, and she wondered what devious thought he was thinking.

The waitress returned with their food a few minutes later. He was right: The waffle was pretty great. Though she thought a person had to be pretty inept to mess up a waffle.

As they ate, more people filtered into the diner. A college couple sat in the booth behind them. A few bleary-eyed people obsessed over their coffee. A group of regulars smiled at the waitress as she passed and chatted with her endlessly when she came to their tables. Liz felt more and more withdrawn the more people who came into the restaurant. As far as she could tell, he was simply happy to have breakfast with her . . . as strange as that sounded.

"You know what I love about diners?" Brady asked, looking up at her out of the blue.

Liz shook her head. She knew why she loved diners, but she was sure it was for different reasons. She never knew where he was going with anything.

"It's an equalizer," he stated simply.

She didn't have any idea what he was talking about. "Hmm?"

"Anyone could be sitting in this booth—a Senator, a businessman, a sorority girl, a bum. We'd all be in the same boat," he said absentmindedly.

"I guess I never thought about it like that."

"You were never in the booth with me." His ever-present charming smile sucked the breath right out of her.

Seriously, where did he come up with this stuff? It was like he knew exactly what to say to disarm her. She didn't know if it was because he was damn good at his job or if he was a master seducer, a Casanova of the twenty-first century. Whatever it was, she didn't want it to stop. Then again, she never wanted her time with Brady to stop.

"I wouldn't guess you were a man who wanted to be equal to anyone," she said finally.

"In politics? Never. In romance? You'll never find my equal. Having breakfast with a beautiful woman? I'll be equal with anyone for that pleasure."

Liz's heart fluttered. He was a smooth talker . . . she knew that much.

"So, why did you ask me here?" She was aware of how many people were in the room, and hoped no one had overheard their exchange.

"I want to see you again," he stated simply. She searched his dark brown eyes for any hint of humor or malice, but there was none. He was telling the truth.

"Again as in now or as in later?" she asked.

"Now and later and many times after that."

Liz swallowed. She didn't know what she had expected, but certainly not that. It didn't make sense. Why had he let her leave the club that first night? Why had he let her walk out of the hotel room? Why had he never called her back, sent his press secretary to fetch her, and then not finished off the job he started? That didn't sound like a man who wanted to see her many more times.

She needed answers.

"If you wanted to see me again, why didn't you call me?" she asked defiantly. She didn't even have the patience to let him answer. "In fact, why did you even start something yesterday at all? You obviously knew you couldn't finish, because you had some dinner."

"Indeed, I did."

"Now you're coming to me saying you want to see me again, but you made no effort before this point," Liz said. "Why did you even kiss me yesterday? Your actions seem rather mixed."

"Because I wanted to kiss you, like I want to kiss you right now," he told her.

Liz blushed. He had said that he wanted her multiple times, and yet he had left her dangling for someone else to scoop up for two weeks, letting her think it was a one-night stand.

"For someone who claims to know what they want, you don't act like it." She could see him tensing.

"Do you want the truth?" he asked, his tone flat.

"No, lie to me," she said, with an eye roll.

His eyes narrowed, and she could see she was pushing too hard. "The truth is, I had to test you."

"Test me?" she nearly squeaked out.

"I didn't know for certain if you were sure about this," he answered her.

"How thoughtful of you to inform me," she said dryly. She was uncertain how the conversation had even gotten here. Brady Maxwell, a State Senator, was testing her to see whether she was sure about the two of them. How did this make any sense?

"People, women in particular, get close to a politician for a reason," he stated bluntly. "I wanted to know whether you were that kind of woman."

"And you decided I wasn't?"

"With the fervor you kissed me back yesterday . . . no one could fake that."

She hadn't faked it, but she wasn't so sure about his reasoning. "That's it? A kiss?"

"You might have cleared the background check as well, but that's neither here nor there."

Oh, of course. A background check. "Seriously?"

"I had to be sure," he told her flatly.

"Totally normal." She wanted that to irritate her, but she found that it didn't as much as she thought it would. If he was serious enough to look into her background, then he must really want to see her again.

"So, what do you think?" he asked finally.

"Well," she said uncertainly, "I don't know."

"You don't want to see me?" He apparently seemed amused at the thought. He knew she wanted to see him.

"I do," she corrected. She couldn't lie about that. "But I don't know why you had to bring me here at seven o'clock in the morning to tell me that. Why didn't you just come to my place yesterday?"

"Because I can't see you when you want to see me," Brady told her, pushing his diner coffee away and meeting her eyes.

Hers were already narrowed. "But you can see me when you want to?"

"Yes." He didn't even try to hide behind his charming words.

"Why? I don't get it."

"I want to see you, but in the position I'm . . . we're in, it's not possible," he told her.

"What, because you're running for office?" She knew she sounded incredulous, but it made sense. He wouldn't want to risk anything . . . especially not on a woman, no matter his big talk.

"And you're a reporter . . . a college reporter," he reminded her.

"And I wrote that article," she said, filling in the blanks.

"You did," Brady confirmed. "While I don't mind you pointing out my faults, the campaign and my opponents will see it as me giving up the nomination."

"Why are you here then?" she asked, her anger mounting once more.

"Because I still want you. Weeks later, I still want you. And you want me too."

Liz's stomach dropped and all the anger she had been holding dissipated. He wanted her. She knew he did, but hearing it like that was intoxicating. She didn't want to give him up. She was having a fucking hard time even concentrating on anything else. After he had left, it felt as if she had a hole in her chest. She didn't know if it was the sex, because that had been fantastic, or if it was just Brady. As much as she wanted it to be the second, that idea scared the shit out of her.

"So, you want me, but you can't see me?"

"I can't see you on your terms," he corrected.

"What does that even mean?" Liz asked, raising her voice. She immediately quieted down and looked around the restaurant. No one had even glanced at them. That was lucky.

"Look, I want us to continue what we're doing, but in private. I don't want to jeopardize my career . . . or your career," he added quickly.

Liz breathed in and out deeply, realizing finally what he was saying. "You want a fuck buddy," she stated as bluntly as possible. If he was going to be all out in the open, she wanted plain words. She wanted to know what he was offering . . . what kind of deal she was willing to take.

He sighed as if she was misinterpreting, but she was sure she wasn't. He wanted to sleep with her, no strings attached, while he was on the campaign and too busy for anything else. She had heard of these kinds of situations before. She never knew how they happened . . . how they got started—apparently at seven o'clock in the morning at a dingy diner in downtown Chapel Hill over coffee.

"That's not what I had in mind," he said.

"No? That's what it sounds like. So, what kind of situation is this?" she asked, her anger resurfacing. She didn't even know where it came from, because it wasn't as if she didn't want to sleep with him, and it wasn't as if she didn't want to keep it a secret. Some innate trigger in her brain was firing and she was listening. "Do you get to sleep with other people? Are you going to be dating someone who fits you better in the spotlight? Should I find someone else to date in the meantime?"

"Liz," he snapped, cutting off whatever she was going to say next. "I'm not here to argue the point. I'm not here to discuss *terms*. I want you, and I want you anytime I can have you. That happens to be a much more limited time frame. If you aren't interested, then good luck with your paper." He pulled out his wallet, threw two twenties on the table, and stood.

"Wait," Liz said, reaching for his arm, "I didn't say I wasn't interested." Her cheeks flamed at the admission, but she sure as hell wasn't going to let him walk out of the diner.

His brown eyes stared right through her, as if measuring the honesty in her statement. "All right," he said, sitting back down.

"Uh . . ." she began, nibbling on her bottom lip, "I've never exactly been propositioned . . . let alone at a diner first thing in the morning."

"As much as I enjoy hearing that . . . I find it hard to believe. No one has ever come on to you?" he asked inquisitively.

"It's not that," she said, trying to find the words. "I've had boyfriends before, but I met them in . . . normal places, like school or work or something. But usually people aren't that interested before getting to know me. Um . . . I've heard I'm intimidating." She shrugged.

"Really?" he asked, looking her up and down. "I guess I could see that."

She didn't know how. She couldn't figure out why anyone thought that.

"You're a well-educated woman at a top university with staggering confidence," he told her, filling in the blanks.

Liz looked down, overloaded by the compliments. "Well, I did bring a Senator to his knees once," she said, trying to break the tension.

He chuckled softly. "I hope it's not just once," he responded.

Liz stared at the napkin resting on the tabletop. She wasn't sure what to say. He was making a proposition that, to be honest, sounded downright appealing. It's not as if they could ever come out and announce they were dating. It's not as if he had asked to date her. He wanted her and he wanted her whenever he could have her. Those were his words . . . the terms he refused to discuss.

"You're thinking too hard about this," he told her with a shake of his head.

"I can't think about it?"

"The longer you think about it, the more likely you are to make a decision I don't agree with," Brady answered.

"So, you're saying if I think about it . . . I'll realize how much of a bad idea it is to get involved with you?" she asked, arching an eyebrow.

"Something like that."

"Well, that's not true. I've already realized that."

"It's not a good idea." His voice lowered and he leaned toward her. "I'm not telling you that it's a good idea. But it's the only idea."

"Is that so?" she whispered, meeting his intense tone.

"Tell me you haven't been thinking about me since we parted." He waited.

She didn't respond. How could she?

"Tell me you haven't been thinking about me pressed against your body, the feel of my lips kissing every inch of your skin, me thrusting in and out of you in the dark hotel room. If you can tell me that, then I'll let you go. No questions asked," he said, sitting back once more and crossing his arms. "Because I haven't stopped thinking about any of those things, and your flushed face tells me you haven't either."

More than her face was heated at his words. She crossed and uncrossed her legs, trying not to look away, but he had reminded her of all the things she wanted him to do to her again. It was too early for her body to be responding in this manner.

"So?" he prompted.

"I haven't stopped thinking about those things . . . about you," she fessed up.

"That's what I thought."

Cocky son of a bitch! she thought.

"That doesn't mean I'm ready to do this with you. Whatever this is," she said, holding her hands up.

Brady sighed. "This is almost whatever you want it to be. It's not public. It's not in the news. It's not a point the campaign can use against me. It's a woman and a man taking what they can in a world where it's not feasible for us to be together. I'm not promising you much, but I'm only asking for discretion. Everything else you give me is up to you."

"Discretion." She said the word like it was a viper ready to strike. Discretion wasn't afforded in journalism.

"I'll be up-front with you. I might hurt you. You're going in knowing that. I'm choosing the campaign. I'm choosing Congress, because it's what I want and what I believe in. Nothing, no one is getting in the way of me and the House of Representatives."

How romantic, she grumbled in her head.

"I'm not going to pretend otherwise. I'm giving you what I can give you, and I'm telling you in advance you might get hurt. But it's worth it to take the risk. I can damn well promise you that it's worth it."

He paused, waiting for her to say something. She wanted to tell him, *Yes, God yes, a thousand times yes!* But so much of this worried her. He was offering her so much, but holding back even more. What if she got invested? What the hell! She was already invested!

She couldn't take more of him than he was offering, but if she turned him down, then she wouldn't have any of him. One night in a dark hotel room wasn't enough for her. It could never be enough.

Sitting there at a turning point, she remembered the feeling when she left the party in Charlotte. It was impulsive and downright insane compared to her normal behavior, but she had known then as she knew now that if she said no, she would regret it forever.

Liz never wanted to regret Brady Maxwell.

"All right," she murmured, threading her fingers together.

"All right?"

"I agree to whatever we're doing."

Brady's smile was entirely magnetic, taking her breath away. She wanted to be the reason for that smile, and every other one after it.

"So, what exactly are we doing?" she asked hesitantly.

"Do you still have that card I gave you?" She nodded, reaching into her purse and pulling it out of her wallet. He pointed out the different numbers. "This is my personal line. It's best that you don't try to reach me on it. I don't check it or give it out frequently, because I suspect it's being tapped. My parents and a couple college friends still use it, but that's about it."

Liz couldn't imagine this kind of life. What were the other numbers for?

"This is my campaign line. It's specifically for campaign-related information. I am always on it. I don't think it's been tapped by the opposition yet, but we'll see how it goes. You can reach me on this one during the day. It would look strange for it to go off any other time. This number goes directly to my secretary. Right now her name is Nancy, but they come and go. She is the easiest way to get hold of me."

Liz was buzzing with all of the information. Three separate lines for three separate things, and all to reach one man.

"So, I just call and ask for you?"

"Yes. She'll ask for your name, and you'll give her a fake one," he instructed her.

"You've really thought his through, huh?" she asked, staring at him with newfound intrigue.

"It's my job to think everything through," he told her.

"If you did, then you wouldn't have passed down that education bill," she retorted.

Brady stared at her blankly, a look she had come to associate as his campaign mask. How had she come to know his faces so well already?

"Are you done?"

Liz shrugged. "Don't use that face with me."

"What face?" he asked, scrunching his brows together.

"Your campaign face. All serious with no emotion. I know you're thinking something underneath there," she said.

"You don't want to know everything I'm thinking."

"I beg to differ," Liz told him.

"We'll get to that later," Brady said, shaking his head. "For now, let's get on the same page, like calling my secretary to get hold of me."

"How are you going to know it's me if I give a fake name?"

"Well, choose one now and then I'll know it."

Liz shrugged. "I don't know what to choose. What do you want me to be—Sandy Carmichael or something?" she asked, chuckling.

"Sure," Brady agreed. "Sandy Carmichael it is then."

Liz rolled her eyes. "Really?"

"You picked it."

"Fine," Liz said. It was an alias, after all. It didn't matter.

"That's the main thing," he said, checking his watch. "There's some more, but we can talk about that later. I think my time is up."

"All right," she said, standing as he did the same. "Should I contact you or . . . will you contact me?"

Brady smiled. "Already anxious to see me again."

"As if you aren't to see me," she whispered.

"Touché," he volleyed. "Until next time, Ms. Carmichael."

She glared at him, hating the stupid name she had chosen. All she really wanted to do was wipe the smirk off his face. Well, kiss the smirk off his face. Okay, she really wanted to do a lot more than that.

They walked away from their booth and toward the front. He smiled at her, but was clearly trying to conceal his pleasure at being in her company. Liz was sure she wasn't hiding it as well as he was.

She stopped him at the door. "Good-bye, Senator Maxwell," she said sweetly, looking up at him with anything-but-innocent eyes.

Liz turned to leave, but he put one hand on her sleeve. She looked back at him curiously. "I'm sure I don't have to remind you about this, but," he said, as the bell clanged overhead, "this is strictly off the record."

Chapter 12

GAME, SET, MATCH

Liz's feet carried her the couple blocks back to her house, but she didn't remember the walk. She had just agreed to carry on an affair with Brady Maxwell. She was jeopardizing her career, her potential (nonexistent) relationship with Hayden, not to mention her privacy, for this man. Not just that, but she was now keeping a secret from everyone in her life. No one could know.

She felt very alone standing in her living room at that moment. Would it always feel like this? Victoria was back home, and she couldn't talk to her about it anyway. Brady wasn't able to come to her. She only got to be with him on his terms. Yet sitting around at the diner with him that morning, she couldn't think of anything else she would rather do. Her world felt upside down, and she had let him do it. Had she really even fought him at all?

But what leverage did she have? She wanted to be with him. He made her feel alive. However she could have him, she would. That was his leverage. He had figured it out when he had tested her backstage at the auditorium. He had her hook, line, and sinker.

She was dead tired, but sleep wouldn't pull her under. Her mind kept repeating what had happened this morning. Over and over she obsessed about every detail of their morning breakfast. He was going to such lengths to be with her; that had to count for something. She knew the terms. She knew what she had gotten herself into, and yet . . .

All she wanted to think about was how good he looked in regular clothes, the stubble on his chin, the way his hands held his coffee mug. Was she losing her grip on reality? This was just a guy!

She buried her head into her pillow in frustration. This was *not* just a guy. This was Brady.

And that was the damn point! How could she feel like this for him? He wasn't a bad guy, but he was the guy she was sharpening her pitchfork over in the paper! And the guy she was spreading her legs for in the bedroom. It didn't make sense. How could she have such duality when she thought about him?

When she realized she definitely wasn't going to be getting any more sleep, she kicked her feet off the bed and shuffled around her room aimlessly. She needed to do something to clear her mind or she would be warring with herself all day. Throwing her hair into a slicked-back ponytail, Liz pulled on a white tennis skirt and top, laced her shoes up, and grabbed her racket on the way out the door.

Thankfully the tennis courts weren't that far from her house. Liz had competed in high school on the state level and won a few championships, but never anything spectacular. She had been recruited for tennis by a few smaller schools in Florida, but she had wanted to go to Chapel Hill, so the offers hadn't even been enticing. She felt a loss at not having hours and hours where she had to play each week. She'd had a tennis instructor since she was little, and moving here without her had been a struggle. It had taken Liz a while to find someone she liked in the area, but the woman was incredibly busy. Liz sometimes found it hard to fit into her schedule.

Today she would have to hope that someone would be there to play with her. Half of the people who frequented the courts were either older and couldn't swing the racket the same anymore, or too young for it to be entertaining. The university students didn't come to this court, since most of them lived on campus and used those courts.

Pulling into the parking lot, Liz cut the engine and slid out of her silver Honda Accord. Her muscles tensed as she swung the racket methodically, anticipating the impending exercise. It was hard to think about much else when a small tennis ball was whizzing toward you.

She walked into the clubhouse with a smile. A teenage boy ogled her from behind the counter as she checked in.

"Is Tana in today?" Liz asked hopefully.

"Uhh," the guy hesitated, trying to look cool and failing. "Let me check." He stared down at a piece of paper for a second and then nodded. "Yeah, I think she's with a student right now, though."

"Oh. Okay. Thank you. Is there anyone else teaching today who isn't paired with someone?" she asked.

He checked the paper again. "Hank doesn't have anyone for the next half hour. Want me to get him?"

Liz groaned. She didn't like Hank. He was all power, all bulk. He didn't understand the finesse that her instructors had always drilled into her. He thought that he could overpower his opponents and typically worked with students with a bit more muscle mass than her. But really maybe she needed to muscle Brady out of her thoughts.

"Hank will do," she said softly.

The boy radioed for Hank as Liz walked out of the clubhouse and toward the tennis courts. The sun was already overhead beating down on her, and it was proving to be a blisteringly hot day. Running around on the court with no protection from the sun, pouring her heart and soul into the movements—yeah, that sounded like the perfect afternoon.

Hank appeared on the court a couple minutes later. He was in his late twenties and had played tennis in college, though not for Chapel Hill. He was one of those guys who had decided to coach to make extra money after he graduated, and never stopped. He was over six feet tall with broad muscular shoulders and a buzzed blond haircut. She secretly wondered whether he was balding and trying to hide the receding hairline.

"Morning, Hank," she said politely.

"Been a while since I've seen you, Liz," he said with a toothy smile that she had grown accustomed to.

"I didn't have an appointment with Tana."

"Well, I only have thirty minutes. So let's get started," he said. Hank walked across to the other side of the tennis court. He stood imposingly across the net from her and she took a moment to ready herself.

She breathed in through her nose and out through her mouth. She could hear the players on either side of her court. *Thwack.* Pause. *Thwack.* Pause. *Thwack.* That was the right rhythm. That was the beat of her drum. The air buzzed all around her, and everything felt singled down to this one second.

Her vision narrowed as she focused in on Hank tapping the ball against the hard green surface and catching it repeatedly. He spun the racket in his hand, letting it rotate three times before grasping it tightly. He bounced the ball against his racket twice and she saw him smile. She knew then that he was ready.

He threw the ball overhead and, when it crested the peak, smacked it with the racket. She took one steadying breath as it sailed toward her as fast as he could muster—and that was pretty fast. Liz jostled her feet back and forth as the ball hit the opposite corner, and then she returned it with a powerful swing.

They volleyed back and forth for position, each coming out ahead at one point or another. It wasn't an even match. Liz knew that going into it. Even if she had more skill in the subtleties, he was overall a more skilled player than she was. When he won, he gloated, but it was better than if she had beaten him. He was a sore loser too.

Liz tossed her racket onto the ground and rested her hands on her knees. Her breathing was coming out in gasps and sweat poured down her back, chest, and forehead. Some of it spilled into her eyes and she had to blink away the salt. She wiped her face with the back of her forearm. It didn't help much, but it didn't make it any worse.

"I'm beat," she said, feeling like flopping over onto the court right then and there.

"You put up a good match," Hank said, paying her a compliment. That was unusual.

"Thanks, but you kicked my ass."

"You held your own. Whatever Tana's doing over there, she's doing it right. You should come work out with me more often," he said with that same toothy smile.

"I don't think my body can take It," she groaned, straightening with difficulty.

"Next time, I won't go easy on you." Hank smacked her back good-naturedly and she nearly fell over. He chuckled and helped right her. They walked back down toward the clubhouse together. Liz's breathing still wasn't even by the time they got there.

"I have another student, but you really should come back and play sometime, Liz. Hard to find good opponents who aren't instructors," he told her.

Liz nodded. Exhaustion was already taking over. "Yeah, I'll be around. I'm working on the paper, running the election column and following the races. I think I'll be swamped, but let me know when you're open and I'll work around it."

"Oh yeah! I read your article about Brady," Hank said, snapping his finger like it had just come to him.

"Yeah, did you like it?" Liz asked.

"I thought it was good. I like Brady, though, man. He's a good guy."

"Do you uh . . . know him?" Even here, when she had let herself get to the point of exhaustion, she couldn't escape him.

"Yeah, he played basketball here my junior and senior years of college. I came home to every game that I could," Hank told her.

"Cool," she said with a shrug.

"Next article should be about his career here playing basketball. Do you know how many points he scored or how many games he started in?" Hank asked.

Liz just smiled. "No, I don't."

"I can write up a profile for you for your next piece. Just quote me," he said with that grin.

"I'm sure it's available on the Internet."

Hank laughed. "You're probably right. Let me know when you're free for another game."

"Will do. See you around," she said, waving as she walked out of the club.

It only took a couple minutes to get back to her house, but she couldn't stop thinking about Brady. Even when she was playing tennis, smacking a tennis ball as hard as she possibly could, he still returned.

She turned the water on cold in the shower when she got home and washed her workout off of her skin. She didn't normally like cold showers, but it had been so hot outside that it was the only thing she could stomach at the moment. Plus, it woke her up some.

Maybe she was being ridiculous about the whole thing. Maybe she and Brady could start whatever they were about to start and everything would be fine. If only she could stop obsessing in his absence. It had to be the reporter side of her coming out, trying to fit the facts into the puzzle. The truth was that there weren't many details to consider, just a whole hell of a lot of hypotheticals. To move forward, she needed to push past the hypothetical and settle in on what she did know. Accept those facts and move forward.

So what did she know?

Brady wanted her. He wanted her badly enough to risk continuing to see her when it had the potential to hurt both of their careers if they got caught.

She really wanted Brady. If the fact that she couldn't get him out of her head and she had felt like she was walking through a black-and-white movie in his absence wasn't enough to prove that, then she didn't know what would.

Yes, well . . . that was it. That was all she knew.

That was all she needed to know.

Liz stepped out of her shower, wrapped a towel around her wet body, and grabbed her phone off of the counter.

"Hello, Senator Maxwell's office," a woman answered.

"Yes, hello," Liz said, trying to keep her voice strong. "I'm trying to reach the Senator."

"Who may I say is calling?"

Liz took a deep breath. "Sandy Carmichael."

Chapter 13

SURPRISE GETAWAY

L iz couldn't have been on hold for more than a couple minutes, but it felt like an eternity. She thought about hanging up. Maybe he wouldn't actually answer anyway. But inevitably she had decided against it. She had mustered up the courage to go through with it, and she wasn't going to back out now.

She heard rustling on the other end and straightened in her seat. He couldn't see her, but it didn't matter.

"Ms. Carmichael, what a pleasant surprise," Brady answered.

Liz swooned in her seat. She had already forgotten how his deep voice affected her. Even when he was talking to her as if she was a reporter and not . . . well, whatever she was, it was still very attractive.

"Brady," she murmured into the phone.

"Yes, it's great to hear from you too," he said cheerfully. He was using his campaign voice. He cleared his throat and all but whispered into the phone, "Give me a minute."

She heard more rustling coming from the other end and she wondered if he was switching rooms or trying to find privacy. Was this what it would always be like?

"Hey," he said, losing the campaign-coated speech for his more personal tone. "I wasn't expecting to hear from you so soon."

"You didn't want to?"

"I wasn't expecting to. There's a difference. I always want to hear from you," he said smoothly.

Liz smiled despite herself. She didn't mind being flattered. "With that attitude, how did you expect me to wait?"

"I didn't," he said. She wondered if he was smirking. She closed her eyes and thought about the way his eyes looked down upon her deviously. It made her swallow and cross her legs.

"I want to see you," she breathed into the line.

"Yeah, I think you mentioned that this morning."

"I know you said it was your terms. I know you said that it was only when you were free . . ." she trailed off.

"And you agreed," he growled into the phone. "Are you backing out?"

"No," she answered hastily. "Quite the contrary. I want you to be free now."

She couldn't believe she had blurted it out. It was what she was thinking, but she usually kept her thoughts reserved. Still, it wasn't a lie. She had gone a long time without him. She knew she had work to catch up on, the paper to do research for, and a portfolio she needed to compile for her professor, but she couldn't concentrate on any of that when he was on her mind.

"I said the things I said this morning because I'm a very busy person."

"I know you are. I follow your campaign schedule," she said.

He chuckled softly into the phone. "I'm sure you do."

"Brady, it's been two weeks. That kiss in the auditorium wasn't enough. Not enough for me . . . or for you," she stated boldly. Whatever was going on with them was something she had to push forward with head-on. If she hesitated too much, she started wondering if she was being used, and she couldn't think about that. She was getting out of it what she could, and what she wanted was Brady.

He sighed as if he was contemplating her assessment. She didn't know what he was thinking. Did he think she was being difficult, when she had relented so easily in the diner this morning?

"What are you doing on Sunday?" he finally asked.

"Sunday?" she said, surprised. She didn't know what she had been expecting, but Brady kept shattering every expectation she had.

"Yes."

"Um . . . nothing. I don't have any plans."

"Good. Don't make any."

Liz bit her lip and felt like jumping up and down. This meant she got to see Brady. She tried not to pout at the thought of waiting three more days. At least she was getting to see him. She knew what kind of schedule he was already working, after announcing his candidacy only a couple of weeks ago. She should be glad for any time with him . . . even if she wanted him sooner than that.

"What are we doing?" she asked.

"It'll be a surprise. I'll send a driver to collect you from the same diner around eight."

"In the morning?"

"Not a morning person, are you?"

Liz was already shaking her head. "No."

"You can nap on the drive."

Liz heard someone call out to Brady through the phone and she froze even though she knew they couldn't see or hear her. She felt as if their time was entirely private. They were sharing a secret that no one knew about, and in that second it brought a smile to her face.

"Yeah, give me one more minute," Brady's muffled voice came through the phone as he spoke to someone in the room. She heard the door click shut again and then Brady spoke. "I have to go. Sunday at eight at the diner."

"Do I need to bring anything with me?" she asked.

"No. I prefer you in nothing."

Liz's entire body heated as she hung up the phone and thought about the last time he had seen her like that. She didn't want to think about anything else until Sunday. Unfortunately, she had a mountain of work, but at least in this moment, she could daydream about her politician.

⸺

Franklin Street was dead as Liz stood in front of the diner. She yawned and tried to wake up. Early mornings were a killer, especially since she couldn't get to sleep last night. She was too antsy about getting to see Brady. She didn't even know where they were going, and it didn't really matter. She just wanted to be with him.

A black town car slowed to a stop directly in front of her. Was this real life? She pulled open the door and sat down on the black interior. She glanced around the car, deflated when she saw that Brady wasn't already in it. She figured they would be picking him up along the way.

"Morning, Ms. Carmichael," the driver said, turning around and giving her a smile.

It took her still-drowsy mind a minute to piece together that she was actually Ms. Carmichael. Of course Brady would tell the driver to pick up Sandy Carmichael and not Liz Dougherty. And thus, her secret identity was now a reality.

"Good morning," she said, stifling a yawn.

The man chuckled. "You can call me, Greg. Buckle up. We have about an hour drive ahead of us," he said, continuing down the empty street.

"All right. Thank you," she answered politely. An hour away. Where was he taking her that was an hour away? She could drive pretty much in any direction and hit a major city an hour outside of Chapel Hill. When they had talked on the phone, Brady hadn't given her any clues, and she didn't suspect the driver would be any help either. He was paid to get her there and no more.

She wanted to nap on the drive, but despite sleep deprivation she was too excited to rest. Plus, she had actually taken the time to do her hair and put on makeup. The last thing she needed was to show up, wherever they were going, with a print from the car on her face.

Instead, she pulled out her notepad that she always kept tucked away in her purse, right next to her handy-dandy voice recorder, and started flipping through her scribbled notes for her next article on the upcoming election. She had received another B paper from her professor. Professor Mires thought she was getting closer to the target, but she still had a lot of work to do. Liz had never tried so hard in her entire life to meet the expectations of one of her instructors. And she would be damn sure that she excelled.

By the time they pulled off the interstate, she had constructed an outline for the article. She tilted her head to the side as she rearranged some of the words. It didn't feel exactly *right* yet. She didn't know what she was missing and it was frustrating her. Maybe it would be better once she actually sat down and typed it all out.

"Nearly there, Ms. Carmichael," Greg said, looking at her through the rearview mirror.

"Fantastic," Liz said, dropping her pen into her purse and straightening to inspect her surroundings.

They were rolling down a narrow street where the lines had all but disappeared. Trees lined the craggy-looking road as tall as the eye could see, and they leaned forward, creating a tunnel through which to drive. They could be anywhere in the North Carolina countryside right now.

The road curved around a smooth bend and opened right up to the lakefront. Liz perked up and leaned forward between the front seats to catch the view. She could just see the other edge of the lake from her vantage point. Stunning lake houses dotted the perimeter, some as small as huts and others as large as mansions.

"Wow," she breathed as the morning light caught the gleam of the blue water. "It's beautiful."

"It is indeed," Greg said, turning to the right and driving around the lake.

Liz wasn't sure what she had been expecting, but a secluded lake an hour outside of the city was not it. She had mistakenly assumed another hotel. They'd had a great time in that hotel, but it couldn't compare to the lake. Did he have a house here? Would they have the place to themselves?

Her mind wandered off in that direction and a big smile crossed her face. A day at the lake house sounded amazing.

She frowned at the thought of not having a suit to wear. She knew that he had said that he preferred her in nothing, but he had to think that they would actually go out on the lake together. Why else would he bring her there, other than for the privacy?

Greg turned down a side street and pulled into the driveway of a two-story log cabin–style house with a wraparound porch and a small set of stairs leading up to the front door. The second story was almost entirely made of floor-to-ceiling glass windows. Trees and bushes perfectly landscaped the yard, and rows of tulips wrapped around the mailbox. Her favorite.

"Here you are, ma'am," Greg said, getting out of the car and running around to her side. He opened the door for her, and she stepped out, mesmerized. "Senator Maxwell has asked that I show you inside. He is delayed by business and hopes that you understand the inconvenience."

Understand? She was at the most gorgeous lake house she had ever seen.

"Follow me," he said with a smile. He trotted down the stone path to the stairs, retrieved a key from his suit coat, and allowed her access to the house. "He's taken the liberty of providing breakfast for you, and wanted to be sure to let you know that there should be swimsuits upstairs that fit you."

Liz nodded, completely bewildered. She tentatively stepped over the threshold and openly gawked at the interior. The entire house was solid wood, from the high-beamed ceilings to the wood floors. A stone fireplace took up the entirety of one wall. The furniture was artfully tailored to match the beauty of the house, set in a neutral earthy palette with deep dark hardwood tables, a soft sand-colored sofa, and olive and light brown chairs with deep sea-blue throw pillows and matching quilts. Lanterns and woodsy decorations adorned the mantel, and candles burned in rustic pillar holders around the room.

The bottom floor was entirely open save for two doors leading off to guest bedrooms. The kitchen connected directly to the living room, with an island in the center and two high-backed bar stools. A balcony from the second floor overlooked the kitchen and dining area, bringing in even more natural light from the surrounding windows. But best of all, the back wall was solid glass overlooking the lakefront.

Liz turned around to face the driver once more. "Is this for real?"

"Beg your pardon?" he asked, linking his fingers together and resting them on his stomach.

"I mean, thank you. Thank you for letting me inside. Was there anything else he told you?" she asked, desperate to know when he would be arriving.

"Unfortunately not, but I'm sure he won't be much longer if he knows what is waiting for him," he said with an encouraging smile.

Liz laughed, feeling lighthearted and free for the first time in a while. She dumped her bag on a chair and walked through the living room to the back of the house. She found a latch on the far wall, switched it to open, and pushed the entire glass wall sideways. It slid easily into a thin seam encased in the wooden wall.

She walked forward onto a wooden deck twice as wide as the house, where a speedboat and two Jet Skis were docked. An outside stone fireplace mirrored the interior, and wicker deck furniture faced the lake. A sturdy hemp hammock swayed between two support beams. A set of stairs led down to a rocky beach, where a pier extended out to a swimming platform with a stepladder. The lake house was almost completely secluded from the rest of the lake's inhabitants. Land curved into the lake to the right and then bent back away from them so that it formed its own little cove. It felt isolated and homey.

Liz loved the water, but she was used to the ocean. The lake looked so calm and serene next to the choppy Gulf of Mexico she was accustomed to back in Tampa. She had grown up on the water, and it made her feel at home.

She spent a few minutes exploring the deck, beach, and pier, but was soon perspiring from the humidity. She returned to the house, where she retraced her steps and found a set of stairs to the second floor. Liz's mouth dropped open. It opened up to a full-size loft with its own smaller sitting area and sliding wooden doors that were currently open to reveal a four-poster king-sized bed. The bedroom itself was so massive it had its own fireplace.

She took a few tentative steps, feeling in some way as if she were intruding. Greg had told her that the swimsuits were upstairs, but she hadn't been expecting upstairs to look like *this*.

As she approached, she saw a note with her name on it on the bed. Her heart accelerated and she picked it up. She felt as if she was in a bizarre world. People didn't do these things. Guys didn't leave handwritten notes at their massive private lake houses or have a driver pick you up in a town car just so they could see you. Whose life was she living?

She opened the card and read the contents.

> *Suits are in the closet on the right,*
> *but you don't have to wear one.*
> *It's just coming off anyway.*
> *—B*

Liz traced her fingers over the words. She could not fucking wait. Tucking the card into the back pocket of her shorts, she made her way into the closet to search out a bathing suit.

She left the room wearing a gold bathing suit with a slight shimmer. It accented her complexion and highlighted her blond hair. The suit was a basic triangle top, but it held her in as much as any of the other ones. She loved bikinis, even though her breasts were generally too big for most styles, and she felt a bit too curvy for the string tie bottoms that she loved.

Walking down the stairs, she reached into her purse for her phone and checked her email. She yawned, still tired from waking up so early, and padded back outside. It was too nice to be cooped up inside.

She thumbed through the news articles absentmindedly. She wasn't really paying attention to what they said. She stretched out on the hammock as a call flashed on her screen.

Victoria.

Liz didn't want to talk to her friend right now. She was in paradise, and she couldn't even tell her about it. Even if Victoria would keep her secret, she didn't feel comfortable risking it. What if they were found out? She would rather tell no one and know that she wasn't to blame.

She ignored the call with a sigh and curled up on her side. A couple minutes later her phone beeped again with a voice mail. Liz pressed it to her ear.

"Hey, bitch! Answer your fucking phone. I hopped on a plane to London yesterday and I'm fucking tanked. Do you remember that hot-ass TA I was fucking at the end of the semester? He's doing some kind of study-abroad teaching thing."

Liz cringed. This sounded like trouble.

"He invited me to stay at his place, so we're basically living at the pub and in his sweet suite that the university actually fucking paid for. I'm living a dream right now. I should have fucking invited you beforehand, and now I feel like an ass. There are about five million gorgeous Brits with accents here."

Victoria was living the dream? Liz looked around the lake house and shook her head. She was on cloud nine.

"You should totally hop the pond and all that. Either way, I'm coming back to Chapel Hill instead of Jersey. We're going to get your nerdy ass out of the office. Anyway, call me back, bitch. Love your face!"

Liz couldn't help but laugh. Victoria was utterly ridiculous in the best possible way. Only she would hop the pond, as she said, to sleep with a TA for a couple weeks.

She stared out across the expansive lake. The temperatures hadn't yet heated the air to an uncomfortable degree, and a slight breeze was rolling in off of the lake. It was peaceful. She felt comfortable here even without Brady.

Her phone buzzed again and she saw Brady's name flash on her screen.

On my way to you.

Liz smiled and jotted back a text. *Good.*

It'll be good when I'm with you. Can't wait to see which suit you picked.

Her grin grew at the comment, and as she was about to respond another text flashed on her screen from Brady.

I'm hoping for nothing.

Chapter 14
HOLDING ON

Liz felt the hammock rock side to side gently, pulling her out of her catnap. Hands traced the sides of her body, and lips captured her own in a searing kiss. She groaned against Brady's mouth, her body waking immediately. Their tongues explored each other and she wound her hands up into his thick, dark hair. She threaded her fingers through the short strands, tugging lightly. His strong hands held her face in place, and his thumb stroked her cheek. She hadn't felt this alive since the last time he had touched her.

"Mornin'," Brady said with a grin before pressing his lips to hers once more.

"Mmm, good morning," she said, unable to control the giddy smile on her face.

"You chose the gold." He fingered the strap.

"I almost opted for nothing."

"We can fix that."

"Please do," she murmured softly.

His hands slid under her knees and shoulders and lifted her off of the hammock with ease. She wrapped her arms around his neck and rested her head on his shoulder.

"I've been waiting all week to get my hands on you," he growled against her neck.

"No more waiting." She let the words tumble out of her mouth. No hesitation and no forethought. He made her feel so confident. It was like everything she had ever been embarrassed to say to guys, she said to Brady. He certainly seemed to like that she spoke her mind.

Brady walked them over to a chaise on the deck, setting her down and taking a seat next to her. She finally got a chance to look at him. She nearly melted where she lay. How had she gotten so lucky?

Her body responded to the pure sexuality that radiated off of the man before her. He was dressed down again today in a white cotton button-down rolled up to his elbows, and khakis with a thick brown belt at his waist. His dark hair was short and spiked a bit in the front. His brown eyes seemed to bore into her, as if he knew the deepest, darkest secrets of her soul. Then again, he was her deepest, darkest secret.

Whatever business he had been involved in before he arrived clearly hadn't required him to be clean cut, because stubble grew in across his strong jawline. She reached up and rubbed her hands against the scruffiness.

"Yeah, I didn't get a chance to shave this morning," he said, gripping her hips in his hands and sliding her down flat on the chaise.

"I like it like this," Liz told him.

"I like you like this," he said, staring into her open blue eyes.

"How?" she asked softly. "Lying down in a bathing suit?"

"Here. With me. Lying down in nothing." He tugged on the string around her neck and let the straps loosen.

The top didn't do a very good job of holding her in when it was tied, and Brady just sat and watched as the top released her breasts. He reached around with one hand and undid the back tie before unceremoniously tossing it over his shoulder and onto the wooden floor of the deck. She lay before him, completely topless in the morning light.

Despite the secluded nature of the lake house, Liz wondered briefly whether anyone could see her. She had never been topless in a public place before, not even on a beach in Europe, when she had gone with her high school friends after graduation. But the way he looked at her washed all of her worries away.

Brady smiled as he bent forward and took one of her nipples into his mouth. Her head arched back as his tongue swirled around the peak. His hand covered her other breast and massaged it demandingly. He moved to the other breast and sucked, pulled, and dragged the nipple between his teeth until she squirmed.

Her hand fumbled out in front of her to try to reach his belt. She needed to get him out of those clothes. He chuckled and pulled back but continued to circle his thumb around her now-sensitive nipple. "You'll get your chance."

I hope very soon, she thought.

She was ready for her chance right now. At the very least she wanted to feel him through his shorts . . . get a glimpse of what she would be having.

He took her hand in his, moved it away from his belt, and then pressed it against his growing dick. Her mind spun as she felt the heat from within and the full length of him pulsing in her palm. Her fingers wrapped around him, gripping him through his shorts, and then slowly pulled up to the tip. He dragged in a deep breath as she repeated the motion.

God, I want you out of those shorts, she thought.

While she was distracted with her own teasing motions, Brady reached down and yanked on the ties holding together the bikini bottoms. Her hand stilled as he traced the edge of the bathing suit with his fingertip, raising goose bumps on her exposed flesh. His fingers moved around the outside of the bathing suit down, so close to her most sensitive skin, and then back up the other side. He hadn't even done anything, and she felt ready to combust.

He smirked as her cheeks flushed; then he moved the bathing suit away from her body. Liz placed her feet flat on the ground and raised her butt into the air so he could get rid of the last remnant of her clothing while he was still fully dressed.

He tilted his head with a devilish smile as she lowered back down. "Let's try that position later."

Liz tried to remain calm while she lay naked out in the open, but her heart was beating double time. She was ready for him. She was ready for everything he would give her and more. So she nodded and seductively said, "Let's try it now."

Brady bent down and kissed her lips. "You can't handle me yet. I think I need to warm you up first."

She thought about arguing with him, until he started kissing his way down her stomach and between her legs. Then she forgot all sense. Why had she thought about arguing?

His tongue licked up between her lips, spreading her open for his viewing. He swept across her clit and her body jumped. The next time he forced her hips down with his hand and used the other one to stroke down her center. She was already beyond ready for him. He was just toying with her, bringing her closer and closer, and then withdrawing until she felt her body gasping for release.

The longer he held her off, the more she felt her body begin to respond in all new ways. She felt her fingers grip the side of the chaise and her toes curl. Heat radiated from her core until it took over her entire body. She didn't know how much longer she could hold out as he alternated licking and sucking on her. His fingers delved into her and began a slow, steady pumping motion. Her body arched off of the chaise as the combination of sensations rocketed her over the edge.

"Fuck, I want that," he groaned as she rode out the orgasm, her core tightening and releasing.

She couldn't even respond coherently. She was pretty sure all she did was stutter, but he seemed to get the picture. He stood and stripped off his button-down. She opened her eyes long enough to stare up at his chiseled chest and shoulders. He was built beyond comprehension. She was glad they had the entire day, because she was going to explore every inch of those muscles.

His hand found the belt to his khakis, and he made quick work of unbuckling it and stripping off his shorts. He wore Calvin Klein boxer briefs, and all she could think about was how his beautiful body belonged in their advertisements.

"Let me," she said, stilling his hand poised at the top of his boxers.

Liz sat up, feeling more and more comfortable in her state of nudity. She slid her fingers along the seam and slowly dragged the boxers to the floor, releasing him from his briefs. She swallowed as her hand wrapped around the base, and she looked up at him with her own smirk.

She ran her hand up and down the hard length, and he closed his eyes with a sharp intake of breath. Liz wet her lips and touched the tip to her mouth. He groaned as she licked around the head before wrapping her lips around him. She went to work licking down the shaft until her hand moved smoothly up and down in time with her mouth rocking back and forth, on and off.

His hands dug into her thick, blond hair, gripping her harder each time she took him deeper. She couldn't believe how much *bigger* it got as she kept up the work of bringing him closer to climax. She wanted him to experience the same mind-blowing sensations he had given her.

She picked up her tempo as she felt him nearing release, and he started guiding her head with his hands. She didn't know if he even knew he was doing it, but soon he was pushing into her mouth faster and faster. She didn't gag easily, but he was pushing her limits. She used her free hand to grip his hip as her lips slid back and forth with each thrust.

"Liz," he grunted, not even stopping the tempo, "I'm gonna come."

She felt him strain against the release, but she didn't want him to stop. She wanted him to come, and she wasn't going to let up until she got what she wanted.

When he saw that she wasn't stopping him, he pumped even faster. She had a split second where she thought she wasn't going to be able to open wide enough to take him all in. He was fucking her mouth, and she was . . . enjoying it. God she actually really wanted this. She groaned as she felt him pulse in her mouth, and the extra sensation did the trick.

"Fuck," he cried. His body shuddered and he released into her mouth. He moaned as he finished, and slowly freed her of his tight grip on her hair. Liz sucked her way back to his head and finally released him.

He looked down at her expectantly. She met his direct gaze head-on and swallowed him all the way down. She licked her lips.

"Jesus Christ," he said, staring down at her with admiration.

She lay back down on the chaise and stretched out for his viewing pleasure. His eyes raked her body as he slowly began to recover his wits. She tried to remain as still as possible as he examined her, but she was sure she was squirming. When his eyes found hers again, he smiled.

"You're coming with me," he said, grasping her around the waist and pulling her to her feet. He scooted her toward the open glass door.

"I prefer that," Liz responded with her pleased-with-herself grin.

Brady smacked her ass, sending her scurrying forward into the living room. "Hey!" she said with a giggle. "Watch how hard you do that."

"You like it," he said, following after her. And she did.

It was strange to walk around the house completely naked, but at the same time it wasn't. She wasn't sure what to make of the warring sides of her nature colliding. On some level, she felt as if she should cover up so his eyes wouldn't see every inch of her, but still, she wanted him to see her like this. The way his eyes followed her made her feel utterly beautiful. It was a feeling that she wanted to remember forever.

They walked up the stairs, and when they touched the landing of the second floor, Brady hoisted her back into his arms and carried her to the bed. Apparently walking at a normal pace wasn't going to be allowed. She almost chided him on being impatient, but really she was getting impatient. How long had it been since they had been in that hotel room?

Way too damn long.

She crawled backward, sinking into the pillow-top mattress, and then pulled the comforter back so that she could burrow into the silky sheets. He slid into the bed next to her and turned onto his side, so they were facing each other. Their legs tangled together under the sheets. His hand ran down to her lower back, pressing her into him. Liz sighed into the embrace.

Soon their bodies heated up at such close proximity. Liz hiked her leg up over his hip, spreading her legs as he moved against her still-wet folds. She groaned at the feel of him between her already aching legs. "Brady," she murmured, her fingers digging into his chest.

"You want me, baby?" he murmured, pushing her shoulders back into the bed and rolling over on top of her. He pushed softly against her opening, and her whole body trembled with desire. She moved her hips forward, trying to get him to move, but he withdrew.

She groaned in frustration. "I want you!" she cried, desperate to get him inside of her.

"Condom?" he all but whispered as he held himself back.

"I'm on birth control," she told him. Any other time she might have been embarrassed talking about it, but right now was not the time. Right now she just wanted him to fuck her.

He kissed her lips as he slipped into her. Her body stilled as he filled her, and she let her eyes close. She hadn't known it was possible for him to feel better than last time, but she had been wrong.

Brady moved in and out of her in one hard, swift motion. Liz tightened around him as the force of it rocked her.

"Fuck, your pussy is tight," he groaned.

He repeated the motion, in and out. Harder, rougher, quicker each time, until he was slapping against her at a rapid pace. Liz was gasping at the power behind each thrust, but she couldn't even begin to deny that it felt good. It felt really fucking good.

There were no pretenses in the way he was driving into her. They weren't making love. They weren't having sex. They were fucking, plain and simple. And Liz wanted nothing more than that in that moment. She wanted him to take her for his own. She wanted him to ravage her body. She wanted to forget that she was Liz Dougherty for a time and be whoever the fuck he wanted her to be, because the Liz Dougherty back in Chapel Hill would never have done this. And now it was all she wanted to do.

He leaned forward on his elbows and kept up the rhythm. "You like when I talk about your pussy?" he whispered. Her body seized at the mention of the word. She had never used it before, but it sounded sexy coming out of his mouth.

"No," she whispered. He arched an eyebrow and slowed his movements. Her body tensed at the sudden change. She was already missing him pounding into her; she was getting close.

"Tell me again that you don't like when I talk about how much I like your pussy," he said.

"I don't like it," she repeated. She took a deep breath and let her walls fall. "I love it."

Brady smiled in triumph. "That's my girl," he whispered huskily into her ear.

He rocked back onto his knees, grabbed her hips in his hands, and pulled her up so that she was resting in the same position she had been in earlier on the chaise. Her feet were flat on the bed and her ass high in the air. He started pumping in and out of her again, and she closed her eyes. Her body was superheating already, and then his thumb started circling her clit.

She gasped and groaned as he hit double stimulation with the move, but he wouldn't release her. Her arms went over her head and she dug into the pillows, trying to stifle her cries.

"Come for me, baby," he demanded.

"I . . . can't " she groaned, feeling her body teetering on the edge.

"Just let go. I want you to come when my dick is inside your pussy."

That pushed her over. She saw stars as her body stiffened and then exploded all around him. Her orgasm sent him over the edge, and he buried himself into her one more time as they came together.

Brady collapsed onto the bed next to her. Liz waited until her breathing evened out and then rolled off the bed and walked into the bathroom. Her cheeks were flushed and her freshly straightened hair was a hot mess. And yet none of it mattered. She felt incredible.

When she finished, she returned to the bedroom and found Brady lying flat on his back dozing off. He was truly an unbelievably good-looking man. She never wanted to erase the memory of his peaceful slumber from her mind.

He cracked an eye open and smiled. "Come here," he said, patting the bed next to him.

She complied, rolling onto her side and snuggling into his shoulder. She breathed in and out, slowly matching her breaths to the rise and fall of his chest. His heartbeat was music in her ears, and she heard it roll down a gradual slope back to a resting beat.

"I'm going to fall back asleep if we stay here," she murmured softly.

"It's still early. You should rest," he said, kissing her hair. "I'm not done with you yet."

She smirked into his chest, liking the sound of that. Gradually her breathing slowed and she drifted off once more, wrapped in his strong, capable arms.

———

They spent the day out on the lake, playing in the water, riding around on his speedboat, and racing on the Jet Skis. He was more skilled at riding, but she managed to unseat him once. That was victory enough.

Liz sped up next to where he bobbed in the water and smiled. She kicked her foot out and splashed him.

"You're going to get it," he said, swimming two powerful strokes toward her.

"You have to catch me first," she said, swinging around on the Jet Ski as he lunged for her.

She watched him swim to his Jet Ski faster than really should have been possible and swing his leg over the other side, and then she took off. The Jet Ski underneath her hummed loudly as she cut across the even water. She could hear him closing the distance between them and laughed out loud at the adrenaline coursing through her.

Liz flew out into open water, veering for the cove that afforded them all the privacy in the world. She felt young and carefree, as if she was finally living. The world was spinning by in a blur and there was only here and now. There was only Brady, and how she felt when she was with him.

She chanced a glance over her shoulder and saw him racing toward her, getting closer and closer by the second. Abruptly she cut to the right, and when he followed her, she darted back to the left. He was so near her that she could see him beginning to pull up alongside her. Taking a drastic turn into the cove, she lost control of the Jet Ski and was thrown off the seat. She landed hard in the water, falling below the surface.

Her hands clawed through the water as she tried to resurface. Her head broke through and she came up gasping. She hadn't been expecting that to happen, and she was more in shock than anything. Air filled her lungs and she treaded water to keep afloat.

Brady pulled up alongside her, laughing boisterously.

"Don't laugh at me, you ass!" she yelled, splashing him again.

"I can't help it if you wipe out so extravagantly," he said, cutting the engine on his Jet Ski. He dove off the Jet Ski into the water and swam the remaining few feet to her.

"I can't believe you laughed at me." She pushed his shoulder lightly.

He grabbed her arm and yanked her into him. His arms circled her waist, pulling their wet bodies together. Liz smiled, instantly forgetting what she had been saying. She wrapped her legs around his waist and slid her hands up around his neck.

Brady held them effortlessly above the water as his lips found hers. She would never tire of kissing him. They tasted like a mixture of sweat and sunscreen, and she couldn't get enough. She pressed her body into him and forgot that they were in the middle of the lake, where other people could see them.

He pulled back before she was ready, and she captured his lips once more. He chuckled. "We should get back to the house. I had dinner delivered. Nothing special, but it's good deck food."

"Sounds perfect," she said, leaning forward and kissing him again.

They docked the Jet Skis back in their ports and toweled off. Plates of food were sitting on the deck table when they returned. Brady peeled back the covering to show her a cheese and bread plate, a fruit plate loaded down with fresh strawberries, pineapple, kiwi, and melon, and another tray with finger food that they picked at as the afternoon sun faded into evening.

Liz sat down next to Brady on the outdoor bench with her feet tucked underneath her and her head on his shoulder. She yawned, the rush of the day and overexposure to the sun catching up with her, but she wouldn't dare slip away when she had so little time left with him.

"So, what else do you have planned for the summer?" Liz asked. It was nice knowing that she was asking not for work, but for personal benefit. Though she worried it might come across that way. "I mean when can I see you again?"

"Those are two very different questions." At least he didn't tense.

"I meant them the same," she said.

"Well, to the first one, I try to take each day at a time and let my staff plan the rest out. I have to win the primary in August, and that's where I'm looking. And in answer to the second, as soon as I can next get away."

She hoped that meant sooner rather than later. She didn't know how much she could handle this waiting game. She would wait for him. She knew that she would, but that didn't mean that she wanted to go weeks without him in her life. In fact, she wanted to spend all of her time with him. And that was a scary thought.

"What about you? What are your big summer plans?" he asked.

Liz smiled. She liked this. It felt comfortable, sitting watching the sunset, discussing the future. She had never been a big one to talk about the future with guys . . . not that this was that kind of talk.

"Working on a portfolio for my journalism class and running a campaign column," she told him. The thought of how much work she had got her all flustered.

"Busy."

"Very. I don't know how I'll find time to keep seeing this guy," she said flippantly.

"You're seeing a guy?" he asked, turning to face her. She wasn't sure whether he was serious or joking. She couldn't read him as well as she thought.

"Well, I don't know if you would call it that," she said.

He narrowed his eyes. "If you're talking about anyone other than me, I'm not going to be pleased," he said, grasping her chin and pulling her in for a heated kiss.

Liz blinked a few times to try to regain composure when he released her. "How could there be anyone else but you?"

And in the summer-heated night, wrapped up in his arms, lost to his touch, she really believed that. Brady had taken over her world. He captured her thoughts, revealed her hidden desires, and made her feel as if she was actually living. In that moment, there was no one else other than Brady.

"I'm having a banquet near the end of the summer, right before the primary. It won't be in any of the websites you've been scraping to track campaign schedules," he said with a laugh. "I assume you're doing that?"

Liz bit her lip.

"That's what I thought," he said with a chuckle. "I can give you a schedule if it makes it easier."

"Then it feels like I'm not doing my job."

"It feels a bit like you're stalking me."

"That is part of my job," she said with a cheeky grin.

"Well, you won't stalk me to this event without a ticket," Brady told her. "I'd like you to be there."

She wanted to ask whether she was going to be going with him, but she didn't. She couldn't ask that. If he said no, she wouldn't be able to keep the hurt off of her face. They'd had such a nice day together that she wouldn't want to ruin anything.

"All right. I'd like to go," she told him.

"In the meantime, will you do me a favor?"

"Sure," she said, offering him the world and more.

"Don't get your picture in the paper."

"What?" she asked, surprised. "Why would I get my picture in the paper?" Liz immediately started looking around the lakefront, as if she were expecting photographers to appear around every corner.

"In your paper. Don't let anyone convince you that you need to have your pretty face next to your name," he said, running his hand down her cheek.

"Why?" she asked suspiciously.

"You're pretty anonymous, right?"

She definitely was. She had been saying not too long ago that everyone knew Calleigh when she was in her position, but no one knew who Liz was. It was probably her own doing. Calleigh liked to be in the spotlight, and Liz preferred the background. Slowly she nodded her affirmation.

"Stay that way."

She didn't understand what that had to do with anything, and it must have shown on her face.

"Right now, you're Liz Dougherty on paper. You've written some articles that are unfavorable to me, but no one knows who you are. If you start showing up at all my events, and people already know your face, then your cover as Sandy is ruined . . ."

Liz started putting the pieces together. That made much more sense. He was protecting her identity and at the same time securing himself a little bit more. So, no pictures in the paper. That was fine by her. She would rather be anonymous than lose out on time with Brady.

"What about your press secretary? Doesn't she know who I am?" she asked, wanting to cover all the bases.

"Heather? No, she knows you're a reporter, but she doesn't know you by face, just by name. And I'll deal with Heather so she doesn't put the pieces together," he told Liz confidently.

"Well . . . I still don't have an answer to my second question," she said, nudging him with her elbow. "When do I get to see you again? I'm not going to have to wait another three weeks, am I?"

"Baby, I never want to make you wait again," he said, picking her up, wrapping her legs around his waist, and carrying her back up the stairs to the bedroom.

Chapter 15

LIKE A DREAM

Liz returned to her house the next morning bright and early. They had spent all night at the lake house and she hadn't gotten much sleep, but it was worth it. She would do it all over again if she had the chance. It felt surreal to come back like this and have everything else be the same . . . when she felt so different.

She wanted to sleep, but life was still moving on all around her. Her world with Brady felt like something out of a dream, and then she woke up to reality.

The entire week felt like that. She turned in another assignment: The one she had been working on during the drive to the lake house. Today was the day she found out whether she had done any better. Overall, she had thought it was a better paper. Maybe Brady was rubbing off on her.

Well, in her opinion, he wasn't rubbing off on her enough. She had managed to see him twice this week at various hotels—once for a pretty spectacular hour and once on Saturday morning before he had to go to work. They had started talking nearly every day, though. She wanted more, but she was already getting more from him than he had said when they had first agreed to do this.

She felt as if they were dating. Maybe they were. Yet their relationship was a complete secret, and not one person knew it was going on besides the driver who had taken her to the lake house. But when they were together, the world slipped away, and he consumed so much of her thoughts.

And still, despite their blossoming relationship, if she could even call it that, her daily life remained the same. She went into the paper every day and submitted articles to be printed, went to class, and resumed her tennis sessions with Tana. Sometimes she even found time to go to the local pool and work on her tan.

Today she had agreed to meet up with Justin after her class. He wanted to talk to her about the AV work he was doing for her for the summer. She was sure he was going to try to get more money out of her. She didn't even have access to the meager funds, and paying him freelance was too much as it was. She was going to have to cut him loose and find someone else to do it if he wouldn't cooperate.

Liz shoved her laptop into her bag and walked up to Professor Mires's podium. "Great lecture today."

"Why, thank you, Liz."

"I was seeing if you had my paper graded," she said with a smile.

"Ah. I actually did get a chance to read yours. I'm a bit behind with the rest of the class, unfortunately." She pulled a paper out of her bag and handed it to Liz. "Good work. This is more on track."

Liz opened the paper to the back and found a B+ circled in red. Well, a B+ wasn't an A, but it was closer. She had enough weeks to bring this grade up. At least, she hoped so.

"I know it's not what you wanted, Liz, but it's getting there. Keep doing what you're doing, and you'll really start to see improvement. In my notes, I suggest broadening your scope and not focusing so much on each individual politician. Maybe work with them all together or look at it more long term or even historically. The reader should be able to relate to your arguments even if they've never heard of the politician. I think you'll figure it out."

"Thank you, Professor Mires," she said, mustering a smile.

She walked out of the classroom with a sigh and veered toward the Pit, where she was planning to meet Justin. She pushed her hair off of her neck as the summer heat beat down on her. It had gone from comfortable to unbearable in the span of a week, and she was really missing the lake house. She knew it was for more than the cool water.

Liz pulled out her phone to text Justin that she was on her way, and she saw that she had missed a text. She opened it and saw the name Carmichael flash on the screen. Her heart skipped a beat. Brady didn't have a lot of free time to text her, and it always made her excited to see his name, even if it was a code name.

Carrboro Town Hall in fifteen minutes.

That's all it said. Nothing to say what was going on or if he was speaking. She checked the time on the text and saw that it was forty-five minutes ago. She was already thirty minutes late, and by the time she got to her car and drove the ten minutes to the outskirts of town she would be an hour late. She bit her lip and debated.

Go to her meeting with Justin or get the chance to see Brady. It was a no-brainer. She could reschedule.

Something came up. Can we reschedule? Liz jotted out to Justin.

We were supposed to meet in ten minutes . . .

Liz grumbled. She knew when they were supposed to meet.

Yeah, sorry. It was an emergency. Same time tomorrow?

Just come to the party at Frat Court tonight, and we'll talk there.

Liz rolled her eyes. How many more times could he ask her to go to his stupid parties before he got the hint?

I don't know if I can make it. I'm swamped with work for the paper, but I'll try. Tomorrow same place, same time, if I can't make it?

Yeah. Whatever, Liz.

Liz sighed heavily. She could not lose her best AV person just because she didn't go to his party. She knew that she was neglecting her work a bit to go see Brady, but Brady was also technically work, wasn't he? Was she just rationalizing? This was ridiculous, and she couldn't deal with it right now.

She put her phone away and tried not to think about it.

Liz parked across the street from Carrboro Town Hall, walked through the crosswalk, and rushed up the stairs into the building. A large group of people were still milling around the room, but it was obvious that whatever had been going on inside was over.

She sighed, disappointed, and searched the room for Brady. She didn't see him and started circling, looking for someone familiar. Standing in a corner was a woman she recognized from *Chapel Hill News*. The local newspaper didn't think very highly of the university paper, largely because of the editorial and opinion columns that took up the majority of the space. Liz didn't blame them for it.

"Hey," Liz said with an awkward wave as she broke into the conversation the woman was having with her photographer.

The woman looked at Liz as if she was trying to place her, then gave her a fake smile. "Hey, how are you?"

She clearly didn't remember who Liz was. "I'm doing all right. I got the memo about this too late. I'm with the university press. What did I miss?"

She saw the recognition shine in her eyes.

"State Senator Maxwell is running for Congress."

"Right. I know. I was at his press conference when he announced," Liz said with a smile. She hoisted her bag higher on her shoulder.

"Oh," she said, turning her head back to her photographer. "Well, he gave a speech about community outreach. It was pretty short and he didn't allow any questions."

"Is he still here?" Liz asked, glancing around the room again. Why hadn't he told her about this earlier? It must have been scheduled in advance. She could have been there on time or at least seen him. Granted, she couldn't miss Professor Mires's class, but Liz might have gotten out of it if she told the professor it was for her project.

"Yeah. He went into a back room after the speech."

"How long has he been scheduled here?" Liz asked.

"Rescheduled to Maxwell this morning after the other guy canceled," Deb said, then turned away from Liz as if the conversation was over.

At least that made her feel a bit better. If it had been rescheduled this morning, then it made sense why his text came last-minute.

A flurry of activity on the other side of the room drew her attention. Brady materialized in the doorway, and Liz sighed softly to herself when she saw him. He was wearing a crisp navy suit with a gray button-down and his signature blue tie. The suit was clearly tailored, because it fit him better than she had ever seen a suit on someone else. It was just too perfect. And all she could think was how she wanted to get him out of it.

She automatically walked toward him and wished that they were the only ones in the room in that moment. He hadn't seen her yet, and she waited for him to look up and feel her eyes on him. She stood at the periphery of the crowd as others shook his hand and some took pictures. He was as smooth as ever, his campaign mask firmly in place as he was introduced to person after person.

Knowing it would be a little while before she got any closer to him, she let her eyes roam. Heather was standing to his right, keeping a watchful eye on everything that was going on. Standing close behind her was that same man from the club who had been a total ass to Liz after Brady had sent a drink. He had been with Heather at the last event. Did he work for the campaign? They hadn't met again since that night, and she wanted to keep it that way.

Maybe she would ask Brady about him next time they were alone . . . if she remembered anything at all when they were alone.

Brady moved through the crowd as much as he could, and then Heather whispered into his ear. He nodded and then addressed the crowd. "Thank you all so much for coming out. I can't wait to come back and speak with you all again, but unfortunately, I'm being told that it's my time to leave."

The crowd dispersed almost immediately as Brady turned to go. Liz took this as her opportunity to get to talk him. "Senator, mind if I ask one question?" she asked, butting around a few people to get to him. She was already pulling her voice recorder out of her bag.

When his eyes found hers, she stopped moving. She couldn't remember him ever looking at her like that. He hadn't even dropped his campaign mask. He was looking at her as if she were another questioning constituent.

She didn't expect him to look at her as though he had been sleeping with her for a couple weeks, but still she had expected something. But she didn't even see a flicker of recognition cross his face. How was he capable of that?

"Sorry, we told the press no questions," Heather said, stepping in between them. "Senator Maxwell's time is very limited."

"I understand," she said with more emotion in her voice than she would have liked.

He turned his back on her without a word and walked through the doors. Heather smiled as brightly as ever and followed him, closing the door. Liz stood there for a minute with mixed feelings warring inside of her. She knew that he couldn't act as if he knew her in public. She knew he was running for office and that he had made it plain what he wanted. First and foremost, he wanted to win the campaign.

But the other, irrational side of her was screaming. Why couldn't he have even smiled at her . . . given her some secret nod as though he was glad that she was there? She had canceled her plans with Justin, however tenuous they were, to come over here just to get shunned. She had a life of her own, and he needed to respect that. He couldn't have her come to every function he was at and not get to spend any time with him. It would break her.

Liz turned on her heel and walked to the door. She wasn't paying attention when a voice cut through her anger.

"Liz! What a surprise to find you here," Leslie Chester said with her overly dimpled chipmunk-cheek smile.

"Hey, Leslie, what's up?" Liz said, continuing her walk toward the exit.

Leslie fell into step beside her. She was short, so she took an extra step for every one of Liz's. "Not much. Lobbying Senator Maxwell. I might take an internship with his campaign," she said. Liz tried not to roll her eyes. "I was surprised to find that you didn't get an interview again this time."

"Why is that surprising, when he said no questions from the press at this event?" Liz asked blankly. She couldn't let emotion show in her voice. She needed to channel Brady's campaign mask.

"Oh, I thought you knew Senator Maxwell," she said, a bit too chirpy.

"Why would you think that?"

"He knew your name last time. Didn't he call you Ms. Dougherty?" Leslie asked, all doe-eyed.

Liz bit the inside of her cheek. Why did Leslie remember every single detail? If Leslie weren't in law school, Liz would be wondering if she herself was going into investigative reporting. "Yes, his press secretary set it up before the event. I wasn't even aware of this one."

"Oh, well," she said with a shrug. "Next time maybe."

"Yeah, maybe," Liz said through gritted teeth. "I have a prior commitment to make. I've got to dash. Good seeing you again, Leslie."

"You too, Liz. And if you need any help with the facts in your column, please feel free to call me," Leslie said, clicking her modest heels across the crosswalk and to her Prius.

Liz puffed air out of her mouth in frustration as she found her Accord. She took a seat and turned the ignition, letting the cool air blast into her face. She rubbed her eyes and tried to calm down. She knew that she and Brady weren't open about their relationship and that they couldn't be. But she couldn't deny that what he had done had hurt. Even though she had agreed to do this with him, it didn't mean that she had agreed to get her feelings stomped on. He needed to take them into consideration before acting so brashly. She hadn't even had any forewarning that he was going to turn his feelings off like a light switch.

Her phone buzzed in her purse and she perked up. Maybe that was him! Maybe he was going to apologize for acting like a jerk.

She pulled her phone out and shook her head when she saw it was Justin.

Here are the deets for the party tonight. See ya then.

The rest of the message listed the time, location, and party theme—one she would likely never follow. Who chose tacky Hawaiian as a party theme?

She finally put the car into drive and started to pull out of her spot, when she saw people exit the side of the Town Hall. Liz's eyes narrowed when she spotted Heather walking purposefully out in front. Even from here, Liz could tell she was talking a million miles a minute. Next came the chubby asshole and then a slew of other people that she didn't recognize, who all piled into black vans.

Last was Brady with another girl she didn't recognize, with superstraight dark brown hair to her shoulders. She was wearing a pink blouse tucked into a high-waisted black skirt with black pumps. She was thin too, and cute . . . really cute. Liz's eyes narrowed as she and Brady talked to each other briefly. Then Brady leaned down and kissed the girl on the cheek.

Liz's heart stopped. After all that stuff about her not seeing anyone else . . . that he wanted her all to himself. She knew they couldn't be together in public, but that didn't mean he could be with someone *else* in public!

She swallowed back the rising bile in her throat and tried to push back the hurt crushing her chest. She just wanted to be angry. Anger was easier to deal with than pain.

The girl hopped into the car before him and Brady followed, closing the door and zooming away. Liz watched the car leave, letting the anger fuel her rash decisions. She stared back down at her phone.

Actually, I think I will make it. See you tonight, Liz texted Justin before throwing her phone into the passenger seat and going home to see if she had anything that could possibly resemble a tacky Hawaiian outfit.

———

No.

That was her general consensus on whether or not she had anything remotely Hawaiian-looking. People were walking around in oversize Hawaiian button-downs, fake grass skirts, coconut bra tops, cut-off jean shorts, foam visors, bathing suits, and leis everywhere.

Liz didn't own any jean shorts or even a jean skirt, which apparently would have been acceptable. She had opted for a white skirt, hot pink bikini top, and flip-flops. It wasn't tacky, but at least it was themed. She had even taken the time to dry her hair, so that it had beachy waves to it. No one seemed to care as long as they got to come up to her and yell, "Do you want to get lei'd?" Then they would throw a lei over her head and laugh maniacally while chugging beer.

Justin dragged her around the party, introducing her to all of his fraternity brothers and some of the girls they were fooling around with, though he didn't always know their names. She wondered briefly whether people thought that she was fooling around with Justin, and drowned herself in hunch punch at the thought.

Her phone was glued to her side, but she had never heard from Brady. After two glasses of the hunch punch, she wasn't thinking straight about anything. She rested her hand on Justin's arm and laughed at a joke some girl had made that she would have normally never found funny. But for some reason right now, it was hysterical.

"What is in this stuff?" she asked, turning to face Justin and trying to stand up straight.

He laughed when he got a good look at her. "Fuck, you're wasted. That is like vodka and Everclear with a hint of Kool-Aid for taste."

"Are you kidding me?" she croaked. "I could *die!*"

"You're not going to die," he said, placing his hand on her waist to steady her. "You'll be fine. Just loosen up a bit."

"A bit? I'm falling over," she said, as she did just that and started laughing again.

Justin reached down and helped her stand up once again. "You're a mess. When was the last time you drank this much?"

Liz shook her head side to side really fast. "Never. No, once!"

"Maybe I should take you home," he suggested. He rested her back against the wall of the fraternity house and leaned closer to her.

"I don't know. I'm having such a good time, though," she said, even though she knew that didn't sound like her at all.

"You're drunk, Liz. Let me take you home."

"I'm drunk?" she asked, poking at his chest. "You're drunk too!"

He shook his head. "No way. I haven't had much at all. I can totally drive."

"I'll just take a cab."

"Seriously, I can drive you."

"Fine! Take me home then," she said, letting him take her arm and guide her away from the house.

Warning alarms went off in her head as they got closer and closer to his car. She was suddenly not feeling well at all. Why was walking so difficult? Why was the entire universe spinning right now? That wasn't a good sign, was it?

"Are you sure you can drive?" she asked, covering her mouth and trying to hold back the rising sickness in the pit of her stomach.

"Yeah, I'm fine. How are you feeling? You look a bit green." He unlocked the passenger door and held it open for her.

"Ugh, yeah, I feel a bit green."

"Are you going to make it all the way home?" he asked.

She nodded, not trusting herself to open her mouth to speak. He walked around the car, sliding inside and pulling out of Frat Court. The car ride did *not* help. It really wasn't a long drive. On the roads this late at night when few people were out, it was less than five minutes from her place to his, but it felt like an eternity. She wasn't sure if her vision was blurring or if they were swerving. Were they swerving?

"Justin, are you drunk?" she asked as they crossed over Franklin Street as the light turned red. She heard tires screech to a halt as they coasted through the busiest intersection in Chapel Hill.

"I'm fine. We're almost there," he said, taking the first right onto Rosemary Street.

Then she saw it in her rearview mirror: blue lights.

"Fuck!" Justin cried as the police car pulled up behind his car.

"Shit, Justin," Liz said, straightening in her seat and wishing she had a fucking shirt. She was in a car, getting pulled over by the police, in a miniskirt and bathing suit top. She felt ridiculous.

Justin pulled over to the side of the road, and the policeman came over to the window asking for his license and registration. Liz watched the next thirty minutes through a drunken haze. Justin was asked to step out of the car. He failed the sobriety tests with flying colors. The police officer informed him that he was being arrested for driving under the influence. Liz watched the officer escort Justin into the backseat of the police cruiser. He would have to spend the night in jail.

"Ma'am," the officer said, coming up to her.

"Uh . . . yes, Officer?" she asked, sobering up.

"Do you have someone who could come pick you up, or do you need us to escort you home?"

"No, I live right around the corner. Only a block away."

"It's late. We can drive you if you need us to," he offered.

"No, thank you, sir."

"All right. Please drink more responsibly next time, ma'am."

"Yes, sir," she said as he walked back to his police car and drove off with Justin.

Liz placed her phone to her ear as she walked the short distance back to her house. She couldn't believe that had happened only one block from her house. That was the unluckiest thing that she had ever witnessed.

"Senator Maxwell's office," a woman answered through the phone.

He had someone answering phones at all hours of the night. What a life . . .

"I need to speak with the Senator." She was pretty sure her voice cracked.

"Who may I ask is speaking?"

"Sandy Carmichael," she said, weakly turning the corner.

"One moment, Ms. Carmichael."

Liz waited a couple minutes, and then Brady's voice came through the line just as she walked through the front door.

"Liz?" he asked. He sounded surprised, or maybe she was making that up.

"Brady." When she said his name, she broke down and the tears burst out of her eyes. The DUI had messed her up more than she had realized. What could have happened was scarier than what actually happened.

"Are you all right? What's wrong?" he asked, clearly concerned this time.

Despite everything that happened, all she could get out was, "Who was the girl?"

"What?"

"The girl you were with at the town hall event?"

"Oh, Liz, did you see that?"

Was he confirming her fears? Was she one of many that he was doing this with?

"That was my sister, Savannah."

Liz froze where she was standing. His sister. Well, that changed things. "Oh," she said softly.

"She lives with my parents, and I picked her up and brought her to the event with me," he said.

"I wish I'd known . . ." she said wistfully, feeling childish.

"Why?" he asked, his tone lowering.

"I went to a frat party."

Brady was silent. Liz was pretty sure that was worse. She couldn't handle his silence.

"A friend of mine was driving me home, and he got a DUI. I just walked home," she said, her voice cracking again. She couldn't believe Justin had gone to jail tonight. She would have to try to get ahold of him in the morning.

"Let me get this straight. You assumed I was with another woman. So you went and got trashed with some other guy who ended up endangering your life," he said, his controlled tone damn near threatening Justin's life at that moment.

"I'm not proud of myself!" she spat back in frustration.

"I don't understand, Liz. I said from the beginning what this was. There are going to be aspects of the situation that you don't like. You can't go off and try to get fucked by some frat boy every time you get your feelings hurt," he growled.

"I wasn't trying to get fucked, all right?" she cried. "Justin is just a friend from school. He helps me at the paper."

"Every guy at that fucking school wants to have sex with you. Every one."

Liz ground her teeth in frustration. "You don't know that."

"I do, and you should too," he said.

"Whatever. I'm drunk and sick and totally fucked up right now. I don't need to be lectured," she said, throwing his words back at him.

"You're mouthy when you're drunk," he said, the words coming off more enticing than she expected.

"I'm always mouthy," she said, flopping back on her bed. Big mistake. The world spun.

"Do I need to come over there and find that out firsthand?"

"Yes," she said. She wanted nothing more than to see Brady, even if she was still angry with him. "Make up for staring at me like you didn't know me by coming over and fucking me like you do."

"Liz," he said with a sigh, "are you going to be all right?" He lost the cocky tone for that briefest period of time, and the fire left her body. She felt sick to her stomach. Tears from the shock of the incident and her experience with Brady welled in her eyes, and she tried to blink them away.

"Yeah. Can I have some forewarning next time I'm not supposed to exist?" she asked weakly.

"I'm sorry I hurt you," he responded sincerely. It was more than she ever expected. She didn't know why, but she suspected it took a lot for someone like Brady Maxwell to apologize.

It seemed she owed him one in return. "I'm sorry I overreacted."

Liz stared up at the ceiling and tried to get it to stop spinning. Brady sighed into the phone, and she wondered if he was still mad at her.

"Can I see you soon?" he asked, answering her thoughts.

"Tonight?" she whispered.

He sighed like he was debating. "All right."

Liz broke into a smile. Tonight.

Twenty minutes later, Brady Maxwell was in her house . . . in her bed . . . stroking her hair and coaxing her to sleep. He planted kisses on her cheeks and hair and shoulders and held her close to him. It was like a dream all over again.

Chapter 16
KNOW WHERE YOU STAND

Liz called Justin the next morning to check up on him. His parents had bailed him out of jail, but they were livid and he couldn't really talk much. She had apologized for what had happened, especially since she had been the reason he had gotten behind the wheel, but he had said he was equally at fault. He was on the same Morehead scholarship that she was on, and she couldn't imagine what it would be like to lose that, especially as an out-of-state student. She knew there were strict policies about alcohol related infractions.

Over a week after the event, Victoria called. Liz panicked when she saw her phone buzz. She had never called Victoria back after she had ignored the call at the lake!

"Vickie," Liz said with a smile. Victoria seriously hated the nickname Hayden had given her, and Liz liked it even more for that.

"If you call me that one more fucking time, I swear by all things holy . . . I will kill you," she said pleasantly.

"I'll take that into consideration."

"So, where have you been, bitch? Can't return my calls?" Victoria asked.

"I've been busy, and it's not like you've tried to reach out to me again. Has your postcoital bliss finally worn off?" Liz asked with a smile. She didn't realize until then how much she missed Victoria always being around.

"Hardly. I made a slight error in judgment, that's all."

Uh-oh! "A slight error in judgment? Care to elaborate?"

"I'd hate to hurt those sensitive virginal ears," she said with a cackle.

"Oh, shove it up your ass, Vickie." Liz had been having nearly as much sex as Victoria typically did . . . soooo . . .

"Well, he did. That's part of the problem."

"Oh my God! You're insane," Liz said, her eyes wide.

"Don't be such a prude, Liz. It was just a threesome."

Liz shook her head. "Do I even want to know what happened after that?"

"Well, the professor I was seeing last semester is the professor for the TA I was with . . ."

"Victoria. You're serious?"

"I'm an equal opportunity offender. Anyway, we were in the TA's office going about our business, and the professor walked in. Lapse of judgment."

Liz burst out laughing. "You were having a threesome in the TA's office, and the other guy you were sleeping with walked in? Fuckkkk! Only you!"

"Anyway, long story short, I think I've worn out the History department for a while."

Liz clutched at her sides as the laughter rolled off of her. She had never met anyone else like Victoria.

"So, I'll be flying into Raleigh-Durham on Wednesday. Come pick me up, bitch!"

And that was how Liz ended up driving into Raleigh after class on Wednesday. Victoria walked through the sliding glass doors at the airport looking as gorgeous as ever in a flouncy cream top, pale pink skinny jeans, and electric blue platform heels. Her long, dark hair was in big curls, and her eyes were covered in heavy makeup. She carried an oversize hobo bag in a soft light brown leather and rolled a sleek suitcase behind her.

Victoria placed her bag in the backseat and dropped into the passenger seat. "Hey, bitch! I've missed you!"

Liz rolled her eyes and smiled. "Missed you too."

"I need a drink. Let's go to a pub," she said, sighing as she looked out the window.

"There aren't pubs in the States, Vic. You probably need to detox for a couple weeks."

"God I haven't been in the lab in so long," she said, tilting her head back. "I'm dying to get back to work."

That was what Liz loved about Victoria: Under all the drama and ridiculousness was a brilliant, beautiful mind. She never thought that someone who cussed like a sailor and dressed like a superstar would be interested in being a lab researcher in genetics and dreamed of isolating genes to reverse the effects of Alzheimer's.

"Lunch instead of booze?" Liz suggested. Victoria nodded and they headed back into Chapel Hill.

Liz parked and they walked across the street to the second-story restaurant Top of the Hill. They were seated at a high top table on the outdoor balcony overlooking the Franklin and Columbia intersection that Justin had blown through the night of his DUI.

Victoria accepted water instead of beer, and they both ordered lunch. The weather was hot, but they had an umbrella to shade them from the sun. It was nice hanging out with Victoria again. Liz had spent half her summer at the newspaper and with Brady. She needed some girl time, time to kick back and relax.

"So, did you do anything other than the TA the whole time you were there?" Liz asked, leaning back into her chair.

"Yeah. We took a weekend and went to Paris. I should have taken more time to see the rest of Europe, but his bed was really comfortable."

Liz rolled her eyes. "Did you like London, at least?"

"Oh, yeah! I loved it. My kind of city . . . busy, busy, busy. Hot guys everywhere, all with accents, who like to dance. Surreal life over there. We should go back together sometime."

"Sounds fun."

"What about you? Anything fun? I see you have a tan. That's new. I didn't think vampires came out during daylight."

"Ha. Ha," Liz said dryly. "I don't work all the time."

Victoria tilted her sunglasses down so she could stare at her.

"Okay, fine. I've been working the whole time, but I've been playing tennis, and I even went to a frat party with Justin."

Victoria wrinkled her nose. "Why the *eff* would you do that?"

Liz shrugged. "Desperate for company?" She couldn't tell her the real reason. "I got trashed and he drove me home . . ."

"Did you sleep with AV Justin?" Victoria asked, her eyes going wide.

"What? No! Have some faith in my taste for once, Vickie!"

"Oh my God, stop calling me that!" she cried.

Liz laughed, loving how much it irritated her. "Actually, he ran a red light and then was arrested for DUI."

"Shit!"

"Yeah, it was a rough night."

"Well, at least you did something interesting instead of following around politicians."

Liz choked on her drink and coughed a few times to clear her throat. Oh how true that assessment of her was.

"What about that guy you were crushing on? Have you talked

to him?" Victoria asked, tapping her manicured finger to her lip. "Gah, what was his name?"

Liz knew who she was talking about. It certainly couldn't be Brady, because she had never spoken about him with anyone. It had to be Hayden Lane. A trickle of doubt formed in her stomach when she thought about him. It felt a little strange to feel bad that she missed him.

She liked what she had going on with Brady. It made her a bit antsy and uncomfortable at times . . . especially when she had thought he had been with someone else. But she really liked being with him. Then why at the thought of Hayden did her insides squirm?

She hadn't heard from him since the emails at the beginning of the summer session, and she didn't know whether he had even thought about her. Actually, she didn't even know whether she was still going to visit him.

Her life felt so removed from what it had been last semester, and she kind of liked it that way. She liked that Brady consumed her thoughts and that she got to look forward to every moment they shared together. With Hayden it was more complicated on some level. At least with Brady she knew where she stood.

"Hayden?" Liz finally offered when it didn't seem that Victoria was going to be able to place his name. She could remember entire DNA structures of a thousand different plants and animals, but names . . . who needed to remember names?

"Right! Hayden Lane. Have you talked to him? He was going somewhere else for the summer, right?"

"Yeah, he has an internship in D.C., but I haven't really heard from him. He emailed me some work stuff at the beginning of the summer, and we talked about me coming to visit, but I doubt that's happening anymore."

"Wait. What?"

"What?" Liz asked, confused.

"He invited you to come see him over the summer?"

"Yeah," she said slowly.

"Why haven't you called him and talked to him? Don't you want to go visit? That boy would not invite you if he wasn't crushing on you hard."

She hadn't thought about it like that. Hayden had been giving her mixed signals, and she didn't want to push him. But Vic had a way of knowing whether a guy was into you. It felt strange, considering how much time she had invested in liking Hayden, thinking he didn't even notice her. Then when he finally did, he pulled back.

"You think?" she asked uncertainly.

"No, I know. When am I ever wrong?" she asked. Liz opened her mouth to speak and Victoria shook her head. "Exactly. Never."

"You're ridiculous. Hayden had his chance to make a move and he didn't."

"Sometimes men are pussies, and they need you to dangle yours in front of them to remember that they're all dicks."

Liz couldn't stop laughing. "Victoria Glass! I'm not *dangling* myself in front of him!"

"Your pussy, more specifically," Victoria said, drinking her water.

"Oh my God, we're not having this conversation. What do you want me to do—walk around his place naked and wait for him to realize?"

"Not a bad plan . . ."

"Correction: horrible plan."

"My plans work!" Victoria said, smacking her hand down on the table.

"Your plans get you double-teamed while a professor you were fucking walks in on you . . ."

"Well . . . there is that," she said with a bemused shrug.

"No shame."

"I mean . . . he could have joined."

Liz buried her face into her palm. How did she end up with the most insanely sexual roommate on the planet?

"Anyway! What I'm trying to say is you need to call him and you need to *remind* him why he invited you in the first place," she said, shaking her boobs from side to side. "I would have invited you because of your rack, but he could be different."

"He's probably not," she said, rolling her eyes.

"No, probably not. So call him. We're just waiting for our food."

"I'm not calling him from a restaurant."

"Why not? Give him a call, tell him how much you've missed him, and can't wait to see him . . . maybe hint at more. You know the gist," Victoria said.

"No way. If I call him at all, which is unlikely, it will be when we get home."

Victoria gave her *the look*. The one that said, *I won't forget.* Liz had seen it a thousand times since they started living together two years ago. She wasn't going to get out of this.

As she suspected, Victoria badgered Liz the entire way back to their house and Liz had had enough when she made it through the door. "Okay! I'll call him. Jesus!"

Victoria gave her a smug look and then sauntered into the bathroom. Liz heard the shower running a second later. She knew that meant she would be occupied for at least the next half hour, and the room would be like a sauna when she exited. Liz could have put off the phone call, but now that it was in her mind, it was like a disease spreading through her body. She couldn't let the thought go.

She wanted to see Hayden even though she was seeing Brady. Well, she wasn't seeing Brady. Okay she was, but it was different.

It's not as if she could walk around in public with him or anything. They were a behind-closed-doors kind of couple. Still, she had freaked out when she had thought Brady was seeing someone else; would it be hypocritical to then go see Hayden? Even if nothing happened, she was sure two years of crushing on him wouldn't disappear just like that.

But she didn't even know if he still wanted to see her. So maybe one phone call couldn't hurt.

He picked up on the second ring. "Liz, hey!"

"Hey. How are you?" Liz said, surprised by Hayden's enthusiasm.

"Good. It's good to hear from you."

"Yeah, it's been a while," she said, walking into her bedroom and shutting the door.

"Sorry about that. I'm sure it's my fault. You know how I said they just had me getting coffee?"

"Yeah," she said, lying back on her bed.

"Well, I still do that and about five hundred million other things every single day. I'm working ten- to fourteen-hour days."

"Geez! You must be exhausted."

"I've never worked this hard in my life. I can't wait for you to come up and visit. That will be my first full weekend off. It'll be good to see you and not have to deal with everything else," he said.

Liz smiled despite herself. It was nice to hear that he hadn't forgotten, and he wanted to see her still. Butterflies fluttered around in her stomach. "So, you're still set for me to visit?"

"Yeah, you do still want to come, right?" he asked a bit tentatively.

He hadn't had any hesitation when talking about seeing her. Why was she so hesitant then? With how enraptured she had been with Brady so far this summer, it was strange to even think of Hayden like that. But he still had a pull, even if it wasn't like Brady. Still, she wanted to see Hayden—that much she knew—but it felt unfair to Brady.

She knew Brady wasn't going to be happy with her going to D.C. to hang out with another guy. He hadn't been happy at the lake house when she had mentioned she was seeing someone, and she had been jokingly talking about him. Then with the incident with Justin . . . it was asking for trouble. She was playing this game on Brady's terms. That was the agreement.

But she still wanted to see Hayden even though she knew it would make Brady angry with her. She and Hayden were friends after all. She was allowed to visit friends if she wanted.

"Yeah, I do. Last weekend in July, right?"

"I think exactly a month from today. Let me check." She heard noise on the other end of the phone as he checked the date for her. "Yeah. I was right. One month. July twenty-sixth is when I get to see you. Are you driving?"

"Yep. It's not that far."

"Cool. I'll have to find you parking. There isn't much up here. But let me worry about that; tell me how you are. Tell me about the paper."

She could hear a smile in his voice. The paper was his baby, and he was probably dying being away from it for so long. She proceeded to fill him in on everything. She informed him about her articles and what she was doing in her class to improve them. He thought that it was good for her, even if he still liked her subjective articles too. They agreed too much on the politics of the matters for him not to like them.

By the time she was getting off of the phone with him, she realized an hour had passed. Where had the time gone? And how had he been able to get away from his busy schedule for a whole hour to talk to her? She certainly hadn't meant to distract him so thoroughly, but damn, it had been good to talk to him. Their conversation had flowed so easily. It actually made her want to call and talk to him more. Maybe she would . . .

"I hate to cut this short, but I really have to get back to work now. Great talking to you, Liz," he said. She nearly corrected him about the amount of time they had been talking, but then she stopped herself. He clearly hadn't noticed the time passing either.

"It was great talking to you too. Good luck with work. I'm sure I'll talk to you again before I come up there."

"I hope so."

When they hung up, Liz stood and walked back out into the living room. Victoria looked up at her smugly, as if she knew what had happened before Liz had even opened her mouth.

"So, I guess you're still going to D.C., huh?" she asked.

"I guess I am."

"That's what I thought," Victoria said, turning back to face the television.

Liz stared at the screen, not really seeing it at the moment. Her mind was elsewhere, racing back to the conversation she'd had with Hayden. They had talked so thoroughly about his job, the paper, her articles, the campaign, and now her mind was working. She enjoyed having someone to discuss her work and what she loved most. She had missed that. She and Brady talked, but it was usually sex first, talk later. They tiptoed a lot around politics, which she didn't have to do with Hayden. It was a nice change of pace.

In fact, Hayden had given her a good idea for the next feature. It was broader than her last article, as Professor Mires had suggested. If she could tie it back to the students, then they would be more interested in who was running for the state legislature.

She smiled, walked back into her room, and started writing.

Chapter 17

WATCHING YOU WORK

Liz spent all afternoon researching the article she was working on for the paper. Victoria complained enough about Liz's obsessive behavior that she finally took a break from the computer to get some dinner. But even when she was away from her work, she was still thinking about it. She wanted to make sure she had all of her facts right first, but she was itching to start writing it.

Even after dinner, Victoria was insufferable. Liz had missed her while she was gone, but it had been nice having the house to herself to work. The girls sat around and watched a movie into the evening, and Liz was bouncing with jitters the whole time. Victoria finally rolled her eyes about three-quarters of the way through and told her to leave.

"Just get out of here. You're making *me* nervous, and I'm not going into the lab until tomorrow," she said, turning back to the movie.

"I love you," Liz said, bolting out of the living room.

She grabbed her laptop off of her desk and was on her way to the office a few minutes later. Hayden had had a brilliant idea about comparing candidate platforms to the student government initiatives. Every spring semester, candidates ran for student government on campaign platforms as wide-ranging as implementing a bicycle-rental facility on campus to decreasing in-state tuition and fees. Hayden thought it would be an interesting article if she could string the two together. Show all of the policies and procedures that mirrored general governmental policies happening within the state and federally. Basically showing the campus that what they cared about here, mattered out there.

It was brilliant. She had always known why Hayden had been chosen editor, but he continued to reinforce it.

When Liz walked into the building, Meagan was sitting at her desk, which was covered in hot-pink Post-its and a collection of brightly colored candies. Liz scrunched her eyes at the display.

"Liz!" Meagan said, whirling around in her chair. "I didn't know you were going to be in tonight. Are you hungry? Have you eaten? I'm kind of starved, and I can't stop eating candy. We could go get something."

"No, thanks. I just ate. Need to work on this article for next week," Liz said.

"Are you sure? Do you need any help with it?"

"No, thanks, Meagan. I think I got it."

She hurried across the room and into Hayden's office. They had less than half the amount of normal staff, and no one had said anything when she had taken it over. She had a lot of work to do and she knew that she was going to be here well into the wee hours of the night.

A few hours later, Meagan came back to her office to tell her that she was closing up and asked her again if she needed any help. Liz smiled and politely told her no, though she knew she would be there well past building close. The article wasn't coming together as smoothly as she would have liked. She had it sitting in pieces on her laptop and even some printed documents that she had scribbled all over.

She was starting to see double when she stared at the screen, and knew it was time for a break. She grabbed her water bottle and trekked down to the water fountain in the hallway. As she was filling up her Nalgene, her phone started vibrating from where it was tucked away in her back pocket. Liz fished it out of her pocket and pressed it between her ear and shoulder so she could continue filling the bottle.

"Hello?" she said.

"I'm going to come pick you up. Be ready in twenty minutes."

Liz's heart skipped a beat. She hadn't seen Brady in three days. He had been busy in Raleigh all week working on campaign-related materials. He hadn't really said much else about it. Now here he was asking to see her when she was busy working on the article Hayden had recommended to her.

She really wanted to, but tonight was not the best night. "Brady, I can't."

"What? Why not?" he demanded. She could tell he was impatient.

"I'm working. I have this huge article I'm putting together. I've been working on it for hours."

"Then you need a break. I'm already in the car. I'm not turning around," he said simply.

Liz sighed. "Seriously. I'm worried if I take a step away I'll lose my entire focus on it. This is a big deal for me."

She really wanted him to understand. She had a life separate from him. Her job as a reporter was what she had been striving toward for a long time. She wasn't willing to give up her dreams any more than he was willing to give up the campaign. And in reality, neither of them should have to. They should be able to make this work while still being the same people. She wondered whether that was ever going to be possible.

"Liz, I haven't seen you in three days. That is three days too many. I'm coming to see you. Where are you?"

"If you want to come watch me work, then you can. I would think it would be pretty boring," she said, closing the lid on her water bottle and walking back into the empty office.

"My time with you is never boring. Are you at home?" he asked.

"Oh, about that . . ." Liz said.

"What?"

"My roommate came back into town. She was in London—I won't even try to explain why—but I don't have the house to myself anymore," she explained.

"So, you should get picked up somewhere else?" he asked dryly.

"Oh my God, you can't come watch me work," Liz said, shaking her head.

"I'm not coming to watch you work. I'm coming to fuck you," he nearly growled at her through the phone.

His voice sent shivers down her spine as she thought about their sex life. They were having sex more each week in stolen secret moments than she'd had when she had been dating her last boy-friend. And she had been practically living with her boyfriend at the time. It was exhilarating and incredible each time she was with Brady.

Plus, she couldn't deny that she enjoyed getting to know him on a more personal level when they met. Some of his walls had started falling the more time he spent with her. After the incident with his sister, he had told her all about his family—his father, the politician; his mother, the professor; his younger brother, Clay, the law student; and his younger sister, Savannah, who would be attending UNC in the fall. She had even learned that Savannah was planning to major in journalism. Liz sure as hell hoped that she didn't try to get on the paper.

She needed to make a decision. She stared at her open Word document and then exhaled softly. She knew that she had work to do, but she wasn't really making all that much progress with it anyway. It might be better to look at it fresh tomorrow. And anyway, she really wanted to see Brady.

"I'm at the office."

"In the Union?" Brady asked.

"Yeah. Do you know where the paper is?"

"Ten minutes," he said before the line went dead.

Almost exactly ten minutes later, Liz heard the door to the newspaper office open. She peeked her head around the corner of Hayden's office and couldn't help but let a big grin spread across her face. Brady Maxwell was in her office. He was on her turf. And he looked really fucking hot.

He looked as if he had come straight from the office in black dress slacks and a tucked-in blue button-down. His jacket had clearly been discarded in the car. It was too hot for pants and a long-sleeved shirt, but she knew that he wouldn't have gone into work in anything else. His dark eyes caught hers across the room, and she smiled. Her whole body ignited in that one look. How did he do that?

She opened her mouth to say something. Greet him, maybe? She couldn't even remember. Because as soon as he reached her, he grabbed her around the middle, pushed them into the office, and crushed their lips together. Liz tilted her head back, reveling in his kisses. She heard him kick the door closed, but all she could think about was his lips, his hands, his body.

Liz couldn't get enough of him. He was sucking the breath right out of her. It had only been three days. Three days didn't normally feel like such an eternity, but now, standing there in his arms, she had no idea how she had been able to go the interminable amount of time without him.

When he broke away, it took her a bit to regain control of herself.

"Baby, it's really good to see you," he groaned against her mouth.

Liz nodded her head. She didn't even have words. With him standing in front of her now, she couldn't even remember what she was doing before he arrived.

"I can't tell if you're happy I'm here," he said sarcastically, with a knowing look on his handsome face.

Arrogant son of a . . . she thought.

"I can't believe you're at my office. That's basically public territory, Brady," Liz said, sliding her hands up around his neck.

"It's the middle of the night. That's hardly public," he corrected.

"As close as it's been since we were at the Jefferson-Jackson gala," she whispered. She hoped she didn't sound as if she were complaining. She liked her time with Brady. Some days it didn't feel like enough, and she wished for more. But not now, not when she was in his arms.

"And probably as close as its going to get," he said, setting clear boundaries.

She knew that all along. They couldn't meet in public. That would defeat the whole purpose of what they were doing.

"As long as I get to be close to you, then I don't care," Liz said, gripping the collar of his shirt in her hands and tugging him back down. "And anyway, maybe I like the secret," she murmured seductively against his mouth. Her tongue darted out and licked across his bottom lip.

His hands gripped her sides and then his mouth claimed her once more. She saw where this was heading fast.

"I like this," he said, his hands running to the hem of her cotton sundress. He slid them up the other side of the material across her thighs. Liz sucked in quickly at the sudden contact.

"My dress?" she asked as he walked her back slowly toward the very cluttered desk.

"Your body," he muttered, his fingers finding the lacy edge of her thong. Liz shivered at his touch. She hit the edge of the desk.

"Brady," she said when he tried to help her onto it.

"Don't," he said, not stopping.

"This is my boss's desk."

Brady smirked as if she had made the decision for him. He reached behind her and pushed all of her neatly stacked papers onto the floor. Her mouth fell open as she watched her assignment scatter.

"I'm taking you on this desk," he said, picking her up and placing her on the now-empty surface. "Don't act like you don't want me to."

She would deal with the article later. At this moment, she could care less.

"Don't move," he said, pointing at her. Liz watched him walk across the small room and turn the lock in the door. "We don't want any unannounced visitors."

"Taking all the fun out of being in public."

"Don't get mouthy with me."

Liz bit her lip and looked down. "I'd never."

Her eyes slowly traveled up to his face, and he shook his head. "Only when I ask you to."

"Come here," she said, crooking her finger. She was getting impatient. He was dangling himself in front of her and then retreating once he got her hot and forced her onto the desk. She thought he might protest that she was giving her own commands, but he smiled and walked toward her.

She grabbed him by his belt and wrenched him in close. His hands landed on the tops of her thighs, and he moved one down between her legs. She unbuckled his belt as quickly as she could manage with his fingers dipping under her thong. She popped the button and slid the zipper to the base before hooking her fingers into his expensive dress pants and sending them over his narrow hips to the ground.

Liz stroked him a few times through his boxer briefs, but he was already ready for her. She slid her hand under the elastic, and wrapped her fingers around his dick. He grunted and leaned forward.

"Yeah. I need you. Right now," he groaned, as she ran her hand up to the head and back. He bent forward and kissed her as hard as he could. Her hand stilled as she lost her train of thought, and he took that moment to scoot her ass forward so she was sitting on the edge of the desk.

He broke the kiss, dropped his boxers, and yanked her thong to the ground. Liz eagerly pulled her dress over her head and unclasped her bra. She knew she was as ready for him as he was standing before her. She could feel her pulse against her throat and her breathing quicken. Her senses seemed to intensify every time he touched her. The heat and electric chemistry between them super-heated the close quarters, and a flush rose to her cheeks.

She had never felt so comfortable naked before a man. This was Brady. He never judged her, was never condescending, and never once demeaned her or made her feel bad for the choices she made. She rarely if ever told him no in the bedroom because of these things. And it was liberating to just *feel*. Because when she was with Brady, she didn't let herself do much else.

Brady gripped her hips in his hands as he pushed forward into her roughly. Liz gasped at the impact as their bodies slammed together. He was right: Three days was too long.

He eased back out of her until the head made a puckering sound and then slid just as slowly back in. He did this back-and-forth motion until she felt as if she was going to burst if he didn't pick up the pace. As if he could read her mind, he started moving faster in and out, gradually hitting into her with more and more force. And the harder he drove in, the louder she moaned, until she couldn't hold back any longer and climaxed at the peak.

Somehow, he held off his own and waited for her to come down off of her high.

After a couple seconds, he started up again. Liz tried to keep from whimpering and tilted her head up to the ceiling. She couldn't believe they were fucking right here, right now, on Hayden's fucking desk. But she wasn't going to stop, especially not when she had Brady on her turf.

"Fuck, Brady," she groaned. "I'm going to turn you down more often if it does this to you. I like holding the cards."

"Baby, I don't know what delusion you're under, because *I'm* fucking *you*," he said, punctuating each word with a harder and harder thrust.

"Oh yeah?" she asked, forcefully pushing him backward away from her and hopping off the desk. She yanked out the chair to the desk and pointed at it. "Sit!"

Brady raised his eyebrows, but did as he was told. It was Liz's favorite chair in the whole building, and after she was finished with Brady, she was never giving it back to Hayden. The chair was oversize and sturdy, with a rounded cushion and big wooden armrests.

Liz climbed on top and straddled him. He watched her with a big, self satisfied grin on his face, as though this had all been his idea. She lowered herself down onto him and started working her way up to his pace. She leaned forward and whispered into his ear, "Now I'm fucking you."

Brady's hands slapped down onto her ass as soon as the words fell from her lips, and she cried out in surprise. He grasped her ass in his hands until she could feel him leaving indents in her skin, and then forced her down on him again and again.

With him guiding her movements, they moved faster than she could have on her own, and soon they were both breathless from exertion. He would lift her up and then force her down over and over again, until all she could hear over their heavy breaths was the smacking of their bodies colliding.

"Baby," he murmured, driving her down harder once more, "I'm still the one fucking you."

Liz threw her head back with a smile. Of course he was. And she didn't want him to stop either.

"And I'm going to be the only one fucking you." He accented his words with an ever-increasing tempo.

"God yes," Liz groaned. She could never disagree with him. Her breasts were bouncing up and down in front of his face as she rocked up and down on top of him. She felt a second orgasm getting ready to tear through her body, and she gritted her teeth and leaned over into his shoulder.

"Baby," he growled. She already knew what he was about to say.

"Me too," she panted.

And then they both let go. Liz felt her body sail away as she closed her eyes and entered a state of euphoria.

Brady wrapped his arms around her waist and pulled her in close. She dropped her head to his shoulder and let out a contented sigh. It was nice to be in his arms, lost in their own world.

They sat like that together until Liz felt herself drifting off. She righted herself, kissed his lips, and then moved off of him. She hated the absence of his body near hers, but there was plenty more time for that tonight, and as many more nights as they could have together.

After they both put their clothes back on and took trips to the bathroom, Liz went to the trouble of locating the papers she had been working on. She wanted them to be there for her when she actually had a chance to get back to them again. With the way Brady was looking at her, it likely wasn't going to be tonight.

Brady leaned over her shoulder and kissed his way up her neck. Liz giggled and rested back into him. His arms moved around her body and wrapped her up. "Is this the article you were so desperate to work on?"

"Something I'm working on for next week," she murmured, lost in his kisses again.

"Comparing campaign platforms and student government?" he asked, reading over her shoulder. His voice had changed slightly. She wasn't sure what it was, but it sounded like campaign mode. She sure hoped he wasn't offended by what she wrote. He normally liked when she wrote controversial material, because at least he knew it was honest.

"Yeah. I thought it was a great way to engage the campus," she told him. She didn't mention that it was Hayden's idea. She had never brought Hayden up before in their conversations. She hadn't really thought about it until now.

"Hmm. Mind if I look at it?" he asked, scooping the papers off of the desk and releasing her.

She had printed what she had written earlier so that she could go through and see what she was missing. She caught more errors that way. "It's not a finished product or anything. It's all jumbled, still needs a lot of work. Don't judge me on the disjointed mess that is the beginning of my first draft," she said hastily.

He smiled and started thumbing through the papers, skimming some parts, and reading other lines word for word. She didn't want to be rude and read over his shoulder or anything, but she was anxious about what he thought. She wanted to know which parts he was reading more carefully than others.

There wasn't really all that much specifically mentioned about him. She usually wrote articles about individual politicians, but this one was different. She was already nervous about it. She hoped he liked it.

"Hmm . . ." he murmured as he flipped to the last page.

"Hmm?" she questioned, dying to know what he was thinking.

"This is good," he said, finally finishing. "I see what you mean about disjointed, but still the writing is good."

Liz blushed. "Thanks."

"I just . . . I have a suggestion, if you're interested," he said diplomatically.

"Oh?" she asked. This was different. Not that Brady wasn't interested in her work. He read all of her articles, and sometimes they discussed them. Nothing too serious. They steered clear of openly discussing politics together.

"Well, I like the idea of comparing platforms to something students can relate to. Youth is the hardest demographic to access. It's difficult to get them motivated or interested in politics, because everyone is busy partying. It's not that that's a bad thing for their age, but there is something outside of college that they're going to have to enter in four years. Some people call it the real world," he said with a shrug. Liz chuckled.

"A lot of students have this idea that the real world sucks and inside the four walls of this institution they're safe, but there are things directly affecting them in the real world. And if they don't take part by voting or campaigning or speaking to their congressman," Brady said, gesturing to himself, "then how can we know how to help them in the future? People thirty to forty years older than this generation are deciding the future, because *they* vote. If all the students participated, that could change."

Liz smiled. She loved this stuff. She had always felt very strongly about youth participation in the elections. It was part of the reason she had become so active in the paper to begin with.

"You're preaching to the choir," she said.

"Of course I am," Brady said. "So what I'm saying is that students aren't actually interested in student government."

Liz narrowed her eyes. "The student government elections on campus are *huge*. Last semester campus was overrun with campaigns. Everyone was convincing people to vote. I think it's a perfect analogy." Plus, Hayden usually had a sixth sense for what people found interesting. He was a natural talent. She trusted his judgment.

"I believe you," he said, holding his hands up as if he wasn't trying to start an argument. "However, I think people might care more if you related it to something like basketball."

"Oh dear lord," she said rolling her eyes. "One of my tennis instructors keeps bringing up you playing basketball."

"You play tennis?" he asked with a smile.

"Yeah. Not that often, though."

"I love tennis," he told her.

"Maybe we could play together sometime!" Then she remembered; they couldn't be seen in public. Her face fell with disappointment. It would have been fun.

Brady leveled her with a look that said the same thing she was already thinking and moved on.

"I'm just saying that this is a basketball school. And think about it like this," he said, warming to his pitch. "Everyone here likes basketball, but not everyone can play. We want to win. We want to make our school look good. So we recruit great players to represent our school, like voting for representatives in politics. We all have a common goal, and we help achieve that goal through various means—participation at games, donating money, tutoring players to help keep them academically eligible, etc. We're all working toward the common good here, and if students took an interest in the game, in this case politics, and helped us achieve our mutual goals, then we might all come out on top."

He had a damn good point. She had never really thought about it like that. She knew that if she wrote that article, though, she would have to start over. It wouldn't be the end of the world, but it would take a while.

"I see your point. It would make a great article," she said. She was sure of it. She just had to decide whether or not that was *her* article. The students would probably love it . . .

"Well, good," he said, tossing the papers back on the desk. "That's my suggestion. I would have been interested in it when I was in college."

He grabbed her by the waist and pulled her back into him.

"Are you finished lecturing me?" she teased.

"Baby, not even close," he said, kissing her slowly and demandingly, until all the tension from their conversation melted from her shoulders. "I think we should go now."

"Yeah. Like right now." She grabbed her bag quickly and followed him out of the building.

Chapter 18
BLACK & WHITE

Her article ran the week of the Fourth of July, with only a couple weeks left before the end of the summer semester. Students were packing their bags for the long holiday, but that article still drove a high volume of readers, especially for the summer. The website went crazy with it, and Hayden called to congratulate her. Despite being so busy up in D.C., he had still been calling her more frequently, sometimes to talk about the paper, but more recently just to chat. She didn't know whether it was because of the article she was writing, or because her planned visit was fast approaching.

Still, it was nice to get positive feedback about her work. She couldn't wait to get this paper back from her professor. She thought it was the one that would be the tipping point for her grade.

Brady was going away with his family for the Fourth of July holiday, and she wouldn't get to see him at all this weekend. Every year the Maxwells went to Hilton Head on the South Carolina coast after the Fourth of July rallies and events that were mandated for them to attend.

The one Brady had asked her to go to was in the early afternoon in downtown Raleigh just off the parade route. He had been extra busy ever since their rendezvous in the newspaper office. The Fourth was a heyday of activity for Brady and his father, who was in North Carolina for the long weekend. He wasn't up for reelection this cycle, but he was there to support Brady. It made them look good having a solid family unit, especially since Brady wasn't married. Liz cringed at the thought.

Finding parking in the middle of the afternoon on the Fourth of July was pretty much the worst experience of her life. It was blistering hot, the hottest day of the year. The air-conditioning in her car wasn't used to handling such extreme temperatures and was having spurts of dysfunction. Luckily, she had opted for white-cuffed shorts and a slouchy red-and-white tank instead of her skinnies. She was just thankful that she had on sandals rather than heels, because by the time she found parking, she had to trek more than a mile to the rally area. She was hot and sweaty when she finally arrived.

The biggest relief was that if she was going to see Brady at all, it wouldn't be until after the event was over. Her hair was already swept up into a high ponytail off of her neck, but she didn't want to think about what her makeup looked like. Maybe she would have time to fix herself up.

Liz entered the park from the southernmost entrance and already found the crowd closing in. Food trucks and various activities for children lined the sidewalks. Ponies tramped in a circle with excited kids on their backs. Local high schools and Scout troops were selling American flags and red-white-and-blue headbands. She could hear a marching band in the distance and the sound of laughter and festivity all around her. She couldn't stop smiling as she walked past a group of people carving up a watermelon. The atmosphere was contagious.

She walked to the center of the park where a stage had been constructed. A band was playing, and people had set up foldout chairs and blankets to cover the lawn in front of the stage. The local band Delta Rae was set as the concert for the evening before the fireworks display.

Liz let her eyes roam the area around the stage for where she thought the Maxwell family might be. She had yet to see the illustrious Savannah, and Brady's younger brother, Clay, was supposed to be in town today too. Their father kept his family so under wraps; she still hadn't been able to dig up much more than elementary school pictures of his siblings. And when she had last tried to look, she had felt creepy, as if she actually *was* stalking him.

As Liz walked the perimeter, she took a bunch of shots of the festivities. She could picture-catalog her activity on site. Students seemed to like that kind of thing. She slid her phone into her back pocket as she approached the stage. A gate was set up so that no one other than staff and guests could wander backstage. Liz wished she had requested a press pass, and then she could have roamed around freely.

She avoided the security guard, found a stretch of unobscured fence, and leaned over the railing to see whether she could see anything. It wasn't exactly stealthy, but she was just curious. What she saw made her grind her teeth.

Lush red hair swished over Calleigh's shoulder as she laughed at something a guy said in front of her. She held a microphone loosely in her hand, but she didn't seem as if she was working at the moment. Liz hadn't been following her work too closely, but she knew that Calleigh was working in the political division of the paper. She didn't have her own column or anything yet, which probably explained why she was in Raleigh for the Fourth instead of Charlotte. Whoever was working above her probably sent her here because they didn't want to make the drive. Or at least that was Liz's guess.

Ever since that incident with Hayden at the end of the spring semester, she'd had a negative reaction to Calleigh. It was strange, considering she had always looked up to her for her work at the paper. Still, she couldn't get over the feeling that Calleigh had snubbed her on purpose. It felt personal.

Calleigh glanced off in Liz's direction, and Liz snapped her head back over the fence. She hoped Calleigh hadn't seen her, but she was pretty sure she had. This was not what she needed.

"Liz!" Calleigh called. Liz sighed and turned back to look over the fence. Calleigh was walking toward her with a smile on her face. She was in professional attire, with a white flouncy blouse tucked into a red pencil skirt and heels that kept sinking into the soft ground.

"Hey, Calleigh," Liz said.

"Surprise seeing you here! I thought you would be in Chapel Hill, or home for the summer," she said, standing against the fence.

"I stayed in Chapel Hill. I'm taking a class and writing my own column at the paper, but I came to town for the rally," Liz told her.

"How nice! I was talking to Hayden the other day and he said someone was covering the information, but he never mentioned it was you," she said with a big bright smile, setting her manicured hand down on the railing.

Liz had talked to Hayden only yesterday, and he hadn't mentioned speaking with Calleigh. Though, why would he? It was none of Liz's business, but she was damn curious as to why he was still talking to Calleigh, when he had said that it was over between them.

"Nice. I'm sure he's so busy with his internship, it just slipped his mind. I'll ask him when I go visit," Liz said, trying not to bat an eyelash or crack a smile.

"Oh, you're going to D.C.?" Calleigh asked, her fingers curling over the fence.

"Yeah, in a couple of weeks."

"Interesting."

"Ma'am," a security guard called, walking over to them, "you're going to have to step away from the fence."

"Oh, she's with me," Calleigh said, flashing her press badge.

"Does she have one of those?" he asked.

"I have hers in my bag," Calleigh said. She gestured to the cameraman standing next to her. Calleigh walked over to her bag and produced a second press pass swinging on a lanyard.

"Make sure she wears it next time," he grumbled. "Now, move quickly. We have to clear the area."

"Yes, sir," Calleigh said sweetly. She handed Liz her extra pass.

"Thanks." Liz slipped the badge around her neck. "That was fortunate," she said as she walked to the other side of the fence.

"Yeah. We always get one extra just in case they throw someone else on the case or we need an additional photographer," she said with a shrug. "You can keep it."

Liz didn't know why she followed Calleigh. She didn't want to be near the woman, but she had given her the pass. It would be rude to walk away now. Also, deep down she knew that this put her one step closer to Brady.

"If they're clearing the area, that must mean the Maxwell family has arrived," Calleigh said, stalking over to her cameraman.

Liz smiled. Brady.

"I can't wait to see Brady's speech. Every time he opens his mouth . . ." Calleigh said. "Well, he's hot."

Liz almost laughed. For a long time she would have never thought that anyone in his or her right mind would turn down Calleigh Hollingsworth, let alone pick Liz over Calleigh. But now, as Calleigh talked about Brady like that, Liz knew that Calleigh stood no chance next to her. It was a damn good feeling.

"Don't you think so?" Calleigh asked.

"Up until he opens his mouth," Liz told her with a condescending smile.

"Yeah, well, you don't have to agree with him to appreciate his good looks. He was just rated North Carolina's most eligible bachelor," she told Liz.

She wasn't aware of that, but she also wasn't surprised. He was gorgeous, ambitious, driven. Liz tried not to think too much about it. It was only a matter of time before women started trying harder to get his attention. And she didn't want his attention diverted anywhere else.

"I'm sure someone will scoop him up soon," Liz said wistfully.

"I can't wait to find out who it is." Calleigh raised her eyebrows at Liz. Calleigh seemed so confident all the time, as if she half expected Brady to find her in the crowd and start making out with her.

Before Liz had to reply, she heard a commotion behind her. She turned back to the gate she had entered, saw it open, and a pair of security guards in slick black suits walked through. The press flocked forward, pressing inward as Brady's family filed into a private holding space.

Liz followed Calleigh through the crowd as Brady's father walked past her. He looked dignified in a black suit, with salt and pepper sprinkled in his hair. Brady was going to age well. The smile left her face at the thought. She couldn't think like that. Senator Maxwell's wife was at his side, but Liz couldn't make out much more than a short bob of blond hair before they disappeared.

Someone shoved Liz out of the way and she missed whoever walked past after them, but found a space to look through a second later. And there was Savannah Maxwell—the girl Brady had been with at the town hall meeting in Carrboro. She was dressed professional chic, in straight black pants, a red fitted tank, and a blue blazer with white buttons. Her dark hair fell stick straight to her shoulders. She looked a lot like a feminine version of Brady.

Then he appeared and Liz's breath caught. There was no way Brady could see her over the crowd of reporters, and he wasn't expecting her to be backstage. It was like witnessing a private moment.

He was all business today. He wore a stern expression, and his campaign mask was in place. His black suit was crisp and tailored to his build. She could tell that he was worried about something even from the distance. She didn't know how. Had she really been spending that much time with him that she could tell something like that? Or was she making it up?

Brady kept walking past the sea of reporters and into the holding room without looking up once. Liz was disappointed she didn't get to see more of his handsome face, but he had to work today. She could understand that.

A few minutes later, the elder Brady Maxwell was announced, and he walked onstage. His speech was as customary as it went for him. Liz hadn't looked through most of his work, but she knew the gist of his campaign. He ran on family values. He always had. It won hearts very easily. Add his personal charisma onstage and he was a guaranteed shoo-in each time he ran for election.

He ended his speech, which had been light and generally emphasized his son's campaign efforts. They wouldn't want to talk policy on a day like today, when everyone was having such a good time. They thanked everyone for coming out and encouraged them to do their civic duty by registering to vote and going to the polls in August for the primary, and November for the general election. The crowd cheered as he thanked them and then walked offstage.

Liz sighed when she heard Heather announce Brady, and she watched from her privileged vantage point as he walked onstage.

Her eyes were glued to him, and she forgot that she was even standing next to Calleigh or that they were in public. All she saw was her man about to charm a crowd.

He started talking with that radiant energy that seemed to flow out of him whenever he started discussing something he cared about. He easily wove in a story about a Fourth of July celebration at the lake house when he was a kid that had all of the families in attendance laughing along. Liz's cheeks colored at the thought of the lake house, and she wondered if he had picked it on purpose, knowing that she would be in the audience.

She listened as the story moved away from his childhood and on to a similar values speech as his father. He talked about wanting to raise children in a world where they could access the American Dream, and fighting for human rights. He related his speech to the battle that the country faced fighting for independence, and how the nation as a people grew and rebuilt from that foundation. He invoked the thoughts of the Founding Fathers and urged the crowd to listen to their testaments.

Liz found herself nodding along with him about halfway through and couldn't seem to stop the longer he spoke. What was he doing to her? She didn't agree with him. Not that she had always disagreed with everything he stood for. There were points she approved of in his policies, but giving the tax incentives to donors instead of funding education had irked her. Yet standing there on a historic holiday and listening to him pour out his heart to an audience moved her.

Brady wanted the country to *work*, and not many people she knew actually cared enough to pursue that. Not many people would give up *everything* to help get the country back on the right track. And he cared about that desperately. He wanted to be there to fight for the people who couldn't fight for themselves and help those who needed the most help. She could feel his words that day as she never had felt them before. He wasn't doing this for the money or to get bigger donors or even to be in the spotlight. He was doing it for Liz, for the people there today, and for every other person he could help. He was speaking to her of his sincerity, and she heard him loud and clear.

It felt as though the world had stopped all around her. She couldn't breathe. She couldn't think. It felt as if it had all shifted. When had she stopped seeing the world in black and white? Where had all the gray crept up from? She was a journalist! She was a reporter! There was no gray in her world. There were the facts and that was all that mattered. Why was she suddenly seeing things that she had never seen before in the one person she had never thought she could accept gray from?

Liz's heart beat harder in her chest at the realization, and she felt like crying. She had never wanted this. She had never wanted any of this. But it seemed that he had been right all along. When they had been dancing, Brady had pleaded with her to just get to know him. If she got to know him, then she could find out that knowing how he voted didn't mean she could judge his character. The more she got to know Brady, the less his voting record seemed to matter. The more . . . *he* seemed to matter. Just him. All of him.

She wanted to reach out to him then, and at the same time run far, far away. What was she even feeling right now? Sick. She felt sick. Her world was tilting off balance, and she was afraid that she would never be able to regain her footing again.

"I, uh . . . suddenly don't feel well," Liz said, touching Calleigh's arm, who was enraptured with Brady's speech. "I'm going to go."

"All right. Feel better," Calleigh said, barely glancing at Liz as she rushed away from the press box.

Liz catapulted herself away from the crowds. She couldn't be near crowds right now. She needed a minute to herself. She needed to breathe.

She walked around the press area to the side of a small building and breathed in and out as slowly as she could muster. Everything was crashing down on her all at once. Despite his politics and despite his voting record, Brady was still a good person. He made some choices she didn't agree with, but that didn't mean that he was a bad politician or greedy or selfish. It just meant he did what he had to do, that he had compromised in office to get what he wanted. Now she saw him for who he really was, and it was like the floodgates opened. Brady Maxwell was giving her a panic attack.

Liz hung her head forward, trying to block out the rest of the world that was going on around her. It was loud and she could still hear Brady, though he was muffled because the speakers were facing away from her.

"Ma'am, are you all right?" a man drawled, coming around the corner.

She glanced up at him. "I'm fine."

"Are you sure? Do you need me to get medical assistance?" he asked. His cheeks dimpled when he talked.

"Fine. Really. Just a bit claustrophobic," she told him.

"I'm the opposite. Wide-open spaces kill me. So, I can understand. I usually just need to breathe and not think about it. I can get you some water if you want."

"No, that's all right," she said, trying to do as he said. She closed her eyes and tried to breathe. The longer she stood there the easier it was to think about Brady.

"Thanks for checking on me," Liz said.

He took the hint, nodded, and left. Liz felt better being alone and not having her panic attack in front of anyone. The only person she wanted to see was Brady, and the only person she shouldn't see when she was like this was Brady. And yet she had to see him. She needed him to talk to him and let him know about her realization regarding his career. In that moment, it felt like if she didn't get it out now . . . then maybe she never would.

Liz heard the crowd cheer, announcing the end of his speech, and knew that she was going to have only a short window in which she could see Brady. So she had to make up her mind right then and there.

When the applause died down, Liz moved into the crowd that was waiting to greet the politicians. They appeared together, shaking hands and kissing babies, as per usual. The press might get a few moments with them before they left, but Liz wasn't going to wait that long. She wanted to see him. She needed to see him.

He found her in the crowd almost immediately. He shook her hand with his campaign smile intact and said, "Pleasure to meet you. I hope I can win your vote."

"I enjoyed your speech very much, Senator," she replied. "I'd love to talk with you about it some more. I do have some questions, though I'd hate to take up all of your time." She was playing a risky game if anyone picked up on what she was saying.

"I'd be interested in discussing it with you after?" he said, like he was offering her the opportunity to speak with him about political matters.

"I would appreciate you taking the time to do that," she said, smiling brightly.

He spent the next twenty or thirty minutes smiling and taking pictures before the crowd started to thin. His father announced that he had another engagement and quickly extracted himself. "Brady, five minutes," he called to his son.

"Looks as if I have a couple minutes," he said to Liz. She smiled as he walked her far enough away from the crowd that their voices wouldn't carry. She could tell that he was anxious that they were together in public. She didn't blame him. She was antsy, but she tried hard not to show it.

"What are you doing?" Brady demanded as soon as they were out of earshot.

"I had to talk to you," she said, wanting to reach out and touch him but knowing better.

"This isn't a good idea," he said simply. Compared to the warmth he was showing onstage and before his audience, to her he seemed frigid. She didn't know what that was about.

"I just . . . liked your speech. I . . ."

"Can we talk about this later? Somewhere not public?" he asked frostily.

"Um . . . all right." She wanted nothing more than to wash away whatever was holding him back. He seemed so distant. She had thought they had connected during his speech, even if it hadn't been directly for her. It had *felt* as if it was for her. This couldn't just be because they were in public. He wasn't like this with her. Even that one time he had given her cold eyes at the town hall, he had apologized for being an ass and hadn't done it since. "What's wrong?" she couldn't help asking.

"What do you mean?"

"Brady . . . what's wrong?" she asked, her voice barely a whisper.

"Why do you think something is wrong?" He checked his watch as if he was bored with her. Where was the man who had only a week and a half ago told her he could never be bored with her?

"I know you too well."

"You put out your article," he stated, as if that explained it.

"This is about my article?" she asked, confused. "I thought you didn't care what I wrote?"

"That's just it. I don't give a shit what you write about. I've always liked that you wrote whatever the hell you wanted and didn't back down. But if you didn't like my suggestion for your paper, why did you agree with me?"

"Well, I didn't exactly agree with it," she said, backtracking. Liz hadn't been able to make up her mind about the article, so she had sat down and written both versions. The one about basketball was sitting on her computer, waiting to be fed into the printer. But it felt wrong taking the idea that Hayden had and then using Brady's example. She had put Brady's take on the back burner and gone with her gut. Standing in front of Brady now, she was doubting her own decision.

Brady just stared. "You said you saw what I meant; that was enough for me. You don't have to use my suggestion, but if you didn't want to, then why didn't you tell me?"

"I don't know," she whispered. She didn't want to upset him. That was why.

"You're a reporter; aren't you supposed to be honest and unbiased?" he scoffed. "I thought you would tell me if you thought it was a bad idea."

"I did think it was a good idea," she said hastily.

"You write what you want to write, and I've always liked that about you. It's why I thought you were different in the beginning. If you can't be honest with me . . ." He trailed off.

Liz didn't think she could strike a nerve with Brady. He seemed so solid inside and out. He didn't get irritated that she cut down his political views, or when she freaked out when she thought that he was seeing someone else. He didn't get irritated about much, aside from whether or not she was seeing someone else. He just wanted her to be up front with him.

It was just a suggestion, but he was taking it so seriously. Did he actually think that she couldn't be honest with him? He was the *only* one she was honest with anymore.

Still, she hated upsetting him. "I'm sorry," she said. "I should have told you. I didn't know you would be so mad."

"Liz, I have to go," he said, but he didn't turn away.

"I know. Five minutes. Give me one more. We're engrossed in conversation." She didn't even stop to wait for him to say anything. "I didn't come to find you in public to argue. I just came to talk to you, because I wanted you to know that you were right."

He stared down at her with interest. "About what, specifically?"

"You told me once that if I got to know you, I would see you for more than your voting record."

"At the gala," he said, a small semblance of a smile appearing on his face at the mention of it.

"You were right," she whispered. Tears were forming in her eyes, and she was so incredibly pissed at them. Why was she getting emotional like this? It wasn't as if they could even move forward in their relationship. They only had secrecy to hold on to. "I see your vision. I see you. I was proud of you onstage today." Her voice was hoarse when she said the last line. "I'm sorry for the tears. They're stupid," she said, wiping gently under her eyes. "But . . . you've got me, Brady. I get it now. I get it."

"Liz . . ." he whispered.

"No, just one more thing," she said, trying to muster the courage. "You won my vote today."

He sighed, as if he had realized how much of an ass he had been earlier. "Baby, do you have plans later?"

She looked up into his face, surprised. Brady was supposed to be leaving for the coast today with his family. She wasn't going to see him all weekend.

"No plans."

"Good," he said softly. "Because I'm going to be spending all night making this up to you."

Chapter 19
OUT ON THE TOWN

Liz stared at the ground uncomfortably before taking a breath and walking into the coffee shop. She had talked to Justin on the phone a couple times since he had gotten his DUI, but he'd had his disciplinary committee hearing this morning and he'd agreed to meet up with her after. She'd offered to go with him to the meeting, since she was the reason for the DUI in the first place, but no one else was allowed inside.

"Over here," Justin called. He waved his hand from the corner, and Liz strode in his direction.

"Hey." He stood when she approached, and she briefly wrapped her arms around him sympathetically before they both took a seat. "How did it go?"

Justin sighed and shrugged despondently. "I wish you'd been there. You could have sweet-talked them for me." He looked up to meet her blue eyes. "They stripped my scholarship."

"Oh my God!" she cried. "What are you going to do?"

"I'm thinking about transferring out. My parents can't afford to pay out-of-state tuition."

"You can't just *leave*." Liz shook her head. "There has to be something that can be done. Can you appeal the verdict? Maybe you can apply for student loans to help with tuition."

"My parents are looking into it, but I don't think there's much that can be done. Student loans look at your records, so I'm not sure how much I could get . . . probably not enough to afford it."

"Ugh," she groaned. "I wish there was something I could do."

"Yeah. Me too."

She felt partially responsible for this. One bad mistake shouldn't bring a lifetime of turmoil. She knew Justin would bounce back, because he was a genius, but it would be hard.

"It just sucks."

"It does. But hey, maybe I should use this as my opportunity to try something new. I was always too smart for college anyway," he said with a wink, but his smile didn't reach his eyes. "Maybe I'll open my own business or take over the Internet. I always thought that would be fun."

"Only you, Justin."

"Thanks for meeting up with me, Liz." He reached out and grabbed her hand across the table. "I made a bad choice, but it didn't turn out as bad as it could have. At least I didn't hurt anyone. I remember running through that light, and I think about how lucky I was that I didn't hit anyone. It's only a scholarship, but it wasn't my life . . . or yours."

"I'm really sorry, you know?"

"I know. Me too."

They finished their coffee and parted ways. Liz was glad that she had met up with him, at least.

She was supposed to go out with Victoria later and she needed to get home and get ready. Liz walked into the house fifteen minutes later to Victoria yelling at her from down the hallway of their house. "You better fucking get drunk with me tonight!"

Liz shook her head and dropped her bag in the living room. She grabbed her latest article from Professor Mires and trudged down the hallway. "I already said I would get drunk with you, Vickie. If you ask me one more time, I'm going to call you that *all* night!"

As she waited for Victoria to relinquish the bathroom, Liz flipped through the paper she had gotten back that morning—the one based on Hayden's suggestion. It had garnered her an A. The professor said that she could really see her improvement and depth of growth. That if she turned in her final paper with similar quality work, she would be comfortable giving her a B+ or even an A- for the class, despite her earlier work in the semester. Liz knew that meant she had her work cut out for her, but she was up to the challenge.

Her last week of classes was coming up; in just over a week, she would be heading out to D.C. to visit Hayden. She found it hard to believe it was that close already. Soon the fall semester would be upon them, then the primary, and then the general election.

Liz shook her head. She was getting ahead of herself. There was still too much that needed to get done before then. Brady's big summer gala event, for instance. It was coming up this weekend, and she was pretty much freaking out about it. Would she be noticed? She already knew that she couldn't go with Brady, but would he take someone else? It didn't help her to get too antsy about it, because at the end of the night, he was coming back to her one way or another. And she had to be confident in that.

Their argument on the Fourth of July had changed their relationship. Liz didn't know what exactly had been the tipping point. It could have been her realization that somewhere under Brady's hard exterior she could hurt him. Or her comprehension of his purpose for running for office, which had softened him to her. Not that Brady was actually any different. He was still gruff, brash, and stubborn, but she wouldn't have him any different. But one way or another, whatever they had been doing before had turned into something . . . more.

Brady had actually postponed his trip to Hilton Head with his family to spend the night of the Fourth at the lake house with her. She hadn't seen the lake that night except through the window of the second-story bedroom, when the fireworks had gone off. She couldn't help smiling now at the thought.

Victoria completed her hair and makeup and walked into her bedroom to change. Liz took that opportunity to do her own makeup before changing out of her shorts and tank top. While she was changing, Liz received a text message from Brady. *Baby, you free tonight?*

Liz couldn't bail on Victoria another time. She had been home for a couple weeks now, and Liz felt like the worst friend in the world. She kept canceling on Victoria to hang out with Brady. She had so little time with him that when he wanted to see her she jumped at the opportunity. But she couldn't do that tonight. If she did, she was pretty sure Victoria would skin her alive.

Going out with my roommate.

How late will you be out?

Liz smiled. If someone else had posed that question, Liz would have found it irritating, but it was Brady. He was different.

Probably very late. Victoria is kind of an animal.

You'll be safe? Can I see you after?

Always safe. Don't worry. Don't you have to work in the morning?

You can't expect me not to worry. I don't make promises I can't keep. I'll take tomorrow morning off. Call me if you're done before two a.m.

Liz felt giddy. Who was this person she had become?

Done. But I'll be wasted, so you'll have to come get me.

I'll come get you. You'll be safe with me.

Debatable.

Don't make me come get you now.

Empty threat. I'm not alone.

Don't test me.

Liz bit back her laughter. She liked teasing him like this. It felt comfortable. They had been together for nearly two months. She couldn't believe it had been that long. They had held on to their secret and nothing had happened. She breathed easier each day that went by.

"Ready, bitch?" Victoria called. Liz opened the door to her room and saw Victoria standing in the hallway.

Liz rolled her eyes at Victoria's appearance. "You look like a baby prostitute."

"That quote is, 'You smell like a baby prostitute.'"

"Boo, you whore!" Liz said with a giggle. She shook her head at her ridiculous best friend. "Seriously, you look like a hooker."

Victoria shrugged. "And you look . . . like you." Somehow she made that sound insulting.

Liz glanced down at her appearance. "I just don't look like I'm going to be selling my body."

"Exactly. Use what you got, girl. You'll only have it for so long. I certainly want to enjoy it."

Victoria was a curvy girl with a full hourglass figure that she loved to flaunt around in very little clothing. She had on a dark blue, skintight V-cut dress that showed off way more leg and breasts than Liz had ever shown in her entire life. She had on mile-high nude wedges and her signature red lipstick.

Liz felt dressed down next to her best friend. She had on a solid coral skirt with a tan ruffle halter-top and brown sandals. She had actually taken the time to blow her blond hair out into messy beach waves. She didn't typically wear much makeup, but she had done herself up tonight. If she hadn't put in some effort, she knew Victoria would have redone her face.

As much as she wanted to see Brady tonight, she knew it was going to be fun to hang out with Victoria. They had known each other a long time, and she always had a good time when they went out.

Victoria chose a bar on the west side of Franklin Street downtown that served beer in giant plastic cups. It was all right on the inside, but everyone went there for the huge patio with benches and live outdoor music. The place was as full all summer as if it were the only bar in town.

Liz didn't recognize anyone, but Victoria waved at a few people. They made their way through to the bar, and Victoria ordered them both beers. Liz wasn't a big fan of beer, but this was the kind of place for it. Victoria handed the fratty-looking bartender her credit card, and they walked back outside with their drinks.

It was a sweleringly hot mid-July evening, and the humidity in the air was thick enough that Liz felt more like she was drinking the air rather than breathing it. She was glad she hadn't straightened her hair, because by the end of the night she would have had waves anyway. Some Jamaican-style band with steel drums was set up on the stage playing music. It reminded Liz of the tacky Hawaiian party she had gone to with Justin, and she sighed as they found a seat at one of the picnic tables.

After a few moments, Victoria spoke up again. "So, what's been up with you?"

"What do you mean?" Liz asked, fidgeting.

"You're different. You're not around that much, and I know you're not working all the time. You normally freak out about your work and obsess. There hasn't been as much obsessing. So tell me, what's up?" Victoria asked, tipping back the absurdly large cup.

"Same old, same old," Liz told her.

Victoria narrowed her eyes. "Don't bullshit me. I know something is going on."

"What's going on, Vic?" Liz asked, deflecting.

"I don't know," she admitted. "But something."

Liz shrugged. She wanted to tell Victoria about Brady, but she couldn't. They had gotten through two months without being caught. She wasn't about to jeopardize that by telling anyone what was happening.

"Does this have to do with Hayden?" Victoria asked, taking a shot in the dark. "I mean, I know that you've liked him for a long time. You're going to see him soon, right?"

"Yeah, next weekend I'm going up there. I'm kind of nervous about it. I mean, he was so strange around me before he left, but he still wants me to come visit. I can't read him. I don't think he has feelings for me, but then sometimes he says things and I think he does. I'm just not on the same page with him."

"Well, then it's good that you're going up there. I can tell he likes you. I think you guys have just been apart all summer, and then when you're together again it'll all come back," Victoria told her.

Liz's stomach twisted at the thought. She didn't want everything with Hayden to suddenly come back. She didn't know what that would be like. With her feelings for Brady swirling around in her head, she couldn't imagine going to see Hayden and dealing with that. Then why was she going to visit him? She didn't have a good answer for that except that she had agreed to . . . and she still wanted to see him.

"Maybe," Liz said, not wanting to concede.

"I think you should just fuck him and stop worrying about it," Victoria said flippantly.

Liz shook her head. There was no way she was going there with this conversation. Not that she and Brady were open about their relationship, but she couldn't sleep with someone else. "No way. He's not that kind of guy, Victoria."

"What *kind* of guy? Every guy wants that."

"That's not what I meant and you know it! I mean, I'm not going to sleep with him to get it out of my system or whatever you said. Hayden didn't make his move at the end of the semester when he could have. I doubt he'd do it now."

"Then why don't you make the move? I swear I've told you this before," Victoria said.

"If he's not interested, then I'm not going to put myself out there like that. Can we drop this?" Talking about Hayden was too confusing with Brady on her mind.

They were friends. Just friends. Hayden had made that perfectly clear last semester. They couldn't do anything because of the paper, and it was even a stretch to say he wanted to do anything with her. All she got from him was mixed signals. She much preferred to have it all out on the table, like with Brady. Hayden was too confusing.

"Fine. We'll drop it, but I still think you should consider walking around naked. You'll find out real quick what he thinks of you," Victoria said with a shrug.

"Thanks for those enlightening words," Liz said with an eye roll. "Anyway, I have a big gala event this weekend that I have to go to."

"Work?" Victoria asked.

"Yeah." It wasn't exactly work, but she couldn't tell Victoria about Brady. Her friend would probably be ecstatic for her, but it was too scary to have people know. The more people with the knowledge of their secret, the more people who could spill it. Even if by accident.

"Do you get to at least wear a rocking dress? Oh my God, have you picked it out already? Can I go with you?" Victoria asked, perking up at the thought of shopping.

Liz shrugged her shoulders as if she didn't know how to answer the questions. "I, uh . . . was going to go in something I already had. That's what I did for the last one."

Victoria leveled a gaze at her that was equal parts *how are we friends* and *are you sure you're female?* "If this thing is a big deal, we need to get you something new!"

"There's really not time," Liz told her.

"We'll make time for this. You'll be less nervous about the event in a brand-new dress! Scientific fact. I would know," she said, then finished off her drink. "Drink up, bitch. I'm getting you another."

Liz stared down into her half-full drink and sighed. It was going to be a rough night.

As the night wore on, Liz felt her intoxication gradually sneak up on her. It wasn't like at Justin's frat party, where the hunch punch had hit her instantly and she had just been gone. This was the best kind of drunk. She and Victoria were barhopping up and down Franklin Street, following friends to new places, and enjoying the company of total strangers in ways that only Victoria could.

She had been trying to convince Liz quite loudly for the past twenty minutes to go home with this guy who had been allegedly hitting on her. Liz tried to tell her that the guy was only interested in her to get to Victoria, but she didn't believe her. When he and Victoria started molesting each other at the bar thirty minutes later, Liz just had to laugh. So much for Victoria being a good judge of those kinds of things.

The guy and his friends followed them to the next bar and one of them actually did try to hit on Liz. He wasn't her type, if she ever had one, and Liz repeatedly had to remove his arm from around her shoulders, touching the small of her back, and stroking her arm. Brady could smash this guy's face in in two seconds. It made her smile to think about it, and the guy leaned in, taking it as encouragement.

"No, really. No, thanks," Liz said, and walked away. She giggled the whole way to the bathroom to locate her roommate. Only two months ago, she would have stayed and been miserable enduring his unwanted attention. It was liberating to feel comfortable enough to stand up for herself. She didn't need to spare his drunk feelings just because he couldn't take a hint.

Victoria materialized a few minutes later, straightening her dress. "Can we get out of here?" she asked.

"Sure. What happened?" Liz asked, following on her heels.

"Too drunk, I guess," Victoria said, "if you know what I mean."

Liz's eyes bulged. "Are you saying what I think you're saying?" They were back out in the open air, wandering Franklin Street for another bar.

"Couldn't get it up. Not my problem. He wasn't very big anyway."

Liz laughed and shook her head. "You astound me."

Victoria walked through a doorway and took the stairs to a rooftop bar. "What was I supposed to do with that, Liz?" Victoria shuddered. "The answer is nothing. I can always call Kirk."

"Who is Kirk?" Liz asked, never able to catch up to Victoria's love life.

"That TA I was telling you about. Remember?"

"The one from England?"

"No, I can't touch the History department for a while. This guy is in Geography," Victoria told her, heading toward the bar.

Liz's head was so heavy and she was having trouble feeling her legs. She didn't know how she didn't stumble or slur or anything. The whole thing was making her want to tell Victoria about Brady. It would be so much nicer to talk to her about him. Then she wouldn't feel so torn about keeping him a secret. If Victoria could so easily tell her about Kirk, why couldn't she talk to Victoria about Brady?

"Anyway," Victoria said before Liz could spill her guts, "Kirk is a bit older and has his own house. Went to get his PhD after spending four years abroad in Somalia or South Africa or something."

"Those aren't exactly close, Victoria. For sleeping with someone in the Geography department, you really don't know your geography very well."

"We don't talk about that," she said, rolling her eyes. "Hold on." Victoria motioned the bartender over and ordered them another round of drinks. Liz's head spun at the thought of another cocktail. She didn't want to feel sick again like last time. At least she had staggered her drinks.

Victoria handed her a bright blue cocktail and smiled. "You're going to like this."

"Why does that scare me?" Liz looked skeptically at the glass.

"Cheers to you, bitch," she said, clinking her glass against Liz's and taking a long swig. Liz shook her head, but followed suit. The drink was beyond fruity, way too sweet for her taste, and, as far as she could tell, straight liquor.

"This is such a terrible idea," Liz muttered, but drank it nonetheless.

Victoria launched into the full details of how she had met Geography Kirk, and Liz tried to concentrate on the story, but she was having difficulty. Victoria's phone went off about halfway through the story and she paused to answer it. Liz wasn't surprised when it was Geography Kirk calling, asking to see her.

"You don't mind, do you?" Victoria asked, batting her eyelashes. Liz glanced down at her watch and saw that it was only one o'clock. She still had an hour in her window of opportunity to see Brady. Perfect!

"Of course not. Go see him!" Liz said enthusiastically. She itched to get her phone out to give his office a ring. It always sent a thrill of excitement through her body when she got to use her fake name. She had hated that name so much, and now it was exhilarating.

Who am I?

"I love you!" Victoria said, smacking a kiss on Liz's cheek. "Take a cab. No DUIs tonight!"

"I'll be careful!" Liz said as she stood with Victoria and exited the bar. Victoria took the first cab that came by, leaving Liz alone on the street.

Chapter 20

AN EMOTIONAL TRIGGER

Liz pulled out her phone as soon as the cab drove off. She tapped Carmichael from her contact list and waited for Brady's secretary to answer. The campaign never slept, and Brady always had someone working the phones so he wouldn't miss anything important.

"Senator Maxwell's office. How may I help you?" his secretary answered.

"Sandy Carmichael for the Senator, please," she chirped.

His secretary paused slightly on the other line before responding, "Yes, Ms. Carmichael. One moment."

Liz froze at the way she said her name. Brady had had the same secretary all summer. Liz wondered whether Nancy knew in some way . . . about her and Brady. She couldn't know for certain, but Liz used this line several times a week lately. She should probably mention it to Brady, but she didn't want to freak him out. Maybe it was better to tell him than take a risk.

"Ms. Carmichael, how nice to hear from you," Brady said into the phone. Liz squirmed where she stood at the sound of his voice. She was pretty drunk and ready for him to come pick her up already.

"Please tell me you're not still at the office."

"I'm in Chapel Hill, actually."

"Perfect. I'm drunk on Franklin Street. Come pick me up. I want you . . . now," she demanded. She took a step forward, stumbled, and latched on to a bench nearby. She giggled into the phone like tripping was the funniest thing she had ever done.

"Baby, how drunk *are* you?" he asked, laughter in his voice.

"Just come get me. I'm going to try to walk to the main bus stop," Liz said, looking at it only a block down the street.

"Maybe you shouldn't move." Liz heard his engine rev through the line and smiled.

"Maybe I shouldn't, but you might not find me."

"I'll find you."

"I'll be at the bus stop."

"Be safe."

Liz narrowed her eyes at the bus stop to keep it from moving and then tried putting one foot in front of the other. It was harder than it looked. Whatever that last drink had been that Victoria had ordered had fucked her up. She needed some water. She glanced over at the store and thought about going in and getting a water bottle. She shook her head. No, she had to meet Brady, and she didn't trust herself to make it inside and back to the bus stop.

She reached the first post at the bus stop and gripped it until she was steady. This was good enough. Holding on to the post made her feel better, more grounded. Her mind started clearing as long as she kept up deep breaths. She didn't want to be sloppy when she was with Brady.

A sleek black Lexus pulled up in front of the bus stop, and Liz smiled. There was her ride.

The ten minutes holding on to the bus stop post had helped her addled mind, and she was able to more nimbly walk around the vehicle. She opened the car door and slid into the black leather passenger seat. It smelled like Brady—primal, enticing, and powerful. If that were a specific smell, she would only associate it with Brady.

He pulled away from the bus stop as soon as her door closed. She tilted her head back and stared at him. She reached out and laced their fingers together. He didn't let go and instead held her hand in his lap. It felt natural, as if he had always been doing it.

"I'm glad you called," he said.

"Me too," she said, tracing her thumb in circles on his hand. Whatever had hit her so hard at the bar was fading away to a nice numbness.

"I have a surprise for you, if you're up for it," he said, glancing over at her.

"A surprise?" she asked, narrowing her eyes. The last big surprise had been the lake house. What other surprise could he have up his sleeve? "We're not going to the lake, are we?"

"No. This is better. More important to me."

Important. That was a big word. "I sure hope that surprise involves a bed."

Brady chuckled and shook his head. "I'm glad you had fun. How drunk are you, anyway?"

"Gone," she whispered.

"Are you feeling up to something else? Or should I take you home?" he asked, concerned.

"At least take me to a hotel so I can sleep with you." She scooted over and rested her head on his shoulder. She was surprised, having not looked at anything aside from his handsome face, that she wasn't resting on a suit. "You're wearing a T-shirt," she mused.

"I do own those," he said, trying to hold in his laughter.

"You should wear them more often."

"Are you trying to get me out of my suit?"

"Don't I always?" she asked with a giggle.

"I think you need some water," Brady said, turning to the side and kissing the top of her head.

"I was going to get some, but I didn't know how far away you were. Where are we going anyway?"

"You'll see. Do you need me to stop?" he asked her.

"No. I'll be okay," she told him.

"All right. But you have to drink some water when we get there."

"I can do that. How far away are we?" She had no idea where they were going, and Brady didn't seem ready to give out any clues. She just wanted to go somewhere where they could be alone. She preferred it that way; then there wouldn't be any tension holding them back.

"Not too far. Maybe twenty to thirty minutes. Just relax. We'll be there soon," he told her. Liz nodded, nuzzled into his shoulder, and closed her eyes.

"Baby," Brady whispered against her hair, "it's time to wake up."

Liz fluttered her eyes open and yawned. She hadn't even realized that she had fallen asleep, but she had been completely out of it for the entire car ride.

They rounded a corner into a complex of brick townhomes. This was a nice area with well-groomed lawns, a gate around the entrance, and rows of clean cars. This certainly wasn't student housing. Brady pulled into a spot in front of one of the buildings and cut the engine. Liz looked around, suddenly feeling much more sober than she had when she had first gotten into the car.

Liz looked at Brady in confusion. "Where are we?"

Brady was smiling from ear to ear. He was beyond happy at the moment, and she didn't know why.

"I'll show you," Brady said, exiting the car and coming around the side to help her out.

Brady opened the door for her and she took his hand as she stood. Seemed that the car ride had helped sober her up more than she thought. She wasn't even that wobbly on her feet. She could still use some water, though. She didn't want to get sick later.

He slid her hand in the crook of his elbow. Liz looked down in surprise, then around the apartment complex, as if she was worried they might be watched. "Brady, is this all right?" she asked, knowing he would get what she meant.

"Right now. It's fine. Calm down," he said with a smile.

Liz walked with him up the stairs to the second floor of one of the buildings. Her earlier buzz had dissipated, and she didn't like not knowing what she was getting herself into.

Brady knocked on the door twice, and they waited there for someone to answer.

A couple minutes later, the door swung inward and a tall guy with sandy brown hair answered the door. He was wearing a UNC T-shirt and khaki shorts despite the late hour. He smiled when he saw who was at the door. "Brady! Man, I thought you were never going to show!" the guy said as the two hugged each other with pats on the back.

"Sorry. Had to pick up someone along the way," Brady told him.

Liz was thoroughly confused. Wasn't Brady going to freak out? Who was this guy? And why was Brady allowing them to be seen together? It felt odd standing there as the two guys acted completely normal.

"Come on inside," the guy said, ushering them through the door, closing it firmly behind them, and locking it.

Liz walked down a hallway and into a modern-looking living room with an enormous flat-screen TV mounted on the wall. His furniture was low to the ground in blacks and whites and a splash of blue here and there.

Brady smiled big and pulled her into his arms as the guy walked into the kitchen. She complied, though she was sure she looked thoroughly confused. What about their closely guarded secret? "Liz," he said, bending and kissing her lips lightly, "this is my surprise."

"Um . . ." she said, not sure what to say.

He released her as the guy walked back into the room with a glass of water. "Brady said you might need this."

Liz took it out of his hand. "Thank you."

"Liz, I'd like to introduce you to my best friend, Chris. Chris, this is Liz, the girl I was telling you about," Brady said.

She was meeting someone. She was actually meeting someone in Brady's life—even if they were meeting in secret, in the middle of the night, at his place so that no one would know about it. This was good. This was a step. That meant that someone knew about her . . . someone important in his life. That must make her important in his life too.

"So nice to meet you," she said, switching the glass over to her left hand and shaking with her right.

"Nice to meet you too."

"He mentions you in his speeches," she said, dropping her hand and thinking of the only time Brady had mentioned Chris around her.

Chris pinned Brady with a glare. "You're still using that same old shit? Can't you come up with something original? I moved to New York, just get over it," he said, shaking his head, then turning back to Liz. "He's such a sap."

A sap. Liz would have never in a million years described Brady as sappy.

"People like to hear that I made the right choice by sticking around. You're a good emotional trigger, or so the speechwriter tells me. Plus, you shouldn't have moved so far away."

"If I hadn't moved, what would you have talked about?" Chris asked.

Brady shrugged. "I'm sure I could have thought of something else to make fun of you for."

Liz stared between the two guys. She had never seen Brady act like this. Was he actually cracking jokes and laughing at himself? She had always thought he was pretty serious. Sometimes he was sarcastic with her, but that was dry humor . . . totally different from this.

"Seriously, convince your speechwriter to come up with new material. People are going to start noticing how full of shit you are," Chris said as he walked past Brady and took a seat on the couch. Liz giggled and then covered her mouth quickly.

"I'll pass along the message," Brady said, shaking his head. He turned back to Liz with a bright, breathtaking smile on his face. He looked so happy and relaxed. "What were you laughing at, huh?"

"Oh nothing," she said, unable to hold back her smile.

"That's what I thought." He reached out for her. "See what I have to deal with? Both of you thinking I'm full of shit."

"Must mean it's true if your best friend and your girl think so," Chris said, lounging across the couch.

Liz's breath caught. Had Chris just called her Brady's girl? She looked up into Brady's face and didn't see any frustration or anger. He hadn't bit back a retort. He wasn't correcting Chris. What was happening?

"Must be," Brady said, planting a kiss on her lips and then pushing her toward the couch.

She was too stunned to even respond. She just sat down.

Brady took the seat next to her and draped his arm over her shoulder. She had so many questions, not the least of which was *Why was this okay?* She wasn't complaining; this was incredible. She just didn't know that this was going to happen. Could she honestly think of a better surprise?

"So, Liz, Brady tells me you're at UNC. What are you majoring in?" Chris asked, switching gears. He picked up a controller off of the table and tossed it to Brady, who caught it one-handed. "You don't mind, do you?"

Liz shook her head. Video games. Seriously, who was this guy she had been seeing the last two months?

She broke out of her trance to answer Chris's question. "Journalism. I work at the newspaper."

"Nice. I used to read the kvetching column every day."

"Oh dear Lord, you're one of *those*?" she asked, unable to hold back.

Chris and Brady both laughed at that. "I didn't care about much in college, so it wouldn't surprise anyone that I'm one of those, as you said." He turned on the XBOX and the icon blasted onto the enormous screen.

The guys set up their game as they talked, and soon they were trying to kill each other on the television screen.

"So, journalism, huh?" Chris said, bobbing and weaving with his player. "What made you choose that?"

"I've always wanted to be a reporter, since I was a little kid. Most people change what they want to do as they grow up, but my goals stayed pretty consistent," she told him.

She couldn't help staring at Brady instead of the screen. He was playing video games. His smile was contagious, and everything that he and Chris said to each other was a riot. They could badger each other and still laugh. It was very clear they had known each other for a long time.

She suddenly felt a loss grip her, as if she had missed a part of him for the past two months. He could very clearly enjoy himself and be normal when he felt completely comfortable and didn't have to hold back.

"Nice. I changed majors about ten times in college. Ended up getting a business degree like Brady. Professors *hated* having us in classes together," Chris told her.

"I can see that. You two seem like you could get in a lot of trouble together."

"Wait a minute," Brady said. "Professors hated having you in class. They didn't have a problem with me."

"Don't believe everything he tells you. He fucked up as much in college as the rest of us," Chris said as Brady grumbled curse words under his breath.

Liz laughed again. "I bet he did."

"Seriously don't believe him," Brady whispered into her ear. His lip brushed against her earlobe and she shivered.

"Are you from the area then?" Chris asked.

"No, my family lives in Tampa. My dad's a professor at South Florida," she told them.

"Your dad is a professor?" Brady asked, stopping his movements on the controller and turning to look at her. Chris proceeded to kill Brady's character off.

"Yeah," she said, staring up into his dark, intense eyes.

"I didn't know that."

"You never asked."

"What does he teach?" Brady asked, suddenly very interested.

"Calculus primarily."

"Huh. And you're not a math person?" he asked.

"I'm a Morehead scholar. I'm perfectly fine at math. It's just not my area of interest," she told him diplomatically.

That got Chris's attention. "You're a Morehead scholar?" he asked, sounding very impressed. "Isn't that the highest merit scholarship in the school?"

Liz shrugged, her cheeks flushing. "Yeah. It is."

"Damn," he said, appraising her.

"That's impressive," Brady said softly.

"Thanks," she said, embarrassed. She turned away from his heated look and let them get back to their game. She hadn't thought her answers would distract them so much, but she couldn't deny that she liked how interested Brady had been in her background.

The guys played a couple games together, and Liz felt herself dozing off again. She rarely got much sleep when she was with Brady, but it tended to be for other reasons entirely.

"Hey, are you falling asleep?" Brady asked, nudging her lightly.

"Oh, no," she said, jumping up. "I'm not."

"You guys need to come up to New York sometime," Chris said. "My place there is smaller than this and I pay ten times as much on it, but you can't beat the location in Manhattan."

Liz looked up at Brady as he turned to look at her. She could read his expression. Chris clearly knew that they weren't out in public. Brady wouldn't have brought them here otherwise.

"What are you doing in North Carolina, anyway?" she asked, changing the subject so Brady didn't have to respond. Brady kissed her lips once before returning to his game. She wondered if that was her thank you.

"Oh, I'm here for Brady's fucking gala event or whatever it is this weekend," Chris told her.

"Oh, really? I didn't know you would be there," Liz said. That was promising. At least she would know one other person besides Brady.

"Yeah. Are you going?"

She looked up at Brady expectantly. "Yeah, I got her a ticket," he said.

"You two are going together?" Chris asked, mashing one of the buttons repeatedly with his thumb.

Brady sighed and looked down at her. She could tell he wasn't happy with that question. She knew they couldn't go together. She really, really wanted to go with him, but he wasn't going to let that happen . . . not right before the primary. This was what she had signed up for, but she couldn't help silently pleading with him to change his mind.

"I don't think that's such a good idea with the election coming up," Brady said.

Chris looked as if he wanted to say more about it, but he didn't. And that closed it. "You know, you could always go with me."

"What?" Brady asked before Liz could speak.

"Hear me out. I don't have a date, and she doesn't have a date. It would be better for both of us if we went together. Then no weird old ladies will try to hand me off to their sons, and, yes, that has happened before," Chris told them.

"I don't know," Liz said, trying to read Brady's reaction.

"It's really a flawless plan," Chris said.

"What do you think?" Liz asked Brady.

He leaned down and whispered in her ear so that Chris couldn't hear. "I don't want anyone else even near you, but compared to the alternative, Chris is tolerable. As long as you know, baby, you're going home with me."

"I don't want anyone else," she whispered back.

Brady smiled and nodded at Chris. "I think that will work better than you both showing up alone. I can send you the details for the weekend."

"Sounds good," Chris said, stretching exaggeratedly. "I think I'm beat. I'm going to go to bed. You guys feel free to stay. I have a guest room down that hallway." He pointed off in the opposite direction of where he was walking. "Really nice meeting you, Liz."

"Nice meeting you, too."

Chris walked up the stairs to the second floor and out of sight. Brady planted his lips on hers, cradled her body against his, picked her up, and carried her into the guest bedroom.

"Look," Brady said, kicking the door closed with his foot and setting her down, "the surprise comes with a bed."

Chapter 21

WHAT YOU'RE LOOKING FOR

Liz walked forward into the ballroom that housed Brady's big gala event. Chris was standing at her side, looking dashing out of his khakis and into a tux. His longer light brown hair was trimmed, and he had shaved. He handed off the pair of tickets Brady had left with them, and they glided through the doors.

The room was a surprising display. Liz had expected the typical red-white-and-blue decor that she had associated with political campaigns, but it seemed that had been replaced with actual evening decorations in black, white, and gold. High tables, covered in alternating silky tablecloths, were scattered around the massive ballroom, where guests mingled with drinks in hand. The waitstaff wandered the premises in tailored tuxedos and shimmery black dresses, carrying hors d'oeuvres and champagne flutes on gold platters.

A sizable number of influential members of North Carolina society were present, along with a few notable politicians, celebrities, and business executives from outside the state whom Liz recognized.

Everyone was dressed to the nines and had probably paid a pretty penny in donations to be at this fund-raising event.

Liz took a deep breath and tried not to think about it. Brady wanted her here tonight even though the party was only supposed to be for donors, friends, and family. She felt extremely on edge in the ballroom surrounded by all of these people, knowing she was essentially Brady's mistress.

No, he wasn't married. No, he wasn't dating anyone. No, she wasn't technically a mistress. But she was a secret and that was enough.

After the time they had spent with Chris out in the open, she had started feeling antsy. She hadn't seen Brady since that night, but she felt like the paradigm of their relationship had forever changed now that someone knew what they were doing. If Chris knew, why couldn't Victoria know? Why couldn't his family know? Why couldn't the whole campaign know?

She didn't like to think about it. She knew it would upset him if she mentioned it, but they were so good together. Would it really be the end of the world if other people knew what they were doing? Would it really jeopardize the campaign and her career? She knew that they had started out a secret for that very reason, but she hadn't ever expected to want to change that. Now that she did . . . she couldn't help wondering if they had just blown it out of proportion to begin with.

Liz followed Chris to an empty table and he smiled at a few people he knew. She was really surprised by how many faces she recognized. Like the governor . . . wasn't he from a different party? And two basketball celebrities . . . had they played with Brady in college? And a news reporter from the *Washington Post* and another one that Liz followed from the *New York Times*. She knew that no press was allowed in the event, and they weren't wearing badges or carrying equipment. Were they supporters?

Liz knew she shouldn't be in reporter mode, but she couldn't help it. It was who she was. Ingrained in her now. This event wasn't open to the press, but her fingers were itching for the voice recorder and notebook she normally carried with her. She only had a deep red satin clutch with her, at Victoria's insistence.

The day after she met Chris, she had gone shopping with Victoria at the mall and some of the local boutiques. Liz had been ready to call it quits and wear what she had, but Victoria had urged her into a few more shops. A few more shops had actually been closer to a dozen, in true Victoria style.

It had been worth it though when they had found *the* dress. Liz hadn't been sure about it until Victoria had forced her to try it on. The champagne-colored silk hugged her figure seamlessly, falling to the floor, the train trailing out ever so slightly behind her. It had a square bustier top with a small V dipping between her breasts. The beaded straps crossed her back and held up the backless ensemble, which was ruched at the base of her spine.

Miraculously, after she matched it with dark red pumps, it didn't need any alterations. Victoria had piled Liz's thick, blond hair up off her neck and into curls. The only jewelry on her whole body was a thin gold necklace and gold-knotted earrings.

"Champagne?" the waitress asked as she passed.

Chris glanced at Liz. "You?"

"Sure," she said, taking a drink from the waitress.

Chris held up his hand and she moved on. "I think I'll head to the bar and get something else. I prefer beer. Did you want something?"

Liz took a sip of her champagne and then set it down. She couldn't get sloshed. She needed to take it easy. "I think I'm good with the champagne."

"All right," he said with a smile. "Don't go anywhere."

"Hey," Liz said, reaching out and touching his arm. "When will Brady get here?"

Brady had told her that he wouldn't be there when the event started, but he would make an appearance once the room started filling up. She just didn't know when to expect him. She was already excited to see him.

"I'm sure he'll be late to his own gig." He glanced down at the watch on his wrist. "Probably in the next twenty to thirty minutes if we're lucky. The sooner he gets here, the sooner we leave."

Liz giggled and shook her head. "What? Afraid of getting pawned off to someone's son again?"

"Don't get me started. I'll tell you that story later, and then you won't be laughing!" he said before turning and walking toward the bar.

Liz took another drink of her champagne and went back to people watching. Brady would be here in the next twenty minutes or so, which meant she had a little bit of time to size up the crowd.

She figured she was the youngest person in the room besides Savannah, whom she picked out in an Anne Boleyn green dress across the room. Most of the donors in the room who contributed to Brady's campaign were up-and-comers riding the bandwagon of success. There were a sizable number of older individuals, women primarily, who all seemed to know one another. She was pretty sure she recognized some of them from her table at the Jefferson-Jackson event.

"Find what you're looking for?" a voice drawled softly into her ear.

She turned around slowly and looked up into an oddly familiar face, but not the one she had been expecting. Where had she seen this person before? He had short blond hair, beautiful blue eyes, and dimpled cheeks. So familiar . . . yet she couldn't place him.

"I wasn't looking for anything," she covered quickly, flushing.

"For you," he said, offering her a glass half-full of dark liquid.

Some guy was bringing her a drink . . . out of nowhere. That felt oddly familiar as well.

"Um . . . thanks," she said, taking it out of his hand.

He chuckled, those cute dimples returning. "You don't remember me, do you?"

Busted! "No, sorry. You do look really familiar . . ."

"We met on the Fourth of July," he offered. "You were having a medical emergency. Claustrophobic, if I remember correctly. How are you handling this event?" he asked amicably.

"Oh my God, that's right! So sorry! I was kind of having a moment," she said.

If only he knew what kind of moment . . .

"You seem all right now," he drawled.

"Much better."

He smiled down at her, and she noticed how handsome he was. "So, what do you think about the party? A bit different from the Fourth of July atmosphere."

"It's classy. I'm just glad it's not red-white-and-blue," she said.

"Ah, how exceptionally unpatriotic," he teased.

"Well, what do you think about it, then?" Liz demanded, taking a sip of the drink he had brought over to her. She smiled as the whiskey slid down her throat.

"Hmm . . . the truth?" he asked with a devilish grin.

"Of course."

"I think the decorations are a bit overdone, the crowd is a bit stiff, and the candidate is a pompous asshole. But hey, we don't vote on character, do we?"

Liz nearly choked on her drink. Had he really just called Brady a pompous asshole? She would have laughed, since it was something she would have thought two months ago, but she didn't think that anymore. She knew Brady too well to think that was true.

"Good to see you think so highly of your representative," she said, biting back a smile.

"Don't believe all of that. They don't represent us. They represent themselves and business and some of the people in this room who give them a lot of money," he told her as a matter of fact.

"What a jaded view of the political process," Liz said. She'd had similar thoughts before, but that was why she was in journalism and not politics. She couldn't deal with the insincerity and duplicity herself. She would rather report on it.

"Only honest one you'll get in here tonight, and don't forget it," he said, gesturing to the crowd.

"You think pretty highly of yourself. I sure hope you never go through the trouble of running for office," she said with a genuine smile.

He laughed out loud and set his drink on the table. "So, you're saying that you approve of the Maxwell family taking over the political field?"

"We'll see how the primary goes first," she said diplomatically.

"Spoken like a true politician. Are *you* running for office?" He leaned forward as if to get the inside scoop.

"Definitely not," she said.

"Maybe reconsider it."

"And would I have your vote, considering what you think about politicians?" Liz asked, leaning forward to match him.

"I don't give away my vote freely, but I think I'd let you take it," he drawled. "You want to run against a Maxwell?"

"Maybe I'll wait for an open seat." She took another sip of her drink. His eyes followed the movement.

The room gradually fell silent all around them, and Liz broke his gaze to look up at the entrance. Standing just inside the double doors, directly across from her table, stood Brady. He looked un-fucking-believable. He seriously got better-looking every time she saw him. He wore a black tux, and his hair had been styled to perfection. Everything just fit him as if it had been made for his body, and all she wanted to do was get him out of it.

She zeroed in on him, and then slowly, as if she were zooming out with a camera, she saw everything else. And what she saw made her stomach drop.

A woman. No, not just any woman. A freaking gorgeous woman. Model thin, above-average height, long, lustrous hair, flawless skin, and an expensive-dress-and-jewelry kind of woman. A woman with her hand holding on to Brady's elbow as if . . . she was there with him. With her Brady.

"Why am I not surprised?" the guy said next to her. "See what I mean by not judging on character alone? I'm sure he's sleeping with her."

Liz's fingers clenched into the cloth on the table as her heart sped up. Three days ago she had been meeting Brady's best friend for the first time. While Brady hadn't said that he was going to the event alone, she hadn't thought he would show up with some other woman on his arm. Not after telling Liz that he didn't want anyone near her. Now he was here with some other woman?

Her death glare must have drawn Brady's attention, because his eyes found her easily in the crowd. They stayed like that for only a couple of seconds, but she was sure he grasped the heat in her stare. His eyes traveled away from her, but jerked back to her almost immediately. He looked at her as if he was trying to puzzle out an answer, and then he looked away.

She felt sick. She needed to get away from there.

"Liz," Chris called, appearing out of nowhere. "Sorry I was held up." He looked over at the guy she had been standing with and clapped him on the back. "Hey, man. How's law school treating you? Are you liking Yale?"

Liz wanted to disappear. She was fuming. She knew deep down she had no right to be angry about this. They couldn't be out in public, but that didn't mean he could bring someone else! She wanted to be that woman right now! His girl. She had never wanted to be in anyone else's shoes as much as she did at that moment.

"Doing just fine. I see you know Liz," he said, using her name without any effort, as if he had known it all along rather than only after Chris had just said it.

"Oh, you know Liz?" Chris asked, sounding confused. "She's here with me." Chris touched her elbow, and it took everything she had not to wrench it out of his grasp. "I didn't know you had already met Clay," he said, turning to face Liz.

That snapped her out of her anger for a second. "What?" Liz asked, her brows scrunched.

The guy Chris had called Clay smirked and extended his hand. "Pleasure to meet you." Liz took his hand and shook it. "Clay Maxwell."

"Maxwell," she muttered, stunned.

"So . . . you haven't met?" Chris asked, trying to judge the situation.

"We met at the Fourth of July rally," Clay told Chris, "and then again just now."

Clay. Maxwell. Fuck. Of course, it was Clay Maxwell. The only other person she had found interesting, attractive, and engaging had been Brady's brother. Great!

Liz glanced back over at Brady, who had started talking to his guests and posing for pictures along the way. His parents were standing behind him and to the left. Heather and that same beady-eyed guy from the club were standing to his right. She would be sure to avoid them. Heather was one of the few who knew her indirectly.

But what was worse, the woman Brady was standing with had her arm on his sleeve and followed at his side the whole time. Liz felt heat rise to her face as her stomach constricted into a million impossibly tight knots. She swallowed down a lump in her throat and balled her hands into fists at her sides. She would have clutched onto the fabric of her dress, but she didn't want to ruin it.

"Are you feeling all right?" Clay asked Liz, reaching out and touching her arm.

Chris looked over at Liz, concerned. "Do you need to sit down?"

"I'm fine," she snapped. She tried to rein in her rising anger, but she wasn't doing a very good job. She kept trying to tell herself that she had no right to be angry, but that felt like a lie.

Liz turned her head away from Brady and the woman on his arm. She couldn't keep staring at them. It made her nauseous to see them together.

"Maybe we should go get you some water," Chris suggested.

"Water. Hmm," she mused, remembering how she and Brady had driven to Chris's house for water. She took a few slow breaths, trying to calm down. "No, I think I'm fine. Already recovering. Must have been the claustrophobia."

"Well, it's good you're feeling better. I unfortunately have to go find the rest of my family. It was good seeing you again, Liz. Chris," Clay said, thrusting his hand out. Clay and Chris shook formally, as if they were on opposite sides of an irresolvable war. Clay flashed her a smile and turned to leave. He only took a step before Brady materialized before him, with his date in tow.

"Clay," Brady said with a smile. It was a campaign smile. Liz could read it a mile away.

"Brady," Clay responded. "Nice party." He made it sound like a joke.

"Thanks. Mind taking a picture? We can do a family one later."

"I sure hope it's for the Christmas card," Clay retorted.

"Christmas in July?"

"Never too early."

"Just take the picture," Brady said, turning to face the photographer. Brady smiled and the camera flashed.

Clay broke away from Brady as soon as it was over. "You should take one with Chris. Have you met his date?" Clay turned to include Liz and Chris into the conversation. "I think I've convinced her to run against you."

"Have you? How kind," Brady said, turning to face Liz.

Their eyes met and she stopped breathing. She wished his campaign mask would slip for a second so she could see what else was underneath that beautiful face. Why was he doing this to her?

"I hear you're running against me. How do you intend to win?" Brady asked Liz.

"By taking out the competition, of course," Liz said without missing a beat.

Clay snickered and Chris squeezed her arm. Brady just kept looking at her, completely unaffected.

"I do believe you would. I hope I can change your mind about running."

"I'm sure you'd try to change my mind about a lot of things," she said coolly.

Brady laughed and Liz tried to muster a smile, but it wasn't without difficulty. "Liz, is it? I believe we met at the rally on the Fourth of July."

"Indeed we did, Senator," she said formally. "And who is your beautiful girlfriend?" Liz turned her attention to the woman at his side.

"Ah, this is my friend Amber," he added, hastily introducing Amber to the group of people.

"Pleased to meet you," Amber said with an overemphasized Southern drawl.

"How do you guys know each other anyway?" Clay asked.

"We met at the Miss North Carolina pageant," Amber filled in.

"A pageant. I sure hope you beat him," Clay said snarkily.

Amber giggled and covered her mouth. Brady shook his head. "Amber is Miss North Carolina. She won this year's competition."

"Is that a scholarship competition?" Liz asked, directing her attention to Amber, because she couldn't look at Brady.

"It is!" Amber answered enthusiastically.

"It must be nice to get a scholarship just for being beautiful," she said, taking a sip of her drink, glancing at Brady, and then setting it back down. "Excuse me. I'm not feeling well. I think I need to go sit down."

"I'll go with you," Chris said. He placed his drink next to hers.

"Good luck with your election, Senator," Liz said, smiling at him, turning, and walking away.

Chris followed close on her heels, waiting until they were at a comfortable distance from other people before speaking. "Liz, calm down. He's not here with her. He only showed up with her. It's not like that. He likes you. I swear. He wouldn't have told me about you if he didn't."

"Chris," Liz grumbled, "do you mind shutting up?"

"Come on. You know he's not interested in that woman. She has nothing between her ears."

"He's still here with her." She continued to walk quickly. She didn't know where she was going . . . just trying to escape.

"He wouldn't have brought anyone if he had the choice."

"Exactly. No one or a fucking beauty queen." She stopped and faced him, making sure no one was paying them any attention. "Not me."

"It's bad timing. That's all. It has nothing to do with you."

"Oh, please," Liz said, shaking her head and starting to walk again. "Its having nothing to do with me is even worse."

"Hey." Chris grabbed her arm and forcibly stopped her from walking farther. "I'm telling you as his best friend that he likes you.

Remember the other night when we were all together? He's not like that with some dumb beauty queen. Now let's get another drink and calm down."

"Did you know he was bringing someone else?" she asked.

"Yes," he said with a sigh, "but not until last night."

"And *why* wasn't I informed of this?" Liz asked testily.

"Because he thought you might back out, and he wanted you here."

"Well, at least he knows me."

"Come on," he said, wrapping an arm around her shoulder. "Let's get a drink."

Liz sighed and shook her head. "No. I don't think I can do that. I can't stand around and watch him with her." She brushed his hand off of her shoulder and started walking toward the door. She had fallen hard for Brady Maxwell, but he couldn't parade that woman in front of her. He couldn't get away with not telling her the truth, not being up front with her, when he demanded it of her.

"Liz . . ." Chris called, following after her. "Don't leave."

"I have to. He doesn't take this seriously."

"He'd be stupid not to take you seriously after that last comment."

Liz shot daggers at him. "Why are you even siding with him?"

"He's my best friend. Look, just come with me for a minute." Chris reached out and stopped her. "Don't leave yet."

"Chris, come on. I'm just going to go."

"One minute," he pleaded.

Liz grumbled expletives softly under her breath before nodding. "Fine. Where are we going?"

"Somewhere quiet," he said, walking toward the back wall.

"For what?"

"Just act natural."

Liz shrugged and decided to see where he was taking her. It was better than sticking around the party and watching the stupid beauty-pageant chick follow Brady around like a lapdog.

They walked through a door on the other side of the room, which led them through a service hallway. They turned a corner and Chris jiggled the handle to the first door on the right. It twisted and pushed inward. Liz peered around him and saw that he had opened a door into a family bathroom.

"What the hell is this?" she asked, crossing her arms over her chest.

Chris looked up and down the empty hallway. "Just go inside. Brady will meet you in a minute."

"In a bathroom?" she asked incredulously.

"Yes. Go," he said, pointing at the door.

Liz looked at him as if he were mentally insane, but walked into the bathroom and shut the door. She felt really ridiculous. She was standing in a bathroom, for Christ's sake. Who did this? What if Brady left her in there all night? Not that she would stay longer than like fifteen minutes . . . okay twenty . . . maybe longer.

She sighed, feeling even more ridiculous. How the hell could Brady bring someone else to this event? Why even invite Liz if he was going to flaunt someone else around in front of her the whole time? After blowing up on her about Justin and not wanting anyone else to get their hands on her, he had the audacity to show up with someone else. As if *she* wanted anyone to get her hands on him!

Just the thought was getting her even more riled up. And she didn't want to calm down.

The door handle rattled as someone wrestled with the stuck knob. It popped open a second later and Brady stood silhouetted in the doorway. Alone.

Liz smiled at the sight of him. Then she remembered she was angry and wiped it away. He moved inside quickly, shut and locked the door. He took one look at her before crossing the small space, taking her face in his hands, and kissing the breath right out of her. Her eyes closed for a second as he took what was his. He was the most intoxicating substance on the planet. Their kisses were like fire scorching through a burning building—hot and destructive.

She didn't want him to stop. She couldn't possibly want that. She wanted to do this for the rest of eternity. Who cared if he burned a hole right through her heart?

Then she came to her senses, and she pushed him back with every ounce of force. She probably didn't move him back more than an inch, but the shock of her stopping him made him stumble a few feet backward.

"What the hell do you think you're doing?" Brady asked.

"Stopping you."

"What have you been doing since you got here?"

"What have *I* been doing?" she asked, her eyes going wide.

"Yes. What have you been doing? Flirting with my brother, making a scene when I come to see you—what is wrong with you?" he demanded.

"I'm not sure I can even justify that with an answer!" she said, shaking her head.

"Is this because of Amber? Because if it is, then you need to get your shit together. Did you forget that I'm on the campaign? That I have an election to win?" he asked gruffly.

"How could I possibly forget?" she demanded.

"I don't know, but you're fucking acting like you have. I thought you knew what we were doing." He clenched his hands into fists.

"That's right. What we *were* doing," she said, trying to brush past him to get to the door.

"What the fuck does that mean?" he asked. He grabbed her by the arm and pulled her into him.

"We aren't doing what we started out doing anymore. If you want the girl who you met in May, then sorry . . . she's long gone," she told him, staring up into his dark, intense eyes.

"You're not leaving, Liz," he told her. She arched an eyebrow, wondering whether he was daring her. "I don't want that girl. I want you. Do you hear me? I want *you*."

Chapter 22

APPEARANCES

Liz felt her anger deflate at his words. She knew it wasn't enough for them to move forward. It wasn't enough to change the course of their relationship. But it was something; it was a start.

"I want you too," she whispered in the silence.

Brady's lips found hers again, soft and warm. He wasn't trying to kiss the life out of her; he was just kissing her. The woman he wanted.

He wrapped his arms around her waist, and she tangled her fingers in his hair. Her chest rose and fell in time with his, and she felt all the remaining fire in her body dissolve.

Brady wanted her.

When they broke apart this time, she was wobbly on her feet and had to rest her hand on his chest to hold herself steady.

"Are you all right now?" he asked, tilting her chin up to gaze into her blue eyes.

"Doing better," she whispered.

"Good. That's what I wanted to hear."

"Brady, why did you bring her? Why didn't you tell me?" she asked softly. She still wasn't comfortable with the idea, but she wasn't angry. Not in the same way, at least.

"I had to bring her."

Liz looked up at him incredulously. "Really?"

"Some things are for appearances. It's complicated. Heather really insisted on this one. My bachelor appearance only accommodates me so far, but in social situations it doesn't look good to show up alone. And it's useful to have someone else there to entertain the people I'm not speaking with directly. As much as I'd prefer to go alone, Amber is the least troublesome of the choices I was given."

"You didn't even ask her yourself?" she asked, surprised. How did all of this work?

"No. I'm too busy to date, or at least that's what I tell my press secretary."

"Does she want you to date?" Liz asked, concerned.

Brady shook his head solemnly. "She doesn't want me to date. She wants me to get married."

Liz let out a peep at that word. Married! He couldn't get married!

"Don't worry," he said, planting a kiss on her lips. "That's not on my horizon for a long time. She can't badger me into something that extreme. That's not like a date at a gala."

Thank God! Liz thought.

"So . . . why were you flirting with my brother?" he asked, a storm cloud forming over his features. So that was what he had been holding back when he'd had his campaign face on while talking to Clay.

"I didn't know he was your brother. Nor did I know I was flirting with him. I was trying to defend you," she said, pointing her finger into his chest.

"Defend me? Why would you need to?"

Liz bit her lip. Whoops! Maybe she shouldn't have said that. It was clear that there was something wrong between him and Clay. But she had already put one foot forward; she might as well take the step.

"He was talking about you and the campaign and politics in general. I didn't know who he was, but they weren't exactly uplifting words," she said as tactfully as she could.

"Fucking Clay," Brady said, shaking his head. "He needs to learn to keep his mouth shut. I promise he was trying to charm you."

Liz swallowed and didn't say anything. Charm ran in their family.

"I would stay away from him."

"I probably won't see him again anyway, will I?" she asked. "He's at Yale. He should be going back soon."

"Not soon enough, unfortunately," Brady said.

Liz wanted to ask what the problem was between them, but it didn't really seem like the time. There were other more pressing concerns . . . like where they were going from here.

"Brady, what are we doing?" she asked, trying to keep from choking out the words. She couldn't ask too much. She couldn't push too hard. She couldn't lose him.

He opened his mouth to say something and was cut off by a sharp rap on the door. Brady hung his head and sighed. "That's my cue. Can we finish this conversation later?"

"Will I get to see you later?"

Brady smiled that gorgeous smile he seemed to reserve specifically for her and pulled something out of his tux. Liz peered down into his hand and saw a little silver key. She glanced up at him, confused. "What's this?"

"A key to my house."

Liz's throat went dry. A key. To his house.

She had never been to his house. She wasn't allowed to go there. They had always met somewhere that couldn't be tracked or traced . . . somewhere the campaign couldn't find them.

"What's that for?" she whispered, not able to tear her eyes away from the key.

"That's where I was planning to have you stay tonight."

Liz's eyes slowly rose to his and her mouth popped open. He bent down and kissed her lightly.

"That is—if you still want to."

He slid the key into her palm, and she closed her hand over the metal, feeling the light weight in her hand.

"I want to," she responded.

"I have a driver tonight, and he can take you. I'll see you tonight, baby."

He placed one more kiss on her lips and then exited the room. Liz stared down at her hand. She had a key to Brady's house.

Liz left the bathroom a few minutes later and walked back into the gala ballroom. Her heart beat a soft rhythm in her throat from her time with Brady, and she couldn't seem to relinquish that feeling. Her emotions were swirling around inside of her like a tempest raging through a storm. She couldn't believe Brady had given her a key to his place. He was slipping. They were both slipping away from their arrangement. The more he let her in, the more she craved from him. Even though she was still mad about Amber, their conversation had tempered her anger so completely that all she could think about was getting back to Brady's house as quickly as possible.

Chris smiled at her as she walked toward him. She wondered what he thought had happened back there. He must think they had worked everything out or he wouldn't look so smug. At least he was a good friend to have arranged a way for them to talk.

He handed her a drink as she approached. "I thought you'd want another," he said with a wink.

"Yes, I would," she said, taking it and sipping on the whiskey sour.

The key felt like the business card Brady had given her the first time they had met and he had told her to call him. She couldn't stop feeling like the tiny thing was weighing her bag down.

The next hour was a blur of Brady, taking pictures, shaking hands, schmoozing all around. She couldn't drag her eyes away from him, and Chris wouldn't let her have more than one more drink. Apparently she hadn't been as sober as she had thought when she had met Chris the first time. He was probably right about it anyway; she shouldn't trust herself to drink in this environment.

Someone handed Brady a microphone and he gave a short speech thanking everyone for being in attendance. A series of other officials spoke after him. It was the same thing from everyone. They all wanted people to donate money to Brady for his campaign. They wanted to take him from a candidate to a shoo-in.

Liz already thought he was. And she had before she had become completely and totally biased.

After the speeches, music streamed through the speakers and the lights dimmed. Everyone began to mingle around the room and some of the younger crowd started dancing. Chris disappeared for a second to get another beer, and Liz thought about leaving early anyway.

She just needed to suck it up and see the evening for what it was. She had gotten herself into this mess. She hadn't thought that she would want anything more from Brady Maxwell than what he had offered her that morning in the diner . . . that she would want a real relationship. And it hadn't mattered, until it did.

Liz found Brady in the crowd standing with his family, Amber, and some official Liz didn't know. Savannah was speaking and

Brady was laughing at whatever she said. At least he got along with his sister. She wondered if he and Clay were too much alike, or if their animosity ran deeper.

Brady said something to the official as Amber spoke with his wife. She wondered what it would be like to stand there with Brady and entertain the wives of officials while he spoke to the husbands. Would she enjoy doing that? A chill went through her. She was getting way ahead of herself.

His eyes found her across the room and she saw his mask fall when he smiled at her. Their eyes locked and her cheeks flushed. He wanted her. She could see it in that one look.

Liz licked her lips. He nodded once, as if he understood what she was implying and turned his attention back to his sister.

She needed to leave. She couldn't stand here any longer. She wanted to be in his bed, snuggled up against his chest, enjoying the time she could have with him. She didn't want to see him parade around a room with someone else. Even if he had no personal feelings toward Amber, it still made Liz feel disgusting. She understood his position, but she didn't have to like it.

"I think this is the last one for me tonight," Liz said, setting down her empty glass.

"Are you sure?" Chris asked.

"Yeah. I think it's time for me to go home."

"You're not still upset, are you?" He leaned against the table and surveyed the people surrounding them.

"No. I'm all right, I guess. Just tired. Sorry I haven't been the best date," she said with a small apologetic smile.

"Well, you weren't the worst one I've ever had," he said with a wink.

"Does this also have something to do with being handed off to someone's son?"

"I swear I'm never telling you anything again. You'll use it against me for all of eternity," he said, shaking his head.

Liz pointed at herself and shrugged. "Reporter. I don't forget much."

"Great," he groaned.

"Thanks for bringing me, Chris," she said, wrapping her arms around his waist and pulling him into a hug. He patted her back twice before releasing her.

"Take it easy. I'm sure I'll see you around. I always end up at functions for Brady."

"Definitely. Hopefully I'll see you soon," Liz said with a smile.

She took one last look at Brady. He looked up, saw her leaving, and smiled. She tried to hold her smile back, but she wasn't successful. He knew where she was heading now.

Liz turned away before he could and walked through the double doors and into the fresh evening air. She turned the corner and stared at the line of cars and limos that stretched around the circular drive. Unless his driver happened to recognize her, she wasn't going to be able to locate Brady's car without a valet.

She looked around and found the valet station, but it was currently unoccupied. They must have been out collecting a car for someone else.

She craned her neck when she heard voices off to the left, hoping it was the valet, but saw someone talking on their cell phone. The person turned and Liz saw that it was Clay. He nodded his head at her and beckoned her over.

Liz scrunched up her eyebrows and stood her ground. The last thing she wanted to do was upset Brady right now.

"Let me give you a call back," she heard Clay say before hanging up his phone and sliding it back into his pocket. "Hey, you're not leaving, are you?"

Clay walked back across the sidewalk to stand in front of her. Fuck! She couldn't take Brady's car if Clay was standing here.

"Yeah, I think I'm going to call it a night," she told him.

"Where's Chris?" he asked, looking around. "Is he getting his car?"

"Nah, I think I'm going to head home alone." She sure hoped he didn't try to read more into that. Chris was technically her date, and now it probably looked bad that she was leaving without him.

"Huh," he said, seeming to mull that over. "Well, do you need a lift?"

"You would miss your own brother's party?"

"Hey, it's not like it's my party," he said with that cute dimpled smile.

"You really don't support him, do you?" she couldn't help asking.

"Why do you care if this guy wins an election?" Clay asked. "I mean, why do you think he's running anyway? In a few years, he's not going to remember anyone in this room who isn't paying him in the upper hundred thousands. Unless you have a trust fund somewhere lying around, which, forgive me if you do, he's not going to remember you either. The man has a plan, and he won't stop for anyone to get there."

"What? Did he step on your toes to get where he is now?" she demanded. This was not a conversation she wanted to have with him after the one she'd had with Brady in the bathroom.

Clay chuckled and shook his head. "Just wait. You'll see. The toes will be the least of everyone's concerns. You don't know him well enough to understand."

"Why are you telling me all of this?" she huffed.

"Because I want to take you home," he told her. "Why don't you let me?"

"I'm just curious," Liz said, holding her hand up. "Does this line actually work on women?"

Clay laughed out loud. "Actually, yes. It does."

"Uh-huh . . . well, maybe you should try some new material."

"Apparently, but that doesn't change the fact that I want to take you home. Nor does it change anything I said about my brother," he said.

Liz smiled slightly. He didn't get it. He didn't get what Brady got about the world. Clay had it written all over him how jaded he was. From the way his hand rested in his pocket, the cockiness in his smile, and the glint in his eyes. She just wanted to . . . fix him.

"I appreciate the offer, but I'm going to have to pass. And about your brother, maybe you're not wrong about him. But next time he gives a speech you should listen to what he says and how he says it. You might be surprised."

"I'll do that . . . just for you," he said with a devious smirk that said he certainly wouldn't.

"Ms. Carmichael?" a voice called behind her.

Shit!

"Yes?" she asked, turning to face him.

"Your car is on its way," the valet said.

She hadn't even gone up to ask the valet for the car. Was this Brady's doing?

"That's me," she said to Clay. "Have a nice night."

"At least let me get your number," he volleyed.

"And what are you going to do with it? Don't you go to Yale?" Liz asked.

"So?" he said with a shrug before pushing his phone into her hands.

Liz rolled her eyes. "I only want to hear from you if you change your mind about your brother," she told him. She typed her number into his phone.

He took the phone back and nodded. "Sounds like a deal. I think I'll find some compassion tonight," he said with a wink before walking away.

Liz blew out softly as he departed. She knew that if she hadn't done that then she never would have gotten away without him seeing that she was getting into Brady's car.

Damn! Why hadn't she thought of using a fake number? Whatever. It wasn't as if she would ever respond to his messages.

Brady's driver, Greg, pulled up in front of the valet station a second later. The valet opened the door for her and she slid into the backseat. Greg stared back at her through the rearview mirror with a smile. "Pleasure to have you back, Ms. Carmichael."

Greg rolled up slowly in front of a brick two-story house in the very back of a gated neighborhood in a Raleigh suburb. It was dark outside, but the front porch light was on, allowing Liz a better view. The house was traditional-looking, with bay windows in the front and a large porch with a porch swing. She knew that Brady had neighbors on either side of his house, but the generous portion of land, curve of the cul-de-sac, and abundance of tall pines obscured the view of any of the surrounding lots.

Liz exited the car after Greg pulled into the driveway and opened the door for her. She thanked him for his time, and he got back into the car and drove away. She couldn't believe she was actually standing in front of Brady's house. She took a moment to relish that fact.

As she walked across the sidewalk up to the front door, she took in the smell of freshly cut lawn and pine that permeated the air. His house was far enough off the road that she could hear crickets and cicadas chirping in the woods, and the stars were bright with life overhead. The temperature had dropped some after nightfall, and a breeze blew in. She had an overwhelming feeling of peace, like the first night she had spent with Brady on the lake.

Liz removed the key from her bag, pushed it into the dead bolt, and unlocked the door. She turned the handle and pushed inward.

The foyer was lit overhead, revealing a giant staircase leading to the second floor. The entranceway was all hardwood floors leading off in three different directions. She closed the front door and took the opportunity to look around the house.

She could make out the outline of a square wooden dining room table off to the left. The room to the right had sliding double doors that led into a library, with an oversize wooden desk taking up the majority of one wall. The bay window was actually a small nook, with a cushion over the seat and bookshelves underneath. She stared all around at the books and wondered whether he had actually read all of them. Where would he find the time?

She backed out of the office and walked into the living room. Dim lighting cast shadows up into the high vaulted ceilings. The living room was nearly the length of the house, save for the kitchen, which she could just make out in the dark. The room was well furnished, and a giant area rug covered the center of the room. Glass doors led out to a back deck used for grilling, and beyond that were trees as far as she could see in the darkness.

Liz wondered whether she should go upstairs. It felt kind of nosy to snoop around his place. She knew that he had given her the key, but this was different from the lake house. This place had Brady written all over it. The house even smelled like him.

Deciding she couldn't help herself, she picked her dress up in one hand and wandered up the stairs. She opened up two guest rooms before locating the master suite. The room was so Brady she had to stop and stare all around her. Navy blue and tan accented the dark hardwood furniture. A picture of the lake house was framed on one wall, and an oil painting of a sailboat on stretched canvas was mounted over his bed. Along a waist-high dresser stood a collage of picture frames. She bent down and examined them, finding some as old as pictures of him and Clay as babies, one with Brady holding what must have been a baby Savannah in his arms with Clay pretending to punch him in the ribs, and some as recent as his college graduation and election to the State Senate. It was like a picture catalog of his life, and it made her smile. She hadn't seen any pictures at the lake house.

Liz tore her eyes away from the pictures and walked over to the tall bed. She ran her hands along the comforter, knowing it was down and likely very expensive, and on the right side of the bed was a note sitting on top of a pillow. She held in her giggle as she took it in her hands, flipped it open, and read the contents.

Baby, it's good to finally have you here.
—B

Liz bit her lip and smiled. He had planned the whole thing out. He would have had to plant this note before he left for the night, which meant he had been intending to give her a key and bring her back here all along.

It still didn't make it okay that he had brought someone else to the gala . . . especially when he hadn't told her about it. But it sure lessened the blow, knowing this was all for her.

Liz removed her constricting dress, located one of his white button-downs, and pulled it on over her head. She hung the dress in his walk-in closet that was full of expensive suits, dress shirts, and ties. Then she wandered back downstairs to wait for Brady.

The sound of the garage door opening made Liz jump up from the couch. She hadn't been sleeping; she had been much too alert for that. But she hadn't known when Brady was going to be back, and waiting had made her antsy.

Liz lounged back on the couch, not wanting to look flustered, and popped one of her knees up. She took a deep breath.

A door off of the foyer opened and closed, and she heard footsteps approach the living room. Brady was shrugging out of his tuxedo jacket when he stepped through the archway. A smile broke out on her face at the sight of him.

His eyes landed on her, and he smirked. "Nice shirt."

She extended her long, lean legs out on the couch toward him and tugged lightly on the material. "Thanks. I think it's a little big."

Brady slung his jacket on the arm of the couch, kicked off his polished shoes, and loosened the bow tie at his neck. "I heard you had another chat with my brother," Brady said, unbuttoning the top button of his shirt and sliding his hands into his pockets.

Liz shrugged and stretched her arms overhead. Was this really the time to talk about this? "He was outside when I was leaving."

"And you decided to give him your phone number?" he asked, his eyes staring intently at her.

"Decided is the wrong word," she told him, propping herself up on her elbows. She had left the top two buttons undone, and cleavage peeked out from her change in position. His eyes dropped to her chest. "I would use coerced. But either way it was only because your driver was about to pull up. I thought it would be better to give him the number and have him leave me alone than have him watch me get into your car. Was I wrong?" She stared up at him through her thick, dark lashes.

"You weren't wrong," he said, "but why does he now know you as Liz Carmichael?"

Liz furrowed her brow. Carmichael. Clay shouldn't know that name. Then it came back to her. "The valet called me Ms. Carmichael," she told him.

Brady tsked and walked forward to sit next to her on the couch. He ran his hands up her thighs with an urgency that said he had wanted to do it all night. He stopped at the edge of her shirt.

"That's supposed to be my name for you," he said, lowering his lips to kiss across her thighs.

"Only for you," she whispered, her chest rising and falling. Her body was heating from his skilled touch. "Are you still angry with me?" Her voice came out hoarse and strained.

"Very," he growled, nipping her leg.

She squeaked as her whole body tensed. "Are you going to forgive me?"

"I'll let you make it up to me."

Brady lifted her shirt from her thighs, scooted it out from under her butt, and then pulled it over her head. He tossed it to the ground and smiled down at her. She hadn't been able to wear a bra with her backless dress, so she was bare before him besides her cream lace thong. "I wanted to take you out of your dress all night."

"You should have," she told him. She watched as he straightened and made quick work of unbuttoning his shirt. "In the bathroom."

"If you hadn't fought me off, baby, I would have had you bent over the sink and taken you right then and there," he said, removing his remaining clothes.

She stared up at him completely naked before her and swallowed. She could never get enough of that body, and he was always so . . . ready for her. She wanted him now. Her eyes traveled the length of him, and she flushed as she thought about all the things he had done to her. Her memory was serving her better than her imagination in that instant.

His hands raked her underwear to the ground, leaving both of them bare. He moved on top of her, settling between her thighs.

"And I'm ready to take you now," he told her before easing forward inside of her. She cried out as he filled her, and tossed her head back onto the pillow. "Just try not to wake the neighbors, baby."

Brady started a slow, sensual rhythm, gliding in and out of her with enough force to push her toward the edge, but not fast enough to get her there. He held her head in his hands and kissed across her cheek to her lips. Their breathing mingled in heated, intoxicating kisses that only increased the passion growing between them.

Her body grew warmer with each passing minute, and she tugged lightly on his hair. He groaned into her mouth as her walls tightened all around him, and he plunged deeper. She pulled her feet off of the couch and wrapped her legs around his waist, which tilted her hips up to him. He used the added leverage to pump faster into her.

"God you feel good, baby," he groaned against her lips.

She nibbled across his bottom lip and sucked it into her mouth playfully. He moaned gruffly when she released him and dropped his head down to her ear, where he returned the favor. She felt her breath coming out in spurts as he continued to drive deeper into her.

"Make me come, Brady," she whispered desperately, feeling the waves of her orgasm tease at the edge of her body. She was getting close, so close, and she wanted him to get there with her. She just wanted to wrap her arms and legs around him and never let the moment fade away. If only they could stay here, like this, forever. Cut through all the misunderstandings and miscommunication, and get to the foundation of it all.

She didn't ever want to let him go.

And then he pushed her to climax. He grunted and released at the same time, burying himself deep inside of her.

"Fuck," he muttered. "Whatever you did at the end." He took a second to breathe. "Amazing, Liz. You're amazing."

She kissed his breathless lips and nodded. She wanted to tell him. She wanted to tell him everything she was feeling and more in that moment.

But he just sighed, nuzzled into her shoulder, and let his breathing even out. She heard him whisper one more time, "You're amazing, Liz," as he held her close.

She couldn't break the moment, not for anything, not even something this important . . . not even to tell him she loved him.

Chapter 23
JUST TELL ME

Liz shrugged Brady's button-down back on, and he pulled a pair of loose basketball shorts out of a gym bag in the hall closet. He slid into the shorts and padded into the kitchen. He pressed a few buttons on the wall and soft music filtered in through hidden speakers.

Brady opened the refrigerator and rummaged through the contents. "I'm starving. Are you hungry?"

She yawned and got to her feet. "I think I'm all right."

"What about some wine? I have a couple bottles of red," he told her.

"Sure. I could go for some wine. What do you have?"

"I think this is a Pinot Noir," he said, holding a bottle up. "That okay with you?"

She walked a few feet forward to examine the bottle. "Perfect."

"You know, I think I could get used to the idea of coming home to you in my shirt, lying practically naked on my couch," he said as he uncorked the wine bottle and poured them each a glass.

Liz's heart stopped. Was he serious? She swallowed back her confusion about where they stood and accepted the statement for what it was.

"I would lie on that couch just waiting for you to come home and fuck me," she said, stretching her arms over her head and letting his shirt ride up her thighs.

He walked a glass over to her. "You keep talking like that and I'm going to have to fuck you again."

Liz took a glass out of his hand and tilted her head up to kiss him on the mouth.

"What the fuck is *this*, Brady?" someone practically screeched from the entranceway.

Liz broke away from Brady, and they both snapped their heads to the side. Heather was standing in the open doorway, wearing a black pantsuit and shooting daggers at them. Liz's mouth hung open and she pulled Brady's shirt down farther to try for some decency.

"What the fuck are you doing here, Heather?" Brady demanded, fury being an understatement. He pushed Liz behind him, but it was well past too late for Heather not to notice.

"The fucking door was open and I had some really important news for you. You weren't answering your phone, so I came over in person, but apparently you were too busy fucking . . ." Heather shook her head in utter disbelief and red-hot anger. "Too busy fucking some college reporter to do your damn job!"

Brady shook his head and clenched his fists. "I don't need to hear this shit from you. Just get in my fucking office, and I'll be there in a minute."

"Are you kidding me right now?" Heather yelled. "Do you know what this could do to you?"

"Heather!" he shouted, losing it completely. Liz jumped in surprise.

Heather stood up straighter, caught off guard by his outburst. Liz had never seen Brady look so angry before, and judging by Heather's reaction, she hadn't either.

"I will deal with you in a minute," he growled.

"I'm going to get Elliott from the car," Heather said, her eyes spitting fireballs at him. "He will talk some fucking sense into you."

"Elliott is here, too?" Brady asked, his hands shaking with anger.

"Yes, and he deserves to know what shit you're getting into, if we're to salvage any of this." She turned on her heel and walked out.

Brady turned around as soon as the door slammed shut and wrapped Liz up in a hug.

"I'm so sorry. I'm so sorry."

He said it over and over again, as if he was trying to convince himself as much as her.

"Are you okay?" he asked, drawing back to look at her.

All she saw in those big brown eyes was concern, not the anger he had spat at Heather, or the hunger he normally showed her, or the campaign mask, or the hardness he conveyed on the outside. Nothing she expected . . . just fear. What could he be afraid of?

"I'm okay," she said softly, taking his hands in hers.

They were still shaking. She knew what had just happened. Their cover had been blown. Brady was going to withdraw from her. Tonight was their last night. She knew it just by looking at him. And yet she was more concerned with comforting him than worrying about that.

"Are you going to be okay?" Liz asked, sliding her hands up his chest and running her hand along his jaw. She stood on her tiptoes and kissed his soft lips. It felt like good-bye.

"Let me deal with Heather and Elliott, okay? Don't go anywhere," he pleaded. She wasn't sure how he expected her to go anywhere when she didn't have a car, but she wasn't planning on leaving him alone.

"I won't. I'll be here, Brady," she said softly, trying to stay strong for him. "But what does this mean?"

"Don't worry." He kissed her hard. "Nothing is going to happen to us. I'm going to deal with it."

"Brady," she said, knowing that couldn't possibly be the case.

"Baby, stop," he said, clutching on to her. "I can't handle this with all of those questions in your eyes. Just trust me."

Liz nodded slowly. "Okay. I trust you," she whispered as the front door banged open again.

Brady pulled away from her with a soft smile. "I'll be right back."

Liz watched him walk away from her as Heather entered with the short, beady-eyed guy Liz had seen following her around the past couple months. He must be Elliott . . . whoever Elliott was. Neither of them looked pleased.

Brady slid the office door open, and Heather and Elliott walked inside. Elliott shot one nasty look in her direction before passing Brady.

Liz sighed. Great. She was the bad guy in this.

Brady followed behind them and slammed the door shut with such ferocity it hit against the other door and popped back open.

She heard voices from the other room, which had to mean that they were yelling at one another. She glanced around and wondered whether she should put her dress back on and get ready to go. She was certain that by the end of this conversation, she would be saying good-bye to Brady and someone would be driving her home.

Liz tiptoed forward toward the door. She would rather hear everything that was being said than wait for Brady to tell her the sad news. What could be the worst thing that could happen if she got caught—she couldn't see him anymore? That was already a real possibility.

Liz tried not to make a sound as she peered through the small opening in the door and listened in on their conversation.

"How long has this been going on, anyway?" Heather demanded. She was standing in front of the bay window, her arms crossed over her chest, leveling a hard stare at Brady.

"I don't see how that is relevant information," Brady growled.

"You've been off your game, Brady. Don't think we haven't noticed," she said immediately. "Has it been going on all summer? Is this why we made that stupid appearance on campus? Because if you changed my fucking travel schedule for your little fuck buddy, I'm going to . . ."

"What?" Brady yelled. "What are you going to do if I changed anything for her?"

"Be fucking pissed off!" she yelled back.

"This is getting us nowhere," Elliott said, placing his hand on Heather's arm in an attempt to calm her down.

"He's ruining everything, Elliott," Heather grumbled. She turned away from them both. "I thought we were all in this together."

"I'm not ruining anything. You're blowing this out of proportion," Brady said.

Liz gave a sharp intake of breath. She hoped it wasn't heard from the other room, because Brady had surprised her. She couldn't tell whether he was defending their relationship or simply saying that this hadn't leaked to the press yet, so the campaign was still safe. Either way it was surprising. She felt as if everything was ruined.

"I'm blowing this out of proportion," Heather said, whirling back around. "Are you out of your goddamn mind? You are sleeping with a college reporter, for Christ's sake. Have you even read her terrible articles? Do you even care what she thinks of you? I read *everything* out there. It's in fucking print that she thinks you're a joke. Don't come at me with some *I want some pussy* remark and expect me to take this lightly."

"Really, Heather? How long have we been working together? Have I ever been the guy to jump at some random pussy? Honestly?" Brady asked, his voice cold and hard.

"Both of you stop it," Elliott said, standing between them. "As your lawyer, I strongly encourage you to reconsider your position and calm down."

His lawyer. *Well, that makes more sense. He is skeezy enough for the job*, Liz thought.

Brady took a few steps away from them, placed his hands on a shelf, and took several deep breaths until his hands stopped shaking. "Fine," he said finally. "What are you guys doing here anyway? It's the middle of the night."

"Yates dropped out," Elliott told him.

Liz's mouth popped open. One of the competitors in the primary had dropped out of the race. That meant Brady had only one other opponent, Charles Hardy. This significantly increased Brady's chances of winning. Hardy was a seasoned politician, but he didn't have the financial backing, the charisma, or the name that Brady had.

"He dropped?" Brady asked, stunned by the new development.

"Yes, we drove all the way over here, because you weren't answering your phone. We thought you would be interested to know what your competition looks like," Heather told him. "It's a different ball field with only one other guy. That makes it a horse race. We can win a horse race, Brady. We can win." She whispered the last phrase as if she wasn't sure he understood what it meant. This clearly meant a lot to her too.

"What does Alex think?" Brady asked, his voice betraying how hopeful he was about the outcome.

Liz had heard Brady mention Alex, his campaign manager, before. He didn't like to talk about him or really anything about the campaign much when they were together, but she had gathered that Alex was a strategy man. He preferred to work behind the scenes and let Brady and Heather take the front on anything in the spotlight.

Heather glanced at Elliott and he nodded. "He said it's a go. You push hard the next couple weeks . . . and I mean hard, Brady, not what you've been doing all summer. If you do that, you have it in the bag, and Alex knows his shit," Heather said.

"Then I'll do it," Brady said simply, like it was the easiest decision he had ever made. "I'll do whatever it takes to win. You both know that."

"Then you're going to have to get rid of the girl," Heather said plainly.

"Heather," Brady growled.

"I'm afraid I have to agree with her. Even if she hadn't written those articles about you, she wouldn't be an ideal choice. She's too young, and she's still in school. Brady, you need someone who makes you look electable, not someone who makes you look like you're robbing the cradle," Elliott piped in.

Liz felt as if she had been punched in the gut. Well, there it was all laid out before her. She was too young and didn't make him look electable, aside from her slamming articles.

"Are you fucking kidding me right now?" Brady asked, shaking his head.

"Brady, you want to win. So stop fucking around," Heather cried. "This election is important."

"Don't you think I know that?" he yelled back at her. "Why does everyone think that I've forgotten? I've been giving everything I have to this campaign, and I've been doing it for a long time now. I know what's at stake, all right?"

"Then you'll get rid of her?" Elliott asked, lacking any compassion in his voice.

Liz felt as if she were sitting with her head resting under the guillotine, waiting for the blade to slice down. It was over. Both of them had told him it was done. That was that.

She couldn't even breathe. She had to hear him say it. She had to listen to him agree even if it would break her.

"No," he said softly, his anger tightly controlled.

Liz wasn't even sure she heard him right, her heart was beating so loudly in her ears.

"What?" Heather and Elliott blurted out at the same time.

"She's not going anywhere," he said, meeting their gazes head-on.

Liz stood very, very still. Was he . . . No, she couldn't have heard him right . . .

Heather rolled her eyes to the ceiling. "Oh, please, you're not going to risk everything for her."

"You're being irrational, Brady," Elliott said.

"I fucking love her, okay?" he yelled back at them without any restraint. "So she's not going anywhere . . . I love her."

Liz stumbled backward away from the door she had been peering through. Her body tumbled forward through the entranceway to the living room, and she collapsed onto the couch, panting. Her mind was whirling all around her, and her hands were shaking.

Oh my God. Oh my God. Oh my God, she thought over and over again.

He loved her. Brady loved her. He had told them no. She couldn't comprehend all of this right now. She just couldn't.

He had never told her that he felt that way. She couldn't have even guessed that he would feel that way. Her heart was fluttering all over the place, and she half felt as if she might throw up.

What would she say if he told her? What was he going to say when he came back out of that room? She couldn't let him know that she had heard. She had to pretend she hadn't. He hadn't wanted her to eavesdrop. She had thought it was because he was going to give up on her, but it was actually because he loved her. She couldn't even think the word without stumbling over it.

Liz heard the voice grow louder and the sound of the doors sliding open. She tried to calm down by breathing slowly and steadily, but she wasn't sure if it was working. Would he know that she had heard him or would he assume she was freaked out? Because she was really freaked out.

The front door opened and closed a second later, and then Brady appeared again in the living room. The anger was gone from his face, but she wasn't sure what it was replaced by. She usually could read him so well, but it was different now. He loved her.

"You're still here," he said softly, walking over and taking a seat next to Liz on the couch.

"I told you I wasn't leaving," she murmured, her voice shaking. She couldn't keep it steady, and she knew it made her sound scared.

"Hey," he said, reaching out and taking one of her trembling hands in his, "you're not going anywhere."

"What did they say?" she managed to get out.

"A lot of bullshit, but we got it worked out. Ted Yates dropped out of the race. I have a pretty busy month ahead of me leading up to the primary," he told her.

"He dropped out?" she asked, hoping she sounded surprised.

"Yeah, you'll hear about it tomorrow. I have a press conference at eight in the morning."

Their conversation stalled and she waited for him to say something. She didn't expect him to blurt out how he felt, but she was waiting for something . . . anything.

She asked the inevitable question. "What are we going to do now that they know, Brady?"

He paused before looking up into her eyes. She saw it then, what she hadn't been able to figure out before. Holy shit! He loved her. He actually did. She swallowed hard and tried not to cry.

"Nothing is going to change, baby," he said, reaching out and running his hand across her cheek. "They want me to win, so they're going to make sure it doesn't get out."

"Oh," she said softly, tears pooling in her eyes despite her best effort.

"Hey. Hey," he said, brushing a tear off her cheek. "Don't cry. We'll be okay. We'll make it through."

She nodded and closed her eyes. So they were going to do the same thing? He loved her and they were going to continue to hide?

"I can't believe they're allowing that. I thought you always said that you would choose the campaign first." She couldn't help throwing his words back at him. She wanted him to *tell* her that he loved her. She wanted his confession to be to her, not to Heather and Elliott.

"I'm choosing both. They don't get the choice," he told her, bringing his lips down and kissing her tenderly.

They broke apart, and Liz looked up into his eyes, wondering what he was thinking. Did he think that they could hide forever? She couldn't be the girl on the side the whole time. He loved her. She wanted to be out in the open with him so badly it pained her. But she couldn't bring herself to say it. She couldn't ruin their moment.

"I'm going to be so busy, and they're worried about me having enough time for everything. I think we should lie low for a little while," he told her.

"Lie low," she said hollowly. What had they been doing?

"I want to keep you in my life, but I have responsibilities to the campaign."

"The campaign," she said. She felt like a broken record, repeating his words back to him.

"I don't think I'll be able to see you as much in the next month as I have. I still want to see you every chance I get, but I have a real shot of winning."

"You're going to win," she told him openly for the first time. She had known all along, but she had never expressed her opinion.

He smiled then. "I hope so. I want to be as sure I'm going to win as you are," he said, then kissed her again. "You know I don't want to take time away from you, Liz."

She waited for it. He had to say it. It was on the tip of his tongue.

"But this is a priority . . ."

"A priority," she said, still reeling. He wasn't going to say it. She could feel it. He wasn't going to tell her.

"Liz," he pleaded, forcing her to look at him fully, "please, tell me you understand. I need to get through the campaign."

She snapped out of it and nodded. "I understand. We're just going to stay the way we are," she whispered.

Stay hidden, she thought sadly to herself.

"Lie low. I can do that," she continued. "I was thinking of going to visit my friend in D.C. next weekend anyway. Then you won't even have to think about it for a couple days. Give everyone some time to cool off."

"D.C.? I didn't know you were going to do that," he responded quickly.

"My friend asked me before school let out. I wasn't sure if I was going to have time to get away, but school ends this week and you . . . well, you're busy," she said softly, staring down at her hands.

"As much as I don't want you to go anywhere, that might be a good idea for the weekend. Who knows what Heather will have me doing this week after our blowout," he said with a chuckle. Liz couldn't even manage one. "I'm going to miss you while you're gone."

"I'm going to miss you too," she said.

He pulled her over into his lap and she wrapped her arms around his neck. "Baby," he said.

"Yeah," Liz murmured, hoping that he would tell her how he really felt.

"We still have the rest of the night together, at least."

"Then we should use our time wisely," she whispered.

"Yes, we should," he said, hoisting her into his arms and carrying her upstairs.

Chapter 24
INTRODUCTIONS

Driving five hours to D.C. didn't sound like a long time in the abstract. But once Liz actually got out onto I-85 it felt interminable. She couldn't believe she was actually going. After everything that had happened and everything that had changed this summer, she was still driving out to see Hayden for the weekend.

She hadn't seen Brady since the night of his fund-raising gala. She hadn't expected to either. They were even more on the downlow, thanks to Heather and Elliott's interference. It made her sigh all over again just thinking about that night. She hadn't thought they could get much more secretive than they had been before, but she was wrong. He had called only once, and that was to tell her that he was going to be too busy to talk the rest of the week. She figured that meant she wasn't supposed to call him either.

Sandy Carmichael would have to be tucked away for the weekend, and Liz would have to try to enjoy herself. She would have to be content knowing the man who loved her couldn't contact her, and that she wouldn't be able to see him until he could see her. They were back at square one.

It was as if they were starting all over again. But now their emotions were much stronger, and so it hurt fifty thousand times more. She couldn't even think about it without her heart constricting, her stomach doing a belly flop, and her throat closing up. She had cried too much recently, thinking about Brady, how he had stuck up for her, that he loved her, that he hadn't told her, that they couldn't be together. She was determined not to cry on this trip.

Liz pulled off of the interstate headed straight for downtown D.C. She and Hayden had decided that she would pick him up after work on Thursday, and he had gotten permission to take the rest of the weekend off. He said even though they all technically had the weekends off, everyone still came in and worked extra hours because there was too much to do. He had even asked not to be on call. He certainly sounded like an overworked intern, but at least he was getting paid.

She followed the directions on her GPS through town and turned off into a parking lot in front of Hayden's building. She cut the engine and sent him a text letting him know that she was here. She was a couple minutes early: Everyone she knew from the area had said northern Virginia had the worst drivers imaginable, so she had built in some traffic time, but there hadn't been as much traffic as she had thought.

Just come inside. I'll come get you. I have some last-minute things to close up, Hayden messaged back.

Liz shrugged and got out of the car. She had dressed comfortably for the trip and wished now that she had put on something cuter. She didn't want to walk inside that building where everyone was in suits and heels without her own heels. She thought about pulling a pair out of her bag, but decided it would look ridiculous paired with her teal cuffed shorts and loose white spaghetti strap top. Her hair was down in waves, because there was no way she was straightening it in this humidity, and she had on light makeup.

She walked across the blacktop parking lot and into the glass building that Hayden worked in. The lobby was immaculate, with marble floors and a large, hard wooden desk. A security guard stood on either side of the desk, and a receptionist sat answering phones in a very professional business suit and tie.

"Hold, please," the man said into the phone, then looked up at Liz. "Can I help you?"

"I'm here to see Hayden Lane," she told him, wringing her hands in front of her body. She didn't know why she was so anxious. She had known Hayden for two years. They had worked together at the paper, and they had been friends the whole time. So she'd had a small crush on him; that didn't mean she had to freak herself out before she even saw him. It was just Hayden.

"I'll let him know. What's your name?" he asked.

She actually had to think about it before answering. "Liz Dougherty," she said softly. All summer she had gone by Sandy Carmichael, so it felt a bit odd to give her real name.

"One moment," he said before pressing a button and holding the receiver to his ear. "A Miss Liz Dougherty here for Hayden. Great. Thank you." He smiled up at Liz. "He's on his way. Feel free to take a seat."

"Thank you," she said. He was already switching back over to the other line to finish his conversation.

Liz took a few steps away from the counter and sat down in the small waiting area. She couldn't get over how weird it felt to be just Liz Dougherty again. It was almost too easy to assume a new identity. She felt lost in the deception and appeal of shrugging off the cares of her world, and now she was rebounding back to plain, average life. It was a bit disorienting.

"Liz," Hayden called, walking out through a side door and

toward her with a big smile on his face. Liz stood quickly and pulled her shorts down to a decent length.

Hayden looked exactly how she remembered except he wasn't in his normal shorts and polo combo. He had on a gray suit with a green shirt and striped tie. His medium brown hair was tousled, as if he had been running his hands through it while working. It was a bit shorter than she was used to. He usually kept it long enough for the curls to start peeking out around his ears, but apparently the Hill had cleaned him up. His hazel eyes were closer to a green color than normal as they reflected his attire.

"Hey, Hayden," she said, walking to meet him halfway.

"Good to see you. How was the trip?" he asked, leaning forward and giving her a hug. She wrapped her arms around him briefly and then they broke apart.

"It was an easy drive," she told him as he continued to smile down at her.

"I'm glad to hear that. Come on back with me. I have one more thing to finish up and then I can introduce you around. Sound good?"

Liz nodded. "Sounds great."

Introductions. How many of those had she had this summer? She could think of one—Chris. She sighed and tried not to think about Brady. It was too complicated and would only frustrate her further.

Hayden held the door for her as she walked into a long hallway. He motioned her toward the elevator and scanned his security card. The door dinged open and they walked inside. He pressed the button for his floor and the elevator shot up.

Liz stood there in silence, wondering what it was going to be like in his office. She half expected it to be a madhouse, but then she also kind of thought it might be like Hayden—calm and controlled. He was efficient, and while the university press was different from a press office, he had always run it so smoothly. It had its moments of insanity, but Hayden tended to keep things under wraps.

What she found when they exited the elevator was much closer to mayhem. The room was covered in desks that were all pushed together and covered in monitors, computers, coffee cups, and hundreds of random pieces of paper. People were running around in a bigger hurry than was likely necessary; some were yelling into phones, and others were milling around chatting with colleagues. It should have been a terrifying sight, but it only excited her. This was what she wanted in her life.

"Come on," he said, walking down the busy hallway. He turned about halfway and stopped at a small desk way neater than any of the surrounding desks. He was possibly the tidiest person she knew. She made a mental note to clean his office before he came back to school. The thought of being with Brady on top of Hayden's desk at the paper made her blush. She needed to get her head on straight.

"Have a seat. I have to copy this stuff and turn it in to my boss before I go," he said, taking a neat stack of papers off of his desk. "I'll be right back."

"All right," she said, sitting down in his chair. She watched the general commotion in the office. It reminded her of the school paper, but with a different kind of hierarchy. She liked the hum of the room and the general sense of urgency. She could fit in here.

Liz turned back to Hayden's desk and examined the area. His Post-its were color-coordinated based on the topic he was working on, and that made her giggle. She wished she was that organized with her stories, but they kind of came out of stream of consciousness.

He had pictures of him with his parents and what looked like his sister. Liz had never met her, but she knew that she was older and had gone to college out of state. There wasn't much else on the desk aside from a few crumpled papers with numbers on them. He must have still been running, because they looked like old marathon race numbers. It wouldn't surprise Liz in the least if he was working sixty-hour weeks and made time to run marathons.

She looked through the collage of newspaper articles he had pinned to a corkboard behind the pictures. She found a few were his from the school press, a few were from other reporters, and one was from . . . her. Liz stared, surprised. It was the article she had written most recently for the paper; the one Hayden had given her the suggestion for. He had one line highlighted in bright yellow that made her smile grow. It was her favorite line too.

> *In an endless sea of overindulgence, find time to indulge in something worthwhile and make an informed, educated decision for yourself. What matters to you in here, will matter to you out there.*

Liz smiled to herself. She liked that he had enjoyed the article enough to post it up where anyone could see it.

"All finished!" Hayden said, rushing back to his desk. "I knew that wouldn't take too long. Want to meet my friends before we head out, or are you beat?" He slung a messenger bag over his head and smiled brightly at her. She had forgotten how much Hayden always smiled. It had been her favorite part of coming into work. Even when she had been exhausted and irritable, he was there smiling away and brightening everyone's day.

"I'd love to meet your friends. Lead the way," she told him.

They walked around the corner and stopped in front of two side-by-side desks. Two guys in suits were seated in front of their computers. They looked as if they were intent on their work, but as she looked more closely she saw they were actually chatting online and playing some video game. Liz shook her head. Men!

"Phillip! Topher!" Hayden said, clapping one of the guys on the back. "Y'all, this is Liz."

They both looked up at once and said hi. One guy stood and introduced himself. "Topher," he said, extending his hand. Liz shook it. He was of average build and height, with really short curly brown hair and chipmunk cheeks.

The other guy she assumed to be Phillip stood next and shook her hand. He was exceedingly tall and skinny, with military-cut hair and crooked front teeth. "Nice to meet you," Phillip said.

"Nice to meet you too," Liz said with a smile.

"Glad you're finally here. Hayden has been talking about getting time off all summer. We were pretty tired of hearing about it," Topher said, crossing his arms over his chest and smirking.

Liz locked eyes with Hayden for a second and then she broke the look. He had been talking about her . . .

"Thanks for ratting me out," he said, chuckling softly. "We were heading out. Are you guys still good for drinks this weekend?"

"Definitely," Topher agreed.

"Depends," Phillip said, leaning in close to Hayden and raising his eyebrows. "Is Jamie coming out with you?"

Hayden groaned. "That's my sister, man."

"So, is that a yes?"

"You're sick."

"We'll see you out this weekend," Topher said, smacking the back of Phillip's head. "It was nice to meet you, Liz."

"You too," she said with a confident smile.

"Let's get out of here," Hayden said, glaring at Phillip, but Liz could see the humor in his eyes.

They left the building and walked out into the parking lot toward Liz's car. Hayden slid out of his jacket and tie before they even made it all the way to where she was parked.

"Do you want me to drive?" he asked. "I know a place we can

park your car near my sister's place. Then you don't have to try to navigate D.C. traffic."

"Um, yes!" she said immediately. "Please drive me back through that madness." She tossed him the keys and walked to the passenger side.

He laughed as he popped the door and sat down. "Geez, how short are you?" he asked as he adjusted the seat back for his long legs.

"You're just tall," Liz said with a shrug.

Hayden pulled out of the parking lot and started driving them away from the capital area. There was a surprising amount of traffic. Not that she was unfamiliar with traffic, but D.C. rush hour pretty much took the cake. Nearly forty-five minutes later, Hayden had the car parked in a street spot.

"This is as close as we're going to get. Is this okay with you?" he asked, putting the car into park.

"Absolutely not. I want to go back out in that terrible mess for another hour, please," Liz said with a laugh as she pushed her door open. "Get me out of here!"

"At least you weren't driving," Hayden said.

"A silver lining!" Liz opened the trunk, and Hayden reached in before she got a chance and pulled her suitcase out. He set it on the ground and rolled it behind him the whole way to the apartment, ignoring her objections.

They stopped in front of a brick building that looked like all of the other brick buildings it was attached to, but Hayden seemed to know where he was going. He pulled a key out of his pocket and let them in.

"Top floor," he told her, motioning up the stairs.

She walked up five exhaustingly long flights of stairs as Hayden walked behind her carrying her suitcase. She did *not* envy him. Huffing, Liz finally landed at the top floor. She dropped her hands to her knees and caught her breath. Hayden appeared next to her with his ever-present smile, not even breathing hard.

"How are you not dying? I feel ridiculous," she said, looking up at him.

"I run marathons," Hayden said with a shrug.

"I play tennis and I'm dying."

"Do you run up stairs while playing tennis?" he asked.

"Do you run up stairs in your marathons?" Liz straightened and looked up into his hazel eyes.

"Fair point. However, I do run over twenty-six miles."

"Shoot me," she said.

He tilted his head and smiled at her as if he was trying to hold back from saying something. She wasn't sure what it was, but his eyes were assessing her. Had she done something wrong?

"My place is down here," he said, pointing down the hall.

They reached the end of the hall and entered the apartment. It was homey, with a clear feminine touch. Paintings of various mediums—oil, acrylic, and watercolor—covered much of the wall space, nearly all of them unbelievably perfect depictions of landscapes with the occasional portrait and abstract thrown into the collection. The furniture was in all earth tones, and candles were on every table as well as the mantel of the fireplace. Liz instantly felt comfortable in the apartment.

"Is she here?" Liz heard a voice call from off in the other direction.

"Yeah, Jamie, come out of the studio," Hayden called back, placing Liz's suitcase off to the side and closing the door.

"Oh my God, hi!" Jamie said, rounding the corner draped in a paint-splattered apron. She looked nothing like Hayden, with a chin-length black bob with red highlights and long bangs that swept across her forehead and tucked behind her ear. She was shorter than Liz, with a naturally tiny frame. The one quality it seemed she and Hayden shared was her charismatic smile.

"Hey," Liz said as Jamie walked right up to her.

"I would totally hug you, but I can't guarantee you wouldn't get paint all over you!"

Liz laughed. "That's all right."

"I'm so glad you're here."

That was a common sentiment, it seemed. Topher and Phillip had said something similar, and now his sister was reiterating the same thing. How much had Hayden talked about her?

It was nice, though. As daunting as it was to come up to D.C., she liked at least getting the opportunity to *meet* people. She had hidden all summer and had forgotten how much she liked to spend time with other people.

"Hayden wasn't sure what you wanted for dinner, but he said he already knew that you liked Italian. I happen to make some kick-ass lasagna," Jamie said, bubbly and friendly. Liz couldn't have kept a smile from her face if she tried. "I hope you don't mind staying in to eat. We can go out if you want. I'm cool with that. Whatever y'all want! I just get super exhausted after driving for a long time and prefer to nap instead of going out. You might not be like that . . ."

"Jamie," Hayden said, shaking his head, "breathe."

Jamie rolled her eyes at him. "Sorry. So, what do you want to do?" she asked, bouncing up and down on the balls of her toes.

"Ignore her. I swear she gets hopped up on caffeine when she's in her studio," he said, nudging Liz.

"Whatever, Hayden. I'm being accommodating, and you're being an ass."

"Lasagna sounds great," Liz cut in, knowing a family brawl when she saw it. "Thank you."

"Great! I'll get started on that then," Jamie said, bounding back into her studio.

"I'm going to go change," Hayden told Liz. "You can bring your stuff into my room. We don't have a guest room, so I'm taking the couch."

"Oh no, I can take the couch. I don't mind," she told him quickly.

Hayden leveled a look at her that she had seen time and time again at the paper. She wasn't getting out of this. He reached forward and picked up her suitcase and started walking it back to his bedroom.

"You are *not* sleeping on the couch," he said. "You're a guest."

Liz shrugged and walked with him down the hallway. She glanced off to the right and saw Jamie's studio. It was a small bedroom covered in easels, canvas, and paint. The floor had a sheet of plastic over the carpet, and the walls were a strange array of colors from where paint had splashed. Jamie removed her apron as they passed.

"One of Jamie's roommates moved out for the summer, so I took over her bedroom. Otherwise I would have had to live in the suburbs with my parents. Really lucky, I'd say," Hayden told her as he opened his bedroom for her.

This was more what she expected from Hayden. The room was perfectly put together and sensible compared to his eccentric artist sister. A queen-sized bed sat in one corner with a green comforter and white pillows. A desk sat against one wall, and that was pretty much it as far as the room went. He clearly spent more time at the office than in his room. It looked more like a place you came home to to change and sleep.

Liz set her bag down in the corner as Hayden rummaged through his closet for clothes.

"I'll go change in the bathroom," he said, walking out. Liz had moved to his bed and taken a seat while she waited. It felt a bit strange to be sitting on Hayden's bed, in Hayden's apartment, hanging out with Hayden. She was sure this summer would be the most memorable she would ever experience. Brady . . . and now she was sitting on the bed of the guy she had liked for two years. Even if they were just friends, it was a bit bizarre.

He reappeared in the doorway in khaki shorts and a fitted T-shirt. "Thanks for coming out this weekend. I wasn't sure you were going to be able to make it."

"I wasn't sure either . . . what with school and everything," she said, not really wanting to get into the real reason. No, she was pretty sure she never wanted to tell him the real reason.

Hayden walked over and took a seat next to her, stretching back on the bed. "How is school going? You're finished with the semester, right? Did you get your grades back already?"

Liz turned to face him on the bed. She stared down at his lean runner's build all stretched out on display and tried not to blush. "This semester was surprisingly a challenge. Professor Mires really helped me do more with my project than I'd ever intended. Thank you so much for your good idea. I got an A on that article."

"Awesome. It was a really good one!" He cradled his hands behind his head.

"Thanks. Couldn't have done it without you."

"You would have come up with something," he said with an easy shrug, as if he'd never doubted it. "So, did you get an A in the class then?"

"I don't find out until Monday. I turned in one last paper this week. I haven't even published it to the paper yet. If I do well on it, then I might put it out there," she told him.

What she hadn't told him was that the paper she had turned in for her final assignment had been the idea given to her by Brady Maxwell. While she hadn't used it originally, she still thought it was a good suggestion, and had written and rewritten it too many times to count since she had published the article off of Hayden's idea. After spending that much time on it, she had decided to turn it in for her final paper to Professor Mires. She was proud of the work and thought it was the right move.

"Nice. You'll have to let me know how you do. Has the paper been good this summer? I know it was pretty dead, since no one is on campus, but did you think it was useful having your own column anyway?" he asked.

It felt like forever since she had talked about her work with anyone in person. It was a bit like opening the floodgates. She told him all about the paper: the people who were still there, the projects she had worked on, the story of what had happened with Justin. Hayden seemed legitimately interested in every detail. It didn't seem to be just because he missed the paper, which was obvious, but that he was interested in her more generally. And he couldn't know the most important thing that had happened to her that summer.

"Hey, you two," Jamie said, peeking her head into the doorway. "Meredith just got home, James is on his way over, and the lasagna is almost done. I'm opening a bottle of wine, if you guys want to venture out to the living room."

Liz looked down at her watch in surprise. Had they really been talking for more than an hour? Where had the time gone? It had been so long since Liz had seen Hayden. She was surprised how easy it was to talk to him.

Twenty minutes later, all five of them were seated around the dining room table. Jamie had lit half of the candles in the room and filled their glasses with red wine. The lasagna was to die for, and by the end of the meal, Liz felt a bit sloshy from the wine, but she also felt wonderfully comfortable with the entire group.

Jamie and James were pretty much the cutest couple in existence, and both more than welcoming to her. Meredith, Jamie's other roommate, worked as a yoga and Pilates instructor nearby and had a total mellow feel to her. Hayden seemed totally in his element, and they spent half of the dinner laughing at one another's comments. Liz didn't know whether it was the alcohol fueling it or the general good company, but she hadn't laughed this much in a long time.

They spent the next couple hours camped out in the living room discussing everything from American politics to French painters to the newest fad diet. The night flew by and soon James was convincing Jamie it was time to go to bed. The two of them and Meredith finally retreated to their respective rooms, leaving Liz and Hayden alone.

"We should probably get to bed if we're going to get up and walk around the city in the morning," Hayden said, standing. He reached his hand out to her and she took it, helping her to her feet. She was happy to find out that she wasn't that wobbly.

"Something is different about you," he said softly as they stood together.

Liz shrugged and smiled sweetly. "Same old me."

Hayden shook his head. "No. I can't put my finger on it, but it's different."

"Good different or bad different?" Liz asked.

"Just different. You were always pretty great."

"Well . . . thanks," she said, stepping around him. "I don't know what it is."

"Me either," Hayden said, his eyes following her.

"I'll see you in the morning," she said, trying to avoid his intense gaze.

"Good night, Liz."

Liz walked back to Hayden's bedroom and closed the door. She leaned her head back against it and let out a long breath.

She knew what had happened to her. Brady fucking Maxwell had happened to her.

Chapter 25
CRACKED OPEN

Hayden and Liz spent the next day walking around D.C. She had never been there before and wanted to go to every museum and monument they could get into. They walked around the Capitol building and managed to get a tour of the White House. They had alternated pretending to hold hands with George Washington in his portrait in the East Wing and had corralled a total stranger into taking a really great shot of them together in front of the building.

Their afternoon was spent inside the National Mall looking at dinosaur bones and walking through endless exhibits at the Smithsonian. The night was filled with dinner and drinks at a laidback tapas restaurant with Jamie and James. Hayden's friends had to stay late at the office and didn't know when they would be off, but had promised to meet them the next night.

That was all right with Liz. After spending all day walking in the summer heat, she was pretty tired. She would have to muster the energy to go out tomorrow. As it was she was ready to pass out from exhaustion.

Liz slept in pretty late the next morning, and then they went out to look at some of the monuments they had missed after spending all day at museums.

She was immediately regretting sleeping in when they got to the Lincoln Memorial and found it packed with people. Apparently families and summer camps made the Lincoln Memorial a regular afternoon stop. People were sitting by the Reflecting Pool eating lunch and covering the steps to the Memorial. They had to nudge past a couple massive groups to even make it all the way up the stairs.

"Guess we should have done this yesterday," Liz said, looking around the shoulder of a parent volunteer. She could see the statue, but it wasn't the most pleasant experience.

"Yeah, this is ridiculous," Hayden said, standing on the step below her.

"Seriously," Liz groaned. The woman standing in front of her had scooted over and blocked her view.

"Come on. Let's come back later." Hayden reached out for her elbow and tugged lightly.

"What? No, we don't have to do that. I don't mind," she said, not wanting to be an inconvenience. Hayden had already been here before; they didn't need to come back just for her if she could get a good enough look now.

"Nah, let's go. It's a better view at night anyway. You'd probably like it," he said. He directed her away from the mass of people.

"All right, if you're sure."

"Definitely. If you want to see it," he said over his shoulder, "then we'll come back."

They walked back down the crowded steps and along the path on one side of the Reflecting Pool. Liz was glad that she had on loose cotton clothing, because it was way too hot to be out in jeans, like some of the other tourists. Her hair was up in a tight ponytail, and she wished she had brought a hat with her to block out the sun beating down.

They passed the World War II Memorial and kept walking to the Washington Monument. The area around the Monument was as packed as the Lincoln Memorial, but luckily they didn't have to get close to see the giant obelisk rising to the heavens.

Passing the Smithsonian Institution again, Hayden chose a restaurant near the National Mall for lunch. It was a small burger joint and the only seating was outside. Hayden paid for both of them, and they carried their food to the empty table. The burgers were pretty incredible, not that she was hard to please. She wasn't sure if it was because of the heat or if they were really that good.

They finished their meal and were about to head back on the Metro, when Hayden stopped.

"Hey, I know one more place we need to go," he said, grabbing her hand and pulling her in the opposite direction. "It's right around the corner. Come on."

He set out at a quick jog, and Liz followed, laughing. "Why are we running?"

"I can't believe I forgot to show you," he said. "I didn't even think about it."

They turned the corner and walked right up to a giant building. Hayden never released her hand the whole time. She was about to extract it from his grasp, when she looked up at the building and saw that it read Newseum on the side. Liz stared forward with awe. It was a building dedicated to newspapers.

"How could you forget this?" she murmured.

"I don't know. But they have the front page of the main newspaper from every state displayed outside, as well as from several different countries," Hayden told her.

They walked and stood before the newspapers all displayed in glass cases in alphabetical order by state. It was pretty incredible to witness. She recognized the majority of the papers, but seeing them all out on display made her happy. One day she wanted to be working at one of these papers.

They stopped in front of North Carolina, and when Hayden saw the front page he had to laugh, because he knew the reporter who had the main story. She felt him circle his thumb against her hand, and she tensed.

She wanted to say that she didn't like it, and that she wished she weren't standing there with Hayden holding her hand, but it would be a lie. The whole moment felt a bit too perfect, and yet so different at the same time.

Here she was completely out in the open in the middle of the day holding a guy's hand. It didn't have to be Hayden; it could be anyone, because it wasn't Brady. She could never have this with Brady.

And at that moment, it wasn't Brady versus Hayden . . . not by a long shot. It was Brady versus *not* Brady, and Hayden happened to be providing the one thing she wanted from the one person she couldn't have it from.

She sighed, hating her heavy thoughts. She had come to D.C. to escape for a little while, and she didn't want to think about all of the confusion that came with her secret life. Regardless, she removed her hand from Hayden's and leaned forward against the glass to point at something. She didn't want to make it too obvious and hoped he didn't think anything of it . . . or try again.

"Did you want to go inside?" he asked, pointing at the museum. "We might still have time."

Liz checked her watch and saw how late it was. "I do, but if we're going to go out tonight, I don't think it's feasible."

"We can go out a little later if you want to see it," he suggested. "I don't mind."

Liz bit her lip and looked up at the building. She did want to go inside. It was such an unbelievable surprise . . . as if he knew just the right thing to make up for the Lincoln Memorial.

"All right. You convinced me."

Hayden's face lit up. He grabbed her hand again, and she let him direct her into the Newseum, where they spent much longer than they should have perusing every aspect of the museum dedicated to journalism.

—

Hayden and Liz met Phillip and Topher out at a bar near George Washington University. The guys went to school there and had a bunch of friends who lived in the area.

The bar was located off of Pennsylvania Avenue with a giant sign over the top of the entrance. When they entered, the room was already pretty packed full of college students and young professionals working on the Hill. The room was all hardwood floors, dark wooden bars stocked with liquor, and a large staircase leading to a second floor. Girls in low-cut tank tops and miniskirts served drinks. Grinding hip-hop beats blasted from the speakers, and people dancing in the center of the room took up the majority of the space.

Liz had dressed up for the occasion in a short mint summer dress. It had thin spaghetti straps that ended in a scoop neck with a wrap look from the waist down. She had paired it with nude high heels and a long, thin silver necklace with an owl pendant at the end. Her hair was down despite the temperature, and she was already wondering if that was a bad idea.

They found Phillip and Topher having zero luck talking to a group of girls by the bar.

"Hey, y'all," Hayden said, approaching his friends.

"Lane," Topher said with a brief nod in their direction before returning to his conversation with the girl.

Phillip turned and then acted as if he was trying to see behind them. "Where's Jamie?" he asked, raising his eyebrows.

"She's not here," Hayden said, shaking his head.

"What? Why not? I thought you said she was coming."

"She'll be here later," Liz told him, saving Hayden from having to say it. "She's meeting up with some friends first."

"Ugh! Let's get drinks before he starts talking about her." Hayden slid his hand around her waist and guided her toward an open space at the bar.

One of the perky blond bartenders came over to get their order. She smiled brightly at Hayden and gave him sex eyes. Liz wondered whether that was how she earned her tips or if it was specifically for Hayden.

He looked good tonight in navy shorts with a gray-and-white striped button-down, a thick brown belt, and matching brown Sperrys. Laid-back preppy, like normal. She couldn't imagine him any other way.

"Whiskey sour, right?" Hayden asked Liz, still not moving his hand from the small of her back.

How did he remember that? she wondered.

"Perfect. Thanks," Liz responded. She leaned her elbows against the bar.

"A whiskey sour and a Maker's and Coke," Hayden ordered. He handed the bartender his credit card. "You can leave it open."

"Sure thing," the bartender said, winking at him.

Hayden turned his attention back to Liz as the girl started making their drinks. "I'm really glad you decided to come visit this weekend," he said with that same smile. His hazel eyes were dark in the dim lighting as they looked down at her.

"Me too. I've had a really good time. It was nice to get away," Liz said with a sigh.

"You wanted to get away from your amazing summer to spend a few days with some random guy, you know," he said, blowing it off as if it was nothing.

"Yeah, just *some* guy," she said, rolling her eyes. "I'd never even met him before or anything."

"Nope. You're a bit of a stalker, Liz."

"Oh, you know, it's what I do in my spare time. Actually, it's kind of my job. I don't know if you know, but I'm a big-time reporter."

Hayden fake-gasped. "I had no clue."

"Here you go, hon," the bartender said, reappearing with their drinks and sliding them across the bar. "Anything else?"

Topher and Phillip appeared behind Hayden at that moment. Phillip shoved Hayden out of the way and into Liz, who grabbed onto him quickly.

"Guys, watch what you're doing!" Hayden called.

Liz's body was flush against Hayden's, and when he looked down at her, she blushed and pulled away.

"We're going to need," Phillip said, and started counting the people, "six shots of SoCo. Got to do it right for my buddy from the Carolinas."

"There are only four of us," Hayden observed.

Topher nudged Hayden; he had his arms slung over the shoulders of two girls. "Meet Anne and Abigail."

Liz shook her head at the display. The girls barely acknowledged them. Liz started making a bet with herself on how fast these girls would ditch them after they took the shots.

"Six shots of SoCo," Phillip said, passing around glasses as the bartender handed them to him. "Hope you don't mind, Lane, but I put this on your tab."

"That's like fifty bucks," Hayden said, exasperated.

"Better you than me," he said, raising his shot glass in the air dramatically. "To nights you'll never remember, and friends you'll never forget."

The group all cheered and clinked their shots together. Liz tilted her head back and let the liquor slide down the back of her throat in one swift motion. She closed her eyes and shook her head. Potent.

"Awesome," Topher said, slamming his drink back on the bar.

"We're uh . . . going to go dance," one of the girls said with a shrug.

"Yeah, thanks for the drink," the second one said, already attempting to retreat.

Called it, Liz thought.

"Aww, leaving already?" Phillip asked, walking with them away from the bar.

Liz laughed as Topher trailed after them too.

"That's a lost cause," Liz said.

"Those guys don't give up easy," Hayden told her. "The girls will give up fighting it before they do."

They picked up their drinks and followed the guys back to where they were chatting up Anne, Abigail, and their friends. The girls all started dancing together to the rhythm of the music. Liz knew girls at home who used this as a defense so they didn't have to dance with certain guys. Phillip and Topher stood and watched them for a couple minutes before coaxing one of the girls to dance with each of them. They were smoother than a lot of the guys she knew, but still.

The dance floor filled up as the alcohol flowed, and soon even Liz found herself dancing with the group of girls. She could only remember that the tall girl was Anne and the short one was Abigail. The rest of the girls blended together and really it didn't matter. It was nice to kick back and enjoy herself. She forgot about everything that was frustrating and confusing about her summer and lived in the dance.

She didn't even think she was that great, but she was living by Victoria's motto tonight: If you're a girl, you can shake it. Apparently that was all that was needed.

Liz danced sandwiched between the other two girls, feeling tipsy and giddy from the drink and heat. She raised her hands high over her head, swished her hips side to side, and dipped down low with the other girls. She dropped her head back and laughed as the girl in front of her touched her toes. It was all entirely too ridiculous, and that made it all the more fun.

Anne, the girl behind her, grabbed Liz's hips to keep from falling over and ended up laughing loudly in her ear.

"Oh my God!" Anne cried.

Liz laughed and steadied herself against Abigail, who stood up and reached out for her friends in front of her. Liz glanced over at Hayden with the biggest smile plastered on her face.

He was standing there only a few feet away, just staring at her. She couldn't judge his expression. It was like a mixture of curiosity with disbelief and a whole lot of *where the hell did that come from?*

Hayden caught her staring back and smiled. He took a few steps to bridge the distance between them and grabbed her hand, pulling her away from the girls. She landed against his chest and he drew her into him.

"Good Lord, what have you been doing all summer?" he whispered into her ear.

"What do you mean?" Liz asked innocently.

"You're so . . . free," he said, as if it was the only word he could come up with.

"It's just me, Hayden."

"You say that," he said, his hands sliding to her hips and swinging them into time with his, "and then you dance like this."

Liz wound her arms up around his neck. "No reason not to dance," she murmured.

"No," he agreed, "no reason at all."

He stared down at her then and she saw in his eyes something she hadn't noticed before—lust. Liz swallowed hard and tried to forget about it. That wasn't what this was. Hayden had his chance at the end of the semester and had made it clear they were just friends. But she knew for certain that he was not looking at her like a friend.

The crowd drew in all around them as couples paired off, but when she was dancing with Hayden, it felt as if there wasn't anyone else in that room.

As they continued to dance, Liz felt her heartbeat rise along with the temperature in the room. She couldn't believe that after two years of crushing on Hayden, here he was finally showing her the attention she had been craving all along. It didn't feel fair that it had taken a summer with Brady to change her, to open her up. It was as if he had unlocked a piece of her that she hadn't even known existed.

Now here she was in a crowded nightclub with the guy she had always wanted, and to say she was conflicted was an understatement. She couldn't turn off two years of attraction like a light switch, but she owed it to Brady. They had too much to work out for this to happen.

Their dancing slowed almost to a stop as Hayden drew her closer and closer to him. She dragged in a ragged breath as her eyes rose to his. She could feel his hot breath on her cheeks and his fingers dig softly into her back.

Oh God, she thought, seeing everything play out before her eyes as if in slow motion.

"Guys!" someone called, barreling against them and clinging to Liz's arm.

Liz broke out of her trance and took a step away from Hayden. Her heart was beating fast and she knew her cheeks were crimson. She broke his gaze and looked over at the person holding on to her.

"Jamie," Liz said, relieved. That had been close.

Jamie smiled brightly at her. She was dressed simply in a striped hi-lo dress and sandals. She threw her arms around Liz with a cheer. "Oh my God, you guys are still here!"

Liz laughed and moved her to arm's length. "Of course we're still here. How drunk are you?"

"The girls gave me too much wine," she said with a giggle. "We should dance!"

"Um . . . your sister is pretty wasted," Liz told Hayden.

"Shhhh, don't tell him," Jamie whispered into Liz's ear.

"Jamie," Hayden said, shaking his head. "You can hardly stand up."

"Don't you start." Jamie pointed her finger in his face. "James will be here any minute, and I'll hear enough from him."

"Do you want me to go get you a water?" Hayden held her steady.

"Yes, I do, but first, bathroom," she said with a giggle. "Liz, shall we?" She gestured out dramatically in front of her.

"Sis, your Drama Club is showing," Hayden teased.

"Smack him for me," Jamie told Liz before striding toward the bathroom.

"I'll uh . . . go with her, I guess," Liz said with a shrug.

Liz walked across the crowded bar and into the bathroom behind Jamie. It was packed with girls fixing their hair, applying makeup, gossiping, and there was always one throwing up into the toilet.

"I'll be quick!" Jamie said, finding an open stall.

Liz stood against the wall with a huff. She tried not to think about how Hayden had almost kissed her. They had been in that position before, except this time she didn't think he'd had any intention of backing off. She was thankful that Jamie banged into them when she did. She wasn't sure if she would have stopped him if he had leaned forward, and that was disorienting.

What am I going to do the rest of the night? she wondered.

Jamie left the stall, walked to the sink, and started washing her hands.

"I just have to tell you something, Liz," Jamie said, grabbing the last paper towel and drying her hands.

"Yeah?" Liz wondered what kind of drunken conversation they were about to have.

"I was really worried at first when Hayden said you were a reporter."

"What?" she said, confused. "Why were you worried about that?"

Jamie tossed the paper towel. She turned to Liz and sighed as if it was such an obvious question. "I didn't want him to be dating someone too rigid. You know, like him."

Liz's eyes bulged. "Oh, Jamie, we're not . . . uh . . . we're not dating."

"Oh, yeah, of course," she said, waving it off. "He mentioned that."

"Yeah, just friends." Liz hoped it would sink in.

"But seriously, you're not uptight or anything! I mean I really *like* you!" she said, tossing her arms around Liz again.

"Well, thanks," Liz said. She patted her back softly and then pulled away.

"I'm so glad that you're here with him. He's so much fun when you're around. It's not all about work this, the paper that." Jamie gestured right and left and rolled her eyes. "He needs a good distraction."

Liz really liked Jamie, but she couldn't have this conversation.
It was like Jamie had already convinced herself Liz and Hayden
were good together. No matter what she said, she wasn't going to
be able to persuade his sister otherwise either.

"Maybe we should head back," Liz suggested.

Jamie glanced down at her phone and nodded. "I think James
is here!"

They walked out of the bathroom and Jamie immediately
launched herself at her boyfriend. They disappeared on the dance
floor a second later, leaving Hayden and Liz alone once more.

"You want another drink?" he asked with a cute smirk on his face.

Liz nodded and followed him to the bar. He ordered them both
another round of drinks. As they waited, he moved her back against
the bar and squared her in with his body. One of his hands brushed
her messy waves off to one shoulder and the other slung across the
back of the bar.

"Did I tell you how amazing you look tonight?" he murmured,
leaning forward to speak directly into her ear.

A shiver crept down her back at his nearness. She shook her
head.

"You look amazing," he repeated.

"Thank you," she said softly, not even sure whether he could
hear it over the music.

The bartender passed drinks to Hayden, who handed Liz hers.
"Come on. Let's dance some more."

They spent the rest of the evening trapped in a mass of dancers
at the bar. Topher and Phillip left with Anne and Abigail later. They
stopped by long enough to say good-bye and smile smugly, as if
they knew Liz hadn't believed they would score. Jamie started feeling sick shortly after that. James apologized to them for her.
Hayden closed his tab and then helped James haul her out of the

bar. Hayden left her with James to flag down a cab. A few minutes later one showed up that would take them back to the apartment.

"Hayden, you're not coming with?" Jamie asked, looking like she might throw up any second.

"We'll be back soon," he said with a smile as he tucked her into the car. Jamie lay back against James just as Hayden shut the door.

"We're not going back?" Liz asked, furrowing her brow.

"I wanted to show you something. Hope that's okay," he said, wrapping his arm around her shoulders and directing her to walk in the opposite direction of his apartment.

A few minutes later, they stood in front of the Reflecting Pool once more. Her feet were sore from walking the few blocks to their destination in heels, but it was a pretty sight. Everything was all lit up, and it was late enough that no one else was around.

Hayden pulled her toward the brightly lit Lincoln Memorial. She trekked up the stairs in her heels until she stood right in front of Lincoln's enormous statue.

"I told you I'd get you your view," he said. She could sense him inching closer to her.

"It's beautiful, Hayden." She continued to stare at the memorial.

"Lizzie," he whispered.

She turned then at the way he said her name. He had never called her Lizzie before. She kind of liked the way it sounded coming out of his mouth. Hayden Lane, who was always completely controlled, was struggling for just an ounce of control around her. When had the world completely flipped upside down?

His hand came up and stroked along her jaw. He stared down into her big blue eyes and then his mouth found her lips softly, as if he was testing the water.

Liz stood very still. Her head was spinning as she felt her body betray her by reacting to his kiss. Tingles blossomed in her chest and awakened that old feeling she had kept hidden inside her for two years. This wasn't supposed to happen. This was Hayden. He wasn't supposed to be interested in her like that. And now . . . he was.

"Hayden," she whispered, pulling back. "I thought you said that we couldn't because of the newspaper."

"I changed my mind," he said.

"Hayden, I . . ." She trailed off as he kissed her once more.

"Shhhh," he urged, "just kiss me."

His hands were holding her face softly, and then when he kissed her again his hesitation was gone. He kissed her as if he had wanted to do it for a long time. He kissed her as if he would never get enough of her. He prodded her mouth open with his tongue and volleyed with her. When he dragged his teeth along her bottom lip, she took a swift breath. His lips were soft and warm and so entirely foreign. Her hands were gripping his shirt and, almost without thinking, drawing him in closer.

Butterflies fluttered in her stomach as the sexual tension between them contracted and then cracked wide open.

Hayden sighed and kissed her lips once more. He moved her arms up around his neck and grabbed her around the waist, holding her in place against him.

"Liz," Hayden murmured.

"Mmm-hmm?"

"I should have done this a long time ago."

Liz laughed lightly.

"Not kissing you last semester when I had a chance was a huge mistake," Hayden said against her lips. "I'm not one to repeat mistakes."

Chapter 26
KEEPING SECRETS

Guilt washed over Liz as fast as a cyclone cutting through a town.

She let Hayden guide her down the steps and to the street, where he hailed a cab. The whole walk she was in a daze. Part of her knew that she had enjoyed the kiss. She had even on some level wanted Hayden to kiss her. And that thought only made her feel worse. She had appreciated her time with Hayden—the openness, his interest in her career, all of the introductions. It was the complete opposite of Brady, and it gave her a headache, because what she really wanted was Brady to give her all of the things that Hayden had given her this weekend. But just because Brady wasn't giving her those things didn't mean that she should have taken them from Hayden.

The cab ride to Hayden's place was quiet but comfortable. When they made it back, up the flight of stairs, and inside the apartment, Liz quickly retreated to the bedroom to change. She just needed a

minute to breathe before saying good night. She didn't know if she
trusted herself to be alone with him much longer. She placed her
hands down softly on the bed, closed her eyes, and tried to get the
image of Hayden's lips out of her mind.

Hayden appeared a minute later in the open doorway and
knocked twice softly. "Hey."

Liz turned to face him, her moment broken.

"Hey," Liz said. He was in more comfortable clothes and his
muscular chest stretched the thin cotton shirt. She looked away,
not meaning to stare. She took a seat on the bed and stifled a yawn.

"I had a great time tonight."

"Me too."

Hayden walked across the room and took the seat next to her.
Liz sat very still, not wanting to encourage him. It had been different when they had been on this bed in the middle of the day and
she hadn't thought anything would happen with Hayden. But now,
with the feel of his lips still fresh in her mind, she couldn't help
tensing at his nearness.

"I'm glad you came this weekend," Hayden said.

He reached forward, stroked her hair back behind her ear, and
stared into her blue eyes. Liz swallowed when he didn't move his
hand from her face. He opened his mouth as if he was going to say
something more, but Liz averted her gaze and he dropped his hand.

She looked down at her hands where they lightly gripped the
bedspread. No matter what she felt for Hayden, she couldn't let this
continue when she had Brady on her mind. She couldn't hear his
sweet words that would convince her otherwise. She couldn't taste
his lips and allow her mind to get all muddled with the feel of him.

Hayden cleared his throat and stood. "Well, I'll let you get some
sleep."

He reached forward and grasped her hand lightly in his. Her
gaze rose to his automatically, and he stared into her eyes deeply as

he placed a soft kiss on her hand. Her heartbeat picked up without warning and her lips parted as the intensity of his affection hit her.

"Good night, Liz," he said, running his thumb across her knuckles.

"Good . . . good night," she whispered.

He smiled down at her once before departing, and Liz released the breath she had been holding.

She liked Hayden. She had liked him for a long time. But she had thought that with Brady consuming her thoughts, her old affections for him wouldn't resurface so easily. And now that she had these feelings bubbling up inside of her, she was torn. She wanted Brady to give her all the things Hayden had given her here in D.C. No matter what Liz felt about this weekend, she knew that it had opened her eyes to what she was missing with Brady.

The drive back to Chapel Hill felt twice as long as the drive to D.C. Alone in her car, Liz had too much time to think, and her conflicted heart weighed on her. She was having a hard time discerning all of the emotions crashing against her like waves. Half of the drive she felt as if she were drowning.

She didn't know what she felt for Hayden. She knew she felt something, but what had once been so clear was all blurry.

And on top of everything, laced into every breath, she felt guilt. She felt it take root in her body the longer she drove.

Did I cheat? she wondered, the word tasting like bile in her mouth.

She didn't know what to do. Brady loved her. He wouldn't tell her and they couldn't be public, but he loved her nonetheless. Not to mention he had made his feelings about another guy being near her perfectly clear.

Still, it had felt nice, even right sometimes, to be with Hayden— being out in public, hanging out, laughing, walking around—the list was endless. Those things felt perfectly right in a way that she had never felt with Brady.

Liz pulled up to her house a couple hours later. She was just happy to be home, and maybe here she could figure out what was warring inside her.

Made it safe, she jotted off a text to Hayden.

The response was nearly instantaneous.

Good. Thanks for coming up this weekend. Can't wait to see you again when school starts.

Liz grumbled under her breath and tossed the phone back into her purse. A couple months ago she would have been jumping up and down for Hayden to respond so enthusiastically toward her, but now . . .

Well, now she was trying to figure out what to do about Brady Maxwell.

Victoria was lounging on the couch when Liz walked inside. She flipped over onto her stomach and propped her head on her hands.

"Hey, bitch! How was your trip? Did you have sex with your Hayden Lane?" she asked all at once.

"Nice to see you, too," Liz said, tossing her bag on the floor and collapsing into a chair. "And no, I didn't have sex with Hayden. I'm not you."

"Ugh!" Victoria grumbled, flipping back over. "You're no fun!"

Liz sighed. She wished she could tell Victoria everything that had happened all summer. She didn't particularly like keeping things from her friend to begin with, but this was huge. This was like the Eiffel Tower of secrets . . . well, as far as secrets went for Liz.

Brady had taken over her life. He had changed her, and Liz was pretty certain that it was for the better. Their relationship was founded on hiding and secrets, yet at its core, she found only truth. And still it wasn't enough.

With Hayden, she had the exact opposite. They were completely free to be open, he told all of his friends about her, and he seemed completely attentive. But he wasn't Brady, and she couldn't ever tell him about Brady.

Her eyes were suddenly cloudy with tears, because she knew then that in her heart what she really wanted was Brady. It had to be Brady. And yet . . . he couldn't give her what she needed.

She could tell him how she felt, but it didn't feel like enough. He had made it clear from day one that it was the campaign over her. It didn't seem to matter to him that he loved her. He stood up for her against Heather and Elliott, but just so that he and Liz could keep doing what they were doing. And that wasn't going to change.

"Vic," Liz croaked, closing her eyes against the tears.

"What's wrong?" Victoria asked. Liz opened her eyes to find Victoria kneeling in front of her. "Are you okay?"

She shook her head, wishing she could let it all out. Hiding things was too hard.

"Are you going to tell me what happened?" Victoria brushed Liz's hair off of her face and rubbed her shoulder.

"I don't know," she muttered.

"Come sit on the couch with me," Victoria said, taking her hand and guiding her to the sofa.

Liz flopped down and pulled her knees up to her chest. She felt ridiculous crying over this. She didn't like to cry at all, and now she was crying over a guy? Ugh! She wanted to tell herself to get it together, but it wasn't working. Maybe just today she would let herself feel the pain that she was experiencing over falling for the wrong guy.

"So, tell me," Victoria said, wrapping an arm across Liz's shoulders. "What happened?"

"He kissed me," Liz sputtered out.

Victoria stiffened and Liz glanced up at her. She had an amused expression on her face. "You're crying because Hayden kissed you?"

"Ugh! No!" she cried, shaking her head. "I can't even right now, Vic."

"Liz, come on. Didn't you want Hayden to kiss you? I'm confused."

"Yes, I did, but not *now*! I wanted him to kiss me before. I wanted him to want me then . . . when it would have mattered!"

Victoria scrunched up her eyebrows in confusion. "You've lost me. Why does it matter if it's then or now? He kissed you. He wants you. I told you so."

"Because . . . I'm seeing someone else," Liz whispered, burying her head in her hands.

"What?" Victoria asked, flabbergasted. "Since when? Who? Why didn't you tell me?"

Liz shook her head. "I can't talk about it, but we've been seeing each other all summer."

"Why can't you talk about it?"

Liz looked up into Victoria's eyes and sighed. "I just can't, Vic. I haven't told anyone about it. I mean, I just told you, but that's it, and I can't even tell you who it is. But he loves me, Vic, and I kissed someone else."

"Whoa, love?" Victoria asked. "He told you he loves you?"

"Erm . . ." Liz muttered, biting her lip. "Not exactly, but I overheard him tell someone else."

Victoria breathed out really fast and glanced away, as if she were thinking about the situation at hand. "Let me get this straight. You've been secretly seeing someone all summer, who you can't tell me about, who you overheard tell someone else that he loves you, and you're crying because another guy kissed you?"

Liz stood very still while Victoria laid out her situation plainly. If only she could tell her more, it wouldn't sound so . . . silly.

"I don't want to break your heart, Liz, but it sounds like that other guy is using you . . ."

"He's not," she answered immediately.

"Why does he have to keep it a secret?"

"I can't talk about it . . ."

"Well, if it *is* that big a secret, then you can't reasonably say that you two are dating. You have to be in a relationship for it to be wrong to kiss someone else. It kind of sounds to me like this guy is stringing you along . . ."

"Victoria, he's not. I swear. He's not." Liz dropped her head into her hands. She didn't even want to consider that Victoria's words were true. She wished she could just tell Victoria what was going on. It would be so nice to have it all out in the open.

"Well, you won't tell me the whole situation! From an outsider's perspective, this sounds like a bad idea. You shouldn't beat yourself up over a kiss with Hayden if you can't even tell your best friend who the other guy is. I bet he doesn't want you near other guys either, right?" Victoria asked, rolling her eyes.

Liz froze. Her tears dammed up. "He doesn't, but I don't know any guy who does."

"I've been with a guy who wanted to keep things on the down-low, and let me tell you, it didn't end pretty. He was seeing someone else on the side, all the while telling me not to see anyone else. I thought it was kind of stupid, but went along with it for a little while, because I was kind of into him. Then I find him sleeping with someone else and he doesn't understand why I would be against that," Victoria said, shaking her head. "All I'm saying is that a guy who wants to keep secrets from other people . . . is going to be okay keeping secrets from you . . ."

Liz wished that she could tell Victoria the whole situation. She wanted to so badly. "It's not like that . . ."

"Then tell me who he is," Victoria said, standing with her hands on her hips. "If it's not like that, then tell me who this guy is."

"I can't tell you, Victoria! If I could, I would have told you already!" Liz cried.

"Seriously, I don't get it. Why is it such a big deal?" Victoria demanded. "Can you *at least* tell me that?"

"No! I can't!" Liz yelled back, pushing her hands into her hair.

"Ridiculous. What kind of guy forces you to keep secrets from everyone?" Victoria asked, pacing.

"I can't explain it. But I don't want to keep secrets anymore. I want to be out in the open. I want whatever we have to be all the time."

Victoria rolled her eyes again. "I hate to be pessimistic about this, Liz. I want you to be happy, but this sounds like a recipe for disaster."

Liz sighed heavily. It did sound like a recipe for disaster. Before, when it had just been about the sex, none of this mattered. But now it did, and maybe all along he was using her and stringing her along and it had been okay, because she was doing the same thing. Now that wasn't what she wanted anymore. She wanted a relationship with Brady, which had its own set of problems.

"I know," Liz finally whispered, pressing her hand under her eyes to wipe away the last remaining tears. "I guess I'll have to talk to him."

"That's probably for the best," Victoria said, sitting back down finally. "I'm sorry I made things worse. I didn't mean to."

"It's okay."

"You're sure you can't tell me. It might make me understand . . ."

"Vic," Liz interrupted, "I can't tell you."

"Okay," she said with a shrug. "Talk to this guy and tell him what you told me. See what happens. But Liz . . ."

"Yeah?" Liz glanced up into Victoria's face.

"You didn't do anything wrong by kissing Hayden. Don't let anyone else convince you otherwise, all right?"

Liz sighed and nodded. If she hadn't done anything wrong, then why did she still feel so bad?

The next day, Liz trudged onto campus bright and early to get her grade from her journalism professor. She hadn't slept much, because she had been waiting for Brady to call her. He knew when she was coming back, so he could have called last night, but he didn't. She would have to wait for Brady, as difficult as that was.

She walked through the journalism building until she found Professor Mires's office. The door was open and a student was already inside talking to her. Liz took a seat in a chair outside of the room and waited.

She hoped that she looked okay, because she hadn't taken any time with her appearance. Yesterday's makeup still covered her face, and she had thrown her hair into a messy bun on the top of her head. She was run-down from not sleeping, and stressing her way through every imaginable scenario with Brady.

"Yes, thank you for stopping by," Professor Mires said as the student who had been in her office exited. "Miss Dougherty, how are you?"

Liz stood and stifled a yawn. "Hello, Professor Mires."

"You're here for your grade, I presume?"

"I know you said in class that we could stop by on Monday and you should have our papers finalized."

"In fact, I do. Come on in," the professor said, gesturing for Liz to follow her.

Liz took the seat in front of the professor's desk. Professor Mires wore her typical librarian glasses. Her brown hair was a curly mess, which explained why she always wore it in a bun. She had on a long blue skirt that dragged the floor, and a cream linen blouse. She took a seat in front of Liz and folded her hands in her lap.

"What are your plans for the next two years, Liz?" Professor Mires asked. "You are an upcoming junior, correct?"

"Yes, I am," Liz said, straightening at the question. "I'm not sure I understand what you're asking. I'm planning to finish my degree in journalism and work on the paper."

"I understand that you're a Morehead scholar and that your senior year, you must have an internship with a completed in-field research project. Had you thought about what you are going to do for this?" Professor Mires prodded.

"I had given some thought to working in-field at a Raleigh newspaper and commuting back and forth. I have a scholarship meeting with my advisor at the beginning of school to discuss possibilities," Liz told her.

"Hmm," she said, leaning forward and thumbing through a stack of papers on her desk. She extracted one from the pile and handed it across the table to Liz.

Liz took her paper eagerly. She flipped to the back page and saw the page filled top to bottom with red ink and a small A+ circled at the bottom. Liz inhaled sharply, unable to believe what she saw. She skimmed through the comments, which was one long glowing review of the article she had written.

"Thank you," Liz muttered, glancing back up at her professor.

"I'm giving you an A in the class," Professor Mires told her. "I know your performance was less than adequate at the beginning, but I'm a strong believer in improvement. And you went above and beyond. I challenged you, and you accepted the challenge with fervor. Each week you got better, but this"—she pointed at the paper—"this showed what you are really capable of. You've done a great job at changing your perspective, broadening your scope, and remaining objective. You should hold on to these skills. They'll take you far."

"Oh," Liz said, "thank you."

The one paper Brady had given her the idea for was the paper that her professor thought had changed her. She had worked hard all summer to achieve this A, really stretching her perspective and working toward what Professor Mires wanted from her. But she knew that Brady had helped with that. He had shown her politics from a different perspective entirely. She had been able to take what she had learned from him and layer it with what she already knew about the world, and that had helped her relate to her audience.

That man will be the death of me.

"Well, you convinced me to believe in your work with that last paper. It showed me that you can improve . . . and drastically in a short period of time. I've been looking for someone like that to help with my research. I've recently acquired a grant, and I'll be doing research with several universities around the country and working directly with the *Washington Post*. Part of the funds will go toward putting together a colloquium regarding political journalism, and most of the North Carolina state papers as well as *Wash Po, New York Times*, and CNN have signed on to participate. I know that you are working on the university paper, and if you continue on the path with politics, then you will surely have your hands full, but I do hope you consider taking the time to work with me. I would be happy to sign off on your internship credit."

Liz stared forward at her professor in shock, her mouth hanging open slightly.

"Are you interested, Liz?" Professor Mires asked.

"Yes! Oh, yes, I'm interested. I would be happy to help you in your research, Professor Mires. What will you need me to do?" Liz sputtered out.

"Great. I'll be in contact more directly when school starts again. It might require some traveling, but all your expenses would be covered. Also, I do hope that it helps you make those contacts you need," Professor Mires said with a smile.

"Thank you so much for the opportunity!"

Professor Mires nodded before standing. "Thank you for your hard work. I'm looking forward to having you onboard next semester."

Liz smiled, her day brightening, and turned to exit her professor's office. Standing in the doorway was the woman's husband. He was holding a bouquet of sunflowers, with a giant smile plastered on his handsome face. Liz suddenly felt as if she was intruding on their moment and quickly ducked out of the office.

Her brain was buzzing as she walked back to her car. She couldn't believe that Professor Mires believed in her work enough to entrust her with her grant research. Not only that, but Liz would be included in work with papers and political journalism outlets all over the country. This felt way bigger than anything she could do on the university paper.

She was so wired she almost missed her phone buzzing in her purse. She quickly answered the unknown number, noting that it had a North Carolina area code. "Hello?"

"Liz," Brady said.

Liz stopped in her tracks in the middle of campus. Her mind quit working and she felt her heart skip. Damn, she had missed that voice.

"Are you there?"

"Yes, sorry," she murmured. "I missed you."

She hadn't even meant to say it. Of course she had missed him. But with everything that had happened since she had left his house, it wasn't the first thing she had thought she would spit out.

"I missed you, too."

Silence dragged on the line for a moment as Liz waited for him to say something else.

"How was your trip?" he finally asked, breaking the silence.

"Good," she said. "I got to see a lot of monuments and museums."

"Sounds right," he said. She heard shuffling on the other end of the line. "Hold on one second."

Liz waited as he spoke with someone else. She imagined him at his office in Raleigh, directing people and deciding on strategies for the campaign. He was probably wearing a standard black suit with his typical red-white-and-blue tie. She was sure he had his campaign mask on, all smiles and charm.

Then she thought about that one night she had gotten to really see Brady, when they had gone over to Chris's apartment. He had dressed comfortably, laughed, joked, and even made fun of himself. It had been relaxing to see him not on edge, as he was all the time. That was the Brady she wanted to be with.

"Sorry about that," Brady said, breaking her out of her thoughts. "I can't talk long. I have a meeting in a couple minutes. I wanted to find out your plans for the remainder of the week."

"I don't have plans until school starts again. Though I do have some exciting news!" she said, wanting to tell him about her professor.

"I can't wait to hear it. I wish I could talk now, but I can't. I'm going to the coast for a few days, mixing business with pleasure a bit. My family is spending the week at the beach before Clay goes back to Yale and Savannah starts at UNC. I'm meeting them in Hilton Head for the weekend. I have a couple meetings and a dinner to attend."

"That sounds nice," Liz said.

"I know I'm going to be really busy up until the primary, but I thought you might come to the coast with me."

"Really?" she asked, surprised. She would have plenty of time to tell him about her job there.

"I would get you a hotel room near my parents' place. I'm going to try to slip this by Heather so we have to keep it on the down-low, but I'll take any opportunity to see you," Brady told her.

"Oh," she whispered, feeling the secrets pile up all over again.

"Baby . . . come see me," he said in that tone that made her squirm. How could she resist him?

She needed to tell him about Hayden. She needed to figure out where this was going. She needed to tell him how she felt.

Most of all, she just needed to see him.

"All right. What do I have to do?"

Chapter 27
THE WAITING GAME

Liz didn't even want to know the cost of a last-minute flight from Raleigh to Hilton Head. She was sure it wasn't something she would be able to afford, but luckily Brady had made all the arrangements.

Now here she was about to board a flight to go see him at his parents' beach house. Or at least, she was staying at a resort nearby. It felt surreal to be living this life. She had so much that she needed to discuss with Brady, but she would have to wait until they were together again to bring it up. Heather had been keeping him more than busy, and Liz hadn't spoken with him except to finalize her travel plans.

Liz was sure Heather was only keeping tabs on him because of their relationship . . . whatever it was. She didn't think Heather needed to push him that hard. She was sure he was going to win. All he had to do was smile.

She stood in line to board the plane and her mind raced back to that first conversation with Brady. Airplanes made him hyperventilate, and she had been the only other thing that had elicited that reaction from him. Liz knew that she still felt that way about him. Brady had changed her. He had made her bolder, freer, and she liked that he had given her that.

Yet they were caught in this unhealthy limbo. Trapped in a place where they couldn't express themselves and couldn't move forward. They were forever boarding the plane, hyperventilating from the intensity and passion of their feelings, but never taking off and seeing where the plane might take them.

With a heavy sigh, Liz walked onto the plane and took her seat in first class. She had only flown first class once, when her parents had sent her to Hawaii to spend a week with her grandparents. She snuggled into her cozy seat and let her eyes close. She pushed away all thoughts of Brady and the decisions that had to be made and fell into a light slumber.

Liz jolted awake when the wheels touched ground at the small Hilton Head Island airport. She yawned and stretched as they rolled to a stop in front of the terminal. The jet bridge attached to the plane and she filed out, grabbing her carry-on luggage, which hadn't fit overhead on the small regional plane.

She made her way to the exit and found a man standing alone, wearing a suit, and holding a sign that read Carmichael. Liz smiled and walked over to him.

"Miss Carmichael?" the man asked as she approached.

"That's me," Liz said.

"Let me help you with that," he said, taking her bag and rolling it out to the awaiting town car.

In that moment, Liz felt so out of her league. Someone had flown her to the beach, arranged for someone to pick her up at the airport in an expensive town car, and she was staying at a luxury beachside resort. She found all of this very hard to believe. But mostly, she wished she could be experiencing all of this *with* Brady.

Trying her best to make light of the situation, she reminded herself over and over of all the good times they'd had together this summer. The sneaking around had been exhilarating, even if she now found it frustrating. Well, the sneaking around wasn't the frustrating part; it was the fact that there was more to their relationship than that, and it was being stifled by their opposing careers.

She ground her teeth. Even when she was trying to think of the positives, the negatives crept back in. She made a mental list of all the things she missed about her time with Brady. The lake, his little notes, the diner, when he dropped his campaign mask, the newspaper office, his intense dark eyes, his coming to see her after Justin's DUI, the Fourth of July, his big gala event when he had given her his key, and then she heard him tell Heather and Elliott that he loved her . . .

Liz swallowed back a lump in her throat. Her whole summer had been Brady. Sure, he was volatile, stubborn, and prone to jealousy, but she knew there was more to him than that, and he had shown her that this summer, whether he wanted to or not.

The town car carried her across the island and pulled onto the grounds of the Sonesta Resort. Liz leaned into the window to look at the beautiful view before her. The hotel boasted more than three hundred luxury rooms with an enormous pool, on-site spa, twenty-four-hole golf course, and beachside access with cabanas and bottle service. It was a dream resort.

As soon as they parked, the driver assisted Liz with her luggage and handed her an envelope. "Here you are, Miss Carmichael. Enjoy your stay."

"Thank you," she said absentmindedly.

She strolled into the air-conditioned hotel lobby, anxious to open the envelope, but all she could do was stop and stare at her surroundings. The lobby was modern chic, with enough of a cozy atmosphere to make it feel like home. Large couches and overstuffed chairs were artfully placed around the room, and couples lounged amid the furniture, reading newspapers and talking to friends. The ceiling rose higher and higher, with gorgeous windows on one side, an impressive mural on another, and a seashell chandelier.

Liz took a seat in one of the chairs and opened the envelope. A plastic keycard, a resort packet with her room number, and a trifolded sheet of paper fell out into her hand. The front of the letter was sealed with a short note on it.

Do not read until you are in your room.
—B

All right, she thought, a big smile spreading on her face. She really freaking liked his little notes.

Liz took the envelope and headed to the elevators, ready to be up in her room to find out what was inside the letter. She pressed the button for the top floor and waited as the elevator took its time. It finally deposited her on her floor, and she found her room near the end of the hallway. She slid her keycard into the slot and opened the door into a beautiful suite twice the size of the one she'd had with Brady in Charlotte after the Jefferson-Jackson gala.

She dropped her bags in the entranceway and closed the door. She couldn't believe that Brady had gotten her this room for two nights in Hilton Head. She was having a hard time believing any of it.

The resort hotel room had a full living room with couch and chairs matching those in the lobby, a dark wooden dining room table set, and a beach-inspired kitchen with light wood cabinetry, granite countertops, and brand-new sleek black appliances. An open door led to a large master bedroom with a king-sized bed, and the master bath came complete with standing glass shower and Jacuzzi tub. But the best part about the whole suite was the exquisite balcony view of the ocean.

Taking the envelope with her, Liz sat down on one of the chairs outside and tore open the letter.

I hope you like your suite. I wanted you to have an ocean view. I've added the spa package to the room, so treat yourself. My schedule for the weekend is attached.

Liz glanced at the second page and saw a list of events that Brady had to attend. Dinner that night with the family and meetings for the campaign after. The next day, he had time blocked off for the family for most of the day, which was disappointing. She would have liked to spend some beach time with him, but of course, that was impossible. That night was dinner and drinks with potential donors. Neither night had an end time, just a start time.

I'll give you a call when I'm on my way, from a private number that isn't being traced. I'd advise you to stay on resort properties at all times. The last thing we want is for you to be seen.

Can't wait to get my hands on you.

—B

Her core heated at the thought of him. Brady Maxwell had gone to all of this trouble for *her*. She hoped she would see him sooner rather than later. Until that moment, she hadn't realized quite how much she had missed him . . . just him, exactly how they were when they were together.

Though she had to admit she wasn't sure what to think about the part about not being allowed to leave. Not that she'd had any plans to go anywhere else, but she did kind of want to see the island. She had never been to Hilton Head, and it seemed silly to stay at the hotel the whole time. Well, she would figure it out.

Not wanting to waste any more time considering it, she called down to the spa to schedule her appointment. By the time Brady came to see her that night, she wanted to look amazing.

Liz spent the afternoon at the beach soaking up the summer sun. It made her miss her parents' house in Tampa, and she wished that she had taken time out of her busy schedule to see them. She still had a couple weeks left before school started. Maybe it would do her some good to go visit her family. Though she found it hard to think about leaving Brady again after what happened last time she did.

As the sun started hanging low on the horizon, Liz returned to the resort and spent her time at the spa. A few hours later, she had been massaged, pampered, waxed, had her fingernails and toes painted, and her blond hair straightened so smoothly that she was afraid to go outside. She walked back to her room feeling unbelievably relaxed.

Brady hadn't called or texted from the private number, but she figured dinner was winding down now, so she would hear from him soon. She ordered room service for a quick meal, and then applied soft makeup. Liz dug into her suitcase and pulled out a black lace babydoll and matching thong. She had packed them last-minute, wondering whether she would ever strike up the nerve to wear them, but after her time in the spa, she couldn't think of a better occasion.

After she was all dolled up, she wasn't really sure what to do from there. She still hadn't heard from Brady, and truth be told, she felt a bit ridiculous sitting around in lingerie. But it hadn't been that long, and she could wait for him.

Liz flipped open her laptop and started surfing through her favorite newspapers. She read the headlines and hooks to see if anything caught her eye, but she was too anxious to be interested. She had an email from Professor Mires regarding her research assistant position for the fall, but even that didn't hold the same excitement it had when she had first spoken to her professor.

A few more hours rolled by and Liz's anxiety had morphed into full-on frustration. Where the hell was he? More than that . . . why hadn't he even called her to let her know that he wasn't going to be here until later?

She felt ridiculous waiting up like this. Here she was dressed in full lingerie, she had taken the time to get her hair and nails done, she was wearing makeup . . . and hell, she had heels waiting by the bedroom door. And still no Brady.

Her gentle yawns turned into full-blown yawns at about two in the morning. Her eyes were fluttering closed, and she felt herself drifting off. By three o'clock, she had almost crashed into her computer a few times, and when she actually did, that was the final straw. She couldn't wait up any longer.

Liz pulled her babydoll over her head and threw it into a corner in anger. She was such an idiot. Why had she gone through the trouble at all of getting dressed up and then waiting for him? She yanked an oversize T-shirt over her head and went into the bathroom to remove her makeup.

By the time she had finished scrubbing her face and crawled into bed, she was wide-awake. At that moment, she hated adrenaline. She just wanted to go to sleep and forget that she had been that girl—the kind of girl to stay up all night waiting uselessly for a guy who hadn't even bothered to call. How could he have planned this whole thing, gotten her to a freaking island, and then not called to let her know he wasn't coming to see her?

She ground her teeth, wondering whether she could feel any more ridiculous. Then she turned the volume all the way up on her phone and stuffed it under the pillow next to her.

That made her feel more ridiculous.

Liz awoke the next morning feeling as if she hadn't slept all night. He eyes were swollen with bags underneath, hair a rat's nest from tossing and turning, and she had a crick in her neck.

She grabbed her phone, hoping to see something from Brady, an apology preferably, but really anything to explain why he hadn't called or texted or *anything* last night. When she turned on the screen, she found what she already knew she was going to find: Brady hadn't tried to get hold of her.

Liz knew that Brady had plans all afternoon today as well, and she wasn't supposed to see him until after dinner with his donors. That meant he had blown an entire night together, and they had only one more left. Whatever happened had better have been important.

Changing back into a bathing suit, Liz trekked down to the pool. She grabbed a secluded spot, ordered a daiquiri, and tried to forget about last night. There was almost no use trying, but she thought it would be worth a shot.

After her third daiquiri, she wasn't sure if she was more or less angry with Brady for standing her up last night. Seriously, how difficult was it for him to make one little phone call?

Liz had spent all of that time at the spa, and here she was adding tension to her shoulders. She knew she should just be grateful that she was at the beach, in a suite, and getting a full spa treatment, but that wasn't the reason that she had flown down.

She wanted to see Brady. She missed him. Plus, they had a lot to talk about.

By the time the sun had moved directly overhead, Liz could feel herself beginning to burn. She hadn't spent enough time poolside this summer, and she wasn't going to be a lobster tonight. Granted, at this point, she didn't even know if she would get to see Brady.

Liz returned to her room a bit tipsier than she left. She took a quick shower and changed into a baby blue backless tank top, a pair of cuffed khaki shorts, and gold sandals. She slung her purse over her head and decided that if Brady couldn't even bother to follow his own written instructions, then why should she?

She ventured back downstairs and walked up to the concierge's desk.

"Excuse me," Liz said with a smile.

"Hello! How can I help you?" a perky brunette asked, leaning forward as if to be more inviting.

"I wanted to see if you had some information on places to eat in town. I'm not too picky, but I wanted something authentic."

The woman smiled brightly and proceeded to overload Liz with choices. By the time she walked away to catch a cab into town, she had a handful of packets, a map with a dozen or more restaurants circled for her to choose from, and no better understanding of where she was going to get lunch.

She hopped into the first cab that pulled up, and was whisked away into the center of downtown Hilton Head. The island retained an old-timey feel, complete with uniform signage. It also had a certain affluent flair, with the high-class golf courses, impressive boutiques, and all of the women coated in diamonds. Hilton Head had been touted as the Hamptons of the South . . . and as Liz looked around, she could see why.

The cabdriver dropped her off in front of the downtown area, Coligny Plaza and Beach Market. Liz wore her dark, thick-rimmed sunglasses through the beachside shopping center. Now that she was actually out and about in Hilton Head, she was feeling more and more self-conscious. She didn't think anyone would recognize her, but she didn't have a legitimate story if anyone did.

Maybe she should have listened to Brady to begin with. Too late now.

Liz wandered around the shops until she found a restaurant that was located on her map. She was too hungry to search out any of the others.

She ate her meal alone and tried to remember why she had left the resort at all. Well, she knew. She was pissed at Brady. Pissed that he would stand her up. Pissed that he hadn't called. Pissed that he loved her and couldn't . . . wouldn't act on it.

She shook her head, tossed the remainder of the meal, and turned to walk out of the restaurant with the intention of spending the rest of the afternoon wandering the shops before heading back to the hotel. Then she heard a voice that was completely recognizable, even though she couldn't see the person who was speaking.

Clay Maxwell.

Liz froze in her tracks just outside of the restaurant, her chest rising and falling rapidly, as she tried to figure out where the voice was coming from. She stuffed her glasses back on her face and swallowed hard. She absolutely could *not* be seen by anyone, especially not Clay. If Clay found out that she was here, she was sure he would start putting the pieces together. After all, why else would she always turn up everywhere Brady happened to be?

Liz was clearly too young to be a big donor, unless she had a trust, and she didn't act as though she did. And people tended to jump to conclusions. Liz would have if she had been reporting, and then she would have dug until she found her evidence. Her gut instincts were normally right.

Like the one telling her to run, run far away at that moment.

The voices stopped, and Liz, thinking she was finally in the clear, turned the corner toward the shops. Her stomach dropped when she saw Clay standing directly in front of her.

A dimpled smirk crossed his face when he noticed her, and the only thing Liz could do in that moment was shake her head and smile.

"Clay Maxwell!" she cried. "I did not expect to find you here."

Clay's grin grew when she acknowledged him, and he pulled away from the woman he was standing with. He was in short khaki shorts, a blue Brooks Brothers polo, and boat shoes. His Ray-Bans hung from his neck by a pair of Croakies, making him look unbelievably preppy.

"Liz," he said, obviously trying to hide his own surprise. "It's great to see you."

"You know, for a guy who begs a girl for her number, you really should have considered using it," Liz scolded.

Shit! Where had that come from? she wondered. She just needed to play a part and then leave. She couldn't have Clay telling Brady he had seen her. That would be the end of the world.

Clay chuckled. The girl he was with raised her eyebrows at the comment. She was pretty, by all means gorgeous, but she clearly had a stick up her ass. If she could look any more snobby in her designer sundress, Chanel earrings, and Tiffany necklace, Liz would have been very surprised.

"Good to see you, too, Liz. Let me introduce you to my girlfriend, Andrea," he said, drawling out her name and pronouncing it Ahn-dreya.

Girlfriend. Liz came up short at that word. The man who had begged her to go home with him and practically shoved his phone down her throat to get her number . . . had a girlfriend. That was rich . . .

"So nice to meet you," Liz said, wishing that she didn't feel like such an idiot.

"Clay, who is this?" Andrea asked. She turned to him pointedly.

"This is my friend Liz. We met on the Fourth of July at Brady's rally."

"Borrring," Andrea said, rolling her eyes.

"She's a big supporter of Brady. I think I've convinced her to run against him," Clay said.

"Ugh . . . whatever," Andrea said. "I'm going to get a drink. God knows I need one. Don't fuck her, okay?" She glared at him and stomped away.

Liz's eyes bulged as she stared back and forth between the couple. What had just happened?

Clay shrugged as if his girlfriend hadn't just told him not to sleep with someone else in public . . . right in front of Liz. "Sorry about that."

"You have a girlfriend," she observed lamely.

"Most of the time," he said nonchalantly. "And you have a boyfriend, I assume."

"I don't actually," Liz said.

"Oh, come on, no single girl refuses that vehemently unless they're dating someone."

"Why are we having this conversation?" she asked, narrowing her eyes.

"Because now I'm confused. You don't have a boyfriend and you didn't go home with me even though you wanted to fuck me," Clay said, as if this were the most confusing thing he'd had to deal with in a while.

Liz shook her head. *Arrogant son of a bitch.* She couldn't stop thinking that when she was around him.

"I didn't want to sleep with you."

"Right," he said, ignoring her statement. "Are you here for that thing Brady's hosting tonight?"

"No, I wasn't aware Senator Maxwell had an event on Hilton

Head this weekend," she lied fluidly. Liz knew that it sounded odd that she would be here and not know about the event, but she couldn't tell him she had flown down to be here for it. That would be even more suspicious. "I'm staying with some friends at a resort for the weekend. Good timing, I guess."

"Well, you should crash the party. Brady has a hot date. You could be mine," Clay said with a shrug.

All of the wind rushed out of her lungs at once. Brady had a hot date. She knew he had dinner and drinks tonight, but he hadn't mentioned a date. Had he flown her all this way just to go out with someone else again? She felt hypocritical getting worked up over this after Hayden had kissed her, but she hadn't gone into that situation thinking anything would happen. Could Brady be thinking the same thing?

She tried to compose herself, but it was not without difficulty.

"You're not bringing your girlfriend?" Liz asked, her voice tight with emotion.

"She'll be there."

"I think I'm going to have to pass," she said, realizing how close she was to accepting the invitation just to see whom Brady would show up with.

His blond hair blew across his forehead in the breeze, and his blue eyes looked down into hers as if he were trying to persuade her with one look.

Liz shook her head, her heart beating fiercely in her chest. Brady had a date and his brother was trying to seduce her. Why wasn't Brady the one after her? Where the hell was he anyway? And why had he stood her up last night?

"I appreciate the offer, but you have explicit instructions from your girlfriend not to sleep with me. I think that's probably a good idea. Good-bye, Clay," Liz said, moving to the right to walk around him.

His hand reached out and touched her wrist. "You know, I did listen to Brady's speech after we talked." He stared at her very intently, all of the humor and joking leaving his eyes. "And I still think you're wrong. He only cares about the campaign and he only cares about winning. I know that he'll do whatever it takes to get there, and I'm sorry he's convinced you so thoroughly otherwise . . ."

Chapter 28
WHETHER OR NOT

Liz hurried back to the Sonesta Resort, eager to be away from her eventful afternoon. Brady had said the last thing he wanted was for her to be seen, and she'd ended up running into his brother. She didn't know whether Clay would divulge that he had seen her after she had turned him down again, but she wouldn't put it past him.

And now all she had left to do was sit and stew over the fact that Clay had told her that Brady had a date for the dinner tonight. He had a date, and he had invited Liz all the way out here. She knew that she couldn't go to the event with him, not after the blowup with Heather, but still it hurt.

Would there always be someone else whom they could be more public with than each other? Would there always be another person putting a wedge between them because they couldn't be together . . . and couldn't even tell anyone that they were seeing each other?

Her hands were shaking when she slid the keycard into the lock. The door swung open and she stumbled forward into the room.

She wished that these emotions weren't roiling through her body. She wished that she could turn it all off and forget how much he meant to her. But she couldn't.

Her actions may have been reckless in D.C., but it was hardly different from him bringing woman after woman to these events. She wasn't accusing him of doing anything with them, but she couldn't keep having people stand in her place. It felt wrong.

They needed to figure this out. And having Clay's words echoing in her ears wasn't helping matters. *I'm sorry he's convinced you so thoroughly otherwise.* Had Brady just convinced her to do what he wanted?

Clay sure seemed to think so. She had changed so much this summer. She hardly even remembered what she had written in her article that was so vile. She didn't remember how it felt not to like Brady or understand his reasoning for running for office. Had he warped her viewpoint so much?

Liz reached for her laptop and pulled up the first article she had written about Brady. Her head pounded as she read her rather cruel recount of Brady's announcement for Congress. She understood why Professor Mires had given Liz the grade she did. The paper had been popular for Brady's picture. Her article was less than stellar, and actually rather mean. She couldn't believe that she had written that Brady was power hungry, with money as his only interest.

She shook her head and flipped to the next article about Brady just as her phone blasted loudly through the room. Liz jumped and hurtled toward her purse.

Please be Brady!

Liz flipped on her phone and answered. "Hello?"

"Hey, Liz," Hayden said.

She bit her lip and all the adrenaline released from her body. *Not Brady.*

"Hayden, how are you?" she asked.

"Good. Though I've been missing you."

"Oh," she said, biting back a smile. "How do you have the time at that busy job of yours?"

"I always seem to find time."

Liz laughed lightly despite herself. She didn't know when Brady was going to come by, and he hadn't called. She was feeling pretty down on herself and the whole stupid trip, and here Hayden was calling when she needed someone to boost her the most.

"Well, mostly I was calling with good news."

"Yeah? What happened?" Liz asked, wandering into the bedroom, pulling back the sheets, and snuggling into the comforter.

"Jamie was exhibiting this weekend. She told you about that, right?"

"Yeah, she did."

"Well, a curator from a museum picked up her work for a slot in their rising stars showcase. Her paintings will be up in the museum starting in August."

"Oh my God, that's so exciting for her! She must be freaking out."

Hayden chuckled. "You have no idea what I'm going through over here. I wish you were here to diffuse the insanity. She likes you."

"Are you calling me to escape Jamie?" Liz asked accusingly.

"That doesn't sound like me at all. Seriously, though, drive back up to D.C. and save me from her constant frolicking around the apartment."

Liz snickered and covered her mouth. "Frolicking?"

"I'm not kidding. She is skipping around and singing Céline Dion at the top of her lungs. I think she might have legitimately lost it this time," he said with an undertone of humor.

"Sorry, no can do. Sounds like you will just have to stick this one out on your own. What would you do if you landed your dream job? I bet you would frolic around the living room," Liz teased.

"I don't frolic," he told her.

"You're no fun."

"Oh please, I can think of much better ways to celebrate."

Liz knew she should have responded with something snarky right away, but the way he said that made her stop her normal retort. He was teasing her. She couldn't grasp that.

He had kissed her in D.C., and still she had a hard time believing that he was interested in her. Maybe she just didn't want to believe it; if she did, then she would have to face too many other complications.

But then he went and said things like that . . . like finding other ways to celebrate. Maybe she just had a dirty mind . . .

He coughed, clearing his throat. "I mean, you know, other than frolicking in the living room."

By the way he said that last part she was pretty sure she wasn't the only one with her mind in the gutter.

"Right," she said, searching for a way to change the subject. This was dangerous territory. "Um . . . when do you come back to Chapel Hill?"

"The Friday before school starts. I have to move into my new place and I'm not looking forward to it. You don't happen to like manual labor, do you?"

"Are you asking me to help you move?" Liz asked.

"Nah, just seeing if you wanted to watch a bunch of runners with their shirts off moving heavy objects," he said sarcastically.

"Well, in that case, sign me up."

"Cool. I'll send you the address."

They continued talking on through the night, until Liz felt herself falling asleep on the line. She'd had a stressful day even though she was supposed to be on vacation, and it was nice to unwind. Her conversation with Hayden remained tame as they discussed the paper and his job. She told him the good news from Professor Mires, and he was happy for her, albeit a bit jealous of the awesome opportunity. It kept her mind off of the fact that Brady still hadn't called, and she had spent the majority of her trip to Hilton Head alone.

"I think I need to get some sleep," she whispered drowsily.

"Yeah. I didn't mean to keep you up so late."

"It's okay. Just tired," she managed through a yawn.

"I'll see you in a couple weeks. Talk to you soon."

Liz got off the phone with Hayden, and she found herself falling into an easy slumber. Her anger from earlier had dissipated. She just wanted to sleep away the rest of the night and forget that once again she had waited up for Brady to no avail.

A crash in the living room awoke Liz from her light slumber. Her eyes darted open and she sat straight up in bed. She was still wearing a T-shirt and shorts from earlier that evening, but she didn't want some random stranger to come into her bedroom.

Liz hopped out of bed and scurried to the open doorway. She pressed herself against the wall, let out of a low soft breath to calm herself, and then she peered around the corner.

Her heart stopped when she saw Brady standing in the doorway. He was in a pair of khaki shorts and an untucked button-down as he all but stumbled forward in the living room area. Was he drunk?

"Brady Maxwell," Liz said sharply, unable to believe that after everything that had happened he would show up at the hotel like this. He hadn't called or messaged her all weekend, and then he had the audacity to walk in drunk in the middle of the night?

Brady stopped walking and turned to face her silhouetted in the bedroom door. "Hey, baby," he said with an easygoing smile.

"What the hell happened to you?" Liz demanded, crossing her arms. She hated acting the part of the bitch, but she couldn't pretend to be okay with this. If he wanted to treat her as if she was a mistress he could toss to the side when he felt like it, then he shouldn't have fallen in love with her.

"It's a long story," he said, collapsing onto the couch. "Why don't you come sit by me?" Brady leaned back and stretched his arms over his head. He sent her the most adorable smile, and she just sighed.

"I think I'd rather hear your story first. I mean, you fly me all the way here, put me up in a hotel, get me the spa treatment, and then don't even bother to come see me. Do you know how long I waited up for you last night? How hard is it to make one little phone call, let alone send one text message?"

She shook her head, feeling all the pent-up anger wash over her.

"Look, I get that we're not together, because it's impossible." She had to fight not to roll her eyes. "But if I'm going to sacrifice my time to come see you, couldn't you at least have the decency to follow through?"

"Liz, stop pacing and come sit down," he said, patting the seat next to him. "You're angry and I want to get my hands on you."

She stopped pacing, not realizing she had been doing it to begin with. "I hate this," she said, shaking her head. "I hate that I'm angry with you. I hate that you're drunk and not taking me seriously. Why didn't you call, Brady?" Her voice was thick with emotion.

He sighed, seeing there was no fighting her. "I couldn't. Heather hasn't let me out of her sight since I got here. She doesn't trust me not to mess up again. Those are her own words. It's like she thinks that I'm going to get something else by her."

"And you're still hiding me," Liz said wistfully.

"Yeah, she stayed by my side all last night while I was out, and told me that my new number had been tapped too, so she would screen my calls. She's just looking out for me, but I couldn't very well tell her that you were the person I wanted to call."

"And when you got back to your place?"

Brady shrugged. "My parents don't have a landline. Everyone has a cell phone, and they were all asleep when I got in. I had to ditch Heather to even get away tonight to come see you. I didn't think she would be quite so clingy after what happened."

"So all of that, and you still can't call today or anything. I'm just so confused, Brady. What are we?" Liz asked, finally sitting down next to him.

"What do you mean?" He wrapped his arm across her shoulders and drew her into him.

Here it was. Here was her moment. She could look up into his dark, intimidating eyes, and tell him exactly how she felt and what she wanted to do. She could let him know that she was tired of hiding, and she wanted to be out in the open. That was what she needed to do.

But it was so close to the primary. Would he even listen to her? Let alone that he was drunk and could hardly take her seriously. It sounded like a recipe for disaster.

Liz held the words on the tip of her tongue, desperate to let him know. She couldn't go on with this torn division in her chest. But she felt as if the words weren't enough. Her simple words wouldn't change anything in the long run. Maybe Clay was right . . . and Brady would do whatever it took to win. Then she would just be collateral damage, and the things she wanted to tell him would be dust in the wind.

She took a deep breath. "Why do you do all of this, Brady? You could have found a marginal amount of time to come see me in

Chapel Hill, or I could have driven into Raleigh. Why go to this extent when it's not even necessary?"

"I wanted to see you," Brady said, pulling her onto his lap and nuzzling her neck. His hands slid down her back, drawing her into him. "I've missed this."

Liz shivered at his touch. They were so right for each other, yet he was denying them so much by hiding.

His hands moved to her ass, and he picked her up and moved her so that she was straddling him. He pulled her hips into him and shot her that devilish smirk.

"Especially this," he said, his voice heated.

Liz shook her head, pushed off of him, and stood. "You can't even take this seriously. Why does it always have to be sex first and talk later? Why can't you just answer my questions? Why am I here, Brady?"

"Because I wanted you here."

"That simple, huh?"

"Yes, why do you have to insist on complicating things? Do you not like what we have going on?" Brady asked, standing and towering over her. "Do you not want me to fuck you?"

"You know what, Brady? Sometimes I *don't* like what we have going on, and sometimes I *don't* want you to fuck me," Liz told him, turning and walking away from him.

She was so red-hot with anger. Her skin was superheating, and she felt tears prick her eyes.

"Don't you see how much hiding this sucks? Don't you even care that it's hurting me? That I was so desperate to have someone acknowledge me in public, I had to go away for a weekend while you were getting bitched at for ever seeing me? Doesn't that feel wrong to you? I just can't keep feeling second best to *everything* else in your life."

"What do you want from me, Liz? I have feelings for you. I wouldn't have had you come here if that wasn't true. But I told you from the very beginning that I wanted you and the campaign. Those two things don't always coincide, and you said you were okay with that."

Brady crossed the room, spun Liz around, and stared intently down into her eyes.

"Those things don't change whether I love you or not."

Liz's breath caught at that word. She was sure he would never use that word to her. It didn't matter if it was in the most roundabout way imaginable. Brady Maxwell had told her that he loved her.

Sure, he had prefaced that with *things don't change*, but she was having a hard time not swooning. He loved her.

It wasn't enough. It could never be enough to make it all better. But it was something to hold on to . . . something that she had.

As her mind replayed Brady's words over and over again, her anger about him standing her up and going to dinner with someone else was slowly evaporating. She hadn't expected him to ever tell her. Not that he had come right out and said it by all means, but it was still nice to hear that word off of his lips.

"Liz," he whispered, sliding his hand around to the small of her back and pulling her in close, "forgive me for not calling. I know this must be hard on you, but I do try to do right by you as best I can." His head dropped down low, and he planted a soft kiss on her lips, before resting his forehead against hers.

"I'm just . . . having a hard time," she admitted, threading a hand up into his dark brown hair and trying to hold on to her fight even though he was draining it all out of her.

"I know, baby," he murmured, pulling her hair lightly to tilt her head to one side.

"I want us to be public," Liz finally told him.

Brady stiffened only marginally before licking and kissing down her earlobe and to her neck. "You know we can't do that. I have the primary in two weeks, and the general election in November. You know that."

"I know," she murmured, goose bumps breaking out on her skin.

His free hand slid up her loose shirt and teasingly traced along her ribs. "We can't be like that, baby."

"Brady," she said, pushing him away, "don't think that all of your sweet words and tempting touches are going to make this better!"

Brady shook his head, grasped her shirt in his hands, and pulled her forcefully toward him. "Listen, I apologized for what happened, but I can't make it up to you if you won't let me. So let me."

She sighed, wanting to stay angry with him. She just wanted to make him see what the hell he was doing to her. "How are you going to make it up to me?"

He smirked. "I didn't fly you all the way out here so I could fuck you in a hotel room. I can do that at home, baby."

Liz's mouth popped open at his words, wondering where else he would have sex with her if not in the gorgeous suite he had rented for her.

"Come with me. I have something to show you."

Liz contemplated continuing their conversation, but knew that it was over. She had told him how she felt about the situation, and he had told her that he loved her . . . kind of. That was going to be as much as she could get . . . for now.

She followed him out of the room and into the elevator. "Brady," she muttered as the elevator carried them down, "who did you go to dinner with tonight?"

"Some college buddies I played basketball with," he told her. "They were giving a donation to the campaign."

"All guys?" she prodded.

He smirked at her as if he knew where she was going with this. "No. I had a date. She was a girl I went to college with who is now an environmental lobbyist. Not much of a date."

"I'd sure hope not," Liz said, feeling the knot begin to untwist in her stomach.

Brady laughed at her words. "I thought you might think that."

"Anything going on between the two of you?" she whispered.

"Baby," he chided, shaking his head.

"Well?"

"You should know there's not."

"How would I know that when you don't even tell me about these people until after?"

"Because you're all I need, Liz," he said sincerely.

They turned away from the main lobby and exited the building through the back entrance, skirted the pool area, and walked the path that Liz knew led to the beach. She sure hoped he had something better than the beach in mind, because sand was not a good idea.

They kicked off their sandals when they reached the beach entrance and carried them as they walked through the sand. Brady's hand found hers, and he threaded their fingers together. Liz froze, surprised that he would hold her hand in public, even if it was two or three in the morning and no one else was awake.

Either way, it felt really nice. He had huge hands, and hers felt dainty in comparison, but it wasn't uncomfortable. They still fit together perfectly.

The waves crashing against the surf were the music as they walked along the beach. As frustrated as Liz was with their situation, she couldn't help but feel at peace out on the beach with Brady. It was as close to public as he allowed, and so she wanted to treasure it for what it was.

Brady stopped them in front of a big cabana. Liz had seen these on the beach when she had been out there yesterday, but unless a person paid for them ahead of time they remained closed and locked. Seemed like such a waste.

"Come here," Brady said, drawing her in closer.

"What are we doing?" she asked anxiously.

Brady threw open the cabana curtains to reveal a plush seaside bed complete with a soft, fluffy comforter and giant pillows. Liz stared forward at the bed, a smile spreading on her face.

He took her sandals out of her hand and tossed them off to the side before picking her up in his arms and laying her down on the bed.

"I've missed you," he told her, running his hand down her body.

"I missed you, too," Liz responded, wondering whether she would always feel the pain of missing him and the heartache of waiting.

Brady didn't leave any more room for conversation as he wound his hand into her hair and tugged on it forcefully. She lay flat against the bed, his body moving to cover her. Her hands fumbled for his button-down. She gave up on the buttons after two and yanked the thing over his head.

She didn't even care that they were in an open cabana on the beach. Anyone could see in and know what they were doing. But Brady had brought her here, and she wasn't going to stop him.

His lips found her demandingly, forcing her mouth open and volleying with her tongue. The urgency in his kisses was contagious and soon she was feverish. She couldn't get enough of him. His hands were everywhere, their bodies grinding against each other. Her legs wrapped around his hips, pulling him harder against her. Their breathing mingled, hot and enticing.

Brady pulled back and stepped out of his shorts while she tugged off her clothes. She just wanted to feel him and know that she had him completely to herself. She wanted to forget the rest of the world, the waiting, the hiding, the need to be with other people for public appearances. With him settling down in front of her, she let her mind fade away and reveled in his touch.

Liz slid her arms around his neck and he pressed his lips down against hers. Brady slid forward into her and she groaned into his mouth. He pushed back and let their bodies meet together over and over again.

She didn't care how angry she had been with him before this. Their attraction when they were together was undeniable. If either of them tried to ignore it, they would only be lying to themselves. They just couldn't get enough. It was why they were risking the world to see each other. It was why, when he was moving inside of her, pushing her toward the edge of climax, she couldn't think of anything else but her utter, unquestionable feelings for this man.

"Brady," she groaned, gripping his shoulders and digging her nails in.

He slammed into her faster and faster, sending her to the brink of release. Liz cried out Brady's name as her body surrendered to him. The intensity of her orgasm hit him and he lost control, thrusting once more, and burying himself deep within her.

He wrapped his arms around her and they lay there, sweat beading between them, waiting for their chests to stop heaving, and their breathing to even out.

"Oh, Brady," Liz whispered, "I love you."

She knew it was true. That against all odds, she had fallen for this man. The one man she couldn't have.

"Baby," he groaned, his voice strained, "I know you do."

Liz remained on her back as Brady dropped his head to her shoulder and kissed a soft trail along her collarbone. She had said it. She had told him. She already knew he loved her, and he had sort of told her, but she would have liked to just *hear* it.

When their breathing evened out, Brady rolled over to his back, with a heavy sigh. His hand found hers and laced their fingers together once more. The moment was so peaceful. Maybe in the end, just knowing how he felt was good enough. And what really showed the way they felt was this . . . in this moment.

Liz turned back over and rested her head on his chest with a sigh, thinking about how easy it would be to fall asleep like this with him next to her.

"No sleeping yet," he whispered, kissing the top of her head. "I got you something."

"You didn't have to get me anything. You already did all of this," Liz said softly.

"Well, it's not all that much . . . compared to this, I suppose. I still wanted you to have it."

He adjusted her so that she was lying on the pillows instead of his chest before finding and sifting through his shorts. He returned a second later, looking a little . . . embarrassed. After everything that had happened between them, she didn't know why he would be embarrassed. Actually, Liz had never seen him like that.

"Here you go," Brady said, handing her a small box.

Liz sat up and took the box from him, narrowing her eyes. "What's this?"

"Just open it."

Liz bit her lip, wondering what she would find inside. She opened the box and stared down at the small necklace. Her heart sped up. Brady had gotten her jewelry. No one had ever bought her jewelry.

She pulled it out of the box, the long chain falling and pooling against the cabana sheets, and brought the face of the necklace closer to her.

"It's, uh . . . called a memory locket," he whispered, running his hand through his hair. "It made me think of you."

Liz was stunned. The necklace itself was a small, circular, see-through locket with a silver border that could be opened, and even smaller charms were placed inside. Her stomach twisted when she saw what charms were in her necklace—an airplane, a key, the number four, and a yellow gemstone.

"I love it," she whispered. How could he be so completely sweet like this . . . knock her right off her feet?

"Good. I was worried . . . well, I don't know if you wear stuff like that," he said with a shrug.

"No, I do," she told him, staring up into his deep dark eyes. "But why the number and the gemstone?"

The other two were obvious.

"I got the four for the Fourth of July, when I won your vote," Brady said, his eyes showing what that day had meant to him. "And the yellow stone is the birthstone for November."

"I don't have a November birthday," Liz said. It didn't even matter to her that he had gotten her birthday wrong; she loved it.

"That's when the election is over," he said quietly.

Chapter 29

PROMISES WORTH KEEPING

Liz didn't see Brady again before school started. The primary was now a week away, and he barely had time to breathe, let alone sneak away to see her. She expected nothing less, though she did find herself wishing more and more that she could be there for him.

The primary made it hard to concentrate on anything else . . . like school starting, or her new research job, or the paper. Knowing that so much was on the line for Brady made her nervous and irritable.

Liz had tried de-stressing by hanging out with Victoria, but by the end of the day Victoria had claimed to need a Xanax to deal with the stress rolling off of Liz in waves. Even though Liz wouldn't tell Victoria what was going on, Victoria still loved her.

By the time the Friday before school got there, Liz had totally forgotten that she had agreed to help Hayden move. He had called her that morning and asked if she had still planned to help. Hoping that it would get her mind off of everything, Liz had agreed and headed over to his old place.

The moving process had certainly been a distraction, as it was physically demanding, but it did nothing to clear things up with Hayden. They had hung out and joked together along with his track friends. When they finished the move, the group got lunch and Hayden drove her back to her car.

"I really appreciated your help today," Hayden said, hopping out of his car and walking with her over to where hers was parked.

"I don't know how helpful I was," Liz joked.

"You were great. Everyone thought so." He smiled his charming smile and moved closer to her.

"Well, I'm glad I could help. Thankfully I don't have to move or else I'd be calling up you and all your friends to help me."

"You know I'd help," Hayden said.

He moved forward to wrap his arms around her, and Liz backed up quickly. "I'm in desperate need of a shower," she said, embarrassed.

She just couldn't have him touch her. She felt bad enough about D.C. She couldn't lead him on to believe this was going anywhere as long as she was still trying to figure things out with Brady.

"Oh, me too," Hayden said, as if he hadn't been trying to get closer to her.

"I'll, uh . . . see you around," she said, unlocking the door. "We start on Monday?"

Hayden nodded. "I'll be in Sunday to finalize the first run, but I'll see you on Monday, unless you wanted to get together sometime this weekend."

Damn he was good. He made it seem so offhand . . . almost as if he wasn't asking her out. Almost.

"I think Monday is probably best. I have to get ready for school and my new job, but thanks . . ."

"Well, Monday then," Hayden said, tucking a lock of her hair behind her ear, with a smile before walking to his car.

Liz opened her door and sank into the car with a huff. She had just turned down Hayden Lane.

She had never guessed she would be in this position. And she had the strange realization that he probably would ask her out again. Maybe he even thought she was playing hard to get or something after D.C. She needed to figure out what she was going to do about that, because she couldn't keep obsessing so much over what she would do if he came on to her again.

The weekend rolled by undeterred by any other mishaps, and soon Liz was back on campus, walking among the familiar brick buildings with Victoria. She had missed the madness of the beginning of the school year. Students were wandering all over campus. Freshmen were holding out maps, trying to find where their classrooms were, and looking winded from walking up the massive hill on Stadium Drive from the dorms. Upperclassmen milled around the Pit, handing out fliers and trying to cajole freshmen into joining their student organization. It was a madhouse, but with an energy and brilliance that few other places rivaled.

Still, she found that what she had missed most of all was walking over to a newspaper bin, picking up a fresh paper, and seeing all of the hard work her friends had put into the first issue. Liz had written her article for that first week a long time ago . . . the same paper she had received an A+ on from Professor Mires . . . the same article Brady had given her the idea for. Hayden had said that he was going to run it the first day, since that had the most traffic, and Liz was eager to see her name in print once more.

"You are much too happy that school has started again," Victoria said as they walked through the crowd in the Pit.

Liz shrugged. It was probably true. She'd had too much time to herself recently to think, and she was glad to have something to do to get her mind off Brady.

"Aren't you glad to be in the lab?" Liz asked. "Plus, there are so many more TAs now."

"That's a fair point, but not good enough. I'd rather be out at the pool than in a classroom."

Liz rolled her eyes. "Says the woman who is taking eighteen hours, and four of those classes are sciences."

"I like science. Nothing wrong with that, Miss Journalism," Victoria said in a high snooty voice.

"Vic, you're brilliant," Liz said, throwing her arm over Victoria's shoulders.

"Of course I am," she responded, raising her eyebrows.

Liz shook her head, laughing lightly. It felt good to be carefree . . . to feel as if she was in college again.

Victoria snagged them an empty table while Liz fetched the first paper of the semester. She stuffed it under her arm and zigzagged back to her friend. Sinking into a chair, Liz pushed her blond hair off of her neck and laid the paper flat in front of her.

She froze when she saw the front page. Her vision blurred and she felt her body sway.

There on the front page was a picture of her and Hayden in D.C. It was the one that they had gotten a stranger to take for them so they could both be in the shot. She remembered vaguely an email going out asking about what people had done over the summer. Liz had brushed it off, since she couldn't tell anyone about her summer. She hadn't thought twice about it.

She couldn't believe this was happening. Brady had told her to be anonymous. He had told her not to get her picture in the paper. And now here she was with a job lined up to work with reporters all over the country, and her picture with another guy front and center. Liz knew she was probably overreacting, but she hadn't told Brady whom she had visited in D.C., and she certainly hadn't expected for that picture to surface.

"Earth to Liz," Victoria said, waving her hand in front of her face.

"What?" she asked, coming out of her trance.

"Is something wrong? You're white as a ghost."

"I, uh . . . made the front page," Liz said, turning to face the paper to Victoria.

"That's fucking awesome. So cool." She bent over the picture and read the little caption. "You and Hayden look great together."

Victoria glanced back up at Liz with a big smile still on her face. She dropped her smile and narrowed her eyes.

"Is this bad?" Victoria asked.

Liz nodded. "Not good."

"Can you tell me why, at least?"

"I've been trying to stay anonymous . . ."

Liz knew as soon as it was out of her mouth how weird that would sound to someone like Victoria, who always craved the spotlight.

"Are you fucking serious? This guy doesn't want you to be known? Does he even know you're a reporter? Does he know that reporters are in the paper? I would come over there and shake some sense into you, if there weren't so many people around!" Victoria cried heatedly.

"Victoria, back off!" Liz snapped, unable to hold her anger in. "He knows who I am. He knows what I do. He knows practically everything about me! There are *reasons* for the things he's asked me to do, and I would do them a hundred times over."

Silence stretched between them. Liz always had a cool temperament. Victoria was the firecracker who would explode at the drop of a hat.

"Fine," Victoria said after a couple minutes. She didn't look too happy about it. "What are you going to do?"

"I don't know," Liz answered truthfully. She should call him and talk to him about it before he found out some other way. She probably should have told him she had visited Hayden a long time ago. After everything, she couldn't seem to find the courage.

Liz fingered the long chain locket at her neck and sighed. She had taken to wearing the necklace Brady had given her every day. She always argued with herself that it went with every outfit . . . that it didn't have anything to do with him . . . that it was just pretty. But she couldn't lie to herself, and she couldn't keep from remembering that she had told Brady that she loved him. Now that the haze of that weekend had gone by, she realized more and more that he had never actually told her . . .

"I don't know either. What do you want me to tell you, since you won't listen to the truth?" Victoria grumbled.

Liz tried to ignore her friend's frustration. The underlying tone said that Victoria wanted to help. She had to hold on to that. "I want you to tell me that it's all going to be all right. That I haven't made a huge mistake. That things will all work out in the end."

She could see what Victoria was poised to say. She could read it on her face clear as day. *You want me to lie.*

But then she didn't. "Everything is going to be all right, Liz . . . somehow."

Hearing Victoria say that only made it worse.

"I'm, uh . . . going to go to class," Liz said, collecting all of her belongings, folding the paper, and shoving it back under her arm. "I'll talk to you later."

"Please be careful," Victoria said anxiously. "I don't want you to get hurt."

"I'll be fine." *Fine. Ugh!*

Liz hurried out of the Pit and away from the ever-watchful eyes. She needed to find somewhere quiet . . . somewhere she could be alone before her class. She knew she would be hard-pressed to find that right now. Students were crawling all over campus like ants after someone stepped on an anthill.

She wanted to go to the newspaper office, but she dreaded seeing and confronting Hayden about the picture. He had no idea what he had done by putting it there. And she couldn't face him without demanding to know why he had put the picture on the front cover without her permission.

It was better that she avoided him entirely.

Liz just started walking. It was better to keep moving than to stop and contemplate everything piling up around her.

Secrets were going to be her downfall. Her secrets now had secrets. She couldn't tell anyone about Brady. She couldn't tell Brady about Hayden. She couldn't tell Hayden about her anger about the paper. And all of it together felt as if it wasn't just caving in on top of her, but it was crushing her.

Worst of all . . . it felt as if by holding on to all of her secrets, she was losing a part of herself.

Liz found a seat on a bench on one of the trails on campus. It was as secluded as she was going to get at this time of day.

She fiddled with her necklace, admiring the mix of charms Brady had picked out for her. The yellow gemstone always caught her eye. It signified the end of the campaign, but did that mean they could be together? She hadn't thought to ask him in the moment, and now she thought about it all the time. If he won, could they move on from the place they were in?

It felt like such a small chance . . . such a small sliver of hope. An unrealistic, tiny sliver of hope.

And she hated having it as much as she reveled in the thought that it could mean something. That maybe a part of him some-where . . . wanted them to be together.

She dropped the locket and reached for her phone. She knew what she needed to do. She couldn't keep sitting here like this wait-ing for Brady to call her, because she knew inevitably he would. Too long she had let life lead her around, and she couldn't keep sitting back and waiting to see where she was going to end up. Fac-ing Brady wasn't going to be easy, but it was the right thing to do, and in the end, they had too much to talk about.

"Senator Maxwell's office," a woman chirped into the phone.

"Hello, Sandy Carmichael for the Senator, please," Liz responded curtly.

Pause. "One moment please."

Liz tried not to roll her eyes. The secretary knew the name was a fake one, and kept reminding Liz by pausing dramatically after she used it. Brady needed to get a new secretary.

"Senator Maxwell is currently unavailable. Can I take a mes-sage?" the secretary asked when she came back on the line.

Liz sat there frozen for a couple seconds. She hadn't expected Brady to be busy.

"Uh . . . just let him know that I called," Liz said.

"I'll make a note of it," she said before hanging up.

Well, then!

Liz didn't know what else to do. She would just stress over it all day . . . until he called her back . . . if he called her back.

Liz rose from her seat and let her feet carry her to class. She sat through three lectures that day, and by the time she left she felt even more restless than before.

Brady still hadn't called. He was sending a message. One she didn't particularly care for.

Liz made her way to the newspaper for their first meeting of the semester. She knew there was plenty to discuss, but she was sure that she wouldn't be able to focus.

Hayden greeted her at the door with a smile, one she was hard-pressed to return. But the heat in his gaze, the pleasure in his smile, and his overall demeanor upon seeing her forced a smile out of her.

"Hey," he said as she approached. "It's good to see you. How was the first day back?"

Liz shrugged noncommittally. "Not bad. Not great."

"Mine was about the same. It does seem to be brightening, though," he said, looking directly at her.

Liz cleared her throat and averted her gaze. She teetered around Hayden as more people filed into the room. Hastily avoiding Meagan, the gossip columnist, Liz took a seat near the back. Hayden stood in the front of the room and greeted the paper's staff. There was a series of cheers for the start of the new school year before he launched into all of the plans he had.

Hayden held a room captivated in a way that was entirely different from Brady. Hayden had a charisma and enthusiasm that seemed to radiate out of him, and he led by example, shouldering as much of the work as he requested out of everyone else.

It made the meeting exciting and full of energy, and reminded Liz why she loved all of this so much. She hadn't even realized how much she had missed it. Working at the paper over the summer felt like isolation compared to the camaraderie that Hayden brought to the table.

Slowly, as time wore on, the tension began to leave her shoulders. She stared off, absentmindedly listening to Hayden's description of all the divisions and heralding in the new prospects.

"And with the campaign in full swing, Liz Dougherty is going to continue to head that division under my supervision. Is anyone else interested in working for her?"

Liz's head snapped up at that. She knew that she was working on the campaign, but she hadn't thought that she would be working *with* anyone. In fact, she hadn't even really planned to consult Hayden on it. She liked the niche she had carved out for herself.

Two hands went up, and Hayden asked the students to stand and give their names and year so he could add them to the notes his assistant, Casey, was taking.

"Tristan King, freshman," one boy said, standing near her.

She would have to figure out what to make of these new recruits. How best to use them. This was now her new task.

"Savannah Maxwell, freshman," another voice said across the room from her.

Liz froze, her heart in her throat. No. She hadn't even seen Savannah in the room. Had she been that out of it that she hadn't even paid attention?

Her eyes slowly drifted to Savannah, who looked so much like her brother. Dark hair and eyes, strong features, confident, thin, beautiful . . . intimidatingly so. She stared back at Liz with an unreadable expression, and Liz wondered whether Savannah could see right through her.

She couldn't work with Savannah. Liz couldn't spend time with her. Would Savannah recognize her? Would she know that she had followed her brother, been to his galas, written nasty articles about him . . . and more, much more?

"Perfect," Hayden said with a smile that said that he, for one, knew Liz's feelings about Brady Maxwell. Or at least, he thought he did. "Welcome to the team."

Hayden continued on with the remaining divisions and talked briefly about things she had heard year after year—conduct, journalism practices, ethics, plagiarism, etc. They were all necessary, but she didn't need to hear them again.

"Thank you all so much for coming to our first meeting. Please meet with your division leaders briefly before departing. If anyone hasn't been assigned a division or wishes to change, please come up to the front and see Casey. I can't wait for another great year," Hayden said, closing the meeting.

Her new team members, Tristan and Savannah, picked their way across the room to stand in front of Liz. Tristan shifted uncomfortably. He was a gangly guy in pressed khakis and a polo, with short, meticulously combed dark hair and pasty skin. Savannah looked unfazed as she stood awaiting instructions. Knowing her brother, Liz expected nothing else.

"Well, welcome to the team," Liz said awkwardly, since she hadn't been aware she would have her own team. "I have a schedule laid out for the semester. I'm working with a professor in the journalism department on a research project with other newspapers, and she is allowing me to publish in the school paper some of the work I'm doing with her."

Liz went on to highlight what she had already been covering and what she wanted to continue to work on. She broke some of the research down for them and assigned them both tasks.

Tristan took feverish notes and Savannah just stood there and smiled, absorbing the conversation. As soon as she was finished, Tristan zipped off to begin his project, leaving her all alone with Savannah, who had barely said anything.

"Thank you for allowing me to work in campaigns," Savannah said finally.

"We're always very welcoming to students' interests," Liz replied plainly.

"I just hope that your feelings toward my brother don't interfere in our work relationship." Her voice was calm and controlled, but something about her tone spoke volumes. She was much too like her brothers.

Liz didn't know how much Savannah knew, but whatever it was, was probably more than Liz would have liked.

"Personal feelings toward politicians have no place in journalism," Liz heard herself responding dryly. "I've been learning that lesson all summer."

It might not have been the smartest thing to say, considering all she had gone through with Brady this summer, but she didn't know what else to say. If Savannah knew only about the articles, then the comment would work as well as if she knew about anything else.

"I agree. I'm sure I'll be learning that lesson in the next several months," Savannah said, a smile finally touching her features. "I just wanted to clear the air between us before we started working closely."

"Don't worry about it," Liz said awkwardly, wanting to end this conversation. "We'll keep personal matters out of it. You're just Savannah and I'm just Liz." She stuck her hand out and Savannah took it. "Pleasure to meet you."

"So nice to meet you too. I'll get started on my assignments right away," Savannah said, withdrawing her hand. "See you tomorrow, Liz."

And every day after that.

Liz grabbed her bag off of the ground and hurriedly exited the newspaper before Hayden could find her. She couldn't deal right now. She was going to have to work with Savannah Maxwell all semester. An ever-present reminder of the secrets she had to hold.

She felt her phone vibrate as she passed through the doors to the Union and out into the oppressive August heat.

Private number.

Great. Of course, Brady would call now.

"Hey," she answered with a sigh.

"Hey. I've been in meetings all morning that I couldn't get out of," Brady said.

It wasn't an apology. Just a reason for not answering. Probably a good one, but she hardly had the energy for it.

"I just got out of a meeting too. In fact, your sister is now working for me."

"What?" he asked sharply. She had clearly thrown him.

"Yep. She showed up at the newspaper meeting and said she wanted to work on campaigns. So, guess what? She now works for me." Liz couldn't keep the frustration and pent-up anger out of her voice.

"Fuck," he growled low.

"Yeah! And imagine my surprise when she asks me not to let my feelings toward her brother cloud my opinion of her! Could you imagine if my feelings toward her brother could do that?"

"She said that?"

"Yes!" Liz snapped. "I don't know how much she knows. She doesn't give anything away, just like you!"

She hadn't even meant to say that. Where was her anger coming from?

"Are you still at the paper?" Brady asked.

"I just left. I'm walking home." She hated that he didn't respond to her outburst. She just wanted to rile him up, make him get as emotional as he did that time he told Heather and Elliott he loved her, force him to do something about those feelings.

"I'm in Durham and have an hour."

He said it so matter-of-factly, as if he had already decided that she was going to see him. Well, of course she was. It was always better to talk about this stuff in person. But she was almost irritated enough to call him out on it.

"Are you going to come get me?" she finally asked when he didn't continue.

"I'll be there in ten minutes."

The line went dead.

Liz ground her teeth and thought about chucking her phone into the side of the building. *Goddamn man!*

———

When Brady picked her up, she didn't know where they were going. It had to be somewhere close and private, because he didn't have much time to talk. She knew Victoria was supposed to be at the lab, but they couldn't risk her coming home and finding a politician in her bedroom. That would mean a whole slew of new questions.

"Where are we going?" Liz muttered.

"I don't know. I'm just going to drive."

"Okay." Liz shrugged and looked out the window.

"Do you know what I woke up to this morning?" Brady asked after a pause.

"An alarm clock?" Liz asked.

Brady's eyes darted over to her side of the car, proclaiming rather loudly that her sarcasm wasn't welcome.

"Fine. No."

"I woke up this morning to Heather thanking me."

"What?" Liz asked cautiously. "Why?"

"For you dating someone else."

Liz swallowed hard, but kept her eyes locked on him even as he drove them aimlessly around Chapel Hill. "I'm not dating him, Brady," she said finally.

"Yes, well, I assumed that," he said sharply. "However, that doesn't explain why your face is on the front cover of the paper with this person . . . another guy."

"I visited him in D.C.," she answered truthfully.

Brady breathed in slowly. It was clear that he was trying to control himself. "I thought you were visiting a friend in D.C."

"Hayden is my friend." She hadn't meant for her voice to come like a whisper, but the coldness to his tone scared her.

"Hayden," Brady repeated the name.

"He's the, uh . . . editor of the paper."

The silence was more painful than his anger. She wanted him to yell at her, scream, tell her how pissed he was, but he didn't. He just sat there his hand lightly clenched on the steering wheel as he drove through town.

"And how do you feel about him?" Brady finally asked.

Ironic, coming from him. Liz clenched her fists at her sides and felt the heat rise in her face. Brady wouldn't even tell her how he felt, and yet he demanded she tell him about Hayden.

"He's not you." She turned her head away from Brady. She had already told Brady she loved him. That had to be clear.

"He likes you," Brady said simply.

"It doesn't really matter! Didn't you hear me? He's not you. This isn't a competition, Brady. There's no room for jealousy. Look, I liked Hayden for a long time, and he kissed me in D.C., and I can't even look at him right now. Why? Why can't I look at someone who I liked for two years before I even met you?" she demanded, turning in her seat to face him once again. "Because the only thing I felt when he kissed me was that I was glad it was out in public. It wasn't Hayden I wanted. It was you. And if it's not you, then it doesn't matter."

"You think this is a competition? That I'm jealous? I made it very clear that I didn't want anyone else near you," Brady said, his knuckles white on the steering wheel.

"It's like you're not even hearing me!" Liz cried. "I love you. I told you that I love you. Don't you hear me? Don't you understand what that means? Just tell me that you love me."

"I don't make promises I can't keep. And I won't hurt you with this one."

Too late.

Liz recoiled as if he had slapped her across the face. His words hurt worse than she even thought they could. Her cheeks heated and her stomach twisted at his refusal . . . his rejection.

"Did you just come here to hurt me?" Liz asked softly.

Brady sighed and pulled over into an empty parking lot. They were on the north side of town and there wasn't much traffic. He slammed the car into park and turned to face her for the first time.

"I came here to find out why you allowed your picture in the paper when you know it's better for you to be anonymous. I came to find out who this Hayden person is when I've never even once heard you mention him all summer . . . though we've been together the entire time. And it seems I was right to come here and get my answers."

"You were right to come and get your answers. I much prefer to see how angry you are at the thought of me being with someone else," Liz spat in frustration. "At least it shows you care under that hard exterior."

"Are you out of your mind?" Brady asked.

She could see his walls crumbling. His anger bubbling over. The emotions he so tightly controlled on a daily basis fragmenting and coming apart at the seams.

Brady shook his head before he spoke. "You're the only person I've ever met who so completely disarms me. I feel like sometimes you aren't looking at me; you're looking through me. Like you know every single secret in my existence . . . like you know exactly what I'm thinking. That was exactly what I meant that very first day we met, when I told you that you were my airplane. You totally fuck me up, Liz!"

He pounded his fist on the steering wheel and stared out across the blacktop parking lot.

"I shouldn't have pursued this. I shouldn't have kept you around all summer. I shouldn't have focused so much damn attention into this pseudo-relationship that we have. I've heard it every single day from Heather and nearly as much from Elliott since they found out. But I didn't listen to them or myself. I said I could control this. I could have what I wanted and see where this went. And it only got worse."

"Well, I'm so sorry," Liz bit back.

"I'm not sorry. I'm furious with myself and you and timing and the campaign. Because the two things I want don't coincide, and I've been groomed my entire life for the one thing that is so close at hand." He turned to look into her eyes again. "I can win this campaign, Liz. I can make a difference."

Brady took a deep breath, steadying himself, and then reached out and laced their fingers together.

"I know," she whispered, her throat tight. "I know you can. I knew all along."

"I have one week before I find out about the primary results. I'm working my ass off, working like I've never worked before. I can't ruin that."

His thumb circled against hers, and Liz's shoulders gradually slumped. She realized what he was saying. He was saying what he had said all along. That when it came down to a choice it was the campaign. And it would always be the campaign.

"So . . . that's it then?" she whispered. "You're choosing the campaign."

"It's never been a choice," he said, reaching across the car for her other hand and looking straight into her blue eyes. She saw all the love in the world reflected back in that gaze. She wished she could see it every day. "I'm stubborn. I want both."

"Both," Liz murmured. His hand cupped her chin and she leaned into his touch. She never wanted to let go, even when she was frustrated with him. "You want us to stay hidden. For how much longer? When does it end? I still have two years of school left. I'm still on the paper. You're still in Congress. You run for office every two years. What happens when the campaign ends?"

Her hand instinctively went to the necklace dangling from her neck. The yellow gemstone mocked her from its place in the locket.

"Let's make it through the primary first. If I win, then we'll figure out November. If I don't . . ."

Liz shook her head and placed her fingers to his lips. "Don't jinx yourself."

Brady's lips kissed her fingers and then he pulled her forward toward him. Her heart was in her throat and she just wanted it all to be right. His lips found hers and she sighed into the gentlest of embraces.

"Let's see how I do in the primary then," he murmured against her lips before pulling away.

Liz nodded reluctantly as Brady maneuvered the car back on the road. The primary and November . . . back to the same place they were before they started this conversation.

Sometimes the decision about whether or not to stay with Brady felt easy, and sometimes it didn't feel like a decision at all. And all she really knew was that every time she pushed Brady to make a decision . . . forced an ultimatum . . . his walls slammed down and his answer was written on his face like a judge giving the guilty verdict to a death sentence. And she was the defendant witnessing her judgment.

Chapter 30
RESULTS ARE IN

Liz stared at her reflection in the mirror. She was all jittery and couldn't stop fidgeting. Today was the day. She had walked into the polling booth this morning and cast her vote for State Senator Brady Maxwell III for the House of Representatives in the primary.

Three months ago she wouldn't have believed she would do that. But standing there with the ballot in hand in a small cubicle surrounded by mostly elderly women, Liz knew there was no other option. Brady Maxwell had won her vote over the course of the summer even before he had unequivocally won her heart.

Then came the unbearable waiting period. Sitting through classes, working at the paper, watching students go about their business without the slightest idea of how important today was. She had spent all week with her new assistants, Tristan and Savannah, encouraging the student body to go out and vote. They all knew the consequences, but conveying that to the student body proved tiresome. And there wasn't much she could do besides use her voice to coax people into going to the polls.

It was finally that time. Hayden would be there any minute to pick her up and take her to the results party for Brady. She had tried to get out of going with him; she would have rather gone alone, but Hayden thought she was going for work. Once again, she couldn't explain her way out of the situation without giving away secrets she meant to hold on to.

With her jitters came an uncontrollable need to *do* something while she waited. She had changed outfits three times before settling on a charcoal pantsuit with a blue blouse and black platforms. She had slid her locket over her head and then back off more than a dozen times before leaving it on. Her hair was flat ironed to perfection, and she had never applied her makeup so thoroughly.

A text appeared on her phone from Hayden, telling her it was time to head out. They still had a full forty minutes before they made it to Raleigh.

Liz exited her house, walked to Hayden's Audi, and sat down in the passenger seat. She tried not to think about the last time she had been a passenger in a car.

"Hey," Hayden said. His smile was full-on charm. "You look great."

"Thanks," Liz said. She appreciated his compliment in spite of her nerves as he pulled out of her driveway.

He looked good too. He wore a fitted black suit with a white button-down and a blue tie that matched her blouse. Brady would surely look better, though. Liz gritted her teeth at the thought. She hated comparing, so she racked her brain to find something else to talk to Hayden about.

"How do you think the paper is doing so far?" she managed to get out.

"Good. We lost a lot of seniors at the end of the last year, but the incoming freshmen are really stepping up. I was surprised to see Savannah Maxwell in the room. Weren't you?"

"I was surprised." Though for reasons he would have never guessed.

"You would think with her family's history she wouldn't have chosen reporting," Hayden continued. "I was worried she would be a liability."

"I think she doesn't want to be under the shadow of her family. Big shoes to fill and all that," Liz told him. It felt strange to have insight into Savannah's head, but she was working closely with her now. Liz could kind of pick up on her vibe.

"Well, as long as you two work well together, then I don't see any problem with it. I know how you feel about our politician."

Liz tried not to cringe at the name Hayden still used for Brady. She needed to change the subject again, but worried that somehow it would always go back to Brady . . . especially today.

Finally Liz relaxed enough to just shrug. She wasn't going to talk about Brady. She was too nervous for him at present.

"What do you think about the other freshmen?" Liz prompted.

Thankfully that incited a long-winded discussion of every new person Hayden had come into contact with. Some Liz had seen or heard about already in the first week and others she hadn't, but she fed him a few questions here and there so she didn't have to give much input.

Even though Hayden kept up a steady stream of conversation, Liz couldn't keep from wringing her hands in her lap from nerves. When Hayden asked about it, she tried to brush it off. She was too invested in the race, since she had spent all summer on it. The outcome was really important and all that. But she was really just anxious for Brady . . . and for what it meant for them going forward.

They followed the directions to the south side of Raleigh, where a ballroom was to be the spot for the Senator's victory celebration and his acceptance speech to run for office. The press passes she had received had Senator Maxwell's Victory Celebration written on them. Liz wondered how well Brady was taking it all. She knew he wasn't as certain of the title as his own party.

Hayden pulled up in front of the ballroom and then into the press parking lot. He flashed his press pass and then drove into their designated lot. The sun was sinking on the horizon when Hayden finally parked, which meant the polls would be closing, ballots counted, and results would be coming in soon.

Liz stepped out of the car into the balmy afternoon heat. She grabbed her bag, complete with notepad and trusted recorder. Hayden carried the camera equipment. Then they walked up to the grand building together.

They flashed their passes and were handed a press information packet, and then were directed to their section of the room. Liz smiled at the usher and followed Hayden into the ballroom.

Her breath caught at the sight before her. The campaign had pulled out all the stops for this event. The room was decorated entirely in the festive red-white-and-blue, with VOTE FOR MAXWELL banners hanging all around the perimeter. A giant staircase opened up on the opposite end of the room from two tiered balconies and led to the ballroom floor below, as well as to a stage that had been erected. A podium rested on the stage with an American flag across it, and another enormous Maxwell sign hung up behind it. A projection screen took up part of one wall and was broadcasting the news as they waited for election results to come in.

A crowd had already formed and people milled around the room, anxiously awaiting the results. Some of the press were interviewing partygoers and speaking excitedly into their microphones, but most were just enjoying the company as they waited to hear the fate of the man they had put their trust in.

She wished in that moment as she surveyed the room that she weren't wearing a press badge, that she weren't dressed in a pantsuit, that she weren't here to work. She wanted to be in an elegant modest cocktail dress backstage waiting and stressing over the results with Brady. She wanted to be something that everyone said was impossible.

"Come on. This way," Hayden said, touching the small of her back and guiding her into the ballroom.

Liz remembered the first press conference she went to with Hayden and what it felt like when he had touched her then. She had been exhilarated and excited, but now all she felt were her nerves threatening to bubble over. She needed to calm down.

Taking a deep breath, she lifted her chin and walked confidently over to the press section, which had a raised platform for the photographers to capture the speeches. Hayden pulled out the tripod stand and began setting up the camera as she dropped her bag on the ground next to his stuff. They would use some of the footage tomorrow in their post-primary reel online. It made her think of Justin . . . and how everything had changed after this summer.

A hush fell over the crowd just as Hayden got the equipment secured into place, and Liz bit down on her lip hard in anticipation. Were they already announcing results? Had the ballots already been counted? Could it possibly be that quick? It didn't seem plausible.

The news commentator straightened his tie and spoke confidently into the camera. "Thank you so much for your patience in these matters. We're all waiting to hear the primary results, and we'll update you as soon as they start rolling in. We already have some winners popping up on the screen now. Follow below to see the list while the rest of us wait for the toss-ups that we have been tracking—the Hardy-Maxwell race over there in North Carolina in particular along with . . ."

Liz tuned out the rest of the commentator's speech. They were still waiting. Toss-up race. She had used the phrase herself in her journalism in the past week while encouraging people to vote, but hearing it on the news made it even worse.

She didn't realize that she had been staring at the screen until Hayden waved his hand in front of her face.

"We're not getting to the results any faster. Are you all right?" he asked, arching an eyebrow.

"Just zoned out, I guess."

"Do you want a drink or anything? I was going to go snag a water," he offered.

"Sure. Water sounds great."

Liz watched Hayden leave the press area and then lost him in the crowd as he went off in search of refreshments. She took that moment to bend down and dig in her bag to see whether she had any text messages. Make sure Brady hadn't messaged her while she was waiting.

"Oh, look," a familiar voice sounded behind her, "you're at another Maxwell event."

Liz stood and turned swiftly, her blond hair flying out around her. She saw the flash of signature dark red hair before her eyes met bright green ones. Calleigh Hollingsworth. Liz dropped the questioning look on her face as soon as she saw who had uttered the accusatory sentence.

"Oh, look, you are too," Liz said with a smile and a tilt of her head. To think she had once idolized this woman. But her naïve blinders were gone and she knew better than to trust Calleigh.

Calleigh smiled, showing her brilliant white teeth. She really was too beautiful for her own good. A skinny little thing with sleek hair and perfectly fitted clothing that accentuated her body in all the right places. Liz would never look like Calleigh, but really, Brady had wanted Liz for exactly who she was. So it didn't matter.

"Are you excited about the results?" Calleigh asked, sidling up close to Liz. Closer than she would have wanted.

"Should be an interesting race," Liz said diplomatically. "Everyone is calling it a toss-up."

"And what do you think?" Calleigh asked, eyeing her coolly. She looked rapt with attention, which made Liz cautious.

"I think it's anyone's game, and the general election is going to be even tougher. So whoever comes out on top had better be ready to show deep pockets. I have a feeling this will be an expensive race."

In fact, she already knew that it was an expensive race. That was why Brady spent so much time with donors and fund-raisers. Why he had gone all the way to Hilton Head to meet with people for a weekend.

"Oh, come on," Calleigh said, nudging her. "Maxwell has it in the bag. You and I both know he does. We were there on the Fourth of July. His speech was very . . . moving."

Liz smiled and nodded, all the while wondering where Calleigh was going with this. She was goading her. Liz knew that she needed to tread very, very carefully.

"Fitting for a Senator's son." Liz hoped it was the right thing to say.

Calleigh smiled wider and waved at someone over Liz's shoulder. Liz took a breath and turned around, not knowing who to expect. With her luck it could be God knows anyone.

"Hey!" Hayden said, hopping up the steps and smiling at Liz and Calleigh. "Here's your water."

Liz took the water bottle out of his hand and tried to remain calm. Calleigh was hinting at something, but Liz didn't know if she actually knew anything. And would she press further in front of Hayden? Liz couldn't judge her next move.

"Hey, Hayden," Calleigh said, lowering her eyelashes and staring up at him. "Liz and I were just talking about Senator Maxwell. We think he's a sure winner. What about you?"

"Oh, I think he wins easy," Hayden said with a lazy smile, turning to look at Liz instead of Calleigh.

If he had paid any attention, he would have seen the irritation flash on Calleigh's face.

"That's what you said all along, right, Lizzie?"

Liz inhaled sharply at that name. That was what Hayden had called her right before kissing her in D.C. The memory of his lips washed over her so suddenly she barely had time to recover.

"Uh, yeah. I think he'll win," she muttered.

"Even with the rumors?" Calleigh asked, her green eyes going wide.

"What rumors?" Hayden asked for her.

"Haven't you guys been following all of the coverage?"

Liz had mostly been freaking out and refusing to watch or read anything. She'd had all her articles already written, and with Tristan and Savannah's help she had been able to obsess all alone. She didn't want to hear about a poll that had Charles Hardy ahead of Brady, back and forth, back and forth.

"Oh, the stuff about his girlfriends?" Hayden asked. "Do you think that's all true, Calleigh? You don't think the guy can be a bachelor politician without sleeping with every girl who walks past him?"

"Really, Hayden? How many women does he need to be photographed with for you to believe that the guy is dating multiple women while running for office?"

"The campaign came right out and said that he had no personal relationships with those women, and they were just friends," Hayden reminded her.

"Convenient," Calleigh said dismissively. "The campaign will make a statement in whatever way is most favorable to them. Whether the campaign wants to admit it or not, it just makes him look like a player."

Hayden shrugged. "Probably. What do you think, Liz?" he asked, trying to include her.

Liz's mouth had gone dry. Of all the days for that shit to surface, it had to be the couple days before the primary that she had refused to watch the news. The only thing she didn't know was whether or not *her* involvement had surfaced. Someone surely would have said something if it had, right?

"Brady's bachelor status is known, as well as the various dates he brings to functions. I don't know why it's being brought up now except as a desperate attempt by his opponent to throw off those who favor more traditional family values," Liz told them, speaking more confidently than she felt.

"Maybe," Calleigh said nonchalantly. "I don't know how they explain away the woman he's secretly seeing."

"What woman?" Liz asked, sure that her voice gave her away. Her hands were shaking and she clenched them into fists at her sides so they weren't visible. She could feel her heart rate picking up. No. They couldn't know.

"There are claims that he's having a secret affair," Calleigh nearly whispered, as if she were telling them a secret, but her eyes stared straight through Liz. Could she possibly know?

"Isn't that all speculation?" Hayden asked. "There really isn't any proof. Or at least, if the competition has it, it hasn't surfaced yet."

Calleigh shrugged. "We'll see. I bet if he wins, it will surface."

Liz found herself nodding, because Calleigh was right. If the competition had any proof of this "anonymous" woman, then it would surely come to light in the coming months. How many times had she been with Brady in a public place where people could have photographed them . . . videotaped them together? She listed them off in her head—gala event, lake house, Fourth of July, second gala event, his house, the cabana, not to mention the time she ran into Clay at Hilton Head, after Brady had told her not to be seen in public . . .

Fuck. Too many places. She had thought they had been so careful, but now looking back on it, it all seemed so reckless. Anything unexpected in politics could hurt a career, especially with a race as close as Brady's. They had been sleeping together in private for months. It all came back to what Victoria had said, "A guy who wants to keep secrets from other people . . . is going to be okay keeping secrets from you." Brady's opponents could paint this so easily as deception, and people would be asking what else he was hiding for the rest of the election. Not to mention that her hard-earned objectivity would go down the drain. She and Brady had been gambling their careers, and now it could all blow up in their faces.

The room fell silent again, and Liz was sure people could hear her thoughts. She forced herself to look away from Calleigh's questioning stare. She didn't know how much Calleigh knew or if, as Hayden had said, it was all speculation. Either way it wasn't comforting.

"We heard that we should be having the final results for the Fourth District over there in the Triangle area of North Carolina any minute now. What do you think about this race, Stacy?" the commentator asked his female coanchor.

"Well, it's really a toss-up, Ryan," Stacy said, furrowing her brow. "There's been so much speculation going around about State Senator Maxwell's bachelor status and the number of women he has been seen with. The question people are asking is 'Who is Senator Maxwell dating?' We've seen him with a North Carolina state beauty queen, an environmental lobbyist, and a swimsuit model. How many women is this politician dating at once? The campaign has come out and officially made a statement. You can see it here on the left."

A clip of a campaign's statement appeared on the screen, and Liz skimmed it quickly as the woman read over it aloud.

"'State Senator Maxwell has had no official relationships with any of the women that he has been photographed with. They are simply friends who agreed to accompany him to events. He is, as ever, focused on the election.' Now, that seems pretty straightforward to me, but I wonder how many more women will surface if he wins this primary. There has already been some talk about him having relations with yet another woman."

"That's right, Stacy," Ryan cut in. "Who is this mystery woman? And will more evidence turn up regarding this situation? If it does, this could look bad for Senator Maxwell if he wins the primary today and moves on to the general election."

Liz felt as if all of the color had drained out of her face. It was all hearsay. Someone had started a rumor that had bloomed into something with the potential to cause chaos. But still, she hadn't heard about any swimsuit model from Brady. Was that just gossip as well? And why was the news even reporting on this?

She knew why even if it was infuriating at the moment. The race was as much selling a person as it was selling a platform . . . maybe more so. People could rally behind a compelling candidate like Brady, but with a potential mishap like this, how far would it set him back?

"Oh, it looks like the results are finally in," Stacy said with a smile.

Liz watched the screen along with the rest of the crowd. She was solely focused on what was about to happen. Brady was going to win. He had to win. This was his dream.

"And it looks like in an incredibly close race with a win by only a thousand votes," Stacy cheered, "State Senator Brady Maxwell has won the primary. Congratulations, Senator."

The room erupted into applause. People were screaming, clapping, hugging one another, dancing with strangers—Liz could even see one lady crying on her friend's shoulder. And all she did was stand there and stare.

Brady won. He had actually won. He had beaten a very qualified candidate, someone who had been working in politics two or three times longer than him. Yet, he had come out on top.

Liz had known deep down that he would win, but still the magnitude of what had just happened washed over her all at once. He had two and a half more months of the campaign to find out whether he won his seat in Congress, but at this point, he had surpassed expectations. If he won his seat in November, he would be the youngest sitting representative. She was *so* proud of him.

Actually standing there, knowing that Brady was the nominee for the House of Representatives, changed everything. Everything.

He wasn't just a chance. A hope. He was a sure thing.

And it was in that moment Liz knew that Brady had been wrong the other day. He had been wrong to say that there was never a choice. No matter how stubborn he was in wanting both the campaign and her, there was always a choice. Always.

But the choice wasn't his. It was hers.

The whole time Liz had been acting as if she didn't have a choice in what happened between her and Brady. That things would work out or they wouldn't. That he was the one who would make the ultimate decision to pull the plug. He had set the rules from the beginning in that little diner, and he had been setting them ever since. Brady decided when and where and even who could know that they had a relationship at all. Brady had decided the risks they would take.

Liz had simply acted like a passenger, letting him guide the car wherever it might go. She had been active and even demanding at times, but she never really pushed the limits. She never did anything drastic enough to make him say enough was enough.

But she knew now that she had to make the choice; otherwise Brady was going to keep making it for her. He had been making decisions for her long enough.

What it came down to was that she loved him and he loved her. It was an inevitable, impossible existence where they stood currently. Their feelings bore down on them with a hopeless, crushing desire, with a need that bordered on addiction. It would forever be that need that she felt, that craving to be with him, to be around him because they were never allowed the opportunity to let their feelings bloom and grow. At this standstill, they couldn't truly develop their relationship.

And the biggest problem. The one above all else was that Brady wouldn't *let* her love him.

Plain and simple.

So the choice wasn't her or the campaign. The choice was whether or not he would let her love him.

And that answer scared her, terrified her.

Because Liz knew that if it was her decision, she would choose his happiness over hers any day.

Chapter 31

BRADY

Brady stared out across the sea of people. The ballroom was full to the brim with his supporters chanting his name, cheering his victory, and waiting for him to give his acceptance speech. He had won the nomination to run for the House of Representatives in his party. He had *won*.

All of the time, energy, planning, strategizing . . . everything he had given up had been worth it. The people in his district had voted, and here he was preparing to step up to the podium to accept the nomination. It was surreal to finally have within arm's reach what he had been working toward all this time.

Yates's dropping out of the race had helped the situation. He had been a more formidable contender than Hardy, though still Brady had beaten him by only a thousand votes. He wished he knew how much of his success rested on the name his father had given him compared to the amount of effort he had put in himself.

In the end, it didn't matter. He was still here, exactly where he wanted to be.

"Congratulations!" Heather cried, rushing toward him with a giant smile plastered on her face. It was the first real smile he had seen from her in a while. She had been even more stressed than he was these last couple weeks.

She wrapped her arms around his waist and pulled him into a hug, the way she used to when they had been running in smaller races. She didn't even touch him anymore; she was too worried about appearances.

Brady patted her on the back and Heather released him, looking a bit flustered.

"I knew you could do it," she said, straightening diplomatically. Even here, right after they had won their greatest feat to date, she still couldn't be herself. Sometimes he missed the old Heather.

"Thanks," Brady said, for once not knowing what else to say.

"How does it feel?" she asked. Her delight was written all over her body. Most other people might not have noticed, since she wasn't skipping around the room and bouncing up and down, but Brady noticed the little things—like the way she gripped her hands together, the set of her shoulders, and her easy breaths. They had been in this business together too long already.

"It feels damn good."

"Don't go saying that to the press," Heather said cheekily.

"Would I ever?" he asked, raising an eyebrow.

Heather leaned in closer and checked to make sure no one was listening. Everyone was milling around them, but they all seemed too engrossed in their own excitement to pay him too much attention. It was a bit ironic.

"Fuck, Brady. We actually did it. We beat the odds. We beat Yates and Hardy. Despite you messing around with that reporter, and the press having a field day, we still made it through. We can win." Her voice was tight with emotion. "We can win."

And there it was. It always came back to Liz. All of the dates that Heather had put on his arm had shown up in the news in a negative light, but it didn't matter. Because to Heather, he had slipped up, he had fucked Liz, and he had carried on an illicit relationship behind Heather's back. Even though he wasn't dating someone else, or married, or had kids . . . it still always came back to that.

Brady wondered whether Heather even noticed how irritated that made him.

"Yes, I believe we can win," he said curtly. "Excuse me, Heather, I need a minute alone before I go onstage."

"Of course," she said. "Congratulations again. Alex said for you to take two days off, and then we were going to sit down and plot strategy. I know that we already have the skeleton in place, but now that we have the nomination, he wants it all finalized."

"Sounds perfect. Friday it is," Brady said. Heather turned to leave, but Brady stopped her. "And hey, Heather . . ."

"Yes?"

"Thanks for all of your hard work."

"Wouldn't have done it for anyone else," she said sincerely before departing.

Brady sighed and walked away from the crowd, hoping to find a moment of peace. He pulled out his phone, glad that he had a new number that wasn't tapped . . . yet. He understood that people wanted to get dirt on him, but the never-ending cycle of new numbers was exhausting.

Not that he could ever let on that anything exhausted him. Some days everything did. He had followed in his father's footsteps, and they were big shoes to fill. At least Brady believed that he could do it. He had been one of those kids who, when asked what he wanted to be when he grew up, had answered without pause, "The President of the United States." That dream had never faded, and luck seemed to be on his side.

He was counting on that luck to get him through this election. He just hadn't anticipated Liz. She was the one game piece that didn't fall into place. Yet for some goddamn reason he couldn't get her out of his head.

Brady entered the empty lounge and took a seat on a brown cushioned chair. He leaned forward with his arms resting on his legs. He had about fifteen minutes until he got up onstage before all of his supporters, staff, and press. He wanted those fifteen minutes to be peaceful, because he knew the rest of the night . . . the rest of the campaign would be without a moment of peace.

He typed in Liz's number by heart; he'd had too many phone changes not to know it.

Hey, are you in the crowd?

Liz's response was almost immediate. *Yes, I'm here with my boss.*

Brady frowned. Her boss. He was sure she didn't mean the professor who had given her the research assistant position, which meant she was here . . . at *his* event . . . with that douche bag.

Brady clenched and unclenched his fists a few times, trying not to let his anger overpower him. He knew he wasn't giving her what she wanted, but he couldn't do anything about it right now.

And then the fact that she had run to someone else . . . just infuriated him. She said that it wasn't like that, but still. Despite it all, he still wanted to be with her. He still really *wanted* to give her what she asked of him.

I have some time and wanted to see you.

Heather will flip her shit if she saw me. I don't want to get you in any sort of trouble. This is a big day for you.

He wished he could tell her what he was really thinking—that he wished she were the woman he was walking out on that podium with, that he wanted her to stand by his side, that he loved her. But he couldn't promise her things that he couldn't give her. He couldn't give her false hope for a life he couldn't offer her right now. He was a man of the state, and he couldn't just . . . fall in love. Not like this. Not on the campaign, when every little thing that came out could damage his career.

Relationships were about compromise, and he couldn't do that. He couldn't compromise his ideals, the campaign, or the country for anyone . . . not even Liz. Not even if he wanted to . . .

At least you'll be out in the crowd. I'll find you from the stage.

I think it'll be really hard for you to find me. I'm with the press. You have your work cut out for you.

Airplanes, baby. I'll find you.

Brady waited for her response, knowing that the time was ticking away faster than he would have liked. He was ready for his speech, ready to move forward. But sitting here chatting with Liz made him want time to stand still.

That was how he always felt with her. Time couldn't move slowly enough. She was always just out of his grasp.

I have no doubts that you'll find me. I'll always be your airplane, but no hyperventilating onstage.

Always. Brady shook his head at that word. Always was a long time. He couldn't give her always yet.

It's going to be a busy campaign . . .

He didn't even know why he had sent her that. Did he just want to instigate this conversation? He couldn't help pressing her buttons and seeing how far he could push her. She always rebounded, but how long could he keep it up? She wasn't completely elastic. There was some part of her that would crack and break if he pushed too hard.

So why was he even testing it? He needed her.

I know, Brady. I'm well aware.

You know this can't be anything else right now. Just don't forget, okay?

God! Why was he torturing her? How many times had he repeated that they couldn't be together? He couldn't seem to convince himself, so he felt the need to beat the words into her instead. Whatever he might want, he couldn't have it until he saw the campaign through to the end.

Who are you trying to convince, Brady? You have a speech to give . . . I should probably let you go.

Brady felt as if she had just hung up on him, yet they weren't even on the phone. He slid his phone back in his pocket and ground his teeth in frustration. That goddamn woman!

He wanted to make things right, but everything he did made it worse. Why had he fallen for her? Why couldn't their relationship just have stayed exactly what it was when they started? Brady had met his match.

He would have to tell her. Tonight. He would tell her that he loved her, that he should have told her a long time ago, that once the campaign was over, he would give her what she wanted. He had been denying himself that long enough. He needed her to know. Once this was all said and done, he wanted to give her the world and more. He would set it right.

Yeah. It would have to be tonight after the primary. She would need to know. He would make her understand.

The door to the room creaked open and Elliott's head appeared in the doorway. "Brady, it's about that time."

"Thanks."

"Are you going to be able to recover?" Elliott asked him, moving into the room and shutting the door.

"Recover from what?" Brady asked, standing and straightening out his suit. He'd had someone pick him out a new one for the occasion, and after he had gotten it tailored, the thing fit perfectly. "I just won the primary."

"As your lawyer, I should tell you that ditching your reporter would be in your best interest." Brady narrowed his eyes. "Yes, I know she's in the crowd. Yes, I know that you've still been seeing and talking to her."

"What's your point, Elliott?" he asked. His voice had a steely edge to it.

"As your friend, I'm sorry that you have such poor timing. I know you wouldn't put your career at risk for just anyone," Elliott said, walking over to Brady. They had known each other a very long time. "What is it about her?"

"I don't want to have this conversation right now," Brady said sternly. He couldn't think about Liz after the abrupt end to their conversation. "I have a campaign to win."

Brady brushed past Elliott and walked to the door.

"You really do love her, don't you?" Elliott asked when Brady reached for the door handle.

"Frankly, it doesn't matter at this point," Brady said, before swinging the door open and exiting.

Brady walked back toward the stage, knowing his time was almost up. Campaign staffers and friends patted his shoulder and congratulated him as he walked by. He forced on what Liz called his campaign mask and accepted all of their praise with poise and charm.

His family was waiting for him at the stage. His father looked happy. Brady knew that his father had always wanted him to enter politics. Brady had practically been bred for it. He was achieving what his father had always hoped for his son.

His father's arm was sitting loosely around his mother's waist. She had short blond hair styled into a bob. She had frequently been compared to Jackie O for her style, beauty, and intelligence. She smiled warmly at her son, a proud gleam in her eye.

Clay and Savannah stood side by side wearing drastically different expressions. Clay, as usual, looked bored and as if he would prefer to be anywhere else. Brady didn't even know why Clay even still showed up to events for him. The longer Clay was around Brady, the less pleasant he became. Savannah, however, was bursting with energy. He and Savannah had always gotten along better than he did with Clay. She was excited for him, and Brady could tell she wanted to crush him with hugs, but she was restraining herself.

That was all any of this was. It was one big game of restraint. No one could be too happy or too sad or too mad. Any of that could be caught on camera and look negative on the campaign. He would play the game and get what he wanted. He knew the costs.

"We're so proud of you, honey," Brady's mother said, walking out of his father's arms and moving forward to straighten his suit.

"Thanks, Mom," he said, looking down at her petite form. She had on a navy-blue skirt suit with a white blouse underneath her blazer. She had on makeup ready enough for the camera crew and bright stage lights, but Brady knew that his mother was beautiful without any of it.

"Not to jinx you, but you're going to win this race," she said with a wink before stepping back.

"Are you ready, son?" Brady's father asked.

"Yes, sir," he responded immediately.

"Then I think it's time."

Brady nodded before turning around and walking to the entrance to the stage. He watched Heather walk up to the podium. She was a natural in front of an audience, and he knew that no matter where he went in his career she would follow him.

"Ladies and gentlemen, thank you so much for attending this party for State Senator Brady Maxwell III," Heather began her speech.

The crowd boomed.

"He's very pleased to be here with you all tonight. We're all very happy to announce that Senator Maxwell has won your nomination to the House of Representatives and will be fighting for your vote at the general election in November."

Brady smiled at her enthusiasm. She had this audience so easily. They were here for him. These were the people who believed in him. It was going to be a close race on Election Day, but the people surrounding him were going to help him get there.

"Without further ado, I would like to introduce you to the man who won your vote, State Senator Brady Maxwell."

That was his cue.

Brady took a deep breath and steeled himself for what he was about to do. He had made hundreds of speeches and he would do thousands more before he was done with his career. The stage was his battleground, and he was ready to fight to win this election.

He stepped out on the stage, into the blaring lights and flashing cameras. The crowd of supporters cheered, and he could hear his name rising from all sides.

Max-well. Max-well. Max-well.

The room was a collage of red, white, and blue. People were holding VOTE FOR MAXWELL signs and waving the signature Stars and Stripes. His logo was plastered everywhere on banners, balloons, T-shirts, and the projection screen on the wall.

Brady's heart contracted as he realized that all of this was because people believed in his plans. He let himself feel that for a second before resuming his confident stride to the podium. He smiled at the crowd, knowing that hundreds of pictures were capturing his every move.

As he stood and waited for the crowd to quiet down, his eyes searched out Liz. He wanted to find her and somehow convey to her across this distance everything he was feeling. She read him so easily, but he wasn't sure whether she would understand when he gave his next speech.

Brady searched through the reporters at the center of the room, and his smile widened when he found Liz. She looked gorgeous in a dark pantsuit and heels with her blond hair hanging long over her shoulders. His eyes shifted to the person next to her, and it took everything Brady had not glare. The guy, Hayden, was talking directly into Liz's ear over the deafening noise while his hand rested on her arm. And Brady couldn't. even. react.

Liz shifted marginally away from Hayden and smiled up at Brady. Her hands moved to a long necklace dangling down past her breasts. His locket.

What is she thinking? Brady wondered.

"Thank you. Thank you," Brady said, raising his hands and attempting to quiet down the crowd. After another minute, the noise had died down enough for him to begin.

"Thank you all so much for coming out to my nomination party. Who would have guessed four years ago that I would be up for nomination for the House of Representatives? I'm humbled and honored that so many people believe in the vision I set forth when I started campaigning for office. It's been a tough road already on the campaign trail, but I never once doubted that y'all would get me here."

Brady focused in on Liz in the crowd. He couldn't read her face from that distance. She was standing very still and seemed to be soaking in what he said.

"I've made sacrifices to get here, and I'm going to keep making them. Everything that I've done to get where I am was worth it to better represent the people of North Carolina."

Liz bristled at those sentences just like he knew she probably would. She crossed her arms and stared straight ahead. He knew he was hurting her.

"When I was growing up, I watched my father working for the people as a Congressman, and I always said that was what I wanted to do as well. I want to work for you. I'm listening to your concerns and taking those concerns with me to Congress."

Brady paused to catch the effect his words had on the crowd. He could still feel Liz staring at him, but he had to scan the room. When he met her gaze once more, he felt his heart rate pick up. His hands were clammy, his cheeks heating, and he found it hard to swallow. He felt his focus shifting away from what he knew he needed to say, but she paralyzed him in that moment. He felt like he was hyperventilating all over again, like he was about to board an airplane. How did she have such power?

Brady swallowed back the panic threatening his body. It was like deep down he knew that by standing in this place, he was sacrificing more than he could ever admit. He wanted Liz to understand. He wanted her to see what she was capable of doing to him.

"I've met a few people on the road to this election who have shown me the example to follow. A man I met in Hillsborough, with more determination than anyone I've ever known, told me that he was going to organize a party with his friends to get the word out. An elderly woman I met while I was in Charlotte made phone calls in my district because she wanted to do her part to help in the process. A young woman I met in Raleigh on the Fourth of July taught me a vital lesson: People can surprise you. They can make you believe in them more than you ever thought they would believe in you. And that's precisely what happened. I believe in you, all of you. I believe in the man talking to his friends to get the word out, the elderly woman helping out the best way she knows how, and the woman who made me understand that no matter what, I could do this."

Liz brushed under her eyes and shook her head. Brady could tell she was torn and emotional from his speech. He was talking about her. Of course he was talking about her. Liz was the one to show him that he could make someone truly believe in what he wanted for the state and in turn, that forced him to believe in her . . . to fall for her.

"And it's those three individuals, every single one of you here, and the rest of the state who make me proud to accept the nomination from the party to run for the House of Representatives in the Fourth District of North Carolina."

The room exploded with excitement. Everyone was cheering and screaming all at once. A huge round of congratulations would follow and then he would go to the celebratory party thrown in his honor with all of his friends and family.

But in that moment, the only person he saw in the room was Liz Dougherty. They stared across the room at each other. He didn't know what she was thinking or feeling. She looked like she was trying to wear her own campaign mask. Not let him in, not let him see what she was feeling.

Then all at once he saw something shift in her. Liz dropped her arms, shrugged like she couldn't explain what she was feeling, then sighed heavily. She didn't look sad or even mad at him . . . she looked resolute. Like she had been on the edge of a precipice deciding whether or not to jump and he had made up her mind.

Grasping the chain around her neck, the necklace he had gotten her, she dropped it down under her shirt and out of sight. She placed her hand over the spot where it was hidden away and gave him the faintest of smiles.

Liz broke his gaze and turned to face Hayden. They exchanged a few brief words, and then she turned and walked toward the double doors at the back of the ballroom. Brady watched her meander through the crowd still cheering his victory. When she made it to the doors, she glanced over her shoulder, met his gaze one last time, and then she was gone.

Don't miss the next book in the Record series by K.A. Linde

On the Record, Summer 2014
For the Record, Fall 2014

ACKNOWLEDGMENTS

This book came to me while I was working on the 2012 presidential campaign in Chapel Hill, NC. Without that experience I never could have written this book, and I'm thankful every day that I took the five months out of my life to dedicate to working for a cause I believed in. So, I think first and foremost, I have to thank the campaign and everyone I worked with on it—Meera, Gregg, Alex, Maddie, Kane, Greg, Rob, and Mary. Additionally the dedicated students at UNC that inspired me each and every day—Hannah, Daniel, Olivia, Anna, Ralph, Avani, and Kathleen. Not to mention the supporter housing that kept me alive during that time—Kiran, Rosie, and Joann.

Several people read early drafts of this book and gave me feedback that proved invaluable. Thank you for your guidance and encouragement—Jessica, Bridget, Christina, Trish, Becky, Lori, and Jenny. Also, Claribel for understanding the life of a politician and reminding me that anything goes.

My agent, Jane, took my experiences on the campaign, offered her advice on this project, and then saw it through to fruition with Amazon Publishing, which I'm happy to now call my home. Thank you to my editor, Carly, for believing in my work and taking a chance on the Record series. Also, my descriptive editor, Tiffany, who pushed my writing and characters to their fullest extent.

And as always, I never would have gotten through this book without my boyfriend, Joel, and my two puppies, Riker and Lucy. Thank you for sound-boarding the book, providing creative plot twists, listening to me rant, offering advice on political matters, and believing in the book from day one.

ABOUT THE AUTHOR

K.A. Linde grew up a military brat traveling the United States and Australia. While studying political science and philosophy at the University of Georgia, she founded the Georgia Dance Team—which she still coaches—and served as campus campaign director for the 2012 presidential campaign. She is the author of five previous novels, *Avoiding Commitment*, *Avoiding Responsibility*, *Avoiding Intimacy*, *Avoiding Temptation*, and *Following Me*. An avid traveler, reader, and bargain hunter, K.A. lives in Athens, Georgia, with her boyfriend and two puppies, Riker and Lucy.